Hidden Sins

A Marti Wells Thriller

Mike Donohue

Copyright © 2024 by Mike Donohue

All rights reserved.

No part of this publication may be reproduced, distributed, or transmitted in any form or by any means, including photocopying, recording, or other electronic or mechanical methods, without the prior written permission of the publisher, except as permitted by U.S. copyright law. For permission requests, contact [include publisher/author contact info].

The story, all names, characters, and incidents portrayed in this production are fictitious. No identification with actual persons (living or deceased), places, buildings, and products is intended or should be inferred.

Book Cover by James, GoOnWrite.com

First edition 2024

ALSO BY MIKE DONOHUE

MAX STRONG SERIES
Sleeping Dogs (prequel)
The Devil's Angel (prequel)
Shaking the Tree
Bottom of the World
Hollow City
Trouble Will Find Me
Burn the Night
Crooked Prayers
The Salt House

MARTI WELLS SERIES
Hidden Twists (novella)
Hidden Chains
Hidden Sins

SHORT STORIES
October Days

For Dash—

My partner in crime through every twist and turn, reminding me that loyalty is the greatest virtue.

What we bury isn't always dead.

—Unknown

HIDDEN SINS

Chapter One

The soft glow of candlelight flickered across the table, casting a warm ambiance over the small table in the Italian restaurant. Marti Wells sat across from her date, trying to muster some enthusiasm for the evening.

"So, Marti, tell me more about yourself. Emily didn't mention much," James said. He was a blandly handsome man with a square jaw and age-appropriate salt-and-pepper hair.

Emily wouldn't, Marti thought, and took a sip of her wine to buy herself a moment to collect her thoughts. The wine was a Barolo that James had ordered. Marti was not familiar with it, but based on the taste, it was likely at the cheaper end of the spectrum. "Well, I'm a private investigator in Jersey City," she said, trying to keep the tone light. "I was a cop for a short time but then went out on my own. I've been doing that for a couple of decades now."

"Oh? That's ... interesting," James replied. She watched his eyes glaze over with disinterest. Which was a little unusual. She'd found, in her twenty-plus years of first dates and small talk, that people were typically curious about her job, at least until they learned it didn't match up with what they knew about PIs from television. In the thirty minutes, and two glasses of red, since they met, she'd quickly learned that the only reliable subject that held James's interest was James, but he wasn't completely oblivious to social norms. He kept trying. Sort of. It was like watching a flickering light bulb in need of a replacement. "And what types of cases do you work on?"

Marti hesitated, not sure if diving into the gritty details of her profession was the best way to keep the conversation afloat. She wasn't sure she even wanted it to continue. The wine wasn't nearly that good. Her clawfoot tub and favorite bath salts would be better company. "Oh, you know, the usual stuff—process serving, missing persons, insurance fraud, corporate work," she said.

"That sounds ... exciting," James said and reached for the wine. Marti had to bite the inside of her cheek to stop herself from laughing. He was a terrible liar. "I'm not sure our firm has ever had a reason to call a private investigator."

"You might be surprised. If the job is done right, you might never know they were there."

"Touche."

They kept at it for another 15 minutes, tried different angles, but it became painfully clear, even to the self-centered James, that they had little in common. Marti's adventurous spirit clashed with his cautious, corporate demeanor. He met her passion for solving mysteries with polite indifference. The more they spoke, the more Marti felt like she was at a business networking event rather than a date. She started looking for a polite way to escape before he ordered another bottle of wine.

She blamed Emily, her sister, for her predicament. Plus the unusual combination of a warm tub, a third glass of Barolo, and a long day in the field looking for a deadbeat spouse. Emily had called Marti, who, in a weak moment, had agreed to this blind date. Okay, if Marti was honest, three of the four weren't that unusual. As she sipped her wine and looked at James across the table, she briefly wondered if her sister's setup was perhaps a passive-aggressive attempt at punishing Marti for all the faults she saw in Marti's life. Marti didn't have a problem with her life, far from it, but Emily always seemed to be harping on her for something, seeing Marti's choices somehow as an indictment of her own, quite different, suburban life.

"I'm sorry?" she said. She realized she'd missed whatever James had said.

"Have you ever considered investing in real estate?"

Marti arched an eyebrow. And there it was. Real estate. Emily's fingerprints on this setup now made more sense. Emily, now that her three kids were getting older, and no longer needed constant attention, was trying to get back into the workforce as a real estate agent. Tonight wasn't a passive-aggressive punishment for Marti, but more of a pimping out.

"I've dabbled in it," Marti replied. "I write a rent check every month for my apartment. But it's not my passion. I prefer the thrill of chasing down a skip or nailing someone committing fraud."

James nodded politely as her sarcasm sailed past his head and then continued on with his pitch on commercial real estate investment trusts. Marti let him prattle on and telepathically urged the cook in the kitchen to hurry the hell up. She was sure the waitress could also sense the sinking ship as she kept giving Marti sympathetic looks when she came to check on them. There really should be a universal safe word on blind dates that either party could invoke and both people could walk away. She glanced at her watch as she reached for her water glass. It was still early. They'd agreed to meet approximately halfway in Wood Ridge off the parkway. If she left now, she could be home in her bed reading a Laura Lippman paperback before 10:00 p.m.

Just then, she felt her phone buzz in her purse, hanging off the back of her chair, with an incoming call. She ignored it. She wanted this awkward social experiment with James to end, but she didn't want to be rude. The phone immediately buzzed again. She unzipped the clutch and glanced at the display. It was her father. Marti frowned. He rarely called her and never this late on a Friday evening. She felt a flutter of worry in her stomach. "Sorry," she said to James as she stood up, "need to take this." She stepped away from the table and back to the more private vestibule of the restaurant before tapping to answer.

"Dad? Are you okay?"

"Hey, Marti," her father's voice sounded weary but otherwise like himself, "Yes, I'm okay. I hope I'm not interrupting anything important."

Marti glanced at James, who was now studying the label of the wine bottle. She smiled. "No, not at all. Just out for dinner."

There was a brief pause on the line before her father spoke again. "I'm sorry to call at this hour, but I have some news. One of my old partners, Detective Bill Thompson, passed away a few months back."

Her father had been a cop and a detective for the Paterson police department for 30 years. Toward the end, he'd become a detective emeritus of sorts and had mentored many younger officers. Marti vaguely remembered Detective Thompson but couldn't remember many specifics. She kept it safe and bland as she tried to figure out why her father was calling about this. "I'm sorry to hear that, Dad," she replied. "He was a good cop."

"Yes, he was," her father agreed. "His widow, Sandy, reached out to me. I'm sure it's nothing, just part of the grieving process, and maybe she just needs a sounding board or someone to vent to, but she thinks he was acting strangely in the last few months, but he never told her anything specific. Now, she wants to know what it was."

"Anything suspicious about his death? What does the department say?" Her dad, though retired for over 10 years, still had many contacts and friends in the department.

"I know nothing official. He was no longer with Paterson PD. About 15 years ago, he took a job in a small town called Cedarwood in the northwest part of the state."

Marti had been born and bred in New Jersey, and she'd never heard of Cedarwood. "Never heard of it."

"No reason to. It's a speck on the map. Tiny town."

"Why'd he go there? Was he chief?"

"No, but he got to run the investigations. He also had family out there. Tired of the crime in Paterson. Wanted to slow things down."

"How did he die?"

"Heart attack. Died in his car on the side of the road. Nothing suspicious, as far as Sandy told me. Do you think you can help?"

"I don't know, Dad. What does this woman expect?"

"I think she just wants someone to listen."

None of this sounded good to Marti. It sounded messy and emotional, and she would likely end up being the target of this woman's frustration, but her father rarely asked for favors. "I guess it can't hurt to hear her out."

"Thanks, Marti. I'll send you her contact information and let her know you'll be in touch."

She disconnected the call and returned to the table.

"Everything all right?" James asked.

"Oh, just a family thing," she replied, shaking her head. "You know how it is."

James nodded, though it was clear he didn't understand. He'd told her earlier that he was twice divorced, though she didn't hold that against him, two marriages were still two less than her own tally, and that his kids were currently at boarding schools in New Hampshire. They fell into another awkward silence. The wine was gone, and the breadbasket was empty. Marti realized she needed an escape plan, and fast, before he started talking about investment trusts and expense ratios again.

She went with the ripping-the-band-aid-off approach. "You know what, James? I appreciate the effort, but I don't think we're a good match. Let's split the check and call it a night. What do you say?"

After initially looking taken aback, Marti wondered how many times he'd been rejected in life. He nodded and smiled, finally looking more at ease. "That sounds great. I'd like that."

It was the first time she'd felt even a tenuous connection to the man.

Chapter Two

Driving her old Subaru along Route 17, headed back to her apartment in Jersey City, Marti couldn't help but smile and feel a renewed sense of purpose. She turned up the radio and sang along to a Belinda Carlise song she'd hated since high school. Her sister had reminded her that life was too short to waste on trying to fit into someone else's mold. She was happy with who she was. Mostly happy, at least.

Marti knew she wasn't good at relationships. She had four ex-husbands to prove it, although the third one had only lasted a few months and she didn't really count it. She was in her 50s and she didn't plan on cultivating any new personality traits. She didn't mind people. She wasn't a complete introvert. She had friends, neighbors, and business associates whose company she enjoyed. On a limited basis. Get too close to someone, however, and suddenly they have a hold on you, a certain power to hurt, wound, betray, and irritate. That's where Marti's ship floundered. Her general philosophy was to keep everyone at a gentle distance and to avoid most of the more messy emotions. There were certainly names for people like her, but screw it, sticks and stones and all that.

She parked the Subaru in her spot behind the building and it sputtered to a stop with a slight shudder. She unlocked the building's back door, climbed the stairs to her third-floor apartment, and took the burning in her legs when she reached her door as penance for the extra glass of wine at dinner. When she entered her apartment, Rita Mae greeted her with a meow and wound around her ankles. This was not a typical greeting. Rita was independent, like most cats, but, perhaps sensing how the date had gone, made an exception tonight. Marti scooped up the tabby and felt a surge of gratitude for the feline companion that had unexpectedly come to share her living space.

"Looks like it's just you and me, Rita," Marti said, scratching the cat behind her ears. "And you know what? That's more than enough for me."

She'd found the skin-and-bones stray out back by the building's dumpster two years ago. She'd left out a bowl of milk and then returned to her apartment. Thirty minutes later, Marti was back outside. She'd borrowed an old carrier from Mrs. Jenkins, coaxed the skittish cat inside with a can of salmon, and taken it to the vet. After the indignity of an examination and quite a few shots, the vet pronounced her healthy. Marti christened her Rita Mae and brought her home. She used to say she was a dog person, but her irregular hours and frequent time on the road wouldn't be fair to a dog. A cat worked better for her lifestyle, and she loved the furball. Maybe she was a cat person now.

They never got their meals, so after Marti checked Rita's water bowl, she pulled out a leftover container of white rice from her Chinese takeout order on Wednesday. Takeout or DoorDash was more her style than cooking for herself, but the disaster with James had sapped even her energy to dial a phone, let alone go back out and pick anything up. So, she pulled out a pan, added some oil, cracked two eggs, and found some frozen peas hibernating in the freezer.

She left the food to heat and walked to her windows. Her apartment was compact but thoughtfully designed, making the most of every inch. It was a one-bedroom but with a very generous bathroom that boasted a charming clawfoot tub, a nostalgic relic from a bygone era that Marti cherished and frequently indulged in with wine-aided, soothing soaks.

The heart of her apartment was the main living room. Along one wall ran a functional galley kitchen, its narrow layout carefully arranged to maximize efficiency. Despite its cramped size and the age of some appliances, it had everything she needed within easy reach, from the coffeemaker to the stove, to an array of knives neatly organized, but mostly gathering dust, on a magnetic strip above the cutting board.

Towering windows adorned with old-fashioned wavy glass amplified the apartment's character. They allowed natural light to flood the space and provided ever-changing views of the surrounding neighborhood. Underneath the vintage windows, dated radiators stood like sentinels, serving as both a source of warmth during chilly winters and an intriguing architectural element.

If she stood at just the right angle and turned her neck like the girl in *The Exorcist*, she had a water view. The Hudson River glistened in the distance, its waters flowing toward the enchanting silhouette of the New York City skyline.

She turned away from the now mostly opaque view and returned to the stove. The fried rice and peas sizzled, and she scooped it all into a bowl and called it dinner. She thought about more wine but opted for a glass of water instead. Thanks to her dad, she was working tomorrow.

A soft pink dawn painted the horizon as Marti laced up her running shoes and jogged down the stairs to the lobby. Stepping outside, the brisk morning air greeted her, invigorating her senses. She began her familiar route, the rhythmic sound of her footsteps echoing along the quiet streets.

The first mile kept her on city streets while she warmed up. She dead ended at the water and turned left. She ran along the Hudson, where the river shimmered under the rising sun. Marti loved this part of her morning run; the tranquil beauty of the dark water always provided a moment of peace no matter what chaos was going on in her life. She never ran with headphones. She preferred to listen to the sounds of the city waking up around her. She took a deep breath, the crisp air filling her lungs, and relished the sweat and solitude.

Forty-five minutes later, she had completed her five-mile circuit and jogged down her block, feeling the satisfying fatigue in her muscles. She slowed to a walk, allowing her body to cool down, and her lungs to catch up, before making her way to the local coffee shop, Cafe Grand. The warm aroma of freshly brewed coffee welcomed her as she stepped inside.

Sophie, the friendly barista, greeted her with a smile. "Morning, Marti! The usual Americano?"

Marti nodded, returning the smile. "You got it, Sophie. Thanks."

As Sophie prepared her drink, they chatted about the weather and their upcoming weekend plans, the kind of banal small talk that eased Marti into the day and the inevitable times she'd have to interact with other people. Finally, with the Americano in hand, and a wistful glance at the fresh pastries, she headed back to her apartment.

Back at home, she set the cup on the table and, after giving Rita Mae a pat on the head, she topped off the cat's food bowl. While Marti was a habitual early riser, Rita Mae was not. Their current schedule worked for both of them. After nibbling at her kibble, Rita Mae nimbly climbed to the top of the couch for a post-breakfast nap. Marti, at least today, did not have that luxury.

Sipping the Americano, she put two pieces of bread in the toaster, close to the pinnacle of her culinary skills, and, when they popped up, added a few swipes of peanut butter. Her stomach gurgled, probably in protest, knowing they were a poor substitute for the indulgent croissant she'd skipped at the cafe.

As she nibbled on her meager breakfast, she pulled her laptop closer and typed "Bill Thompson detective Cedarwood" into the search bar. A flurry of results appeared, a mix of older articles detailing local investigations Bill had been involved in and stories praising his charitable work for the Police League.

The fourth story in the results was a news story about his death. She clicked on it and read the details of his passing. The more she read, the more she thought she remembered her father's old partner, but she couldn't be sure. Her father had collected a lot of partners over the years. She could be projecting or combining different fragments. They found this Bill Thompson in his personal truck on the side of Sawmill Road on the outskirts of Cedarwood. He lived on the opposite side of town. It was after midnight and the car was on the shoulder, engine running, lights on. It was called in by a passing motorist and a Cedarwood police officer responded. The story quoted the Cedarwood police chief saying there was no sign of foul play and it was a tragic, but natural accident. Marti translated that to a heart attack, but she'd be able to confirm that later.

She scrolled back to the top and studied the department headshot accompanying the story. Bill Thompson appeared to be in his early sixties. The portrait hinted at a solid build, leaning toward heavy. He had a round face with full cheeks and a soft jawline, a slight double chin. His eyes were his best feature—large, sympathetic, and expressive. His remaining hair was thinning and combed over to the side in a haphazard part.

She scrolled back through the results and found his obituary, a poignant tribute to a man who had served his community with honor and integrity. The obituary mentioned his years of service on the force, his accomplishments, his charity work, and his devotion to his family. He was survived by his wife and three stepchildren.

After a moment of reflection, Marti closed the laptop. It was still early, not even eight yet, but after she showered and drove out to Cedarwood, it would be late morning. She wasn't exactly sure what she could do to help Bill's widow find closure, but she knew it would mean a lot to her father, and a part of her she didn't like to listen to knew she didn't do enough for the old man. Stupid messy emotions. She stood up from the table, washed her plate, and tossed her paper coffee cup in the trash.

Twenty minutes later, she locked the apartment, headed down the back staircase, and out to the Subaru. After a quick spiritual, but not religious, blessing and two ignition attempts, followed by a less spiritual outburst, the Subaru turned over and she was on her way.

Chapter Three

Cedarwood Township was a 50-mile straight shot west on 78 before bending north on the local roads until it emptied into a picturesque town center complete with a town green and gazebo. It took just over an hour but was a pleasant enough drive once she cleared the congestion of Jersey City and Newark.

Mature trees with a high, leafy canopy lined the road into Cedarwood and created a tunnel of red and gold in the autumn light. A weathered blue and gold sign by the roadside welcomed her to town and told her the population was 5967. She cracked the windows, letting in crisp air that carried a faint scent of nature that was almost foreign in Jersey City.

A mix of quaint businesses and charming residences lined the main street. The architecture of the buildings was traditional Colonial charm. It was not a recent faux, retro remodel, either. She was sure some, if not all, of the structures dated back to the 19th century or earlier. She had a brief sense of timelessness that was quickly dispelled by the sight of an auto repair shop on the left and the glowing blue of a Chase bank sign on the right as she entered Cedarwood center.

The next building was Harmony's Brew, a cozy little cafe, its exterior adorned with flower boxes overflowing with colorful fall blooms. It looked like it was doing a brisk business, and Marti was tempted to stop for a second breakfast, hobbits had the right idea, or early lunch. Why label such things? But she'd always been a business-first type of woman, so she drove on.

The four blocks surrounding the town green carried a mix of chain franchises, boutique shops, and necessary small businesses like dry cleaners, liquor stores, and take-out pizza joints. She steered around the square, bustling with a weekend farmers' market. A redbrick town hall and a community center flanked the square to the right. To the left, she spotted a historic inn that was likely standing when George Washington still had real teeth. If the shops weren't supporting the residents' needs, the primary industry appeared to be tourism or the outdoors. She'd seen two prominent signs directing people to rail trails and nature preserves.

As she finished circumnavigating the square and approached a forking intersection, the landscape opened up to reveal a stunning view of the surrounding countryside. She was sure there was a scenic overlook begging for Instagram influencers lurking nearby. Everything was pleasant, cozy, and nostalgic. It made her a little queasy and homesick for the smog and grit of Jersey City. She was a natural city girl and felt her shoulders relax a fraction after she made the turn and put the village at her back. Her father had texted her Sandy Thompson's address and she followed her phone's GPS directions to the east onto Old Turnpike Road. Marti thought the road was likely just one of many things preceded by the word old in Cedarwood. Many probably even spelled it olde, but the Turnpike wasn't one of them.

She found the Thompson residence five minutes later, after one more right on Hollow Road. She pulled into the driveway behind a burgundy Honda Accord and a silver Ford F-150 pickup. The house was a mid-Atlantic Colonial with a symmetrical design and a central entryway surrounded by evenly spaced windows on either side. It was a mix of brick and shingle siding with black shutters. The large wraparound front porch was the exterior's defining feature, spanning the width of the front facade and adorned with decorative spindle railings and hanging planters.

Marti got out of her Subaru, stretched out the kinks in her back, and looked around. The house itself sat on a generous plot of land, maybe two acres or more. Through the natural border of leafy trees, Marti could barely make out the neighboring houses on either side. As she walked up the crushed stone path, she noted the well-maintained lawn and beautiful landscaping. Bill Thompson had died over three months ago, but someone was still taking care of the yard work.

She rang the bell and stepped back. But no one answered. Marti frowned. Her father said he had called ahead and told Sandy Thompson she would stop by this morning. She rang the bell a second time. After a pause, she heard footsteps approaching.

Sandy Thompson opened the door and Marti saw a woman older than her, but not by much, maybe in her late-50s, with wavy, shoulder-length hair, streaked with gray, pulled back in a simple ponytail. She wore comfortable yet tasteful attire—a simple blouse and dark-colored slacks. A gold locket hung at her throat. The weight of grief was visible in her hazel eyes and the dark pouches underneath. Her complexion was pale, and it was clear she was trying to rally for her visitor.

"Ms. Wells?"

"That's right."

She held out a slim hand. "Sandy Thompson. Thank you for coming." Marti took it. It was ice cold and delicate and Marti thought of brittle bird bones and let go quickly before something snapped.

"I had dinner with your father a few times over the years, but I don't believe we ever met."

"No, I don't think so either. I would not have still been living there by that time. This morning, I was trying to remember any stories or details about your late husband, but I'm not sure I managed. I'm sure Dad told me some, but he had a long career and a lot of partners."

"Not to worry, I appreciate you coming out and humoring me." She said it with an attempted smile, but Marti saw a shadow cross her face at the same time. "Please come in," she said and held the door open.

Inside, the foyer had gleaming hardwood floors that almost made Marti squint. Maybe doing yard and housework was Sandy's way of dealing with Bill's death. She followed Sandy down a short hallway. To the left was a living room with large west-facing windows that would grab the afternoon light. To the right was a formal dining room with white wainscoting panels and a stylish chandelier centered over a large oak table.

Marti slowed as they passed through a short hallway that served as a portrait gallery. There were three rows of neat eight-by-ten frames forming a large square. She watched three children, a girl and two boys, grow and transform from elementary school through high school graduation. She was sure she and her sister had similar photos taken at one point, but they were likely stuffed in a drawer or a box somewhere. Maybe not forgotten, but not on display. Many of those years were best left forgotten. Marti continued on behind Sandy.

Sandy led her into a spacious and open-concept family room and kitchen. The family room featured a brick fireplace, a large screen television mounted above, and matching sofa and loveseats. A sliding glass door led to a deck in the backyard.

"Coffee?" Sandy asked.

"That would be great," Marti said.

The kitchen was white and soft grays with stainless steel appliances, granite countertops, and refreshed cabinets with ample storage.

"Please, have a seat," Sandy said and indicated a nook with a small table and built-in benches.

Marti settled in while Sandy set up the coffeemaker. The counters were clean of clutter or dirty dishes and the room smelled vaguely of lemon and lilacs. A renovation had updated the kitchen in the last five years. It was nothing over the top, but it was modern and stylish like the other rooms Marti had seen. The house was not showy or ostentatious, but something well put together and definitely not cheap. As Sandy filled two mugs, Marti wondered if Bill's widow came from money or had her own career. It was rare for cops to come from money, at least detectives and beat cops. She made a mental note to follow up. Maybe it was financial stress, mounting bills, or late payments that were bothering Bill in his last few months?

"Milk and sugar?"

"Black is fine."

Sandy took a carton from the refrigerator and added a splash of creamer to her mug before carrying both cups over to the table and sliding into the seat across from Marti. Up close, or maybe under the harsher kitchen lights, the toll of the last few months was clear. The dark patches under Sandy's eyes were more pronounced. The lines around her mouth carved deeper. Marti noticed the blouse was misbuttoned near the top. Perhaps feeling the scrutiny, Sandy raised a hand and patted at her hair. "I'm sorry. Today has been a hard day."

It was an apology seeking a reason. Marti recognized it as more grief.

"I understand," Marti said. "No need to apologize. I'll try not to take up too much of your time." Which Marti realized made no sense since Sandy was the one who asked for her time, but she wasn't sure what else to say.

Sandy vaguely waved a hand. "Doesn't matter. I'm glad you're here. Have you ever lost anyone?"

Marti immediately thought of Joel, the partner she'd lost in the line of duty during her brief time as Jersey City police, and the fugue state she'd wandered around in for weeks, but she was not about to tell Sandy, a virtual stranger, those personal details, so she simply said, "Yes."

"A silly question, I know. Who hasn't after a certain age? But then you know, grief can be physical and mental. Some days I feel like I've been in a car accident or come down with COVID again. I'm achy and tired and my head feels like it's full of cotton. I can't think straight. Today isn't the worst day, but it isn't the best either and I'm happy for the distraction. More than happy. I'm grateful you took the time to come out. You can't hide from the grief, but you can occasionally get a moment's relief."

Marti glanced around again at the sparkling kitchen and thought of the potted plants and weed-free beds outside. This woman was working hard to find that relief. "That makes sense," she said.

"What did your father tell you about Bill?"

"Not much, really. I read some news stories on the internet this morning. You became a widow a few months ago. Bill died while he was in his car. Did not appear suspicious. That's about it."

"That's right, but it's not the entire story. He had a heart attack. There must have been some signs or symptoms because he pulled over to the side of the road. He was in his truck on the other side of town near the Fairmont line. It was a little after 11 o'clock at night. A passing motorist made a 911 call. The responding CPD officer recognized Bill's truck. The door was locked, but they managed to get it open. Bill was slumped over. The officer tried CPR and called the ambulance. Paramedics also tried CPR on the way to the hospital, but the ER doctor declared him DOA. The chief's knock woke me up at midnight. I always sort of worried that Bill would somehow die in the line of duty …" she trailed off.

Just not like that, Marti thought. Sandy told the story in a flat monotone. She'd either given up the pretense of being the chipper housewife who answered the door and offered coffee, or she was on some sort of medication and it was kicking in.

Again, Marti struggled to find the right words to say. She'd been in situations like this before, close to people or family who were profoundly hurting, but it never got easier. Nor should it. "That must have been hard," she finally said.

"Impossible. I still can't think about it. Makes me catatonic. I can't understand it."

"No symptoms or health issues?"

"No. None. Wait, no, that's not quite right. None that he told me about. He'd had a physical six months ago. It's an annual requirement for the department. He wasn't the picture of health. The doctor put him on a beta-blocker and told him to exercise more. He took the pills, but not the exercise. Work always came first and that left little time for other things, including himself. He didn't smoke, but he liked his junk food, drive-thru lunches, caffeine, and bourbon. He'd have a cocktail or two most nights."

"How old was he?"

"Sixty-one. Four years older than me. Getting close to retirement. We'd talked about it but vaguely, more like hopes and dreams than actual plans."

"My father mentioned you thought Bill had been acting strangely recently?"

Sandy nodded. "Strangely might have been a poor word choice. Perhaps stressed would have been better. He wasn't sleeping well. I'd find him up in his office at two or three in the morning. Or he'd leave the house and go on these drives to God knows where. Just picked at his food. Always seemed to be somewhere else. I'd come into the room and a Giants game would be on TV and he'd just be staring out the window."

"That certainly sounds like stress. He never said anything?"

"No, not to me, and it's driving me crazy. I feel like I need to know. Or maybe I feel like I should know. In either case, now, I have to know. It's become like a popcorn kernel stuck between my molars. I keep poking at it with my tongue and until I get it out, I won't be satisfied. That's why I called your father."

Marti leaned back and nudged her coffee cup aside. It had gone cold. "Don't take this the wrong way, but does it really matter? Knowing will not change anything."

Sandy showed a little spark for the first time since she opened the door. "Of course, I know that and I've told myself that. I've tried to move past it. It's why I waited all this time before reaching out, but it hasn't gone away. I'm starting to wonder if I ever really knew the man. It was a second marriage for both of us. We both grew up here. Bill was a few years older than me in school. He eventually joined the Army and moved away. I stayed, other than four years of college at Penn State. We reconnected when he moved back, but he was always a man who kept his own counsel. Kept things close to the vest. He'd get annoyed if I pressed him on things that he felt didn't concern me. I'm not a person who likes confrontation. I learned to steer around the subjects that prompted those mood swings. Now, I regret not pushing harder."

"Can I ask you a personal question?"

"That's why you're here."

"How long were you married?"

"Almost 13 years."

"Were you happily married?"

"I used to think so. My first marriage ... was not a good one. I can say that with confidence. I was much happier with Bill, but was he happy? For the first 10 years or so, I wouldn't have hesitated to say we were happy. Or, at least, he never said he wasn't. But these last six months? A year? I guess I just don't know. Something was eating away at him. Some secret. That's part of what's bothering me."

Marti thought there was a big difference between being happy and being merely satisfied or content, but she'd dig into that later. "Where was he going that night?"

She shrugged. "I don't know, and I don't want to wonder for the rest of my life."

Chapter Four

Sandy stood and refilled their coffees. Marti could feel her bladder assert itself, but she bore down. She wanted to keep Sandy talking.

"Do you think it might have been about work?"

"Maybe. Bill was old-fashioned. Tight-lipped. Very stoic about everything. But he was almost a fanatic about his job. He might have brought it home with him, but he never shared. He never discussed work at home or at parties. With me or with anyone outside the department. If he had, I'm not sure he wouldn't have bored everyone silly. Most of the crimes in Cedarwood are property crimes. Petty larceny, theft, vandalism. All of it usually teenagers acting out. There are very few violent crimes in Cedarwood."

"Why did he come back?"

"He has family here. A younger brother and some cousins who might as well be brothers. Also, his father got sick. The man was mostly an asshole, and Bill would be the first to tell you that. The way his dad beat up his mom when he was a kid was a big reason Bill went into law enforcement, I think, but," Sandy shrugged, "he was still family, and Bill had a strong sense of duty and loyalty."

Marti put the familial stuff aside, something to think about though, and went back to the work question. If it wasn't his health, the next most logical stressor would be a work issue.

"Did you ask anyone in the department?"

She smiled. "Cedarwood PD is a small outfit. Department makes it sound so much bigger than it is. Bill was the only full-time investigator. He had a sort-of partner, more of an apprentice over the last couple of years, a current officer, who they thought might take over when Bill retired. Her name is Jessica Lawson. Nice woman, seems smart and competent from what I could gather. I talked to her after the funeral. She picked up most of Bill's current work. She said a lot without saying a lot. You know what I mean?"

"She gave you a gentle blow off."

"Exactly. She was polite and sympathetic, but no one really knows anything."

"There might be nothing to know, Sandy."

"I know and I've considered that, but I think you're wrong."

"Do you think Bill's death was suspicious?"

"No, no. That's not it. I know I'm being vague. I can hear it too, I just think I deserve an answer of some sort. I don't think I'll be able to move on with my life without knowing. There might be nothing for Jessica Lawson, or the chief, or his friends, or the kids, but there is something for me. I know it."

Marti found it hard to argue in the face of Sandy's certainty, so she sidestepped it for now. "You mentioned kids. I saw the photos in the hallway."

That brought a brief but bright smile to Sandy's face. "Yes, Bill's step-kids. Three from my first marriage. The only good things that came out of that train wreck. Ethan is the oldest, then Olivia. The youngest is Brian. Ethan is 26 and lives in Manhattan. He does something in marketing that I can never quite understand. Olivia is two years younger and lives here in Cedarwood. She's getting her master's degree and waitresses at the cafe in town. Brian is still in college. He's studying business at Rutgers."

Marti did the math. Tough ages to get a stepdad. "Did Bill adopt them?"

"Not formally, no, but in every other way. My ex, their biological father, has been completely absent since the divorce. Bill got them through their teenage years, so he earned it."

Marti ran the conversation back in her mind but couldn't think of any more questions. More importantly, she couldn't think of any way she might help this woman. In her opinion, Sandy needed to talk to a therapist, not a PI.

Her hesitation must have been clear on her face because Sandy jumped in before Marti could speak again. "Just start with his office. I can't even go in there.

I've tried and I just … can't. It's too much. Take a look and then spend the day, talk to a few people. I'll pay you for your time. If you still think there's nothing, then I'll drop it."

Marti didn't think that was true, but she didn't want to just walk away. "I can try, but are you sure you can't think of anything else? What you told me really isn't much to go on."

Tears suddenly dripped down Sandy's cheeks. "It's all I've been thinking about since he died, and I can't think of anything. Not a single damn thing."

Marti didn't have any other pressing active cases, but she knew she really should just walk away. That sounded cold, even in her own head, but even if she found an answer for Sandy, it was likely to be painful or banal, not helpful. "Why don't you show me Bill's office?"

Sandy led Marti through the orderly first floor of the house. Marti was sure even the dust was in the proper place. Eventually, they reached a closed door at the end of the hall. Sandy pushed the door open but didn't enter. She stood aside to reveal a cluttered and chaotic space, the complete opposite of the rooms they'd just passed through, filled with teetering boxes, assorted knickknacks, dirty mugs and glasses, and haphazard piles of paper almost obscuring a large desk.

"This was Bill's home office," Sandy explained, with a hint of sadness in her voice. "He didn't like anyone in here. I learned early on to just shut the door and leave it be I kept the rest of the house clean."

Marti could only nod in understanding as she stepped into the room. Heavy curtains hung, closed, over two windows, creating a dark cave-like atmosphere. Marti didn't doubt Sandy's story. The room had a neglected feel to it, as if it had been untouched for a while. The musty smell of old paper and faded ink filled her nostrils.

The dimensions of the room were modest, a little deeper than it was wide, with shelves lining one wall, sagging under the weight of old files and yellowing documents. The desk, once grand, now looked worn and weathered. Random doodles and scribbled notes covered a blotter on the desk's surface. In one corner, file and banker boxes leaned precariously, almost defying physics.

It was clear that Bill had spent a lot of time in this room, but it was equally clear that he hadn't been too concerned with keeping it organized. It might have made sense to him. Her own basement office on any random day might look similar if she was in the middle of a case. Maybe not to this extreme, but Marti didn't take the disorganization as a personal failure, more as ample evidence of a busy detective. But if Cedarwood was mostly petty property crimes, what was all this?

As she scanned the disarray, the paper appeared to multiply in front of her like bacteria colonizing in a petri dish. Marti noticed more stacks of paper piled up along the baseboards, others crammed into overflowing boxes. She walked carefully around and stood behind the desk, but didn't immediately sit in the chair. She stared down at the desk from above. The papers and blotter were a maelstrom of scribbles, scrawls, half-scratched notes, and phone numbers. No pattern or meaning jumped out at her. She counted herself lucky that Bill's penmanship was mostly legible.

She glanced back at the door, but Sandy was gone. She sat down in Bill's old leather office chair and, after moving the furry coffee cup off the desk to the neighboring windowsill, spent the next 30 minutes in the office doing a cursory review of the papers and files in and around the desk. She figured their proximity might make them the most relevant. She began with the paper and sticky notes on the desktop and then went through the desk drawers, but she found no smoking gun that might shed some light on Bill's behavior. She quickly realized that to make any sense of it all, she'd need to catalog and organize the chaos, a task that would take more time than she had available today.

Along with all the analog paper on the desk, there was an older laptop that was connected to a separate monitor and keyboard. She shook the mouse and the laptop's screen blinked to life, asking for a password. This could be a potential treasure trove of information, but she needed to gain access.

She gathered up the various coffee mugs/science experiments and left the office. She found Sandy in the kitchen, staring out the back window. She turned when she heard Marti enter the room, an expectant look on her face.

"It won't be that easy, I'm afraid." Marti placed the dirty dishes in the sink and then asked, "Do you know the password to Bill's laptop?"

Sandy shook her head, her expression troubled. "I'm sorry, I don't. Bill's quiet nature extended to his password. I didn't even know his ATM password either, despite having a joint account. It was just how he operated."

Marti nodded. "No worries. It's another piece of the puzzle we'll have to figure out. It might be in a desk drawer, or I may need to call in some help to crack it." She thought of her friend Neon, who could likely get past the password in less than two minutes with his eyes closed, but she wanted to explore other options before calling in her favorite hacker.

"I'll do my best to help you," Marti assured Sandy. "But that room will take some time to sort through properly. Plus, I think you were right, I should also talk to some of the other people in Bill's life."

"Yes. Great. Of course."

"I'm thinking I'll come back on Monday and start fresh."

"Thank you, Marti. I'm grateful for your help. Truly."

Marti watched the woman's face cycle through relief, anxiety, and fear as she spoke. How would she feel when this was all over?

"I'll bring a contract with me on Monday just to make the details of our arrangement official and to avoid questions later."

"Okay."

"Please let me know what you think, but here's what I'm thinking. I'll start on Monday and give it three days. After that, we regroup and see where we're at and if you want to continue."

"That sounds fine."

"Okay, good. I'd like a three-day retainer to start to cover my time, expenses, and lodging."

"That won't be a problem. Is a check okay?"

"Sure, that would be fine."

Sandy nodded, stood, and moved to a kitchen drawer. She seemed steadier with a task to complete. She removed a checkbook and looked expectantly at Marti.

"One thousand should be fine to start. I'll provide receipts and reimburse you the difference if it comes to that."

Sandy nodded again, bent over to fill out the check, then held it out.

"Thank you," Marti said, tucking the check into her pocket. "I'll do my best to find some answers for you."

Sandy gave her a fragile smile. Marti was getting whiplash trying to follow the woman's moods. It must be exhausting.

"I appreciate it, Marti. It's been a difficult time, not knowing. I just want some closure."

"I'll do everything I can to help." She tried to keep her tone neutral. False hope could be as dangerous as no hope. "Do you have any recommendations for hotels out here?"

"You could stay at a chain out by the highway. There are a few of the larger ones two exits down off 78. Marriott. Holiday Inn. Probably a couple more, too. The other option would be to stay at The Cedarwood Inn here in town."

"I think I saw that when I drove through," Marti said, thinking of the old inn near the town square. "Being closer would be great, waste less time commuting, and I don't mind supporting local businesses."

"That's a good choice. The inn has cozy rooms and the owner, Mrs. Harrison, is a lovely woman. She attends St. Mark's, and we volunteer together at the food pantry. I'll call her and see if she can offer you a special rate."

"That would be great. Thank you."

They said their goodbyes and Marti got into her car and drove a short distance away, out of sight of the house, before pulling over. She took out a new pocket-sized notebook from the Subaru's glove box. She always carried one with her to jot down field notes as soon as possible, capturing important details while they were fresh in her mind. She spent the next 15 minutes going over her conversation with Sandy in her mind and recording the salient details in the notebook. She took the folded check from her pocket and stuck it between the pages of the notebook before putting the whole thing in her purse.

Notes done, Marti made the 10-minute drive back to Cedarwood center and parked her car on Evergreen Street. Marti observed that most of the nearby streets had names of trees. Harmony's Brew, the bustling cafe she'd noticed on her drive in, stood nestled on the corner with a black-and-white striped canopy and old-fashioned hand-lettered script on the wide, street-facing window. She entered and found the interior more modern and funky than she expected. The exposed brick walls were adorned with local artwork, and the tables and chairs appeared to be scavenged items. The Replacements played from a pair of box speakers behind the coffee bar. A mix of families, couples, and singles filled up half the tables. The overall ambiance was warm, bohemian, and inviting. The cafe would not be out of place in the East Village.

A friendly waitress breezed past Marti and invited her to choose a seat. Marti sat at a circular, wooden two-top with hot pink chairs. Moments later, the waitress was back with a glass of water, a neatly arranged silverware setup, and a small menu to peruse. Marti inquired about Olivia, Sandy's daughter, and learned that Olivia was not working that day. Marti decided to linger anyway and adhere to one of her cardinal private eye rules—eat while you can. The other was pee while you can. With a touch of nostalgia, she ordered a classic BLT with a side of fries and a Diet Coke.

As she ate, she watched the other patrons in the cafe, come and go, noting the friendly chatter and the sense of community that permeated the air. Most people were greeted with a smile and by name. Cedarwood Township was a small town, and Marti's PI brain couldn't help but wonder what secrets it held beneath its charming exterior.

After finishing her meal, she paid the bill and left. With her belly full and her spirits lifted, Marti returned to her car and coaxed the Subaru to life. Seventy-five minutes later, she was back in her apartment listening to a litany of complaints from a chatty Rita Mae.

Chapter Five

Sunday morning arrived, and Marti woke up early. She hadn't always been a morning person but, through age or maturity, now accepted it. She yawned, stretched, and dug out some relatively respectable running gear from the closet, then laced up her worn-out sneakers and headed out for her five-mile run. The sun was just beginning to rise, casting a warm golden glow over the city. She tilted her face up, trying to catch the warmth. Marti loved running now, when the streets were quiet, and she had the Hudson River path mostly to herself. She stared across the water toward Lower Manhattan and the steel and glass needle of One World Trade. It still looked wrong to her. She wasn't sure if she would ever get used to it.

After her run, she felt she deserved a treat, so she made her way to Cafe Grand. Sophie, as always, even on a Sunday, was working the counter and greeted her with a smile.

"Good morning, Marti! How was the run?"

Some runs felt great. Some felt like a slog. This one fell somewhere in the middle. "It's done."

"The usual?"

Marti nodded. "Yes, please. With a splash of cream. And a pastry, please."

"Chocolate croissant or cinnamon roll?"

"That's like asking me to choose between my children."

"I would never make you do that," Sophie said with a laugh. "I will make the choice then."

As Marti waited for her order, she exchanged pleasantries with Tiago, Sophie's brother, or uncle, or cousin. Marti couldn't keep track of the twisting genetic ties of the family-run business. Sophie put her to-go cup on the counter and Marti grabbed her Americano, along with her pastry reward bag, and headed for home. She had some business to attend to in her basement office.

Marti smiled as she walked home and peeked into the pastry bag. Sophie hadn't made a choice, either, and included both a croissant and a cinnamon roll in the bag. When she reached her building, it did not surprise her to find the stooped form of Mrs. Jenkins, the octogenarian caretaker of the building's flowers, out front, tending to the small patches of autumn tea roses and other blooms. Marti offered the cinnamon roll to the elderly woman, who dusted off her hands, sat on an upper step, and accepted it with a grateful smile.

"Thank you, dear. You always bring such delightful treats," Mrs. Jenkins said, patting the space next to her on the step. "Why don't you sit and enjoy yours with me?"

Marti obliged, settling down next to her neighbor. "It's my pleasure, Mrs. Jenkins. You work so hard to keep these flowers looking beautiful. It's the least I can do."

As they tucked into their morning treats, Mrs. Jenkins asked, "Have you met our new resident yet?"

Marti raised an eyebrow, taking a sip of her Americano. She'd noticed the U-Haul last week in passing but didn't really think about it. The Silvios were expecting their third child and had decamped for a house in Hackensack. "No, I haven't." Their building was rent-controlled and quite stable, so new residents were not common. "Have you?"

Mrs. Jenkins beamed, eager to share the news. Gossip was the coin of her realm. "Her name is Sarah Adams. She's a young woman, probably in her 30s, I'd say. She's a graphic designer. Very artistic and friendly, or so I've heard."

"That sounds nice," Marti commented, intrigued by the thought of a young artist joining their tight-knit building, which, to Marti, often felt like it was a canasta game away from a retirement community. Marti was one of the younger residents, and she wasn't far away from her AARP card.

"Oh, she's a cat lover too," Mrs. Jenkins continued. "I saw her bring a carrier inside from the moving truck."

Marti smiled, knowing Mrs. Jenkins had probably logged every box and suitcase from her first-floor window that Sarah had brought inside. "That's wonderful. I'll have to stop by and say hello."

Mrs. Jenkins nodded, taking a moment to unwind part of the cinnamon roll and pop it into her mouth. "She appears to be settling in nicely. We're all happy to have her here."

"Is she getting along with the other neighbors?"

"Seems so," Mrs. Jenkins replied. "She's reserved, but friendly. No complaints so far. She even helped me carry a bag of potting soil to the shed."

"It will be nice to have someone new around."

"Yes, indeed," Mrs. Jenkins agreed, a twinkle in her eyes. Marti could imagine her delight in having a new story to discover. "And you know, dear, you should consider getting to know her. It's always good to have friends in the building."

"I have plenty of friends in the building."

"Friends that don't have Ensure in their cupboards."

Marti smirked. "You and Mrs. Consuelo, and Mrs. Potts, and Mrs. Sanchez. You're all going to outlive me. Plus, I'm not exactly the most sociable person, Mrs. Jenkins, you know that. I have just as many friends as I need."

The elderly woman chuckled. "I know, dear, but maybe it's not you. Maybe she needs a friend."

Marti laughed. "Touche, Mrs. Jenkins. I'll think about it."

"That's the spirit," Mrs. Jenkins said, patting Marti's hand affectionately. "Now, finish your croissant, dear. You don't want to waste such a delectable treat."

"That's something you never have to worry about." She finished the croissant in two bites and crumpled up the bag. She said goodbye to Mrs. Jenkins and took the rest of her Americano upstairs.

Back in her apartment, she did a half-hearted yoga routine that she counted as a cool down and post-run stretch, even if it was 30 minutes late. Then she showered, changed, fed Rita Mae, who ignored her, grabbed the new notebook from her purse, and headed downstairs to her basement office.

She wanted to keep the momentum going from her run. If she slowed down, she knew she'd feel tired and want to nap. She used her phone to deposit Sandy's retainer check. After her visit and seeing the Thompson house, she didn't doubt it would clear, but better safe than sorry. Assumptions had burned her before. Next, she spent a few hours at her desk tidying up some business odds and ends, organizing files, and updating her notes on other cases. She didn't expect this additional work for Sandy to last long, but it was always nice to start a job with as few distractions as possible.

Once she'd cleared her desk, she pulled up the standard boilerplate contract that she used for most jobs and filled in Sandy's information, plus the daily rate and work details they'd discussed yesterday. She pulled up an invoice document, added a receipt for the retainer, then printed out the contract and the receipt and placed them in an envelope to deliver to Sandy the next day. Finally, she flipped through and read over the notes she'd transcribed yesterday. She didn't learn anything new, but she firmly believed going over notes and details was never a waste of time.

After satisfying herself that she had done all she could on a Sunday, she went back upstairs and rewarded herself for her early-morning diligence and discipline with a short nap to recharge. Maybe she should make 'sleep while you can' another of her rules. When she woke up, the shadows were longer and day was creeping toward night. She checked her phone. Sandy had sent her a text telling her she'd been able to arrange a reservation at the Cedarwood Inn.

She kicked off the blanket, stood, and packed a small bag with a few changes of clothes, toiletry essentials, and a paperback mystery. After a moment's hesitation, she tossed in her sneakers and workout clothes. She knew she might not have much time, but she felt good at least pretending she might get out for a run.

She puttered around the apartment, half-heartedly cleaning, before flipping on the television and getting sucked into the second half of Billy Wilder's adaptation of Agatha Christie's play, *Witness for the Prosecution*, on the classic movie channel.

Once the film ended, she scoured her freezer and found enough frozen bits and bobs to put together a makeshift dinner. It wasn't the most gourmet meal, but it would do the job. She ate her meal, washed it down with a glass of water, and then fed Rita Mae, double-checking the cupboard to make sure the cat had enough supplies for the next few days. She had one last task before calling it a night. She spent a few minutes scanning her shelves and pulling out paperbacks.

Marti stepped across the hall to Mrs. Potts' apartment. She could hear her neighbor's television as she knocked on the door. Mrs. Potts still had her wits and faculties about her, but most of her hearing had fled the scene during George W's presidency.

Mrs. Potts opened the door with a warm smile, her kind eyes shining behind her bifocals. Mrs. Potts was in her mid-80s and had lived across the hall from Marti for more than a decade. Her silver hair was neatly arranged in a bun atop her head and her glasses perched delicately on her nose. Despite her age, she still had a spry energy about her, and her genuine care for the building's other residents made her an invaluable neighbor.

"Good evening, Marti," Mrs. Potts said, opening the door wider to invite her inside.

"Hi, Mrs. Potts," Marti said with a matching smile, stepping inside. "I hope I'm not interrupting anything important."

"Oh, just some PBS news. Nothing too exciting. At my age, you've seen and heard it all before," Mrs. Potts replied, chuckling softly. "What can I do for you, my dear?"

Marti explained, "I'm heading out of town for a few days on a case, and I was wondering if you could look after Rita Mae while I'm gone? She's got enough food and water for a few days, but she enjoys the company."

Mrs. Potts' eyes sparkled with delight. "Of course, Marti! I'd be happy to keep an eye on her. You know I love having that goofy furball around. She's such a sweetheart."

Marti wondered if they were talking about the same cat. "Thank you so much, Mrs. Potts. Here, I brought you a stack of cozy mysteries I've finished. Thought they might keep you entertained."

The older woman took the books, leafing through the titles with a smile. "Oh, these look lovely! You know me so well." Besides their mutual love of animals, Marti and her neighbor shared a voracious reading habit. "And you even threw in a spicy romance. How scandalous! I'll have to read that one under the covers with a flashlight."

Marti laughed, picturing that. "Well, it's always good to keep things exciting, right?"

"Oh, my dear, those parts froze over years ago. But I'll enjoy the romance from afar."

"I'm sure you will," Marti said. "Thanks again, Mrs. Potts."

With a last wave, Marti returned to her own apartment. She filled the old clawfoot tub with warm water and added some lavender salts. The warm, inviting water in the tub was a welcome treat, and she submerged herself, escaping into the gentle world of a new cozy mystery.

When the water had cooled, Marti climbed out and put on her pajamas, an oversized St. Peter's sweatshirt and pill-balled sweats, before climbing into bed. Rita Mae joined her and stretched out against her side. As she drifted off to sleep, she couldn't help but feel a sense of gratitude for her small community of friends and neighbors. She wasn't alone. She had a support system she could rely on. She closed her eyes and dreamed of quaint towns, warm baked goods, mysterious poisons, and daring detectives.

Chapter Six

Marti was on the road by 6:30 the next morning, leaving behind a disgruntled Rita Mae, who gave Marti's overnight bag a scornful look before bounding up to her perch on top of the couch.

"Typical," Marti muttered, knowing that Rita Mae, like herself, was never one for goodbyes.

The typically congested metro area traffic unexpectedly showed mercy, especially on a Monday morning, and she made great time. On the flip side, this put Marti in Cedarwood before 8:00 a.m., a little too early to call on Sandy at her house.

Her plan, if you wanted to call it that, was to start with Bill's chaotic office. She knew it wouldn't be a pleasant task, but it had to get done, so she might as well get it done first. Despite finding little during her cursory look on Saturday, she still hoped that the answer to Bill's stress might be superficial and easy to find. She'd mulled it over during the drive and was still a little unsure of what she was doing or what Sandy expected. Grief did strange things to people. But she would give it her best shot to provide some kind of answer. The woman was clearly struggling with her husband's death and if Marti's expertise could help, so be it. She'd do it. But not before 9:00 a.m.

Stopped at the little town center's one traffic light, she looked up and down Cedarwood's main drag and decided a repeat of Saturday afternoon's stop would be her best bet at killing some time. Eat while you can. She parked her car on the street half a block away and strolled inside Harmony's Brew to the pleasing aromas of fresh coffee, bacon grease, and maple syrup.

Right away, Marti recognized the waitress hustling out the breakfast orders as Sandy's daughter Olivia. The family resemblance was undeniable—they both shared a similar slight build and cheekbone structure. Marti found a seat and, after a moment, Olivia approached the table, dropping off a menu with a quick smile and a promise to return shortly.

A moment later, she was back. "Hi there! Welcome to Harmony's Brew. I'm Olivia, and I'll be your waitress this morning. Can I get you started with some coffee or a juice?"

Up close, Marti saw she had her mother's hazel eyes and defined jawline. She wore a frilly vintage-inspired apron over flared jeans and a peasant's blouse, matching the sense of offbeat charm in the rest of the cafe.

"Good morning, Olivia. Nice to meet you. My name is Marti. I'm actually working for your mom," Marti replied.

The smile slipped a fraction and the woman's eyebrows knitted together. "Oh. You're the private investigator."

"Yes. I was hoping we could have a quick chat at some point. It doesn't have to be now."

Olivia glanced around. "No chance of that, but it usually cools off around nine and I take a break. Would that work?"

"Sure, that would be perfect."

"Did you want anything in the meantime?" Olivia asked, slipping back into her chipper waitress persona.

"Yes, please, a bucket of coffee and a ham, egg, and cheese sandwich on sourdough."

"Coming right up!" Olivia said, before dashing away again.

"Sorry if I appeared rude in there. You caught me a little by surprise," Olivia said. They were sitting on a bench across the street from the cafe.

"Not a problem. I didn't go in there looking for you, just coffee, but you look like your mother. I recognized you right away. You seemed to know about her plan to hire me. She mentioned me, then?"

"Yes. I guess Bill used to work with your dad or something?"

"That's right. They were partners back in Paterson. Before your time. So, Bill adopted you?" Marti knew the answer to this from her chat with Sandy but was interested in how Olivia might put it.

"No, not exactly, but my real dad is … well, I don't know, I barely remember him at this point. He's a hazy smudge in my memories. He's gone and Bill was the next best thing."

"How did that work out?"

She shrugged and looked less like a young woman and more like an indifferent teenager. "Okay, I guess. He was always around, always there, which was important, but he could be a little strict. He was really into rules, as you can imagine with his job, but in retrospect, it was probably a good thing. My brothers and I were a little lost for a bit after my parents divorced. He helped us."

"That's good. Your mom said you're going to school. What are you studying?"

"Psychology. I'd like to be a social worker, I think."

"The world could certainly use more of those."

She smiled. "How's it going so far?"

This time it was Marti's turn to shrug, though she doubted anyone would mistake her for a teenager. "Not much to report. Really just getting started. I looked through your dad's office briefly and talked to your mom on Saturday, but haven't done much else yet."

"Good luck with that office. He never allowed us in there."

"Did Bill ever talk about his work with you?"

"No, never. That was not the type of guy he was. He wasn't quiet. We'd talk about school, or my work, or Mom, but that was it. He never mentioned work. Not just with me or Ethan or Brian. Mom, too."

"He mentioned nothing in the last three months?"

"Nope, never work. Not even as I got older."

"He say anything, not necessarily about work, but anything that stuck in your mind in those last few weeks?"

"No, and I know that's Mom's theory, but I just didn't hear anything like that. If pressed, maybe he was a little withdrawn, a little quieter than usual, but it wasn't something I would have picked up on if you hadn't asked or Mom hadn't made it a thing."

Marti let it go. It was a data point, but Olivia was young and maybe a little self-centered. She'd keep asking everyone she interviewed to get a better picture of Bill's last few months.

"Any idea where he might have been going that night?"

Olivia shook her head. "He did like to drive. He said it was a good way to think. Sometimes I think he just missed being young, being on patrol. Maybe missed the action from Paterson. Cedarwood is pretty quiet."

"Was he happy?"

Olivia paused. "I'm not sure I ever thought about it." She looked across the town green as she considered it. "I honestly don't know. I don't think he was unhappy. I think he was content. He'd moved back here to take care of his own father and later found himself with a family. He was doing his duty. That was very important to Bill."

"Got it. Anyone you suggest I talk to?"

"Jessica Lawson, maybe."

"Okay, your mom mentioned her, too. A woman he was mentoring at work. Anyone else?"

"Kevin. That's my uncle. Bill's brother. He's also a police officer. I'd start with him. He can give you the names of the rest of the family and maybe some of Bill's friends."

Marti stood. "Thanks. I'll let you get back inside. I appreciate the time." She handed Olivia a card. "If you think of anything, call or text me."

Marti nodded as Sandy opened the front door and let her into the house. She could see the woman looked more at ease than she did on Saturday.

"You look better," Marti said.

"I feel better. I think I'm just glad something is happening, even if nothing comes of it," Sandy replied.

"I get it."

They walked down the hall and into the kitchen. "Can I get you some coffee?" Sandy asked, picking up her own mug.

"Thank you, but no, I just stopped at the cafe in town and probably drank an entire pot," Marti replied. "I had a nice chat with Olivia, though. She's a lovely woman."

Sandy smiled. "But she thinks her mother has a screw loose hiring a private detective, right?"

"She didn't say that. I think she realizes it's something you need to do, but she just doesn't understand."

"I know. I don't totally understand either, but this feels right. I woke up feeling lighter and better than I have since the funeral. I know," she winced and corrected her tense, "knew my husband and something was bothering him."

"I'm a little worried you're putting a lot of pressure on the two of us to come up with something. I believe you when you say that something was bothering him. Olivia said it was a possibility too, but you need to understand that we might never know."

"I understand, but by hiring you, I'll know that I tried. I'm too screwed up with his death to do it myself."

Marti wasn't sure the woman really believed what she'd just said. She was afraid Sandy was expecting an explanation that would make Bill's unexpected death make sense. Even if they found a credible reason for his behavior, it still wouldn't take away the shock of losing him or moving on in his absence.

There was a pause, and Marti took the opportunity to pull the contract and receipt for the retainer out of her bag and hand them to Sandy. "Here are the papers, all signed and ready. And thank you for arranging the reservation at the inn."

Sandy took the documents and glanced over them quickly before she added her own signature. "It was no trouble at all. I spoke to Lucille, and she was more than happy to help. She'll send me the bill directly."

"That's perfect. Saves me the paperwork," Marti replied. "I'm going to spend most of the day going through the paperwork in Bill's office. But I might also look around the other areas of the house, his closet, dresser, just to see if anything jumps out. Did he have a workshop or use the garage?"

"He puttered around with his truck a bit. Changed his own oil. Things like that."

Marti nodded. "Then I'll poke around out there, too."

"Of course, look around wherever you need to. I have to head out in the afternoon for some errands, but you're welcome to stay as long as you like."

Marti gave a small nod of appreciation. "Thank you. I'll be in the office if you need me," Marti said, retracing her steps from Saturday toward the room on the far side of the house.

She started with the curtains. She stepped around the teetering piles of papers and pulled them open to let in some natural light. Then, hoping to let some fresh air in and ease the musty smell that hung in the air, she tried to open the windows. They didn't budge. She suspected the windows might be frozen shut from disuse. She leaned in and put some muscle into it and eventually they both creaked open a few inches and a cool breeze wafted in, bringing with it the scent of blooming mums and other flowering shrubs from the landscaping outside.

Satisfied that she would not pass out from dust or paper mold, she turned her attention to the files. She spent the rest of the morning doing a thorough survey of the cluttered space. There seemed to be little rhyme or reason to it. It appeared Bill had arranged it all by tossing the files, notes, and papers in front of a blowing fan. She felt as if she were trying to unwind a twisted ball of fishing line, but she did her best. She carefully combed through the papers and separated them first into big related piles, and then smaller ones.

She found a mix of personal and work-related documents. There were files from past cases, half-formed notes without context, maybe from ongoing investigations, and photographs from various events. Plus, the usual mix of home office clutter you'd find in any house. Phone and credit card bills, mortgage statements, tax returns, and junk mail.

She did not find a smoking gun, but she started to build a picture and feel a sense of connection with this man she had never met, seeing glimpses of his life and work in these papers. After reviewing the bank statements and tax returns, she didn't believe money was the problem. The Thompsons weren't rich, but they were comfortably middle class with money set aside for retirement and just six years left before they owned the house free and clear.

After two hours, she needed a break and wandered back toward the kitchen where she ran into Sandy heading toward the front door, carrying her purse.

"Find anything?"

"Does the carpet or the top of the desk count?"

Sandy smiled. "Everyone has a system."

"And everything has a place," Marti replied. "I'm sure my office would look much the same to an outsider."

"You said you might look around, right?"

"That's right."

"Don't forget to check the basement. He had some things stored down there."

Marti groaned inwardly; she couldn't face more paper but tried to keep it out of her voice. She was being paid after all. "Okay, thanks for the heads up."

"No problem. I was just leaving. I'm picking up some donations and driving them over to the collection center in Fairmont. I should be back in an hour or so. There's deli meat, plus containers of egg salad and pasta salad in the fridge if you're hungry. Help yourself."

Marti was not a big fan of mayonnaise, so she steered clear of the salads and made herself a simple turkey sandwich with stone-ground mustard and Muenster cheese. She helped herself to a couple of Pepperidge Farm Milanos and a glass of iced tea to complete her lunch. While she ate, she took out her notebook and jotted down some thoughts from her chat with Olivia that morning. It was something she should have done earlier, but better late than never. Next, she wrote down the pertinent financial findings and a few other bits she found interesting. Or potentially interesting. It wasn't always easy to tell, especially at the beginning of a case, what mattered and what didn't. Better to put it all down and sort it out later.

When she'd reluctantly finished the last cookie, she washed the plate and glass and replaced them in the cupboards. She decided to delay going back into Bill's man cave made of paper and do some snooping around the house while Sandy was out. Even if it wasn't snooping, since Sandy knew what she was doing, it still felt like snooping and was best done with an empty house.

Marti started in the master bedroom, her experienced eyes scanning the room for any signs of hidden secrets. The king-size bed was neatly made, but the blinds were half drawn, creating a dim and cozy atmosphere. She walked over to the bed and crouched down, peering under the bed and sliding a hand between the mattress and boxspring to see if anything was tucked away. She reached under the bed. Her fingers brushed against the cool wood of the floor, but there was nothing hidden there.

Moving to the bedside table, she pulled open the drawer and found a stack of paperback books, a small clip-on reading light, and some random things that might be dumped from a pocket at the end of a day. She carefully went through the contents but found nothing of interest. Next, she moved to the dresser drawers, searching through shirts, socks, and underwear, but still nothing stood out.

She then turned her attention to the closet and just as meticulously checked each item of clothing. She only wanted to do this once. She looked inside pockets and felt for anything unusual, but it seemed like an ordinary collection of clothes that belonged to a retired police officer. No hidden notes, unmarked keys, or other mysterious objects. She checked the closet for loose floorboards but didn't turn up any hidey holes.

After finishing her search in the bedroom, Marti proceeded to the bathroom. It was a clean and well-organized space, with fresh towels neatly folded and various toiletries arranged on the counter. She opened the mirrored medicine cabinet and found two prescription bottles for Bill. She took out her phone and snapped photos of the labels, making a mental note to ask Sandy about them.

She stood there for a moment, contemplating whether there might be anything else of interest. In her experience, people hid things up high and near where they slept. She moved back to the bedroom and glanced at the ceiling. Then checked the closet again. Maybe there was a crawl space somewhere, but she didn't see any access in the master bedroom. Another thing to ask Sandy about. She moved on.

The garage looked like most garages she'd ever seen. Concrete floor. Various stains. The scent of motor oil, gasoline, and slightly fetid garbage. The far wall had tools hanging on the wall and paint cans stacked neatly on slim metal shelves. Marti checked the narrow workbench and rolling toolbox, but there was nothing unusual there either. She was getting frustrated with the lack of tangible, tactile progress. Maybe it wasn't something outward. Maybe it was something inward. Maybe he was suffering from depression or another mental health condition. Marti found that just as terrifying, if not more, than a more mundane physical threat. When the mind turned against you, how did you fight back? She suppressed a shiver and moved outside to search Bill's truck.

She realized she should have asked Sandy for a key, but found the door was already open. She sat in the driver's seat. The truck smelled faintly of old coffee and fast-food wrappers. After a moment's deliberation, Marti decided it was not an altogether unpleasant smell. She searched the glove box, side pockets, and center console. She even checked under the seats and lifted the floor mats, but the truck didn't hold any secrets to Bill's distress, either.

She had just climbed out of the pickup and shut the door when a police cruiser pulled into the driveway.

Chapter Seven

"Great," she muttered. She thought maybe a neighbor had seen her in the garage or around Bill's truck and called the police as a concerned citizen. See something, say something.

A tall man with wide shoulders stepped out, wearing a crisp uniform and a serious expression. It was the type of neutral facial expression Marti thought of as polite cop-face. But then he locked eyes with Marti, raised his hand, and gave a hesitant wave that softened his features. "Are you Marti Wells?" he called out as he walked up the drive.

"Yes, that's me," Marti replied, extending her hand for a firm handshake. Up close, she suddenly saw the resemblance. "You must be Bill's brother."

"That's right," he confirmed. "I'm Kevin Thompson. Sandy told Kate, that's my wife, that you'd be here today. Thought I'd stop by and introduce myself."

Marti could sense a touch of defensiveness in his tone, and she understood why. She was a stranger, poking around in his late brother's life. "I appreciate it. I wanted to talk to you, too," she said, trying to put him at ease.

Kevin nodded, glancing back at the house and then at his shoes. "I gotta be honest, I'm not sure what to make of this."

"That makes two of us."

"I just want to make sure whatever you find isn't dressed up to tarnish my brother's memory," he said.

"That's not my intention at all. I didn't chase this or come looking for it. I was asked to do this as a favor."

"Your father."

"That's right, and I just want to help Sandy make peace with this. Maybe find some answers that help. I'm not here to dig up dirt on Bill."

"You're not going to find any dirt on Bill. He was a good man. A good detective. A good brother."

"I don't doubt it and if that's what I find, that's okay, too. That's a type of answer, too, and I've told Sandy that."

"Sandy won't like that. She likes to get her way."

Marti cocked her head at that. She hadn't seen that side of Sandy. She could certainly sense Sandy's stubbornness. She'd clung to the notion of Bill being upset and she'd gotten Marti to agree to the job, but Marti hadn't sensed any real hostility. Sandy had appeared almost numb with grief.

"How so?" she asked.

Now that she'd put him on the spot about his comment, he seemed reluctant to follow up. "Oh, I probably shouldn't have said anything. We just have opposite personalities, I suppose. I tend to go along to get along."

"And Sandy doesn't?"

He scratched his chin. "She tends to get her way in the end."

Marti didn't push it but made a mental note. "How much older was Bill than you?"

"Almost 15 years. I was the family surprise. I was always trailing after Bill and my cousins like a little puppy, but he never made me feel left out. Like I said, he was a good older brother."

"You must have been happy when he came back to town."

Something flashed across his face almost too fast to notice. "Yes. I had just started on the force at that point. Moved over from the sheriff's department."

"Sort of a family reunion."

He gave her a weak smile. "Something like that. I was happy to know my brother had my back."

There was something there, Marti thought, but steered the conversation away from any potential tension for the moment. Her instincts told her it wasn't the time to push. "I've been going through Bill's office. Your brother was well respected in the community and the police force," she commented. "I'm sure he had a positive impact on many people's lives."

"He did," Kevin replied, a flicker of pride crossing his face, and maybe relief at being on safer ground. "Bill was a dedicated officer, always striving to make Cedarwood a better place."

"Sandy must have been proud of the work he did."

"Sandy has always been there."

Which struck Marti as an odd turn of phrase, but before she could follow up, they heard an approaching engine. They both turned and watched Sandy's Acura pull into the driveway.

Kevin nodded to her as she pulled past them into the garage and then began walking back to his cruiser. "I hope you can find something that puts her mind at ease," he said. "Bill's passing has been tough on all of us."

"I'll do my best," Marti promised. "And I will keep you informed of any progress."

"Thank you," Kevin replied. "If you need anything or have questions, don't hesitate to reach out."

Sandy and Marti met at the garage and watched Kevin pull away. He raised a hand as he drove off and then Marti followed Sandy into the kitchen.

"Coffee?" Sandy asked.

"Sure."

"It's just instant. Is that okay?"

"Not a problem. I'm mostly in it for the caffeine."

Sandy took out two mugs, filled them with water from the tap, and put them in the microwave. As the water heated, she turned and leaned against the counter.

"You met Kevin."

"Yes. He stopped by while I was looking in Bill's truck. You two don't get along?"

"Did he say that?"

"No, actually he didn't. Your face right now is saying that."

Sandy smiled and shook her head. "We don't not get along. We just haven't found our footing yet since Bill's death. He doesn't think hiring you is a good idea," she said. "I can't blame Kevin for being protective. He loved his brother, and he's probably just looking out for me. But I was his wife, not Kevin, and I have a right to know what was going on with Bill."

Marti gave her a sympathetic smile. "Of course you do," she agreed. "And don't worry about Kevin. I'm used to dealing with skeptical family members."

Sandy chuckled softly. "I can imagine. You must have some interesting stories to tell," she said.

"Oh, you have no idea," Marti replied. "What about the rest of his family? What's your relationship with them? Any issues?"

"No, nothing beyond the usual family drama."

"Family is always tough in my experience," Marti said, thinking about her own often strained relationships with her father and sister. "It must be doubly tough when you all live on top of one another in the same small town." At least Marti could keep her sister a few interstates away.

"It can be a fishbowl," Sandy said. "And the dynamics of the Thompson family aren't exactly simple. I'm closest to Kevin's wife, Kate, but I'm friendly enough with the rest of the family. Since Bill's passing, I do feel like I've become a bit of a pariah, though. After they all dropped off the casseroles, thoughts, and prayers, I've heard little from them. No invitations for dinner or going out to Bluey's or Tuckerman's. We all used to like to do that when Bill was around." She smiled. "For such a strait-laced, introverted, rule follower, the man could really dance. I know some people thought we were a bit of an odd match, but that's how he won me over."

"A man who can dance can have any woman he wants."

"Ain't that the truth."

"Maybe the family is just trying to give you some space."

"Maybe. Or maybe cut me loose."

"I'm sure it's not that," Marti said.

"Don't be too sure, but you're probably going to talk to the lot of them. I'll let you decide."

Marti was getting the sense that talking to the extended family was going to be like walking through a minefield. She finished the coffee and put the mug on the sideboard. "I'm going to head down and check out the basement. I took a break from all the office paper after lunch, thank you for that by the way, and looked around the house but came up dry."

"All right," Sandy said. "I'll be around the rest of the day if you need anything."

Marti flicked the light switch at the top of the stairs and then felt her heartbeat quicken as she descended the creaky stairs into the dimly lit basement. She added weak 40-watt basement bulbs to her list of pet peeves. On the plus side, the low light kept her from noticing what was probably an abundance of spiders. She disliked spiders and other creatures with extra legs almost as much as she disliked mayonnaise.

She glanced around. She had braced herself for the same sort of clutter and disarray as she found in Bill's office, but what she found surprised her. The unfinished basement was tidy. Excruciatingly so. She pulled her phone from her pocket and turned on the flashlight app. The brighter light revealed a water heater and boiler in the far corner. Old cardboard moving boxes, now marked as containing holiday decorations, were piled on a pallet to keep them off the floor. A set of rough-hewn wooden shelves lined the opposite wall. Long white banker boxes sat on each shelf, meticulously labeled with months and years. He must have periodically purged the office, shredding or discarding old files and packaging up the others if he thought they might be needed or useful in the future.

Curiosity piqued, Marti walked over to one box labeled '2015' and carefully pulled it down. She opened it to find file folders filled with copies of official reports and case files. Her investigative instincts kicked in, and she flipped through the folders. She paused and looked down the length of the row. These shelves contained meticulous documentation of Bill Thompson's career as a police officer.

Then, tucked into one side of the box, she found something she recognized—a series of field notebooks, bound by a rubber band, similar to the ones she used herself. A little bigger than hers with a spiral-bound top, but there was no doubt about their purpose. She pulled one loose and flipped it open.

She recognized Bill's precise, neat handwriting. The pages documented various interviews, observations, hunches, and leads. Some notes were in a type of shorthand only he would recognize, but she got the gist of most of it. As she skimmed, she realized these notebooks were a treasure trove of insights into Bill's investigative techniques and thought processes.

Putting the notebook back in the box, Marti's eyes scanned the other boxes on the shelves. She walked down the row, box after box, each representing a part of Bill's career. Some years had two or three boxes, others only one. But as she reached the last box labeled '2022' her heart sank. There were no more boxes beyond this point. Bill's meticulous documentation had stopped six months ago. Maybe that was natural. Maybe he did a sort of audit every six months or just once a year, depending on the ebb and flow of his casework. But maybe there was something else going on.

Frustration mixed with determination surged within Marti. Part of her wanted to write this all off as Sandy's grief. But she couldn't. Not yet. Maybe there was something crucial in those last six months that would explain the behavior Sandy noted before Bill's passing. If that was the case, his notes might be the key. She needed to get her hands on Bill's last field notebook. She hadn't come across it in his office. Maybe they were with his personal items and still at the station. Or maybe he had it on him when he died.

She glanced at her watch and realized that the afternoon was slipping away. Deciding to call it a day, she made her way back upstairs. Sandy sat like a sentinel in her chair by the kitchen window.

"I didn't find anything specific down there," Marti said as she closed the basement door. "Did the coroner return any personal effects?"

"Yes, his clothes, watch, keys, rings. It's all in a box in my car. I … didn't know what to do with it."

"Did you notice if it included a notebook?"

"A notebook?"

"A small one that he might have used on the job?"

"Oh, one of those. Bill always had one in his pocket. I was terrified I'd end up putting them through the wash and he'd lose some clue or important number."

"Did you?"

"No, I never did, but there is no notebook in the box."

"You're sure?"

"Yes, they went through each item with me as they put it into the box and gave me a receipt. I'm sure."

"Okay. I can't find the one he was using at the time he died."

"Huh. If it's not in the office, I haven't seen it anywhere else in the house. Maybe Jessica has it at the station?"

"That was my thought. I'm going to call it a day soon and go check in at the inn, but I plan on talking to her tomorrow and then come back and tackle more of the office."

"Okay, I might be out, but I'll leave the door unlocked. Just let yourself in."

"Thank you."

They chatted for a few more minutes. Sandy gave her the contact information for her oldest son, Ethan, in New York. Marti would prefer to talk to him in person, but if things changed, or she had a question, it would be good to have the information at hand. She also asked Sandy to write a list of the rest of the extended Thompson family members in Cedarwood and their spouses. Sandy said she'd have it ready the next day.

Marti could sense the disappointment coming off of Sandy in waves as she prepared to leave. She didn't want to promise answers or results, but after watching Sandy slowly wilt throughout the day, she didn't want to leave her alone like this for the night. "Don't give up yet," Marti said. "We said we'd give it three days, right? We'll keep looking. Let me talk to some more people."

"You're right," Sandy said as she walked Marti to the door. "See you tomorrow."

Marti could tell Sandy didn't see two days still left, only one day already gone, but it was the best Marti could offer right now.

Chapter Eight

The Cedarwood Inn stood on the corner of Main Street and Elm Avenue, an elegant three-story building with a charming white facade adorned with intricate gingerbread wood trim. The exterior also boasted a wraparound porch with a line of rocking chairs where guests could sit and watch the happenings at the gazebo or town square. An old-fashioned wooden sign stood on the lawn surrounded by beds of landscaped flowers and low shrubs.

It was almost too charming, Marti thought as she carried her small overnight and laptop bags up the front steps. The scent of old wood and polished brass greeted her as she pushed through the wooden double doors. Dark oak floorboards creaked under her feet. The lobby exuded a nostalgic charm of a sort, with antique furniture and vintage oil paintings adorning the walls. The air smelled strongly of floral potpourri.

An older woman stood behind an ornate wooden desk at the end of the hall that served as the check-in counter.

"Ah, Marti, dear, I've been expecting you all day!" the woman exclaimed, leaning forward as if she was about to share a secret. "I'm Lucille Edwards, the owner. Sandy told me you'd be staying with us."

Lucille was an older woman, big boned, in her late 60s, with a mischievous glint in her eyes. Curly silver hair framed her face, and she wore a colorful floral dress that seemed to match her vibrant personality.

Marti raised an eyebrow, recognizing the mating dance of a classic gossip hound. She knew she'd have to be careful not to reveal too much to Lucille, but at the same time, she couldn't help but feel that the innkeeper might be a valuable source of information. Or a tool to spread information.

"Well, that's me, and here I am," Marti replied.

"And how's it going so far?" Lucille asked.

Marti deflected as best she could. She was not ready to engage with the town busybody just yet. "Not too much to report. This was really the first day. I'm just going through Bill's home office and personal effects. Getting things organized. Meeting people. Getting the lay of the land. That sort of thing."

"Uh-huh." The evasive non-answer clearly disappointed Lucille, but she had just enough manners not to push it further. Not yet. She left a pregnant pause, but Marti was a pro at the silent waiting game. She smiled and stared right back.

After a moment, Lucille cleared her throat and looked down at the desk.

"Well then, Sandy already took care of the payment details, but if you'll just sign the register, we'll get you officially checked in." She picked up a large leather-bound ledger and turned it around to face Marti. She must not have disguised the look on her face. "A bit of an antiquated formality, I admit," Lucille said, "but we have a written record of every guest going back to 1810. John Adams and James Polk both stayed here."

"Never much cared for the Polk administration," Marti said.

Lucille frowned for a moment. "That was a joke."

"Yes."

"I see." As if she knew James Polk and took personal offense.

Marti dutifully signed her name but began to wonder if the room would have a pull-chain toilet and a spittoon. Lucille slid the register onto a shelf behind her and then turned back around.

"Did you know Bill?" Marti asked.

Lucille's eyes softened with a touch of sentimentality and the innkeeper immediately brightened at the question and Marti wondered if she'd been rehearsing what she'd say if asked.

"Oh, yes, I knew Bill very well," she replied. "We went to school together, all the way from kindergarten to graduation. He was a bright and cheerful young man."

"Was he a jock? A nerd? What was he like in school?"

"Oh, he played sports but wasn't the star. He moved between all the cliques, never in the spotlight, but never shunned either."

Marti remembered high school far less fondly. "Difficult to pull off."

"Yes, I suppose, but Bill was tough to dislike."

"You lost touch after graduation?"

"I went off to college, then came back here and slowly took over from my parents. Bill joined the Army after graduation and moved away, but he came back when his daddy got sick."

Marti nodded. "And he had other family here too, right? I met Kevin." She prodded further.

Lucille nodded back. "Yes, indeed. Kevin, I did not know as well. He's the youngest, but the Thompsons have been here for generations. Family was important to Bill. He had lots of relatives in the area. After his daddy passed, he decided to stay. Wanted to be close to family, I suppose. Losing a parent, even one like Donald Thompson, can make you reevaluate things."

"And when he came back, what was he like? Did you still like Bill?"

"Of course, I still liked him. He was the same man, just a little more gray, a little more mature like all of us, but he was still easy to like. A good man—loyal and moral. You won't find anyone in town saying anything different if that's what you're after."

Lucille's sniff implied she would be the ultimate judge of Bill's character.

"That's not what I'm after, Lucille. It was just a question. If I'm going to help Sandy, I need to know about Bill."

"Of course, I'm sorry. I'm not used to dealing with private investigators." Lucille came around the desk and led Marti up the interior staircase to the inn's second floor.

"No problem. What about Sandy? She would have been a few years behind you and Bill in school." Marti let the question hang and knew Lucille would fill it in. She was clearly not a woman comfortable with silence.

Still, unlike her quick defense of Bill, Lucille paused for a moment before answering, or maybe it was just the act of climbing the stairs. "Sandy is more complicated," she began, choosing her words carefully and a little breathlessly. "She's efficient, that's for sure. If you need something done, she's the woman you want. We work together at the food pantry, and she's always taking charge and getting things organized. The same goes for other projects through the church. But ..." Lucille hesitated.

"But?" Marti prodded gently, sensing there was clearly more to the story. They reached the top of the stairs and turned left.

Lucille sighed. "She can sometimes come off as a bit abrasive. Granted, she's just holding people to their word or expectations, but some folks take offense to it. I think she means well, but her straightforward manner can rub people the wrong way."

Lucille stopped outside a second-floor room. "Here we are." She handed Marti a brass key the size of a soup spoon.

Marti nodded. "Thank you, Lucille. Your perspective has been really helpful."

Lucille smiled warmly. "You're welcome, dear. If you need anything else or have more questions, just let me know. Enjoy your stay," she said, turning to head back downstairs.

Marti fit the key into the lock and, with some effort, it turned with an audible snap. The air inside felt warm and cottony as if someone hadn't turned the room over in quite some time. The room's interior matched the cozy charm of the rest of the inn, but it was entirely outside of Marti's taste. A queen-size canopy bed with faded, frilly curtains hanging from an ornate wooden frame dominated the space. Marti placed her bags on the lumpy mattress, went to the window, and pushed the curtains (frilly, of course) aside. The window faced the front of the inn, toward the gazebo, and along the main street. She could just see the edge of the Harmony's Brew awning off to the left. She tried pulling the window open, but it didn't budge. There might be literally centuries of paint keeping it in place. She let it be.

She turned back to the room and sat on the bed. The quilt on the bed looked like it had seen better days, its colors now muted with age. All the remaining furniture, dresser, bedside tables, chair and matching ottoman, were old, but not in a chic way— more in a worn-down way as if they had been there since the inn first opened its doors and Polk was eating in the dining room. The room's wallpaper had a pattern of large, climbing roses, and the carpet was threadbare in some places.

The Cedarwood Inn was well loved, but it hadn't seen an update in decades.

The room felt suffocating with its stuffy air and dated decor, but it was only a minor inconvenience. She'd spend most of her time here sleeping. She would make the best of it and focus on the case at hand. After all, solving the mystery behind Bill Thompson's distress was more important than her personal comfort. Mostly.

With that thought, she pulled out her notebook. She dropped into a doily-laced chair and jotted down more observations about the day. Had she made any progress? Maybe. She'd certainly gathered more string. As she recounted the day in her mind, she realized she'd forgotten to ask Sandy about the prescription pills in the medicine cabinet. She made a note and circled it. She felt her eyes getting heavy in the warm air.

Where was Bill's last notebook?

Chapter Nine

Marti sat up with a jolt and for a moment the room's dim light played tricks on her waking mind and she was lost in the unfamiliar shapes and shadows before the musty scent of the potpourri and dusty quilts jolted her back to reality at the Cedarwood Inn. She sat back in the chair and her notebook slid from her lap and landed on the floor with a soft thud. With a sigh, she stood, stretched her arms and legs, then made her way to the window.

Outside, darkness enveloped everything. The town green was still, only a few scattered streetlamps provided dull yellow light. No one was out. She listened to the quiet whistle of the wind through the inn's upper eaves before she stepped back. She fumbled in her bag and pulled out her phone. Its digital glow revealed it was nearly eight o'clock. She'd been out for almost two hours. Her stomach rumbled a gentle reminder it had been a while since her meager turkey sandwich and Milanos for lunch at Sandy's house. She found the switch on the table-side lamp and flicked it on, temporarily banishing the shadows, but perhaps not improving the room's decor.

After a quick visit to the bathroom to freshen up, Marti made her way back downstairs. She steeled herself for another interrogation, but the familiar face of Lucille was absent from the front desk, replaced by a young woman who appeared to be in her early twenties. Marti offered a polite smile as she approached.

"Good evening," Marti said.

"Hi there," the young woman replied with a friendly smile and set her phone aside. "How can I help you?"

"Marti Wells," she introduced herself, extending her hand.

The young woman shook it. "I'm Holly. A pleasure to meet you."

Marti nodded. "Likewise. I was wondering if you could recommend a place to grab a bite around here. It's been a long day and my stomach is begging for some attention."

Holly's eyes flicked to the clock on the wall. "Well, at this hour, your best bet is probably the Blue Haven Pub. It's just a few blocks away unless you want to drive back out to the interstate."

"No, I was thinking of walking."

"Bluey's it is then. Stay away from the meatloaf or any specials they're pushing. Stick to the burgers or chicken and you'll be fine. It's close. Just head north, away from the square, take the first right, then two quick lefts. You'll see it."

Marti nodded her appreciation. "Sounds good. Keep it simple. The easy choice is no choice."

Holly grinned. "You'll like it here then. No chance of overanalyzing things in Cedarwood. Except for gas stations, banks, or churches, we only have one of anything. So it's Bluey's or the Circle K, and I think the pub wins hands down unless you're a connoisseur of three-day-old hot dogs."

Marti chuckled. She liked this girl, liked her bubbly sarcasm. "No, I like my dogs boiled and fresh. Pub it is, then. Thanks for the tip, Holly."

"You're welcome! Enjoy your meal, and if you need anything else, just ask."

"You on all night?"

"No, just until eleven. We lock up after that. Lucille lives in a guest house at the back of the property. There's an after-hours buzzer near the front door that rings her. Or, if you think you'll be later, we can give you a key for that door, as well."

"Got it." Marti thought about waking up or even encountering Lucille at that time of night. "I'll take a key, just in case."

Holly smiled and nodded as if she could tell what Marti was thinking, then reached into one of the desk drawers and withdrew a key with a small red ribbon tied to it. "Here you go. The lock can get sticky sometimes. Just wiggle the key a bit. It'll turn eventually."

"Thanks." With a last nod, Marti headed down the hall toward the door, but then stopped and came back. "Quick question. Do you know Olivia Thompson? Around your age, I think."

"Oh, sure. Olivia. We were only a grade apart in school. Most everyone knows everyone here, you know. Small town, small lives, et cetera." She shrugged as if the cliche was an accepted fact. Maybe it was. Marti had grown up in a metropolis compared to Cedarwood and even then, Paterson had felt small and insular to her teenage self. She couldn't imagine how desperate the itch might be for some to escape a place the size of Cedarwood. Then again, Bill Thompson had escaped and had come back.

Marti smiled, slipping into her PI persona. "I'm working for Sandy Thompson, Olivia's mom. Trying to help her figure a few things out since her husband passed away."

Holly put up a hand. "Lucille filled me in, but even without her, most everyone knows why you're here, Marti."

"Oh," Marti said. She'd been here a day and everyone knew? The look must have shown on her face.

"Small town," Holly said again. "Get used to it."

Marti shook it off. Maybe everyone knowing her purpose might actually make her job easier. "Okay, great. That saves me the explanation. What can you tell me about Olivia?"

"Well," Holly started, "she shouldn't be hard to find. She's still in town and waitresses over at the cafe most days. I think she's going to school too, but I'm not sure for what. We were better friends in elementary school. We still smile and say hi, or whatever, but we don't really hang out anymore. I don't know, we just drifted apart in high school. Olivia was pretty quiet, kept mostly to herself, especially after Samantha."

"Samantha?" Marti inquired.

Holly nodded somberly. "Yeah, Samantha. She was Olivia's best friend, but she … she killed herself in 10th grade."

Marti's expression turned serious. "I'm sorry to hear that."

Holly's response was a half-hearted shrug. "Yeah, it sucked. She took a bottle of vodka out into the woods during a snowstorm, drank the entire bottle, and then passed out. She died of hypothermia. No one knows why she did it." Then, with a dismissive gesture, "But life goes on."

Marti pondered the weight of such an event in a small town, and the weight of whatever event pushed Samantha out into those woods. "Intense," she murmured, as if speaking to herself, but then recalled her own misspent youth where everything, good and bad, had felt intense. Teenagers often felt invincible or above the consequences of their often reckless actions. The permanence of death was almost something they couldn't conceive. Despite Holly's casual attitude, Marti had been around enough death to know that Samantha's suicide would have rolled through the town, and the town's young people, like an irrepressible wave.

"Life goes on," Marti repeated. Another cliche. She understood the sentiment but wasn't sure she totally believed it. It certainly didn't go on for Samantha. What about Samantha's parents? Or siblings? Or friends? It might have gone on for Olivia but veered off in another direction without her best friend.

"Thanks again for the recommendation on the food."

"Sure thing. Remember to stay away from the meatloaf," Holly said with a smile.

"Will do." Marti wrapped her knuckles on the old check-in desk and headed out of the inn and into the chilly night. The crisp air was a welcome change after the stuffiness of the inn. She walked briskly through the empty streets toward the Blue Haven Pub. A breeze rustled the leaves of the oaks and maples that lined the square. Holly's directions played in her mind: head north, a right turn, and two lefts. She followed the route, the quaint streets of Cedarwood echoing with the soft scuffs of her footsteps.

Chapter Ten

The Blue Haven Pub bore a timeless charm, its facade constructed from rustic brickwork and mullioned windows. Maybe she was just hungry, but all the charm was beginning to grate on Marti's nerves. The building's architecture embraced a two-story structure with a gently sloping roof, giving it an unassuming yet inviting silhouette against the night. To its left, a small antique shop exuded a similar sense of history, its weathered storefront window adorned with faded curiosities. On the other side stood a bookstore, its window display showing stacks of new and used books. Like a moth to a flame, Marti stopped briefly and perused the titles on display before continuing on.

Entering the pub, the aroma of food and the murmur of conversations mixed with the television over the bar greeted Marti. The interior was a blend of old countryside charm and modern comfort. Large-format black-and-white landscape photos, Marti assumed of the surrounding area, adorned the walls, while intermittent dimly lit sconces added a cozy ambiance. The bar ran along one side of the room, polished wood reflecting the warm lighting. Scattered tables and large booths on the opposite wall filled out the space.

It was a Monday night, so the pub wasn't bustling, but it was far from empty. A handful of patrons occupied tables and stools, engaged in quiet conversations. As her gaze swept the room, she noticed an interesting sight—a lone figure seated at the bar, engrossed in her thoughts, half-eaten burger pushed away, half-empty glass still in front of her. Olivia Thompson. Marti's curiosity stirred as she considered why Olivia might dine alone at the bar. Was it by choice or necessity? She started toward Olivia when she felt someone watching her. Marti's eyes scanned the scene again until they settled on a back booth. There, she spotted a man with a strong resemblance to Bill Thompson, sitting across from a woman. He raised a hand slightly.

Marti altered course and walked over. As she approached the booth, she studied Kevin Thompson's face, his features a mix of curiosity and uncertainty. The woman sitting with him was in her late 30s, with chestnut-brown hair that cascaded gracefully in loose waves around her shoulders in a way that made Marti jealous of her own unruly locks.

"Hey there," Marti greeted as she reached the table.

Kevin's expression remained guarded, still the polite cop, but his tone was friendly. "Hi, Marti. Marti, this is my wife, Kate."

"Pleasure. I'm Marti Wells. I've been talking to your sister-in-law about Bill."

Kate extended her hand with a friendly smile. Her grip was cool and firm. "Nice to meet you. Sandy mentioned you would be around. Pull up a chair."

Marti grabbed a chair from an empty table and sat. "Is that Olivia at the bar?" Marti asked.

Kevin kept quiet, but Kate answered. "Sure, that's Olivia. Have you spoken to her?"

"Yes, we connected this morning. Why is she eating alone?"

"Oh, that's just Olivia," Kevin said. "She came over to say hello when she came in, but she likes to keep to herself."

Marti filed that away. Olivia was family to Kevin by marriage, not blood. His brother's stepdaughter. She also recalled what Holly had told her about Olivia being quiet. Marti hadn't sensed that when they'd met at the cafe, but maybe a single bar patron was her true persona and she was just playing a part as the perky waitress. No one liked a sullen server. No tips in that.

She focused back on Kate. "Do you have any idea what might have been bothering Bill in the last few weeks before his death?"

Kevin put his bottle of beer down on the table with an audible tap but didn't say anything, just stared off over Marti's shoulder, maybe watching the football game from a distance.

"No, I don't and I've told Sandy that. I told her she'd be better off letting sleeping dogs lie. As far as I saw, Bill was Bill. He was a nice guy, but I don't think anyone would describe him as … exuberant. Being a little moody or short-tempered is hardly a crime, right?"

"Of course not, but it might show that something was bothering him. I didn't get the sense that Bill was always that way."

"No, he was always pretty serious, especially about his job. Kevin is similar, but Bill was typically polite. Like I said, not chatty, but he was social. You will not find many people in town that will say a bad word about Bill."

Marti was getting a bit exasperated by this knee-jerk reaction to every question she asked about Bill. "Good, that's not what I'm after. I'm pretty sure that's not what Sandy's after, either. She knew her husband which is what makes his behavior, or demeanor, at the time of his death so troubling for her. But I never met him. I'm totally in the dark, so I'm just trying to get a sense of the man. Was he smart? Silly? Prickly?"

Kate looked at her. Marti felt Kevin's attention shift. She could feel him tense across the table. He was still watching the game, but he was also interested in what his wife might say. Kate tilted her head and rolled the glass in her hand. "The best I can do is say he was a cop. First, second, and third. He was a good man. I can't speak about him as a husband. He was smart, but he liked and respected rules. He did everything by the book. On the job and probably at home, too."

She sensed Kevin relax a fraction. She shifted her eyes to him. "That sound about right? As his brother?"

He nodded. "That sounds fair. Makes him sound like a bit of a hard ass, which maybe he was, but he wasn't a teetotaler for the rules, either. He might try to give you a break or warning on the small stuff, but she's right, he wouldn't let you slide on the big ones. He believed in accountability."

"Did that ever lead to any problems? Being an officer in a small town, it has to lead to some tangled relationships."

Kevin shrugged. "Sure, but that's part of the job. You can't make it personal. It's just business."

A waitress, a young woman with bright-red hair pulled back in a messy bun, approached the table. Kevin ordered another beer for himself, and Kate and Marti said, "I'll have the same."

"Sure thing," she said.

"Did everyone feel that way?" Marti asked as the waitress departed for the bar to fill the order.

"Don't know. I'm sure some people felt a shared history was worth something but, for Bill, it didn't put them above the law. Above accountability for their actions."

"Can you think of any examples?"

Kevin spun the empty pint glass between his palms for a moment and then said, "There was this one time, five or six years ago now, when Bill had to arrest his own best friend from high school. They weren't still super close, but there was a lot of history there." Kevin shook his head, a mixture of nostalgia and regret in his eyes. "It was a white-collar crime case. The crime itself was a financial mess, but bloodless. One of those crimes where it's sort of hard to tell if anyone actually got hurt. To an outsider, it might look like a victimless crime. Just a guy manipulating spreadsheets. Maybe he's getting rich but he's not out front waving a gun in a teller's face, you know?"

"Sure, but I'm guessing that cut no ice with Bill."

"Mark Anderson was the vice president at the local bank branch. Turns out, Bill's old friend had been manipulating accounts for years, opening dummy accounts and dummy loans and collecting performance bonuses based on the new client volume. The bank branch's internal audits couldn't quite pinpoint the source of the irregularities, but they knew something was off."

He paused as the waitress dropped off their drinks. "The tip came from an anonymous source, a bank employee who stumbled upon some suspicious documents. They slipped a note under the door of the local police station, honest to God, and that's how Bill ultimately got wind of it."

Kevin's fingers tapped lightly on the rim of his glass, his gaze distant. "Bill began digging deeper. Taught himself accounting principles. He pored over financial records, interviewed bank employees, and traced the money. It was meticulous work, and the more he uncovered, the clearer it became that Mark Anderson was behind it all. It was a tough case for Bill. Anderson had lied right to his face. More than once. But the evidence was undeniable. The paper trail, the money transfers—it all pointed to his old friend's guilt."

"What did he do?" Marti asked.

"Only thing he could do. He laid out the evidence, Anderson stopped the denials, and Bill arrested him. That was his job, his sworn duty. He didn't take that oath lightly. He would have rather pulled out his own teeth with rusty pliers than let Anderson slide. I was there. For his part, Anderson didn't cajole or blame Bill. I think he was relieved, to be honest. Last I checked, Anderson's got four years to go up at Bayside. Most people get it. They don't hold us personally responsible. Some do, of course. You just learn to deal with those guys."

"Sounds like Bill could have made a pretty good career of it in the military. I'm surprised he opted out."

Kevin gave a wan smile. "You're right, and I think he was going to be a lifer, but our family genes betrayed him. It was a medical separation. He failed a physical. Heart arrhythmia."

Marti thought of the prescription bottle in the bedroom medicine cabinet. "But he could still get a job as a police officer?"

Kevin half nodded, half shrugged. "He didn't talk about it, but I guess the issue wasn't that severe. He didn't have a pacemaker or anything. It was big enough for the Army to say no, they can afford to be choosy, but not big enough for Paterson or Cedarwood to pass him up."

The conversation petered out, though Marti sensed there was more to learn. She needed to work on her bullshit. She was good at digging out facts, good at interviewing when she had an objective or a string to pull on, but bad at prospecting. She would have gone broke in sales.

But this time, Kate saved her.

Marti was about to say goodnight and try her luck with Olivia at the bar when Kate said, "What about the Manning case?"

Marti watched something flash across Kevin's face at the mention of Manning's name. She'd almost missed it. Maybe it was nothing. Just a fleeting burp, swallowed down to be polite, but maybe not. He'd looked annoyed at his wife's comment. Maybe even angry.

"What's the Manning case?" Marti prompted when neither Kate nor Kevin spoke up. It wasn't nothing. Kate had caught the look or felt the vibrations coming off her husband. She was suddenly very interested in the label on her bottle of beer.

"A cold case," Kevin finally said. "Missing person. It happened maybe five years ago now. Big news around here, but maybe not up in the big city."

Marti let the comment go. "Did Bill do a lot of cold case work?"

Kevin shrugged. "We all do. It can get slow out here. You pick up a file and try to crack one. What else are you going to do? You can only write so many parking tickets."

"Why was the Manning case big news?"

"David Manning was a popular high school science teacher with a passion for nature photography. He was always walking the parks and trails around here at dawn or dusk with his camera.

"He was last seen at Emerald Lake, a popular tourist spot, and a place he was known to visit often to photograph the sunset over the water. A passerby found his camera and tripod abandoned on the shore, but no one ever saw Manning or his body again."

"Hard to disappear these days," Marti said.

"No obvious motive in this case. No reason he'd disappear on his own. No note. No blood. No other nearby footprints other than the guy walking his dog who found the camera. Despite divers in the lake, searches of surrounding woods, and interviewing just about everyone in town, no concrete leads ever materialized. No leads period. It was big news because there was no news."

"And conspiracy theories make for better headlines than tragic accidents."

He tipped his now empty bottle in her direction. "Exactly."

"And Bill was working this in his spare time."

"That might be putting it a bit strongly. I don't think it was that formal. For a long time, it was just a local mystery. It was the topic that would come up during poker games or backyard barbecues. Batting around theories. Bill might have been a little more serious about it than others, but I don't think he was losing sleep over it."

"Got it," Marti said. "That doesn't seem like something he'd need to keep from Sandy. It sounds like it was pretty widely known in town."

"Well, Sandy is a different story," Kevin said. This time, Marti caught a look on Kate's face. There were apparently two different conversations going on at the same time.

The waitress had cleared away the empties as she brought fresh rounds and Marti wondered how long and how much the Thompsons had been drinking.

"How so?" Marti said.

"Bill adored her and practically worshiped the ground she walked on, and he loved those kids like his own, but she can be difficult. She likes to get her way and she'll prod and push until she does. That will eventually leave a mark."

Marti glanced at Kate, but the other woman wouldn't meet her eyes. Marti would be interested in her opinion. What Kevin was describing could be true or could just be how some men saw certain types of women, strong women who knew what they wanted and didn't sit back passively and wait for it. She didn't know Sandy well enough to make a call, but she also hadn't seen the person Kevin was describing. To be fair, though, Lucille's description when she was checking into her room could have been a more polite way of saying the same thing.

"Were you surprised they got together when Bill moved back to town?"

"A little. I don't remember them interacting much back in the glory days, but I was far behind Bill in school, so maybe I missed something."

"Were they happy?"

"I thought so, but looking in from the outside on anyone's marriage and making a guess like that is a sucker's bet. I've gotten calls on domestics to places and addresses you'd never suspect."

It felt as if they were heading out onto thinner ice and Marti wasn't sure she saw much benefit in pursuing it further with Kevin. She wanted to get Kate alone at some point, but that could wait.

She finished her beer and put her palms on the table.

"Okay, I've taken up more than enough of your time tonight. Thank you. It's been helpful to hear about this side of Bill." She smiled and replaced the chair. "Nice meeting you, Kate."

Marti headed toward the bar and looked for Olivia, but the young woman was gone. She perched on a stool at the end of the bar with a wide view of the room. She watched the Thompsons talk to another couple on their way out and then leave. She didn't recognize anyone else, so she ordered a burger, pulled a paperback out of her purse, and drank a glass of mediocre pinot grigio while she waited for the food. The burger was better than the wine, but the book was better than both. She was feeling more relaxed with a stomach full of beef, cheese, and alcohol. She debated another drink but then thought better of it. She needed to be rested and sharp in the morning. She planned to find Jessica Lawson at the precinct. She settled her bill, slid off the stool, and headed for the door.

Chapter Eleven

As she walked back to the inn, Marti's footsteps echoed through the deserted streets of Cedarwood, creating a ghostly cadence in the still night. There were no cars or other pedestrians on the street. Cedarwood rolled up the sidewalks early. The small town seemed subdued in the dark, a canvas without its charming colors. As she walked, the sporadic lights away from the pub cast long shadows that seemed to reach out and grasp at her like silent specters. The back of her neck tingled. She felt a growing unease, a subtle sense of vulnerability. She tried to shake it off, but it stuck. She tucked her chin and picked up her pace. Three hours ago, she never thought she'd be rushing back to the quilts and frills of the inn, but that's all she wanted at the moment.

She made the second left. Poplar Street was another desolate corridor. There were more streetlights, but no people. Didn't anyone walk their dogs in Cedarwood? The harsh glow of streetlights now cut sharp shadows that highlighted the lingering pockets of dark alleys. Her footfalls bounced and echoed off the buildings that seemed to hunch and loom over her. She forced herself to keep walking. She felt her heartbeat quicken and a growing sense of anxiety gnawed at her resolve not to break into a run.

She rebuked herself for ordering the bar's cheap pinot, whose aftertaste coated her mouth now like an old sock. "It's all in your head," she muttered to herself.

Until it wasn't.

The sound of an approaching car drew her attention. It moved closer and she expected it to pass, but it didn't. The car stayed behind her and matched her pace. Its high beams cast a blinding halo around her and elongated her shadow out in front of her. She stopped and turned. The car braked, then stopped. She shielded her eyes, but she could see nothing beyond the light from the square headlights. A knot of tension twisted in her stomach, and she fought to keep her composure. Maybe it was a cop on patrol. Or someone stopping to take a phone call. Her rational mind threw out other sensible possibilities, but a deep, ancient part of her brain told her something else. She was being hunted. She was the prey. She turned around and resumed walking. Her steps now punctuated by the steady rhythm of her racing heart.

She hadn't brought her gun. It remained locked up in the floor safe of her Jersey City apartment. She didn't like guns, saw them as a last resort, and who would have thought she'd need it on this case? But she wasn't completely unarmed. Working alone, as a woman, often in dangerous or fraught situations, she might not carry a firearm, but she carried pepper spray and a personal safety alarm in her purse. She slipped her hand inside her purse and found the slim canister of mace

Suddenly, the engine roared behind her, and without thinking, she leaped to the side, her body tense with fear and flooded with adrenaline. The roar was quickly followed by a screech of tires as the car rocked to a stop beside her. She looked to her right. Her gaze met the eyes of the driver. The eyes were all that was visible inside the dark car. The driver wore a ski mask with the mouth stitched together in a crooked line with thick red string. The sight chilled her to the bone—the stitched mouth and hollow eyes felt like a nightmare given physical form.

As Marti stared, a gloved hand raised, a finger and thumb extended like the gun she'd left behind. Marti's breath caught in her throat. The nightmare apparition pulled the imaginary trigger, a gesture that seemed to cut through the night air like a gunshot. Marti took an involuntary step back. Then, just as abruptly, the car sped away, red taillights disappearing into the night. Marti stood there, trembling, as the distant rumble of the engine faded into nothingness.

She didn't check herself now. She ran the rest of the way back to the inn with the canister of mace tight in one hand. She looked over her shoulder a few times, but never saw the car or the headlights or anyone else behind her. She sprinted past the empty gazebo and almost slipped and fell on the damp grass of the town square before she made it across the street to the inn. The yellow porch light by the door acted like a beacon.

She stopped and clung to the wrought iron rail at the bottom of the porch steps. Her breath heaved in her chest and small, bright spots danced in front of her eyes. She closed them and took three deep, calming breaths. Relief washed over her as she climbed the steps. She was okay. She was safe.

With shaky hands, she pulled at the doorknob. It didn't budge. The itching sensation on her neck returned. She desperately twisted the knob back and forth until she remembered Holly said she locked the door at eleven. A compulsion to look back seized her, but she resisted. She would not give in.

She clawed at her pocket as she felt the anxiety return. She finally pulled out the extra key and then almost dropped it. Her hand shook too badly to fit the key into the lock. She felt her heart in her throat. She closed her eyes and squeezed the key until she felt the sharp edges cut into her palm. The pain cut through the panic. The doorknob stopped doing the jitterbug and the key slid into the lock. She turned the key firmly and felt the lock snick back. She slipped inside and threw the bolt back. Relief washed over her as she leaned her forehead against the door's cool glass.

Slowly, she looked up. Beyond the gazebo, she spotted a single flicker of red—the glowing tip of a cigarette. Her gaze locked onto it. The embers burned like a malevolent eye in the night. Then, with an almost casual gesture, it tumbled away, swallowed by the darkness. Could be anyone, Marti thought. Didn't have to be the man in the mask. Could finally be that dog walker or a local cutting across the green on their way home. Still, a shiver raced down her spine. As Marti retreated upstairs to the safety of her room, her thoughts were a whirlwind of questions and unease. What had she stumbled into?

Marti paced the dimly lit room, too wired to go to sleep right away. Her footsteps creaked across the warped wooden floor. She glanced at the outdated lock on the door and wondered if it would hold against any real threat. She propped the spindly desk chair under the knob, a potentially futile attempt at creating a more substantial barrier against potential intruders.

She stood a few feet back from the window, gazing out, watching for movement or more cigarettes. The moon hung low, casting a pale glow over the town center. To most, it would be a serene scene, a Rockwell portrait of a small town at rest, but to Marti, it belied the unease coursing through her veins. The events on her walk back to the inn had caught her off guard and shaken her, but it had also ignited something.

As she resumed her pacing, her thoughts buzzed with conflicting emotions. One voice urged her to pack her bags, leave Cedarwood behind, and let Sandy find another way to deal with her grief. She was not required to risk her life for the woman's peace of mind. This was not a personal quest or vendetta for Marti. It was a job. Another voice, the one she recognized as her true self, protested. It whispered about integrity, her word, and her reputation as a relentless investigator. If she bailed on this case, what would happen on the next one where she was pushed, shoved, or threatened?

Fighting off her frustration, Marti sat on the edge of the bed. She ran her fingers through her hair, the tangled strands seeming to mirror her tired mind. Frustration mingled with curiosity. She'd only been here a day. Who had she ticked off enough to warrant a reaction like tonight?

She finally felt the edges of sleep as tiredness pulled at her eyelids, a reminder of the early start and exhausting day she'd had. She gave up on the rest of her nightly routine. Nothing about tonight had been ordinary or routine, so she felt justified not brushing her teeth. She left her mace on the side table, her shoes by the bed, and slid under the bed's heavy quilt. She looked at the old-fashioned canopy above her, its ruffled edges casting shadows on the far wall.

Sleep was out there but did not come easily. She missed her own bed. This room felt suffocating. Outwardly, she kicked at the weight of the heavy quilt as she tossed and turned. Inwardly, her mind continued its tug-of-war. She counted her breaths and tried to distance herself from the events of the night. She'd always been good at shutting out emotions. Just ask any of her ex-husbands or her sister.

As seconds turned to minutes, her thoughts gradually quieted. She looked past the fear.

She'd only officially been on the case for a day, but clearly she'd spooked someone enough for them to follow her out of the pub and try to intimidate her. But who? She'd barely talked to anyone yet. She'd basically puttered around Bill's very cluttered office and talked to his immediate family. Then again, Holly told her the entire town knew Sandy had hired her. Maybe it wasn't anything she said or anyone she talked to. Maybe her presence alone in Cedarwood represented a threat.

Just as she drifted off, Marti realized it might also mean something else. Sandy might be right. Bill might have been anxious about something but kept it to himself. And someone in Cedarwood wanted it to stay that way.

Chapter Twelve

Sleep helped. Marti woke up feeling more determined and clear-headed. The morning air was crisp as she stepped out of the inn's side door. Her breath formed small puffs in the early light. The secondary door led to the inn's garden and the well-cared for space greeted her with an array of colors—a symphony of late-season flowers that swayed gently in the cool breeze. Stone pathways meandered through the lush greenery, inviting guests to explore. It wouldn't last much longer, and she felt lucky to see it now. Summer was long gone and even autumn was fading. She was okay with that. She enjoyed the change of seasons, and fall was her favorite. It brought its own colors and mindset. She tilted her head up to the sun. She needed the warmth and light after last night.

Beyond the garden, Marti's gaze fell upon a small Cape-style cottage nestled at the rear of the property. It exuded a rustic charm, of course. The cottage's exterior boasted a low white picket fence, a vegetable garden, and potted flowers along a slate walkway that led to a bright purple door. It had to be Lucille's home. No one else could pull off that shade of purple. She felt a slight pang of guilt at dodging the woman by using the side door. Marti had no doubt she was waiting for her at the reception desk but knew she couldn't face the woman without caffeine.

Leaving the serene garden behind, Marti walked toward Harmony's Brew. The aroma of freshly brewed coffee was like a physical fish hook in her cheek, pulling her toward the eclectic cafe.

As Marti entered the cafe, the bell jingled softly above the door. The atmosphere, like her previous visits, was warm and inviting, with the murmur of hushed conversations and the clinking of cups filling the space. A few people glanced her way, but her entrance didn't stop conversations. If she was a topic of conversation in town, she wasn't the only one. She did a quick sweep of the bustling space but didn't see Olivia. She weaved her way through the tables to the counter and ordered a large coffee to go along with a blueberry muffin.

Five minutes later, with her order in hand, Marti exited and made her way back up the street to the gazebo. She settled onto a bench, again letting the sun's rays warm her skin. The new day scrubbed clean the ominous feelings that had coated the spot the night before. The town square bustled with activity—people walking their dogs, grabbing coffees, dropping off dry cleaning, going about their routines, and greeting each other with nods and waves. She marveled at what a difference just a few hours could make. Munching on the muffin, Marti observed the ebb and flow of life in Cedarwood. Was the morning's Rockwell-esque tranquility real or just a mirage? Did it only hide the mysteries beneath the surface? Did she believe in hope or despair? She'd seen plenty of the latter in her years as a private investigator. She'd met evil more than once and seen the destruction it could leave in its wake. But the scene in front of her now spoke of hope and kindness, too. What did it say about her if she bet against that?

Marti checked her phone for the address of the Cedarwood police station. Like most things in town, it was close by. Still, she lingered on the bench a moment longer, a pause before diving into her day, then stood with a soft sigh, ignoring the pop in both her knees, popped the last bite of muffin in her mouth, and drained the coffee before throwing the trash in a nearby can. She would bet on hope. It was too early, and the muffin was too good, to take the odds on despair, but she knew by the end of the day her feelings might change. She set off toward the town hall, her steps purposeful. She could be hopeful, but she was still being paid to do a job. It was time to piss more people off.

The town hall reflected Cedarwood's long history. Its architecture morphed and blended between different prominent styles of the last three centuries. It was a sprawling three stories tall, made mostly of red brick with gabled roofs, and large windows that captured the morning light. An American flag and a New Jersey state flag fluttered in the breeze on twin poles above a memorial commemorating the townspeople who had fought and died in various wars.

Following the sign indicating the police station entrance, Marti continued along the sidewalk, down a slight hill, and around to the back of the building. The police station's exterior was unassuming, just a plain industrial beige door, but the insignia on the wall to the right confirmed her destination. She realized the town hall was actually four stories and was built into the side of the modest hill. The police station occupied the basement, a small structure designed for practicality, or a low crime rate.

Alongside two empty spots, two marked police cruisers and a nondescript sedan were parked in a line near the door. The unmarked, dented, gray sedan seemed to shout 'police' more than the modern black and gold cruisers. Four other cars, maybe for civilian employees, were parked in a second row. Marti assumed the town shared some services with the county sheriff or the state police. She also realized losing Bill Thompson so suddenly might have been a big blow to such a small department.

Marti entered the station and found herself belly up to a room-length counter, a clear boundary between the town's residents and its law enforcement personnel. She took in the tidy office space. Cubicles divided up the main area, each separated by medium-height partitions, giving an impression of semiprivate workspaces. She could see an office in the back corner. The chief's office, she guessed, its door slightly ajar. She couldn't tell if anyone was inside. A hallway extended from the main work area to the right, deeper into the basement, suggesting a place for holding cells or interview rooms.

A woman noticed Marti at the counter, rose from a nearby desk, and approached. She carried an air of authority tempered with approachability, her gaze sharp but not unkind. A seasoned bureaucrat. The department had a chief, obviously, but Marti guessed in this room, at least, she was the actual power. She had short auburn hair and bifocals perched on the end of her nose. Her hazel eyes held guarded warmth and a glimmer of curiosity. She was wearing a simple blouse and slacks that spoke of practicality and efficiency.

Marti introduced herself and pushed a business card across the chipped counter. The woman's gaze flicked to it briefly before returning to Marti's face. "Nice to meet you, Marti," she said. "I'm Lisa Wilkins. I handle administrative tasks and dispatch here. How can I assist you?"

"I'm here on behalf of Sandy Thompson. She hired me to gather some information about her late husband. I'd like to speak with Jessica Lawson if possible. I just have a few questions related to his work."

"Of course. Let me see if she's available. Give me a moment." She picked up the card, turned, and headed down the hallway to the right.

Marti took the moment alone to look over the office again. The quiet hum of activity was a contrast to the bustling exterior of the town. She saw two officers going about their duties in the cubicles, maybe typing up reports. She could just see the tops of two other bent heads on the far side of the room, as well.

Lisa returned a moment later, trailed by another woman who Marti assumed was Jessica Lawson. She was young, maybe early 30s, her brown hair pulled back tight in a low, simple ponytail. Her blue eyes were bright but lacked the warmth or curiosity she'd seen in Wilkins'. Her face, even her bearing, communicated more than a hint of wariness, if not outright suspicion. She carried a navy-blue sports coat over her arm that matched her pants. She slipped it on before lifting the end of the counter and stepping through next to Marti.

She extended a hand. "Jessica Lawson."

Lawson's grip was cool and firm.

"Marti Wells," she replied and smiled, trying to soften what had unexpectedly become a tense introduction.

"So, Marti Wells, from Jersey City. What can I do for you?"

Jessica Lawson wasn't being rude, exactly, but she wasn't rolling out the welcome mat, either. Marti had a feeling this visit would be a waste of time, but she had to try.

"Yes, that's right. Raised in Paterson. My dad was police. He worked with Bill before he moved back to Cedarwood," Marti said, fishing a little for common ground.

"Uh-huh."

That earned her nothing and she moved on. "I understand you were working with Bill recently. I'm hoping you might shed some light on a few things for us."

"Us? Who's us?"

"Sandy Thompson. She's the one who hired me. She has some questions about Bill."

"Right, Sandy."

There was that tone Marti was becoming familiar with when she mentioned Sandy, but she wanted to stay focused on Bill. For now.

"She mentioned you were Bill's partner?" Marti typically liked more pointed questions to generate more specific answers, but she wanted to give this woman some rope and see where it led.

And it led right out the door.

"I'm headed out, but we can walk and talk."

Lawson's eyes skipped to Lisa Wilkins who was still standing by the counter, avidly watching the pair like a spectator at a tennis match, before she stepped around Marti and pushed through the outer door. Marti took a moment to swallow her annoyance and then followed.

Lawson stood at the corner of the building near a dented and overflowing upright ashtray. As Marti approached, she pulled a pack of Camels from her jacket pocket, tapped one out, and lit it with a practiced motion.

"I didn't think anyone under the age of 30 still smoked. I thought they beat it out of you in school these days."

Lawson sucked in a lungful and then blew it out through her nose and squinted at Marti through the drifting smoke. "I'm 32 so I don't make your cutoff and if you've been in town for more than a day, you probably know there's not much to do other than smoke, drink, and stare at the trees."

"I think you're forgetting at least one other vice. It's more fun and rarely leads to cancer."

"I didn't forget. Have you seen the men around here? That vice leads to rug rats, domestics, and bankruptcy. I'll stick to smoking."

"Does that description include Bill?"

She took a last drag and ground the cigarette into pulp under her scuffed black pump. "Christ, you aren't going to give up, are you?"

"I've sometimes been told that's an admirable character trait."

"Not all the time. Sometimes it's just kicking up dust on a good man's grave."

"That's not my intent."

"But that's what you're doing, right?"

"Says who?"

Once more, Marti couldn't help but notice the excessive hostility directed at her inquiries, a reaction that seemed disproportionate to simple, polite questions.

"Says me. Look, for the record, Bill was a good man and a dedicated cop who didn't deserve what happened to him."

"What happened to him?"

Lawson gave her a look that said she'd like to grind Marti under her shoe like a cigarette butt. "Shit happened. Life happened. This job happened. His death wasn't suspicious or strange or fate. It was just a heart attack, an accident, and nothing Sandy says or does is going to change that fact."

"Why would she want to change that fact?"

"Listen, here's the truth and if you try to put this on me later, I'll deny it, but, despite Bill worshipping the ground she walked on, God only knows why, Sandy is likely feeling guilty for hounding and hectoring him into an early grave. She was always up in his business for no reason other than she was bored. The woman is exhausting. She's an emotional vampire. And now that he's dead, she's using you to absolve her own guilt."

"Could he have been worried about a case he was working?"

Lawson smiled and just shook her head. "I will not get into any department business with a civilian."

"Did you take over his cases?"

"Ditto for talking about any active cases."

"Were you aware of any personal problems?"

"Get someone else to do your dirty work." Marti watched her rein herself in before she continued. "Do everyone a favor, go back to Jersey City and let this go. Sandy's a narcissist. She thinks everything is about her."

"And her husband's death isn't?"

Lawson just gave one last shake of her head and walked to one of the parked unmarked cars, got in, and pulled out fast, narrowly missing a cruiser that had just pulled into the lot. The officer in the car gave her a 'what gives' look, but Lawson either didn't see or didn't care.

The cruiser parked in the empty spot in front of Marti where she was still standing, processing the conversation with Lawson when the officer stepped out. He smiled as Marti shuffled back a few steps to give him room to pass.

"Don't mind Lawson," he said. "It's not personal. She's like that with everyone."

"Even puppies and babies?"

The guy laughed. "Probably." He extended a hand. "Scott Ackerman."

She introduced herself. His grip was firm and dry. His teeth were bright white and straight. Officer Ackerman looked like he'd stepped out of a recruitment poster. Maybe mid-20s, six feet with a clean-cut appearance and a square jaw. Marti had no doubt he dreamed every night about honor and commitment to duty. She had a brief desire to sully those thoughts when she realized Ackerman had likely been born in this century. The worst part of aging was sometimes having these mind-bending thoughts.

He was looking at her, and she realized he'd asked her something.

"Sorry?"

"I just asked if there was anything I might be able to help you with, Marti?"

"Maybe. Did you know Bill Thompson?"

A shadow flitted across Ackerman's face. "Of course. The department is pretty small, but I also grew up here. I've known, sorry, knew Bill for as long as I can remember."

"I'm a private investigator working for his widow."

"I know Sandy. Great lady. I was good friends with Ethan and Olivia. We all sort of grew up together."

"You're not still friends?"

"I guess, but it's never like when you were kids, right? I still see Olivia at Harmony's from time to time. Ethan not so much since he moved to New York."

"Got it. Sandy tells me Bill was distracted, stressed, and maybe troubled about something in the weeks before his heart attack. Did you notice that?"

He looked over her shoulder and then shook his head. "No, not that I recall. I work patrol, so I didn't see him much, but when I did, he seemed like the same old Bill."

She nodded. "Well, if you think of anything," she handed him a card, "gimme a call."

He gave her a full 120-watt smile as he pocketed the card and turned for the door. "Will do."

Chapter Thirteen

Marti went back inside. Lisa Wilkins still stood at the counter. It was clear she had been trying to eavesdrop and, given the volume Lawson reached by the end, she'd probably succeeded. She gave Marti the same efficient and blandly welcoming smile the second time.

"Yes?"

"I'd like to speak with the coroner or medical examiner who handled Bill's case."

Marti wasn't familiar with Cedarwood or the county policies for dealing with sudden, unexpected, or suspicious deaths. She knew there had been a statewide effort in recent years to move many towns and municipalities from using contract coroners to the medical examiner system because of the increased complexity of death investigations and the need for specialized medical skills that a forensic pathologist could provide. Not to mention the expert testimony potentially needed at a trial.

Lisa hesitated a moment, as if debating whether to provide the information, but must have decided, as Marti knew, that it was public record and she'd only look petty and difficult if she withheld it. "Cedarwood contracts with the county for use of their medical examiner's office. There's a small team. I'm not sure which one specifically handled Bill's case."

"Do you have an address or a number I could call?"

Again, that minute hesitation before she said, "One moment," and walked back to her desk. Marti now suspected that it wasn't personal. Lisa Wilkins weighed the pros and cons of every one of her actions. Her entire day was a series of micro pauses as she calculated the cost-benefit analysis of each response. By the time lunch rolled around, she must be exhausted. Wilkins returned a minute later with a yellow sticky note that contained a phone number and address in precise block lettering. "The ME's office is over in Pittsdown. You'll have to jump on 78 and head west. It's about a half hour this time of day."

"Thanks," Marti said, taking the note. "One last question."

"Sure."

"Bill's personal effects from the office, his desk? Did those go to Sandy or ..." She let the question linger. She knew they were not at the house and must still be somewhere in the office.

"I'm not sure. Someone cleaned out his space, but I'm not sure who. I'm sure his belongings, minus any confidential department files, have been boxed up and preserved."

Marti thought preserved was a strange choice of words. She was also sure Lisa Wilkins was lying through her teeth. She knew exactly where Bill's things were. She'd likely preserved it all herself. So why was she lying?

"If you could ask around, I'd appreciate it. Sandy mentioned a few photos, a pen, and a couple of other personal things she'd like back."

Sandy had said no such thing, of course. Marti's competing lie came just as easily. She was practiced at it. Often, in her line of work, lying was the only way to get to the truth. And Marti really wanted to get to Bill's missing notebook.

As Marti retraced her steps back to the inn, she thought about the reactions of the two women at the police station. One smiling and lying. The other prickly and straddling the border of hostility. On the whole, she preferred Jessica Lawson's upfront candor. Put your cards on the table, so to speak. But she still couldn't square the caginess of either woman. She'd need to talk to Lawson again at some point, but she'd give the woman time. She'd also like to confront the woman with concrete information. Fumbling around in the dark, half blind, promising to protect Bill Thompson's reputation and legacy, had, in retrospect, not gotten her very far.

She made it back to the inn. Much of the early-morning traffic around the green had slowed. It was quiet and peaceful. She was warm from the walk and she felt the urge to curl up on the grass near the gazebo and take a nap. That would certainly get people talking. She smiled to herself and kept walking through the gate, and then followed the gravel path to the right toward her car. She noticed an older man in worn overalls and an oversized straw hat meticulously tending to the inn's topiary, his movements with the shears deliberate and practiced. He looked like a detail from an Andrew Wyeth landscape. A perfect fit for the small town's atmosphere.

Farther back, past the gardens, at the rear of the property, she spotted Lucille on the porch in one of the rocking chairs. Marti raised a hand briefly in greeting and then looked away before the woman could engage her any further. She didn't want to be rude. Or, at least, accused of being rude. She reached her old Subaru in the inn's small lot and felt a sense of relief wash over her as she slid into the driver's seat.

With the address of the county public safety building in Pittsdown programmed into her phone's navigation app, Marti began the drive. The route took her through the town's outskirts and then onto a wider road as the scenery transformed from quaint neighborhoods to open fields to sporadic thickets of forest before she reached the onramp to Route 78. She headed west. Traffic was light. She found a radio station billing itself as classic rock; she turned up the volume and tried not to be offended that the music reminded her of high school. If this was now classic rock, how did the world label her?

The Pittsdown Public Safety Building stood as a testament to functionality over aesthetics. Or, the architectural cost of the local government going with the lowest bidder. Its brick and concrete exterior exuded an air of stern authority and a complete lack of creativity. Marti parked the Subaru in the lot and entered the building through its glass doors.

The interior was bustling. Several town and county services, including the Pittsdown Emergency Management, Health Department, Medical Examiner, Weights and Measures, and Consumer Affairs, used the building. The directory posted on the wall just inside the doors told her the ME's office was in the basement. No surprise. She'd never been in a morgue that wasn't underground.

Following the signs, Marti navigated her way through the building's corridors until she reached the stairs. She went down one flight and found the office of the medical examiner. She knocked lightly on the door.

"Come in."

As Marti pushed open the door, a wave of antiseptic scent enveloped her, immediately reminding her of every hospital and clinic she'd ever been in. The air inside was cool. Soft fluorescent lights hummed overhead, casting everything in a stark, clinical glow.

The office itself was a blend of functionality and efficiency. It was a large open space, spanning much of the width of the basement. Desks and shelves ringed the outside. The shelves held various medical supplies and reference books. A series of autopsy tables, scales, and instruments dominated the center of the room.

The steady tapping of keys emanated from a computer stationed at a desk in the corner. Otherwise, the room was empty. Even from across the room, Marti could see that scattered papers, evidence bags, and labeled vials covered the desk. A large magnifying lamp with an illuminated lens hung off one corner of the desk.

"Good morning," Marti greeted the woman from the doorway with a nod, offering a polite smile. "I'm Marti Wells, a private investigator. I was hoping you might answer a few questions about Bill Thompson. His widow has hired me to look into his death."

The woman tapping on the keyboard turned in the desk's swivel chair. She was middle-aged and heavy through the middle. Her white lab coat billowed out around her. Her salt-and-pepper hair was pulled back in a practical bun. She wore a pair of thin glasses. The glasses gave her face an air of scholarly authority, along with a touch of weariness that Marti imagined had been earned from years of examining life's harsher realities.

The woman stood and met Marti halfway across the room and extended a hand. They shook. "Victoria Turner."

Up close, the weariness faded. Dr. Turner exuded professionalism and curiosity, while a smile softened her features. "Please, come on back. Let's talk in a conference room. No need to do this over one of these tables."

She led Marti past her desk, where she paused to open the bottom drawer and sort through a thicket of papers before selecting a thin file, then she opened a door to the right and motioned Marti inside a small conference room that held a round table, four chairs, and a whiteboard, currently clean, mounted on one wall. They each took a seat and Dr. Turner said, "You mentioned Bill Thompson. How can I assist you today?"

Marti took a moment to gauge Dr. Turner's demeanor, sensing a blend of professional detachment and genuine willingness to help. It was a refreshing change from the residents of Cedarwood whom she'd met in the last 48 hours. She took a few minutes to sketch out Sandy's reasons for hiring her and finished with a more specific request. "I wanted to check with you about the circumstances of Bill Thompson's death and the autopsy findings."

"I'm afraid I might not be that helpful. Mr. Thompson's death was not suspicious, and we only performed the autopsy because it was an unexpected death, slightly unusual circumstances, and he was in law enforcement. If he had died at home on the couch, I'm not sure they would have considered it necessary."

"I understand. Anything you can tell me might help. I'm not here to nitpick or cause trouble. I'm just trying to put Sandy's mind at ease."

"It's not a problem. I made a copy of the report." She pushed the slim folder across the table to Marti.

"Thanks. I thought I might have to talk you into sharing."

"It's public record. If Mrs. Thompson had asked, I could have mailed it to her."

Marti took the file and flipped through it. A life summed up in five sheets of weights and measurements. She'd study it later. She closed it and set it aside. "Even though Sandy is desperate for answers, this is probably not a keepsake she'd want. Anything I should pay attention to?"

"Not really. You know he died in his truck on the side of the road. He might have had some warning, enough to pull over, but not a lot. Not enough to call for help. As part of the autopsy, we received his medical records from his primary care physician. He'd had a physical just over six months ago. It hinted at potential heart problems and that was our guess, but until they are on the table, you never know. There are a few other things that could have produced a similar result. An aneurysm or pulmonary embolism comes to mind. One of my team, Michael Reynolds, did the autopsy. Myself and another team member assisted and observed. Nothing unexpected or surprising showed up. Bill Thompson died of a massive heart attack. Or, acute myocardial infarction if you want the jargon."

"Was there an underlying cause?"

"The primary cause was atherosclerosis. One artery was almost 98 percent blocked. Tie that into what we know from his doctor and colleagues about his generally unhealthy lifestyle, like his penchant for fast-food, physical inactivity, moderate to heavy drinking, and chronic stress and it's sort of amazing that he lasted as long as he did. His chest was a ticking time bomb."

"Nothing else outside the heart?"

"In terms of abnormalities? No. Lungs, kidneys, spleen. All the internal organs were normal or within normal ranges. His liver wasn't in great shape, which you'd expect with that level of drinking. But overall, there were no other signs of chronic or malignant disease. Toxicology was clear. Why?"

"His brother mentioned a family history of arrhythmias. It's why the Army discharged him. And Sandy said he hadn't been sleeping well and was losing weight. I wondered about pain or other disease."

Turner nodded. "The file from his primary care physician noted the arrhythmia. It could have been a contributing factor. It certainly didn't help, but we didn't pick up on any larger issues. There were no cancers or tumors. No clots or hemorrhaging other than his heart. Personally, it wouldn't surprise me to learn he'd suffered at least one minor heart attack before that night."

"So maybe he knew it was coming. Or sensed it."

"I only met him a few times personally. Cedarwood doesn't get many murders. He always struck me as a dedicated and conscientious detective. You get a sense of which guys are going through the motions and which ones really care. Maybe he saw things a little too black and white, but as a scientist, I'm the same way. Of course, being a good caretaker for his cases didn't mean he took good care of himself." She pointed at the folder. "The proof is right there in black and white."

Chapter Fourteen

Marti sat in the Subaru in the parking lot with the windows down and read through Bill Thompson's autopsy report. She jotted down the occasional note, but Dr. Turner had been correct. The thin file was all very matter-of-fact. Age, date of birth, social security number, home address. The place and cause of death. Details of the viscera. The ultimate handling of the remains by the funeral home. Bill Thompson arrived at the ER as a DOA. He'd been on Dr. Turner's table the next day. They buried him the day after that. Bing. Bang. Boom.

Having made a first pass at his home, Marti had harbored some hope that the explanation for Bill's behavior might be health related. If he'd seen his doctor for that physical and had found himself staring down cancer or an inoperable brain tumor, his stress and brooding would have been understandable. But that didn't appear to be the case.

The one interesting tidbit from the trip was the photocopy attached to the end of the report. It was a handwritten note from the responding officer. Likely from their own notebook prior to writing up an official report. She didn't know the reason for including it here. Maybe it was just expediency given how fast the autopsy and internment happened. The note itself didn't contain any new information on Bill's death. It just contained more specifics on the timing and the steps that brought Bill's body to the ER. But it included the responding officer's name. B. Martinez. She wanted to go out and look at the place where Bill had died. Maybe Martinez could tell her a little more.

After her ritual incantations and three attempts, the Subaru sputtered, hesitated, and then settled into, if not a comfortable hum, an adequate whine. Marti glanced at the oil change sticker on the upper left part of the windshield. Overdue. She should probably drop it off at Gerry's soon, or at least make sure her AAA membership was in good order. With that cheery thought, she pulled out of the parking lot and headed back toward Cedarwood to check in with Sandy.

Marti used the time to think about what she'd learned to date. Not much, she decided, other than the people of Cedarwood seemed to think positively of Bill Thompson. Everyone she'd talked to so far talked about his dedication to his job and his family. She had a feeling those platitudes, however well-intentioned and kind, were not the type of answers that Sandy was looking for from her.

As she pulled off 78 and onto the smaller roads that wound into Cedarwood, she mentally reviewed the two conversations she'd had today. First, Jessica Lawson and her sharpened claws. Marti couldn't figure out if she knew something, was protecting Bill out of a sense of obligation or police fraternity, or was just annoyed at Sandy for hiring a private investigator.

Her second conversation with Dr. Turner had been more cordial, but not any more fruitful. The ME had confirmed the heart attack, Bill's generally poor health, and a lack of anything else remotely suspicious. That didn't mean it might not have happened, but Dr. Turner struck Marti as a consummate professional and not the type to slack on her duties, especially when it involved a cop. Marti believed Bill's cause of death was a heart attack. Other than the minor mystery of Bill's missing notebook, which could be nothing, she found herself where she'd started. With nothing.

She might not know much yet, but something, maybe it was intuition, maybe it was the lack of anything else, Bill's death was too quiet, too normal, for lack of a better word, made Marti now believe Sandy might be correct. Something was bothering Bill when he died out on that highway.

Sandy opened the door as Marti climbed the front steps. "Lunch?" she asked.

"I could eat," Marti replied.

"Nothing fancy, I'm afraid. Chicken salad and chips, okay?"

Sandy appeared to be fond of mayonnaise as a main ingredient, but Marti didn't want to be rude. "Sounds perfect."

They went into the kitchen where Sandy took another plate and glass from a cupboard and started assembling a second sandwich. Marti washed her hands at the sink. A carton of pre-mixed iced tea sat on the counter and Marti poured two glasses and carried them to the kitchen table.

"I still haven't found Bill's last notebook," Marti said.

"No?"

"It's the only loose thread I can find. Everyone agrees he used them. Plus," she waved a hand toward the door in the corner, "the basement. But no one admits to having that last one. Might be nothing, but it's a little strange. As I said, a loose end. Are you sure the medical examiner or another officer didn't return it with the rest of Bill's personal effects?"

Sandy cut the sandwiches and added a handful of Classic Lay's potato chips to each plate before carrying them to the table and sitting across from Marti. She shook her head. "I mean, those first few days are still a little foggy, but I really don't recall seeing it. You're welcome to check the house again. Did you ask Jessica Lawson?"

Marti chewed and swallowed and tried to ignore the mayo. "Yes, I spoke to her this morning." Marti would not pass on Lawson's opinions about Sandy. "Both she and Lisa Wilkins said that Bill's desk had been cleaned and boxed up, but they would double-check. I haven't heard from them yet."

Nor did she expect to without pushing the issue. Even if Lawson had the notebook, Marti was sure she would continue to claim the notes contained details of ongoing investigations and it was department property. Marti thought she might have better luck finessing the issue with Lisa Wilkins.

"Well, I think Jessica would know best. She told me she would do anything to help. She was probably closest to Bill at the end. But what about Kevin? Did you ask him?"

"Good idea. I can ask Kevin, as well."

Marti spent the rest of the meal filling in Sandy on the steps she'd taken already and the ones she planned to take next. She might have spun a little bullshit to dress up the little she had uncovered so far, but Sandy seemed happy enough with the state of things. Marti did not tell her about the man in the mask or the feeling of being followed back to the inn from Blue Haven.

As they were clearing the dishes, Marti thought of the note at the back of the autopsy file. "Do you know a B. Martinez? Works at Cedarwood PD?"

Sandy's brow wrinkled briefly and then cleared. "Yes. Brenda Martinez. She's one of the newer hires in the department. I don't know her well. I think I only met her once or twice. Why?"

"She was the initial responding officer on the scene. I just thought she might be a good person to talk to. Cover all the bases." Clutching at straws, Marti thought to herself. "If you don't know her that well, I can ask Kevin or Jessica for an introduction." Though, given the veiled hostility she'd brushed up against with both of them recently, she wondered how receptive they'd be to her talking to Martinez.

After rinsing and putting away the dishes, Sandy left to volunteer at the church and Marti retreated to Bill's office. She plopped down in the old leather desk chair and looked over the piles she'd created on Monday and wondered if there was a secret worth dying for in all that paper. While the man appeared dedicated to his job, maybe to an unhealthy extent, Marti had to remind herself that the secret might have nothing to do with his job. If Marti had learned anything in her long career as a private investigator, it was that everyone, every single person, had something they'd prefer to keep to themselves. Bill's vice or shame or embarrassment could have been cross-dressing, or an eye for young boys, or skimming money from the department slush fund, or an affair.

It didn't seem likely to Marti given the picture that was emerging, but she couldn't dismiss it either. "We all wear masks. We all have secrets," she mumbled to the empty room.

She spent an hour re-reviewing the piles of paper she'd sorted on Monday but found nothing new and nothing that sparked any suspicion about a secret vice. His credit card statements for the past year matched neatly with the trips and notes from the squares on his desk blotter calendar. There was no pattern that she could see. No regular or lavish outlays of cash that drew her attention. Any personal charges that related to work were later submitted for reimbursement with copies of receipts. The man didn't ding the town budget for one extra penny. She gave him posthumous credit for honesty when no one was looking.

Fed up and restless with the lack of progress with the piles of paper, she moved on to the bookshelves lining one wall. Banker boxes full of paper, plus other accumulated trinkets and knickknacks crammed the available space. A collection of work mementos, photos, and various odds and ends collected over a long career.

Marti's eyes swept over the shelves. Among the items, she found a small trophy with a silver plaque that read: Cedarwood Police Department Bowling Championship - 2009. Next to it was a framed newspaper clipping with a headline that proudly declared: Officer Thompson Receives Community Service Award. Marti noted the genuine smile on Bill's face in the accompanying photo.

Next to the newspaper clipping was a shelf dedicated to family photos. Most were family gatherings, holidays, and trips. She caught Cinderella's castle at Disney World in one. Marti could feel the awkward smiles and forced poses in the snapshots through the frames, but one photo drew her attention more than the others—a five-by-seven image of three young children in a church or chapel. She picked it up to get a better look. Sandy's children from her first marriage. Ethan, Olivia, and the youngest, Brian. Marti's eyes followed the gazes of the children's, and she could just make out the crucifix in the background. Marti recalled the many hours of her own youth spent huddled in a pew on Sunday mornings.

The oldest, Ethan, stood confidently in an altar boy's robe, while beside him, Olivia, also in a white robe, seemed to exude a mix of excitement and reverence. The youngest, likely too small for an official role, wore a miniature suit, his untucked shirt and missing tie adding a sweet touch of youthful disarray.

She felt like an uninvited guest at a personal moment, yet the photo provided a glimpse into the Thompson family's history—a reminder that even a dedicated police officer like Bill had a life beyond his badge and investigations. She replaced the photo and moved back to the desk.

Marti diligently sorted through the drawers, one after another. Each drawer seemed to hold a jumble of unrelated items—old receipts, paperclips, pens, and a smattering of random notes. She set aside anything that seemed remotely important.

Wanting to clear some space, Marti paused and headed back to the kitchen. She opened the cabinet under the sink, found garbage bags, and returned to the office to dispose of items that were clearly trash. With a swift and methodical efficiency, she cleared the drawers of unnecessary clutter, determined to uncover any hidden clues. Weren't clues always found buried in old desk drawers?

Her search for clues came up empty. She hadn't turned up Bill's laptop password conveniently written down, either. She realized she would need to turn to Neon's expertise to bypass the security and get her access to the laptop. She was ready to call it a day. She felt caked in dust and grime after emptying the drawers. She gathered her belongings and tucked Bill's laptop into her bag.

As she scanned the slightly cleaner room to see if she'd missed anything, she heard Sandy return from her volunteer work. Good, they could make a little more progress. Marti picked up a pile of documents she'd set aside and headed for the kitchen.

Sandy was emptying the contents of a grocery bag into the refrigerator when Marti entered.

"How was church?" Marti asked.

"Oh, it was good. It was just a committee meeting for the church's fall festival. It's our annual fundraiser. Live music, kid's games, a silent auction. That sort of thing."

"What church is this?"

"St. Mark's, in town."

"Is that the one with the white steeple I can see from the inn?"

Sandy shut the refrigerator door and folded the empty brown bag.

"No, that's St. James. The Episcopal church. St. Mark's is the stone one at the opposite end."

Marti sensed her warming to the topic of churches and religion. "I think I'm going to call it a day," Marti said heading off further comment. "But I have a favor to ask."

"Sure, of course. Anything I can do to help."

Under the overhead lights of the kitchen, Marti could see the dark circles chiseled under Sandy's eyes. She wants to help, Marti thought, but she also wants a distraction. Maybe that's what grief was, looking for a distraction until you began to forget. No, that sounded too harsh. Marti didn't think Sandy wanted to forget. Maybe grief was looking for a distraction until you can start living again. Fake it until you make it. If Sandy was faking it, she was going to crash soon. Her hair was still in place. Her smile, too, but Marti could see the edges fraying.

She almost thought about holding off on her request, but if she was going to make any tangible progress before their three-day deadline, the laptop and cell phone were becoming increasingly important and couldn't be delayed. She felt a twinge of guilt but pushed on. This was what Sandy wanted. Or, thought she wanted. She put the stack of paper on the kitchen counter. "I was wondering if you could go through Bill's recent cell phone bills and highlight any numbers you recognize. It will save me time tracking down the ones you don't."

"Of course, that makes sense."

"Here's the last six months," Marti said and tapped the pile of statements. "I'm also taking Bill's laptop with me." She patted the bag on her hip. "I didn't find his password anywhere, so I'll get my friend to crack it and we can see if there's anything on it that points to what was bothering Bill."

"All right, if you think that's the best thing to do."

Marti could sense her hesitation but didn't see a way around it. "I'll get it back to you. I don't think it will take my guy more than a few minutes." Sandy just nodded, and Marti left it at that.

With their plans set, Marti and Sandy parted ways. As Marti drove back toward the little town center, she felt the pull of home growing stronger. As the sun set, Marti's resolve solidified. She wanted to be in her own bed tonight. The thought of returning to the Cedarwood Inn and Lucille and the dusty quilt and lumpy mattress held no appeal. She'd call Neon on the way and drop off the laptop. She felt her spirits lift as she drove past the turnoff and continued out to the highway to make her way back to Jersey City.

Chapter Fifteen

As the Subaru rattled along Route 78, she called Neon, her mind set on making the most of the remaining daylight hours. She hoped he was awake. Even if most of the rest of the East Coast was preparing to leave work or prepping dinner, she knew the hacker's schedule was anything but ordinary and he was like a cranky toddler when woken up too early. Nevertheless, the risk was worth it, she thought. She'd rather get the laptop to him tonight instead of waiting until tomorrow.

She dug the Bluetooth earpiece out of the cupholder and connected her phone. After a couple of rings, Neon's voice crackled through the phone's speaker.

"Good morning, Marti."

"Hey, Neon."

"What's going on?" Neon replied, his voice cool and collected. She hadn't woken him. That was a good sign. Marti wasted no time. "I'm on a job and I've got a password-protected laptop that needs your touch. Think you're up for a minor job?"

There was a pause, then a chuckle from Neon. "Depends on the laptop. You know I'm used to more exciting requests."

"I know, I know. This one might not be as thrilling, but it still pays the same and could be a big help in my case."

"Fair enough," Neon said. "Give me the details. What kind of laptop are we talking about?"

Marti tugged the laptop out of her bag on the passenger seat and glanced at it. "It's a Dell Inspiron 15. Nothing fancy, but I couldn't find the password in the client's office and didn't want to keep searching or hoping."

"A consumer Dell is not exactly Fort Knox. I can probably talk you through it."

Marti was far from a Luddite. She couldn't afford to be in her profession. She needed to know the current apps and trends. Many of her cases never left her basement office. They started and ended on her laptop. Even so, she knew what Neon considered simple and what she considered simple were on the opposite ends of the spectrum. She knew her limitations and when it was worth paying for expertise.

"I appreciate the offer and I should probably learn a bit more from you, but now is not the time. There's a ticking clock and the case is not near the city. I've got to drive back to Cedarwood tomorrow."

"Where?"

"Exactly."

Neon chuckled. "All right, all right. I'll do it. It should take about as long as it takes to heat a cup of ramen."

She realized she didn't know where Neon lived. She had a distinct mental picture of a low-rent Jersey City studio apartment filled with very high-end computer equipment, but that was a complete fabrication of her own mind. They'd met in person a few times, but it was rare. Most of their business was conducted online or on the phone.

"I'll do you one better. Consider it a bonus. Meet me at JJ's in," she glanced at the dashboard clock, "an hour. I'll buy you dinner."

Jersey Joe's was a hidden gem nestled along Montgomery Avenue, a dangerously quick 10-minute walk from Marti's Jersey City apartment. Its unassuming exterior blended with an adjacent thrift store and a small family-owned electronics shop, but its reputation for mouthwatering shawarmas and addictive garlic fries was a well-kept secret among locals. The establishment had an air of shabbiness that only added to its appeal in her opinion. Any profit went into the food, not the decor. It was one of Marti's favorite places for lunch or dinner. Hell, she'd stop in for breakfast if they offered it. She lived in constant fear of the day Instagram and the hipster foodies sniffed out the fries and ruined the place.

The restaurant was the brainchild of a husband-and-wife duo, Sam and Maria Khoury. There was no Joe in the family. The name existed solely for its American-ness and for the alliteration. The couple had immigrated to the United States from Lebanon in the 1990s with a passion for cooking and a determination to share their love for Middle Eastern cuisine with their adopted community.

As Marti sat and peered out the small front windows and waited for Neon, a familiar voice diverted her attention. Sam, the owner and primary waiter, Maria handled the back of the house, stood by her table with a friendly smile.

"Hey, Marti, long time no see," he greeted her. "Everything okay?"

Marti returned the smile. A long time between visits for Marti meant three or four days. "Hey, Sam. Yeah, it's been a busy week. I'm mostly out of town on a job."

He nodded in understanding. "Well, you know you're always welcome here. What can I get for you today?"

"Just my usual chicken shawarma wrap and a side of garlic fries," Marti replied. "Wait, make that two. I'm waiting for someone."

Sam raised an eyebrow at that, but Marti replied. "Not that type of someone. Just a," she struggled for a moment with a way to both explain and categorize Neon and eventually settled on, "work colleague."

Sam chuckled. "Didn't your second husband start off that way, too?"

"You're hilarious." Though Sam was indeed correct. She and Jimmy had met on the job.

Marti couldn't help but smile when she thought about Jimmy. She had been tailing a suspect through Jersey City's bustling Caribbean Street fair, trying to blend in discreetly with the crowd. Nothing about the parade or the costumes was discreet, but they offered a great distraction for following bail jumpers. As she navigated through the sea of people, she accidentally bumped into a street performer who was expertly juggling fire torches.

The torches went flying, and a small gasp rippled through the crowd. Marti instinctively jumped up to help and grabbed a torch midair before it could crash into the funnel cake cart and a bucket of hot oil. Amid the relieved applause, she locked eyes with Jimmy, who had been the performer she had inadvertently disrupted.

With a boyish grin, he walked over, his eyes dancing with amusement. "Well, if you wanted to get my attention, you could've just said hello."

They struck up a conversation that lasted well beyond the street fair. But not much longer than the marriage. The combination of demanding work schedules, emotional baggage on both sides, and a lack of balance between their personal and professional lives led to their unraveling and ultimate divorce. Their marriage lacked the stability and shared goals needed to weather the challenges they faced individually and as a couple. Still, she thought of Jimmy fondly and often wondered where he was in the world.

"Coming right up," Sam said, pulling Marti back to the present as he jotted down her order.

Before he walked off, Marti leaned forward in the plastic booth and asked, "Sam, let me ask you something. What's the one thing that could keep a guy like you up at night? Or a secret you'd never tell Maria?"

Sam's eyes flickered with a mix of amusement and then contemplation. He took a moment to think, his face growing serious, and then he leaned against the table and lowered his voice. "Well, Marti, I'd say one thing that might keep me up at night is wondering if I'm giving Maria the life she deserves. We work hard, but I sometimes worry it's not enough."

Marti nodded. "And what about secrets? You must have heard a lot of them around here."

Sam leaned in even closer, his expression more serious. "True, I have. I would tell you that the secret to a long and happy marriage is to have no secrets." He paused. "But that is a fantasy. Everyone has secrets. Some big. Some small." He glanced over his shoulder. "The one secret I've always kept from Maria is how close we came to losing this place a few years back. Business took a nosedive and I did everything I could to keep it from her. It was a tough time, but we made it through."

Marti raised an eyebrow, intrigued. "I had no idea."

He straightened up with a grin. "Well, that's the thing about secrets, right? Sometimes they're just chapters we'd rather keep closed." He pushed away from the table as if trying to get out from under a cloud, and Marti felt a pang of guilt for dredging up those memories. "Your food will be up in a jiffy."

"Thanks, Sam."

Through the windows, she watched as Neon arrived on his bike. He locked his bike to a parking sign with practiced efficiency. The streetlights cast a soft glow on his casual attire. Neon's appearance was as distinctive as ever—a black hoodie, a band tee peeking out from underneath, and faded jeans paired with scuffed white Chuck Taylor sneakers. His hoodie partially hid his bright green spiky hair.

Marti kept her eyes on him as he scanned the street briefly before spotting her at the window-side booth and making his way inside. Marti knew Neon as almost two different people. His online persona was brash and confident and this was the person she encountered most, both on the phone and online. On the occasional times they met in person, Marti had found a reserved, shy, and introverted young man with almost stunted social skills.

As Neon approached her table, his gaze flickered up to meet hers for a moment before bouncing back to his shoes as he offered a faint, shy smile. She greeted him with a nod he didn't see, the familiarity between them bridging the wordless gap. Neon slid into the seat across from her.

Sam came by with a tray and dropped off their food without a word, but cocked an eyebrow at Marti as he turned to leave.

"Hey, Marti," Neon said after Sam left, his voice quiet yet warm.

"Hey, Neon," she replied. "Thanks for meeting me on short notice."

He shrugged, a glint in his eyes. His online persona was in there somewhere. "I'm always up for a challenge, you know that."

Marti couldn't help but smile. Despite his reserved nature and dual personality, there was an undeniable camaraderie between them.

"Let's eat first. Fries are always better when they're hot."

He didn't argue, and they spent the next 10 minutes quickly devouring the chicken shawarma sandwiches and fries. She kept the conversation light. She asked about any recent interesting projects, then his bike, then computers. She received mostly one- or two-sentence answers, but that was alright. She appreciated the effort, and the food was more than enough to make up for the lack of stimulating conversation.

After they were both done and wiped their fingers clean of the grease, she picked up the laptop from the seat beside her and pushed it across the table to him.

"Take your time," she said. "I just need to unlock it and see what's inside."

Neon nodded. He took a thumb drive out of his pocket and plugged it into the laptop's USB port. He paused and studied the screen, and then his fingers deftly flew across the laptop's keyboard. Marti watched as his focus deepened, his face relaxed, and his complete attention became consumed by the digital world in front of him.

Before she could even ask Sam for a refill of Diet Coke, Neon spun the laptop back around and Marti could see the familiar Windows desktop.

"That's it?" She knew he would crack it, but she just thought she might have time for dessert along with another Diet Coke.

"That's it. I removed the password, so you can shut it down and next time it will boot right up to the desktop." He grabbed his messenger bag and slid out of the booth. "Thank you for the food," he said and then walked out.

Chapter Sixteen

She ended up staying for dessert. In truth, it took little convincing.

"Maria made her cinnamon baklava today," Sam had said as he cleared the plates from the table.

"Yes, please."

He left and returned a moment later with a generous slice of the sweet pastry made of layers of filo dough, filled with chopped nuts, and sweetened with honey. He placed a cup of karkade tea alongside.

"Thanks, Sam." He nodded, smiled, then moved off to serve other customers.

As she sipped the steaming hibiscus-flavored brew, she thought about what Sam had said earlier about not providing for Maria but didn't see how it might help her case. Was Bill feeling something similar? A level of guilt for not giving Sandy the life she deserved? Marti hadn't gotten that vibe from Sandy. Nor had she expressed anything remotely like that to Marti, either. She just seemed confused and out of sorts by grief. Marti also didn't think Sam's secret about the restaurant's recent dire financial straits applied, either. While she couldn't be sure about Bill Thompson's emotions, she could be more confident in his financial footing. She had been through all the papers in Bill's office and money didn't appear to be a big issue for the Thompsons. They weren't rich, but they were comfortable. She certainly didn't think it was something that might lead Bill straight into a heart attack.

She finished the baklava and tea and ducked her head into the kitchen to say thank you to Maria before leaving. She'd found a parking spot for the Subaru midway between her apartment and JJ's and she decided to just leave it there for the night. The extra little dose of exercise wouldn't hurt. She took the long way around the block, listening to the city sounds, happy to be back in her neighborhood, and let her unconscious mind chew over the case but by the time she reached her building's front door, she still didn't have any insights into what killed Bill Thompson.

She opened the door and climbed the stairs to the third floor. Doorways and hallways were dark. Many of the residents of her building were in their 70s and 80s and turned in early, even if they regularly woke up again at three or four in the morning. She opened her own door and, despite being well cared for by Mrs. Potts, received the silent treatment from Rita Mae. That was fine with Marti. It had been a long day, and she was in no mood to do a psychological tango with her cat.

She walked to the bedroom and put Bill's laptop on the bedside table. She should really start going through the computer, but she didn't have the energy right now. Her bathtub beckoned through the open door, but she decided on a quick shower. She was eager to sleep in a bed that wasn't covered in 14 pillows or smelled like rosewater.

After she'd toweled off and put on her pajamas, underwear, and an XXL St. Peter's T-shirt, she walked back into the bedroom and found Rita Mae already curled up on the pillow and Marti supposed all was forgiven. She slid under the sheets and fell asleep thinking about secrets. In her experience, people kept secrets because they were afraid. Afraid that people would judge them. Afraid that people would misunderstand them. Afraid that they'd lose something. So what was Bill Thompson afraid of?

The morning sun filtered through Marti's bedroom window, casting a yellow light on her rumpled bedsheets. Beside her, Rita Mae stirred and stretched her furry limbs before she decided that more sleep was in order and curled up again with a contented purr.

Marti yawned and stretched. She didn't have that option. Someone had to pay the bills. Her lower back and hamstrings felt tight as she slid out of bed and onto the cool hardwood floor. Too much time in the car and office chairs of late. She glanced at the clock. She'd left her overnight bag and running shoes at the inn, but she would not let that be a convenient excuse. Not today.

Her morning runs were an anchor in her life. It set up the day and set up her mood. She put on shorts and a long-sleeved T-shirt and then dug through her closet until she found a passable older pair of sneakers. She laced them up and secured her hair in a ponytail before heading out.

Mrs. Jenkins was sitting by the window in her first-floor apartment, and she waved as she jogged down the building's front steps. The streets were just beginning to wake, and the rhythmic sound of her sneakers on the pavement gave a sort of soundtrack to the thoughts bouncing around in her head. As she jogged along the familiar route, her body on autopilot, she picked over what she knew (not a lot) and where she might go next. By the time she made it home, she had compiled a list of four or five things she could tackle today.

After her run, she indulged in a long shower, the warm water soothing her muscles and rinsing away the sweat. The fragrance of her shampoo filled the steamy bathroom as she took her time, allowing herself a few moments of solitude before the day's obligations took over.

Dressed in clean clothes, Marti ventured into the kitchen, greeted by the cheerful chirping of a family of house sparrows that nested in the eaves. Rita Mae had gotten out of bed herself and now sat expectantly by her food bowl. Marti scoured the cupboards for some breakfast. The search yielded more for Rita Mae than herself. She pulled a tub of instant oats out of a back corner. She really needed to get over to Delgado's and get some food, at least some canned soup and bread. Sort of pretend she was an adult. She couldn't eat shawarma and fries every night. Well, she could, but ...

Her stomach growled audibly as she measured out kibble, poured fresh water, and gave the cat a reassuring pat on the head. "You're not the only one hungry this morning, Rita."

Just as she was about to prepare her own breakfast, the jingle of keys in the front door lock caught her attention. Marti turned, surprised to see Mrs. Potts stepping inside. The older woman blinked in surprise at the sight of Marti. "Oh, my. You gave me a start. I thought you weren't back until Wednesday or Thursday."

Marti smiled. "Sorry, I got in late or I would have knocked. I just came back for a quick trip. I'm heading out again, but I made sure Rita got her breakfast. Could you pop over in the evening?"

"Of course," Mrs. Potts chuckled and put a hand to her chest. "Always good to give the ticker a little jumpstart every once in a while."

"Gotta keep the engine running."

With a friendly nod, Mrs. Potts shuffled back out the door. "Well, I'll leave you to it then. Safe travels, dear."

"Thank you, Mrs. Potts. Have a great day."

"I will. At my age, every day is a bonus, so it's hard to complain."

As the door closed behind the older woman, Marti turned her attention back to the box on the kitchen counter. Plain instant oatmeal. What had possessed her to buy it? But it was that or sip from takeout ketchup packets. She microwaved a bowl of oatmeal, added a pinch of salt, and then, despite a well past expiration date, added a splash of syrup. Sugar didn't go bad, did it?

She carried the steaming bowl over to the table and then retrieved the laptop from her bedroom. Going through the laptop was the first item on the mental to-do list she came up with while running. She felt a surge of optimism despite her bland breakfast. The secret she sought might be just a few clicks away.

Or not.

As Neon promised, the laptop booted up straight to the Windows desktop, bypassing the password prompt. But that is where the good news ended. The laptop seemed almost too clean, its contents orderly and mundane. It was as if Bill had used it strictly for personal matters. A few insurance documents, some scattered notes, half-completed household budget spreadsheets, PDFs of tax and escrow statements for the house. An excise bill from the town. It was the detritus of everyday life. There was little trace of his professional life.

She combed through his internet browser history, paying attention to sites he visited more than once: online banking and brokerage sites, online email, a few news sites, Cedarwood PD, St. Mark's church, a health insurance HMO, and a few medical sites. No porn or gambling or anything else that might be considered a sin, an addiction, or a terrible secret. She jotted down the sites mostly because she wanted to note something for her report to Sandy. She felt the frustration replace the optimism at another dead end. She closed the laptop and finished her oatmeal, ignoring its distinct taste of elementary school paste.

Determined to keep her spirits up, she pulled out her phone and tapped Sandy's contact number. When in doubt, keep moving forward. After a few rings, Sandy's voice came through the line, accompanied by the sounds of heavy breathing. "Hello?"

"Hi, Sandy. It's Marti. Are ... you okay?"

"Hi, Marti. I'm fine, just out for a run."

"A run?"

"Yes, well, maybe more of a walk with intermittent periods of faster walking, but I decided I would not keep spending every morning curled up in bed, staring at the wall."

"Good for you," Marti replied. "Listen, Sandy, I ended up coming back to Jersey City last night to drop off Bill's laptop with my friend. But while I'm here, I thought I might talk to Ethan. I know you gave me his cell number, but I thought I might stop by in person. You said he worked in the city, right?"

"That's right. I don't know where exactly. It's in Midtown, I think. Hold on, I just got back to the house. I have his business card inside."

Marti could hear the background noise change as Sandy moved indoors. After a moment, she continued, "Yes, here it is. I can text you a picture. Would that work?"

"That's perfect, thank you."

They disconnected and a moment later her phone dinged with a text notification. Marti opened it and saw Ethan McGill's business card.

Marti left her car on the street by JJ's and decided to take the train into the city. She didn't want to battle the inbound rush hour traffic on the roads. She walked the two blocks to the nearest PATH train station and descended underground. The train was just as crowded as the roads. People stood shoulder to shoulder, absorbed in their own worlds. She held onto a pole, her fingers grazing the cool metal as the train rattled along the tracks and under the Hudson River.

She got off at 34th Street and transferred over to the NYC subway line, crisscrossing the station until she found the uptown 1 line and boarded another jam-packed car. The scent of coffee mixed with the musk of the crowd created the distinct urban aroma that she had grown accustomed to over the years. Her eyes wandered, observing the diverse range of people sharing this small space, their expressions a mosaic of emotions from exhaustion to excitement. She glanced at her reflection in the window, taking in her own appearance. Her attire was casual, a simple pair of jeans, a light jacket over a T-shirt, plus comfortable boots.

She did some quick research on her phone as the subway made its stops and moved north. As she read, Marti felt herself drawn into the ebb and flow of Manhattan swirling around her. The chatter of voices, the rustling of newspapers, the occasional burst of laughter or music—it was all a symphony of urban life that she had come to appreciate.

She rode the 1 train three stops north and exited at Columbus Circle. When she emerged from the subway onto the crowded streets of Midtown, the towering skyscrapers seemed to reach for the heavens. The cacophony of honking horns and the buzz of activity surrounded her. She got her bearings and walked briskly south along the sidewalk, dodging other pedestrians for a block before turning west toward the river.

Chapter Seventeen

The building housing Ethan McGill's office was an old, converted brick warehouse on the edge of the fancier Midtown high-rises. Maybe a block or two away from having the right address, but close enough to catch the shine. If the business took off, it could move into the neighboring skyscraper digs. If it didn't? It could quietly pack up and very few people would be the wiser. Marti's footsteps echoed on the weathered pavement as she approached the entrance, a simple red door marked with the building's numbered address. There was a large sign with detachable nameplates next to the door listing the building's occupants.

Inside, the building's lobby had an understated grace. The exposed brick walls and rustic fixtures offered a chic but welcoming atmosphere. The harried receptionist appeared to be doubling as gatekeeper and security guard.

"Ethan McGill, TradeQuest," Marti said.

The woman was engaged on a call but buzzed her through the gate and with a hand over her headset mic said, "Third floor, up the stairs to the right."

Marti smiled and nodded her thanks and then went through the turnstile. She took a moment to collect herself before ascending the worn steps. She climbed the steps to the third-floor landing. Marti looked down a corridor with worn carpets and closed doors. The modern decor and updated furniture appeared to have stopped at the lobby.

Ethan McGill was the VP of Marketing for a startup founded by a group of finance and tech enthusiasts. TradeQuest aimed to revolutionize the stock trading experience by combining sophisticated technology with a user-friendly approach. The company's mission, breathlessly detailed on the website Marti had perused on the train ride, was to democratize trading and make it accessible to a broader range of individuals by gamifying the process. They believed that by introducing interactive elements and educational tools, they could engage a younger generation of potential investors and traders. The team at TradeQuest comprised innovative individuals from both the financial and tech sectors, working toward bridging the gap between Wall Street and Main Street.

That last bit of marketing jargon made Marti want to hold her nose. Getting more people into the stock market who only believed the market went up seemed like a bad idea. But she was just a humble PI.

Marti found the door with TradeQuest's name and logo and pushed through the door. Inside, the office suite was simple and unassuming. A farm of beige cubes in the middle with a few glassed-in offices and conference rooms around the outside. The reception area shared space with a vending machine, sink, coffeemaker, and a few pieces of mismatched furniture.

A young woman sat near the kitchenette in a cube without walls and welcomed Marti with an infectious smile and an air of eager efficiency.

"Good morning. How can I assist you today?"

Marti had to resist the urge to scratch behind her ears and see if she rolled over on command. Instead, she returned the smile. You catch more bees with honey than vinegar.

"Hi, I'm here to see Ethan McGill. I don't have an appointment, but I'm hoping to have a quick chat."

The receptionist nodded and typed into her computer. "Sure thing. May I have your name?"

"Marti Wells," she replied.

She tapped a few more keys, then looked up. "Mr. McGill is in a meeting at the moment, but he'll be free in 15 minutes if you'd like to wait. I sent him a note that you're here."

Marti thanked her and settled into one of the mismatched chairs, likely left over from previous tenants. Glancing around some more, she noted the functional furniture and a corkboard with job postings and rooms for sublet from employees and the various other small businesses sharing the building. The atmosphere was definitely more scrappy startup rather than polished corporate giant.

Ten minutes later, a man walked into the reception/kitchen area and looked around. Ethan McGill was tall and lean. His physique, under the white Oxford shirt and black jeans, hinted at an active lifestyle. He had his mother's pale complexion and sharp cheekbones. His height and build must have come from his biological father. His sandy-blond hair was neatly combed, and his brown eyes held a mix of curiosity and wariness as he looked at Marti.

"Hi, I'm Ethan McGill."

Marti stood and extended a hand. "Marti Wells." His grip was firm and ice cold. He smelled strongly of sage and mint. "Your mother hired me to look into …" She suddenly felt her cheeks redden slightly. She wasn't sure what Bill Thompson was to this man. Father? Stepfather? Just Bill? "Her husband's death."

"Of course, the PI." He turned and looked at the receptionist, who was clearly listening. "Mary, is conference room A open?"

"Yes," she said.

"Follow me, please. Let's do this somewhere more private than the water cooler."

The term 'water cooler' sounded antiquated and affected, but maybe that's how marketing people talked. She followed him down the corridor to the left, past two empty glass-fronted offices before he stopped and held the third door open. She entered a conference room with a striking view of Midtown Manhattan. It was an aspirational view. The city unfolded before her, a panorama of towering steel and bustling streets that was a reminder of the city's relentless ambition, wealth, and energy.

Marti put the view at her back and sat down. "I hope I'm not intruding. I was in the city and wanted to talk to you about your …" She'd walked into it again. "Bill," she finished.

"Yes, Mom mentioned she had hired someone. I guess you're it."

"I'm it," Marti agreed, trying to lighten the tension she felt creeping into the room. His aftershave was even stronger in the closed conference room.

He stared at her across the conference table, and she realized that for whatever reason, he'd taken a dislike to her and was going to make this as difficult as possible. If that's how he wanted to play it, she was determined, then, to at least be direct. "I take it you don't agree with your mother's decision?"

"To hire a private eye to investigate his death? No, not really. What's there to investigate? Everyone else has accepted Bill's death but her." Marti was about to respond, she felt like she'd gotten pretty practiced at deflecting this particular thrust, when he continued. "Let me ask you something. How long have you been working on this?"

"I did a little on Saturday but started in earnest on Monday," Marti replied, wondering if he was going after the money.

"We'll call it two full days and change with Saturday and this morning."

"Sure."

"And presumably you've gone through Bill's disaster of an office and talked to several people other than just my mom."

"That's correct." She could now see where this was going.

"And what exactly have you found so far?"

"Two days isn't that much time—"

But he cut her off. "I can probably guess. You've found out that Bill loved his job. He loved being a cop. He loved law and order and rules almost to a fault. He married my mom and he was a pretty good stepdad all things considered, but the job always came first. How am I doing so far?"

"Not bad. I guess I should have talked to you first. Could have saved me some time."

"I can keep going. I don't think they had money issues. My brother's tuition is still being paid and they must almost own the house. They lived pretty frugally. Bill didn't have time for lavish vacations or expensive hobbies. He did, however, love fast-food and bourbon. I don't know for certain, but I'm guessing he was in lousy shape."

"I talked to the medical examiner. His chest was a ticking time bomb."

"There you go. It sucks, but it happens. The man died of a massive heart attack. End of story. A somewhat tragic story, sure, but nothing worth investigating."

She waited a beat, then two, but he seemed to have blown himself out at this point.

"I don't disagree with you, Ethan, based on what I've learned so far, but Sandy really does seem troubled and believes Bill was really worried about something when he died. Something that might have contributed to his ultimate heart attack."

"She wants to believe."

"Why would she want that?"

"Because it makes for a better story. More drama. Less banal. She'll be a widow now for another 20 years maybe, and she'll have to tell the story countless times. A vanilla run-of-the-mill heart attack is boring."

"She's not marketing her widowhood."

"No? We're all telling stories to the world in some form."

That felt like a really cynical worldview, especially from someone only in his mid-to-late 20s, but she didn't want to argue or heighten the tension any further, so she pivoted.

"You had a decent relationship with Bill, then?"

He shrugged and fiddled with the button on his shirt cuff. "It was all right. I'd like to think it was getting better. The teenage years weren't all that great, but maybe that was normal."

"How so?"

"You gotta remember that Bill was always a cop first. He couldn't turn it off. It was law and order 24/7. Maybe he saw a few shades of gray, but he was strict and it wasn't just on the job. It extended to the home. He had an Army background. He followed the rules and he expected the same from you."

"And that was a problem for you?"

"I was 12 when he moved in. I'm guessing it would have been a problem for most normal teenagers." Marti had no children, but she'd been in plenty of homes and seen her own nieces and nephews change and she thought Ethan was probably right. That type of discipline would be tough enough with any parent, never mind a stepparent.

"My dad, my biological dad, was pretty flaky and rarely around much after I was seven or eight and my mom was always a pushover with us kids, so Bill was a real change. I challenged his authority pretty much every chance I got."

"That must have led to some fun family dinners."

"He came around eventually." Ethan gave a wry smile and then continued, maybe aware of the picture he was painting of his deceased stepfather. "He wasn't all bad. He stuck around. Now that I'm older, I can see how it was a tough situation to walk into. Three adolescent kids. He really loved my mom, and he encouraged all of us to get involved in different things. Drove us to Scouts, track practice, karate, all that kind of stuff."

"Did he ever talk about his cases or work with you?"

Ethan shook his head with no hesitation. "No, never. He was still Mr. Law and Order at home, but he was not Detective Thompson. Not around us kids, anyway."

"And nothing when you were older? Maybe in the last three months or so before he died? That's why your mother hired me. She's convinced that something was bothering him, something big enough and bad enough that eventually the stress killed him."

Ethan looked slightly embarrassed before he said, "I've been busy at work. The hours at a startup like this are intense. I didn't always call or check in regularly, but when we talked, he never mentioned anything specifically. Not like that."

"Okay. One last question. Since the funeral, have you seen your father's most recent work notebook?"

"The little notebook he carried on him while working cases?"

"Yes."

"It's missing?"

"Maybe not exactly missing, I'm not sure, but I can't get my hands on it. Having that would get me closer to him. Maybe close enough to see what, if anything, was bothering him."

"No, I haven't seen it. When it wasn't in his jacket pocket during the day, he locked it up with his service weapon and ID at home. Like I said, he took his casework really seriously. I'd sometimes see it in the cupholder of his truck."

"It's not in either of those places. I've checked."

"That's weird. Did you ask Jessica Lawson? She was his partner of sorts at the end. Maybe they're at the station?"

Marti thought about her brief encounter with Lawson. "I've spoken to her."

Ethan had a point. Maybe it was time to push a little harder.

Chapter Eighteen

Marti sat on the subway, heading back to Jersey City. With rush hour over, the train was relatively empty, with only a few passengers scattered here and there. Dim fluorescent lights flickered overhead, casting a pale glow on the worn seats and the drab interior as the express train flashed through the local stops.

As she rode beneath the streets of New York, Marti reflected on her conversation with Ethan. It lined up with what Olivia had said about Bill, too. He was a solid stepfather, there for them, but also there with rules and discipline. He wasn't a pushover or a shoulder to cry on. It sounded like he was the stricter parent compared to Sandy. But both Ethan and Olivia appeared to be doing all right so maybe Bill was who they needed at the time.

Ethan had also emphasized that Bill was devoted to the job and never discussed work or his cases at home. That was also consistent with what Olivia and Sandy had said. And the basic crux of the problem. Bill might have confided in his fellow officers, but they weren't talking either. If there was even anything to talk about. She found the circular logic discouraging. What started as a simple favor for her father was turning into a major frustration for Marti. Sandy was convinced that something was bothering her late husband, but no one would back her up. Today was the third day she'd been on the case and the initial deadline they had agreed to at the start. Marti knew if she tried to end her own involvement tonight, it would be a tough conversation. Sandy wouldn't like it.

The day wasn't over yet, however. Marti knew she needed to focus on the immediate steps at hand. First, she wanted to visit the spot where Bill had been found, despite the assurances from Lawson and Ethan that it was likely irrelevant. Something inside her urged her to see it for herself, to connect with the physical scene where this had started.

Her other priority, tied to visiting the site, was to speak with Brenda Martinez, the first responder. While contacting her directly through official channels might be met with resistance, Marti thought of a potential alternative way to get an introduction. Sandy had said Martinez was a newer employee. That might mean younger and that might mean a social media footprint.

She pulled out her phone and started searching. Brenda Martinez was a common name and it took some time to sift through the results on the different apps. She struck out on Facebook and Twitter but thought she might have a hit on Instagram. A few swipes, a couple of clicks, and she found herself on Martinez's Instagram profile page. There were no references to the Cedarwood police department, and most of the photos were of food or drinks, Brenda Martinez apparently liked to bake, but Marti thought she recognized Harmony's Brew in the background of two shots. She tapped out a quick private message and hit send just as the train pulled into the Jersey City station.

Martinez had responded by the time Marti had climbed the station steps and walked the three blocks to where she'd left her car at JJ's the previous night. Marti revised her estimate of Brenda Martinez's age down a few years based on the speed of her answer.

'Sure, not a problem. Are you around today? I'm not on shift until 3 p.m.'

The quick reply and breezy tone caught Marti off guard. She had become accustomed to having to practically pull teeth to get any information out of people on this case. She had the location from the autopsy report. She wanted to get Martinez's impressions, as well. She checked her watch, then tapped out her own response.

'Can we meet where you found Bill at 2?'

Again, the response was almost immediate.

'See you then.'

Marti unlocked the Subaru and climbed in. With a pang of regret and a mild rebuke from her rumbling stomach, she drove past JJ's and navigated over to Montgomery until she could swing around and merge onto 78 West. She settled in for the hour drive with NPR broadcasting the BBC World Service. She was 20 minutes into the hour-long drive and had just finished listening to a story on the recent revolution in Sudan when her phone rang. Marti glanced at her phone propped in the cup holder and frowned. It was her sister, Emily. Marti didn't have a poor relationship with her sister, they just weren't particularly close. They were very different people. And they rarely, if ever, called each other at 11:30 on a Wednesday morning. She felt a flutter of panic in her gut. Her nieces and nephews? Their dad?

"Hey, Em," she answered, trying to keep her voice steady as she navigated the traffic. "What's going on?"

"Hi, Marti," Emily replied, her tone unusually serious. "I'm at Dad's place, and there's something I need to talk to you about."

Marti felt a stab of concern, or maybe it was guilt, in her gut. She was doing this favor for her dad, but she hadn't been out to see him in weeks. "Is everything okay?"

Emily hesitated before responding. "Well, that's what I want to discuss with you. I've noticed a few things lately that have me worried about his memory."

Marti frowned. "What do you mean?" Emily was the worrier in the family. Marti was the one who plunged in headfirst and dealt with the aftermath. Emily was more hesitant and picked at things.

She heard Emily take a deep breath before continuing. "It's been happening over the past few months. He's been forgetting things—appointments, where he put things, and sometimes even people's names. Eleanor stopped me today and told me he got disoriented the other day trying to find his own apartment after lunch."

Marti listened, her grip on the steering wheel tightening. "Em, those things could happen to anyone, especially as they get older."

"I know," Emily admitted, "but these occurrences are happening more frequently, Marti. And they're not like him at all."

Marti sighed. She also knew what her sister wasn't saying: You haven't been here. You haven't seen him lately. "I get that you're concerned, but there's a whole memory unit at that place, right? Doctors, specialists. That sort of thing. Wouldn't they pick up on these things?"

"Yes, there are," Emily confirmed, "and I've consulted with the staff here."

Marti felt a hot lance of anger bubble up. "You consulted them without talking to me?"

To her credit, Emily didn't rise to the bait. "Consulted might be a strong word. It wasn't a formal appointment. I stopped by when I was visiting and asked one of the memory specialists. They think it might be early-onset dementia, but he hasn't been tested or diagnosed. I think we need to be proactive about this, Marti. The sooner we address it, the better Dad's quality of life will be."

Marti took a moment. This wasn't Emily's fault, she reminded herself. She made her hands relax their grip on the steering wheel as she considered Emily's words. "I just hate the thought of him being in a place like that. Dad's always been so independent."

"I know," Emily said. "But sometimes, the best thing we can do for the people we love is to make sure they get the care they need. Even if it hurts."

"I'll come out this weekend and visit him and then we can talk. Don't make any decisions or have any more consultations until then."

"Okay. I'll wait until then. Call me after you visit."

Marti spent three miles stewing on the phone call before she called her dad.

"How's it going out in Cedarwood?" he said. She'd braced herself when she heard him pick up the phone, but all she heard was the same gruff voice she'd been hearing her entire life. It was always like stepping in mid-conversation. He liked small talk even less than Marti.

"Have you ever been out here?"

"Why would I do that?"

"It's ... peaceful. Okay, good point. I can't really see you out here either." Her old man was a city mouse through and through just like her. He'd gritted his teeth and tolerated their annual trips to the beach at Asbury Park when she and Emily had been kids. Marti continued, "Had you talked to Bill recently?"

"No. He and Sandy came to my retirement party. We promised to keep in touch, that sort of thing, but you know how that usually goes. Sandy called out of the blue with this request. You're not getting anywhere?"

"She says he was distracted and distant the last few months, but I'm not finding anything, personal or professional, to show that nor anything that might give her the type of answers she's looking for."

"The locals tell you anything?"

"Not much. They're being tight-lipped, but I'm not sure it's for any specific reason. I think they just don't want to talk to a PI and would prefer to put it all behind them."

"He definitely died of a heart attack?"

"Yes, no doubt about that. The autopsy was conclusive. I spoke to the ME. She didn't hold back. She said she has no doubts. The only question appears to be why he was out on that road driving the night it happened. I'm actually headed out there right now to take a look."

"Sounds like you're doing all the right things. If there's nothing to find, there's nothing to find."

"I'm meeting with Sandy at the end of the day to figure out if we'll call it. People already think I'm in it for the cash. I don't want to hang around."

Her father made a noncommittal grunt but remained silent.

Marti had one last question. "Dad, did anything ever keep you up at night?"

He was quiet for a long time before he said, "Worrying about you girls. You and Marti. That kept me up."

Marti felt her stomach twist. "Me and Emily."

"What?"

"You said 'you and Marti.' I'm Marti."

"Of course you are."

As Marti continued her drive along 78, she flipped through the FM radio stations and let the noise wash over her, a welcome distraction from the weighty conversation with her sister and the follow-up with her father. Her mind meandered as she watched the landscape change from suburban sprawl to more rural. The occasional farm and rolling field passed by her window. The colors on the trees had exploded in the last week; she tried to focus on that and push aside thoughts of her father's condition. And she was largely successful. She was very good at avoiding problems in her own life.

When she reached her exit, she pulled into a small gas station to fill up and grab a cup of coffee. The air was warm for September and filled with the scent of gasoline and dying leaves. She took a sip of her coffee as she waited for the tank to fill and felt the bitter warmth invigorate her senses. It wasn't great coffee, but it did the job. She smiled to herself. By and large, the same could be said about her ex-husbands.

As she settled back into her car, she flipped through her notes from the autopsy report that contained the details Brenda Martinez had provided about where Bill Thompson's truck and body had been found and Martinez's initial steps in the incident until the ambulance arrived. She pulled up the map on her phone, her fingers expertly pinching and zooming until she felt she was in the right vicinity.

The road she was looking for was a two-lane state road, a few miles outside of Cedarwood, that acted as a connector to the surrounding townships. She noted another gas station or maybe convenience store, The Corner Country Store, within a mile of where she thought Bill had been found. She plugged that address into her GPS for reference and pulled back out onto the road.

Twenty minutes later, Marti pulled into the The Corner Country Store's lot. The store sat at the crossroads of two quiet rural roads, its faded plank pine facade blending harmoniously with the rustic countryside. A small farm could be seen in the background. Cows milled about in a large fenced-in area. Large bales of hay were scattered about. It looked pretty in the afternoon sun even though Marti knew farming was likely a hard grind of a life.

The store had clearly seen better days, the years having etched their marks on its peeling paint and creaking wooden sign. The gas pumps out front, aged and weathered, whispered tales of simpler times. A porch with a scattering of benches and chairs invited travelers to rest a spell, if there had been any travelers. A collection of colorful potted plants added a touch of life and vibrancy to the otherwise bland exterior. Marti could see the appeal of the crossroads location 50 or 60 years ago, but she wasn't sure how the management kept it open now. All the rocking chairs were empty. But the parking lot wasn't.

Marti was 15 minutes early, but as she navigated around the two old fuel pumps, her eyes fell on a young woman in uniform, leaning casually against the driver's side door of a red Acura, sipping from a can of iced tea. This, Marti assumed, was Brenda Martinez.

Martinez appeared to be in her mid-twenties. Her uniform was crisply pressed, and she wore it with a relaxed confidence. Her short, dark hair was pulled back into a tight ponytail, and her brown eyes held a hint of curiosity as she watched Marti pull into an adjacent parking spot.

Marti approached Brenda with a friendly nod. "Officer Martinez, I presume? I'm Marti Wells. I appreciate you taking the time to meet with me."

Brenda nodded and tossed the can of iced tea into a nearby trash can. "Sure. Bill was a good man. He took the time to talk to me when I joined the department and gave me some good advice. If I can return the favor in some way, even if he's gone, I'll try. What can I help you with?"

Her tone was cool professionalism. Marti wasn't sure how far this courtesy would extend once she started asking questions, but it was a better start than her very brief chat with Martinez's colleague, Jessica Lawson.

"First, I just want to say I'm not out here looking to dig up dirt on Bill or the department. His widow, Sandy, has some questions and feels like she's owed some answers."

"Owed?"

"Her word, not mine."

"What are your words?"

"Why did I take the job?"

"That's right."

"I don't think anyone is immune to loss, but I think everyone processes grief in their own way. I think Sandy is struggling. She said Bill was acting strangely in the weeks leading up to his heart attack. She thinks he was worried about something, but he didn't confide in her what it might be, and she never worked up the courage to ask. Then he dropped dead before she could. Maybe she's feeling guilty about that. Maybe it's nothing. Maybe she's looking back and seeing ghosts. I don't know. If it helps her to have me ask some questions," Marti flipped a hand, "why not? She deserves that much."

"Not sure that gives her the right to root around in Bill's business."

"Even as his wife, I might agree with you to some extent, but that's why she hired me. She feels like she needs to make amends. And I need to earn a living. In her place, you might do the same thing."

Martinez said nothing for a moment. She looked out at the road as a dirt-crusted pickup drove past. When she looked back at Marti, she had those flat, unemotional cop eyes that Marti recognized all too well. She wondered if Martinez realized that this meeting might get her into trouble, but all she said was, "Alright."

"I'm just looking for the truth. No trouble in that," Marti said.

Martinez looked at her like she was a naïve child if she really believed that hokum, but surprised Marti by smiling. She had big, square, straight teeth and the smile transformed her face. She no longer looked so severe and dour. "If you tell the truth, you don't have to remember anything."

It felt like a quote, but Marti couldn't place it. She nodded and returned the smile. "Not a bad mantra for a cop."

"Doesn't have to apply to just cops. Shouldn't apply to just cops."

"True enough."

"How did you get my name?"

"I found it on a note in the back of the medical examiner's report."

"Why go through Instagram? Why not the department?"

Marti had been hoping Martinez wouldn't ask that question. She stepped gingerly. "I did talk to Lisa Watkins and Jessica Lawson. I was actually in Jersey City this morning before coming back out and I thought going through social media might be more efficient." Not a lie exactly. She parried with her own question back at Martinez. "How long did you know Bill?"

"I started a little over a year ago, so I knew him, but not all that well. I wouldn't even say we were friends. We were friendly. It's a small department, but more colleagues than friends. Maybe that would have changed with time. Maybe not. He was older, obviously, and retiring in a few years, but his death shook me a bit, I'll admit. Shook everyone. Bill was a fixture around town."

"Can you walk me through how you found him? I'm trying to get a feel for the scene."

"You want to go up and look at it? Would that help? It's just a mile or so up the road." She pointed off to the right, where the road disappeared around a bend. "We could ride together."

"If you have time, that would be great."

Marti sat in the passenger seat of Brenda Martinez's red Acura as they drove west, away from The Country Corner Store, and deeper into the heart of Cedarwood's rural landscape. The township itself was large, but the vast majority was wilderness. The residential sections outside the concentrated town center comprised scattered lots and the occasional farm.

The narrow road stretched out before them, flanked by a tapestry of changing foliage. On either side, tall trees rustled gently in the breeze. Their looming canopies provided intermittent shade to the sandy shoulder of the road. They drove past utility poles, broken-down fences, faded signs for businesses long gone, and abrupt cuts in the roadside wood that led to who knows where. It was a quiet, undisturbed place. It would be dark and lonely at night. What had Bill been doing out here?

Martinez slowed and pulled onto the shoulder. They couldn't have driven over two miles. "This is it. I remember the pole." She pointed out the windshield at a cracked utility pole canting at a 20-degree angle toward the trees. Marti watched her eyes go foggy as she replayed the scene. "I came up on him from this direction, from behind. I recognized his truck. It was on the shoulder. Hazard lights were on. I thought initially it might be an engine problem or a flat, but once I approached, I could see him slumped over the wheel. The doors were locked. I tapped on the driver's window with my flashlight because I thought he might be asleep."

"How'd you get in?"

"Driver's window was cracked. We keep a loop of wire in most of the cars. Comes in handy for a variety of things. I popped the lock. He didn't look good. Drooling. Gray. His eyes were open. I remember that."

"He was still alive?"

"I don't know. I'll be honest. I was a little rattled. My hands were shaking. I tried to remember the protocols. I pulled him out of the truck, got him flat on the side of the road, and did CPR. I did check for a pulse at some point. I remember his skin was cool. I eventually remembered to use my radio. I kept up the CPR until the paramedics arrived. They took him, but I heard he was declared DOA at the hospital."

"Did you notice anything else?"

"No, nothing unusual."

Marti glanced up the road. Five feet off the shoulder, the asphalt petered out. It had eroded over time into a hard dirt shell, but a little closer to the woods she could see a drainage ditch, maybe put in by the utility company. You wouldn't want to get your axles snagged in that, especially in the dark.

"He must have known it was coming, right?" she asked. "Car was lined up and basically parked. No skids. He didn't slow to a stop in the road."

"That would be my guess. Chest pain or tightness. Maybe shortness of breath, right?"

"You didn't see Bill's notebook in the truck, did you?"

"His notebook?"

"Small notebook. Kept it on him for notes or interviews. Things like that."

"No, I know what you mean, but I didn't see it. Wasn't really looking for it though either. Someone told you it was in the truck?"

"No," she admitted, "but it hasn't turned up. I thought maybe you'd grabbed it and turned it in to the department."

"I certainly would have if I'd come across it."

Marti reached for the door handle. "I want to take a quick look." She hopped out of the Acura and walked until she was even with the utility pole. There was no traffic in sight in either direction. She looked at the dirt and gravel on the shoulder. No trace remained of anything that had happened. Martinez came up and stood beside her.

"Quick grid search, say 50 feet in either direction?" Marti couldn't see Bill going any farther in his condition.

Martinez looked at her. "What are we looking for?"

"Any trace of that notebook."

"Why?"

Marti couldn't answer that question with any certainty. "Humor me? What if Bill tossed the notebook out the window or tried to hide it in some way before he died?"

"But why?"

"I don't know. But it just bothers me that the notebook is still missing. What if Bill was working on something sensitive? And tossing the notes or hiding them was some attempt at keeping them secure or confidential?"

"Big assumption. No one at the office has mentioned anything like that. And it's a small office."

"I understand. You're right. The flip side could also be just as true. The notes and notebook aren't relevant at all. It will go faster if we both search."

Martinez shrugged. "Sure, let's do it. Can't hurt."

They each covered a careful 50 yards in either direction of the damaged pole. Marti kicked over rocks, brushed through piles of leaves, and walked along the edge of the woods, but neither of them found a trace of the notebook. No scraps of paper or torn up bits of suspicious litter. Plenty of litter, but nothing that resembled a pocket notebook.

They met back at the pole. Martinez glanced at her watch. "We'd better head back. I'm on duty in a half hour."

Martinez drove Marti back and dropped her off near the pumps. Marti pulled out a business card and handed it over. "I appreciate the time. If you think of anything, let me know."

"I will, though I can't imagine what that would be. Bill was a good man. And a good cop."

"That's what everyone keeps telling me."

Her next step was to head over to Sandy's house and have the difficult conversation that no other answers were coming her way. But first, her earlier gas station coffee was making its presence felt. She needed to find out if The Country Corner Store had a bathroom.

Inside, Marti found herself transported back to a world where time moved a little slower. The shelves, worn with age and lined with a haphazard array of merchandise, seemed to groan under the weight of history. Among the clutter, snacks in colorful packaging and tubs of taffy and penny candy beckoned. Stacks of canned goods stood like sentinels, ready for duty in the event of a culinary emergency.

The heart of the store, however, was a collection of dusty antiques that whispered tales of days gone by. Faded books with cracked spines perched alongside weathered porcelain figurines. Vintage signs boasting long-forgotten brands adorned the walls. It was a haven for collectors and treasure hunters alike, each item seeming to have its own story to tell.

The air was a panoply of distinct scents. Coffee beans, aged wood, soap, and the faint trace of leather, maybe from the huge, weathered armchair in the corner. It was a place where time didn't so much stand still as it did leisurely meander along.

Behind the counter, stood a woman with limp dishwater blonde hair that matched her beige T-shirt and brown apron. She couldn't have been older than 30 or 35, but the harshness of life had etched deep lines into her face. Her pinched expression seemed to come from a lifetime of frowns. She appeared unnaturally thin, as though her frame was held together by twine and stubbornness.

Her eyes, though watchful, didn't hold the warmth of welcome or even a hint of a smile. Instead, Marti saw the weight of countless days and nights spent tending to the store, and perhaps, enduring the trials of life itself. It was as if she had become part of the store, a fixture rather than a proprietor, and she silently observed Marti's entrance with a stoic demeanor.

"Do you have a bathroom?" Marti asked.

"For customers," the woman replied.

"Got it," Marti said. She walked to a chest cooler toward the back, pulled out a grape Moxie soda, and walked over to the register. "Never seen these outside of Maine."

"Lee Cody likes them," the woman said in a lukewarm response that didn't invite further inquiries. Marti took the hint, kept her mouth shut, and paid for the soda.

The woman made change and they stared at each other across the scarred wooden counter. "So, could I have the bathroom key or whatever," Marti eventually said.

The woman reached under the counter, took out a key tied to a large piece of rebar, and pointed toward the back corner. Marti resisted the urge to beat some basic customer service into the woman and took the key.

She did her business in the customers-only bathroom, returned the key, and walked out onto the porch. She was tempted to sit in one of the vacant rockers and drink her Moxie but was worried the woman inside would chase her off with a hatchet if she stayed any longer than necessary. Instead, she went down the steps and climbed back into the Subaru.

She sipped the strange regional soda and thought it tasted more like licorice than grape. But that was the least of her worries. As she drove, she tried to think of a way to tell Sandy that even with no answers, she was going to have to make peace with Bill's death. Death didn't discriminate and there were always loose ends in its wake. With Marti's profession, she should know. Life was a long accumulation of minor mysteries. Death didn't magically reveal any answers. Not to the living at any rate. She had a feeling she could work this case for three months, talk to everyone in Cedarwood, and never find out what might have been bothering Bill in his last moments.

A half hour later, Marti was in Sandy's kitchen, but she wasn't alone. She sat at the kitchen table and listened to Sandy and Lisa Wilkins argue about the seating chart for the upcoming Police Officer's Charity Ball. A large piece of posterboard and various colored sticky notes covered the table. Marti sipped from a cup of tea and nibbled an oatmeal cookie while she listened to the debate.

Lisa Wilkins looked at one of the Post-it notes skeptically and adjusted it to the left. "I think Patty should sit at table seven instead. Remember the Mildred incident?"

Sandy frowned, her brows knitting in concentration. "Mildred incident? That was years ago. Are they still holding onto that grudge?"

Lisa chuckled. "Oh, they are, believe me. You remember how at the last ball, Patty accidentally spilled red wine on Hannah's dress, and Hannah accused her of doing it on purpose?" She made air quotes around 'accidentally.'

Sandy laughed, maybe recalling the dramatic scene. "Yes, I do. Hannah thinks that was retaliation?"

"Yes, it was another chapter in the ongoing feud."

"It's amazing how long these things can simmer."

Lisa nodded. "The rumor is Hannah's been waiting for the perfect moment to get back at her. I wouldn't want to be in the same room with those two, let alone at the same table."

Marti couldn't resist. She leaned in, "So, what's the Mildred incident?"

Chapter Nineteen

Sandy smiled and shook her head. "Like all good small-town stories. The town's annual bake-off is to blame for the Mildred incident and the feud between Hannah and Patty.

"Hannah is renowned throughout the town for her exquisite baking skills, particularly her mouthwatering red velvet cake. She won first place five straight years. Patty, on the other hand, has never won the bake-off. Hannah's cakes always overshadow her chocolate chip cookies.

"Determined to outshine Hannah and finally secure the coveted blue ribbon, Patty decided to fight fire with fire and change her entry and use her great-aunt Mildred's red velvet cake recipe, which featured a secret ingredient only whispered about in family circles."

Lisa picked up the story. "The thing you need to understand about Patty is that she likes to talk. She would have no trouble winning the blue ribbon for gossip. So, word of her plan and secret family recipe soon reached Hannah.

"As the competition unfolded, Patty's cake, which she had lovingly dubbed "Aunt Mildred's Sweet Surprise," drew raised eyebrows from both the judges and other contestants. It was an excellent cake but also a very familiar cake. Hannah had been watching the judges' reactions with growing suspicion. Soon, Hannah's competitive spirit got the better of her. She decided to investigate, lurking around Patty's cake booth, until she could sneak a taste herself, and soon confronted Patty with a dramatic accusation. She'd stolen Hannah's recipe. Patty insisted it was a family recipe and demanded an apology from Hannah. Things quickly escalated into a wild cake-throwing melee that sent frosting and crumbs flying in all directions. Eventually, the women were separated and the judges called in. Both women ended up with egg, as well as frosting, on their faces if you'll excuse the pun. It turns out Aunt Mildred's secret family recipe and Hannah's award-winning recipe shared a common ancestor: Betty Crocker."

Sandy finished the story. "Their cake clash quickly became the talk of the town, and the Mildred incident, as it became known, is forever etched in Cedarwood's history. But neither woman is happy with the notoriety, and each blames the other. While it began as a comical misunderstanding over a secret ingredient, it ultimately transformed into a much more personal feud that has continued to simmer over the years."

"I wonder just how many secret family recipes are copies of Betty Crocker or Fannie Farmer?" Marti said.

"I'd say more than a few," Sandy agreed. "The secret ingredient is usually Tollhouse or mayonnaise. Anyway, you didn't drive back out here to listen to two biddies like us. Any news?"

Marti glanced at Lisa and Sandy caught it. "It's okay. Heck, if you've been doing your job, most of the town probably knows about it by now."

She definitely wasn't wrong about that. Time to pull off the band-aid, Marti thought. "I'm coming up empty, Sandy." She held up her hands as the expression on Sandy's face soured. "I don't doubt you or the fact that Bill was anxious about something. A few other people have mentioned something similar. My trouble is, I just can't find any indication of what it actually was. I'm just about done in his office, talked to his colleagues, talked to the medical examiner, talked to you and Ethan and Olivia, and I'm no closer to knowing what it was now than when I showed up on Saturday."

Sandy's frown deepened. "You've only been working it a few days."

Marti glanced across the table and caught Lisa looking uncomfortable as she straightened out a few Post-it notes on the seating chart. "That's true," Marti said, focusing back on Sandy. "I keep hoping the next rock I turn over will provide some answers or even a hint, but I want to be honest. The longer this goes with no progress, the more difficult it will become. People will start thinking I'm hanging around just to take your money."

"I don't care about that. And I know it's not true."

"I appreciate that, I do, but once people start thinking that way, it's hard to turn that opinion around and they are less inclined to help. They'll see it as me taking Bill's money. I don't need that rep following me."

"I guess you can only do your best," Sandy replied.

Marti felt like Sandy was now acting, or worse, fishing for pity because she had an audience. She remembered Ethan's comment about his mother's need to control the story. Marti pushed back her chair and stood. "I'm going to finish up with Bill's office. I can give you a more detailed rundown and we can go over those phone numbers when you and Lisa are done."

Sandy just nodded and turned her attention back to the table and the delicate balance of seating everyone at the gala. Marti knew when she'd been dismissed. She put her empty mug in the sink and walked down the hall to Bill's office.

She stood in the doorway and fought the temptation to turn around and leave, even if it meant driving back to the inn and dealing with Lucille. Boxes, files, and papers covered the room. She had been trying to be logical and systematic with her search, but the results just looked scattered and half done. Marti had assumed that if Bill were up to something there would be some trace. Something, anything, somewhere. But now, turning up nothing, she felt adrift. She wasn't sure what pile to tackle next. She'd lost what little enthusiasm remained somewhere between The Country Corner Store and the afternoon tea. Still, a sense of obligation forced her to stay. If she couldn't earn her money getting answers, she could at least be an adequate cleaning woman.

She'd left off yesterday cleaning out Bill's desk. Much of that could be quickly discarded. She picked up a half-filled garbage bag and approached the desk. Anything that was clearly trash, she tossed into the bag. Anything else went into an empty box in the name of straightening up and bringing some order to the chaos.

Twenty minutes later, she was dirtier but feeling a little better. She made a mental note to retrieve Bill's laptop from her car and return it to Sandy. The desk was now clear. Or mostly clear. The laptop's secondary monitor, landline phone, and small notepad remained. She picked up the notepad. She hadn't looked at it before because other files and papers had covered it. It was a chunky, spiral-bound, square block meant for taking quick notes. Doodles and phrases covered the top few pages. They were the type of notes that you might halfheartedly make while listening on the phone. She flipped through the sheets. Bill had some talent for dogs, cats, and umbrellas. There were also various notations, letters, and numbers, maybe phone numbers. Some were boxed in or underlined, while others were crossed out.

She set the garbage back down, went to the bookshelf, and sorted through the papers until she found the stack of phone bills again. She took them back to the desk and sat down. She'd given the recent couple of months to Sandy, but she had the earlier part of the year. This suddenly felt like something. She tried to tamp down any feelings of excitement. It might just feel like this because everything else had come up empty. She cross-referenced the list of numbers on the notepad with the last six months of phone bills. She got three hits, all on his business cell. The first number had been called eight times in the last three months, but most of the calls took place earlier, late June, early July. She'd need to check the recent bills to see if there were any calls in the last few weeks before he died. She didn't recognize the 302 area code. In the age of cell phones, area codes had become largely irrelevant.

On a whim, she grabbed the desk phone and dialed. After five rings, it rolled to an automated voicemail that just repeated the phone number, with no name or identifying information. She left her own name and phone number and asked for a return call regarding Bill Thompson. She would not hold her breath.

She decided to try the rest. The second number had a little set of stylized wings next to it. She tapped in the numbers.

It was answered almost before it rang. The voice was short and clipped. "Air National Guard, Warren Grove Range. How may I direct your call?"

She disconnected. At least the little wing doodle made sense, but why was Bill calling a National Guard Base in central New Jersey? He'd once served in the Army, she knew that, maybe this was related? Maybe it had nothing to do with Bill's mood change. She pulled the phone bills closer and ran her finger down the column. It was a two-and-a-half-minute conversation, so it wasn't a wrong number. It was something. She made a note to ask Sandy.

The final match was a number that had been boxed in and then crossed out on the top sheet. It had been called just once back in May.

She dialed and a real person picked up the call on the second ring, which surprised her, so many people screened their calls these days, only this wasn't a personal number. It was a business.

"Sundowner. How can I direct your call?" It was a male voice. He sounded slightly bored or distracted. Maybe both.

"Is the Sundowner a hotel?"

The question seemed to amuse the man on the other end. "Sure, some people call it that."

"What would you call it?"

"My boss would call it a short- or long-term lodging option."

"Still not what you would call it though, right?"

"Okay, I'll play. A downtrodden, slightly damp, mostly depressing motel for newly divorced dads."

"And where are you located?"

"Rehoboth Beach."

"That's in Delaware, right?"

"Last I checked."

"Okay, thanks."

She hung up and leaned back in the chair. Rehoboth Beach was a boardwalk, coastal town. She'd never been, but she'd been to plenty of places like it on the Jersey Shore and she was sure if she closed her eyes, she'd have no trouble conjuring up the Sundowner. Why would Bill call them? If she was right, and she'd check later, it wasn't the type of place where Bill and Sandy would stay.

Then she remembered something else and quickly stood and went back to the bookshelves and moved piles and boxes around until she found Bill's credit card statements. He'd made the call in late May. She sorted the sheets until she found the June statement and ran her finger down the list. He hadn't just called the Sundowner. He'd driven down and visited. There were charges for gas and food in Delaware two weeks after he made the phone call.

Chapter Twenty

Marti finally felt the buzz. This was something. This was a thread she could pull on. She stood and paced around the office. Her legs itched to jump in her car and drive to the Sundowner right now. She wanted to look that sarcastic voice in the face and ask him more questions. Instead, she pulled out her phone and did a quick search. It would take four hours. That would put her in Rehoboth Beach at close to eight. She weighed the pros and cons. She wanted to keep pushing, but if the man on the phone had no answers, she'd have to find other people to question and that might be tough at that time of night. People didn't like opening their doors or answering phone calls from strangers after dark.

Her finger hovered over the recent call. She could quickly call back and ask the desk clerk more questions but felt this might require some finesse and face-to-face interaction. She hated the thought of waiting even just overnight but knew that was mostly her own frustration and impatience. Whatever had pulled Bill down to Delaware could wait another night. She put her phone back in her bag. Better to finish up the office as much as she could, then talk to Sandy, get some dinner, and get some sleep.

She let out a long breath and granted herself five seconds of self-pity, then got back at it. The bookshelves that lined the left wall had cabinets on the bottom. She'd glanced inside while doing the initial survey of the room and saw that most were empty or only partially filled with boxes. At the time, she sighed with relief, thinking that at least part of the office was organized, and then mostly forgot about the bookshelves. Now, she had to deal with them. She pushed more boxes aside and cleared a space in the middle of the floor, then she opened the doors on all three cabinets and pulled out the boxes. Much of it appeared to be personal memorabilia from Bill's early career and life before Sandy. She was getting a feel for Bill now and it fit that while he was dedicated to his job, he did not like to call attention to himself or his work. She found plaques, recognition certificates, and old files and notes from his time working with her dad in Paterson. One box contained his dog tags, boots, discharge papers, and faded photographs from his time in the Army.

In the last box, Marti found a surprise. She discovered three big binders with photocopies of official Cedarwood crime files. She flipped through them. They were not just Bill's cases, either. The files went back over 20 years, before Bill started with the department, and appeared to be a log of the department's cold cases. Why did he have these? A hobby? Curiosity? Something else? She flipped through a second time, going more slowly. There were no notes or annotations. No sign of which case Bill was interested in, if any.

"Marti?"

Marti flinched, startled by the sudden voice. Lisa Wilkins stood in the doorway. Marti hadn't heard her approach. She slid the binder off her lap and out of sight.

"Jeez, you scared me," Marti said.

"Sorry, I didn't mean to," Lisa responded.

"You figure out the seating?"

"Yes, we did. At least for now. Listen, I'm just on my way out, but I wondered if I could talk to you for a minute?"

"Sure." Marti stood, went around, and sat behind the desk.

"Sorry, maybe someplace a little more private." She glanced over her shoulder. "Could you walk me out?" She didn't wait for an answer, just turned and disappeared down the hall.

Marti clambered out of the rickety desk chair and followed. As she passed through the kitchen, she saw Sandy in the living room talking on the phone. She gave a brief wave as she followed Lisa into the entryway and out the front door. The sun was setting and there was a bite to the air that hadn't been there that afternoon. Marti rubbed at her arms.

Lisa opened the driver's side door of her SUV and threw her purse inside. Now, she stood by the open door looking a little lost. Marti stopped a few feet away and waited. The stern and efficient office manager from the police station was gone. Marti thought she looked nervous and uncomfortable as she shifted her weight from foot to foot and looked over Marti's shoulder toward Sandy's front door.

"I'm sorry. I should have said something sooner, but I just couldn't find the right moment." Her eyes flicked to Marti's face and then away again. "Or maybe the right words." Marti wasn't sure where this was going, so she just kept silent. "Bill was a good man. A good police officer. You'll hear that from anyone. I'm sure."

Marti nodded. "That's true. That's what everyone's been saying." Marti paused for a moment. "They don't always say the same thing about Sandy. Even the cops. I didn't expect to find you in there."

Lisa gave a thin smile. "We're not exactly friends, but Sandy has her good points. In many ways, we're pretty similar, so maybe that says something about me. We tend to end up working on projects like the gala or things for the church. We both attend St. Mark's in town. Either we are both pushovers or have some knack for it."

Or you both like things done in a particular way and people have decided it's not worth the effort anymore to butt heads with the pair of you, Marti thought, but kept her mouth shut. She still didn't know why Lisa had called her outside, but the light was fading fast and she really wanted to get back inside the warm house, even if it meant returning to the cluttered office.

Lisa seemed to sense that she was stalling and blew out a breath before continuing. "The fact that Sandy hired you is not a surprise to me. She'd been complaining to me about Bill for months when we met to go over different projects. First, it was the silent auction in the spring, then the clothing drive, and then the gala. It started with little things, minor complaints, sort of trivial things if you ask me, but it was a constant stream. I didn't really see this at work. Bill mostly kept his own counsel, and I didn't interact with him as much as some others. He could be quiet and you might interpret that as standoff-ish, but I didn't really see what Sandy was complaining about. Then, about three or four months before he died, there was a forensics conference that Bill and a few other officers and staff attended. It was a two-day thing. Thursday and half a day Friday."

"Okay," Marti said. Even though the story appeared painful for Lisa to tell, Marti was still at a loss about how it might tie into Bill's death.

"I started hearing a few rumors the next week. Just little comments or jokes about Bill. Apparently, there was a woman at the conference, or at least at the same hotel as the conference, and she was spotted more than once with Bill."

"Lisa, you're just telling me this now?" Marti tried not to snap at the woman. "I've been chasing my tail and wading through mountains of paper trying to find some answers for Sandy and this might all be down to an affair?"

"I don't know. That's just it. It was all rumors and innuendo. Office gossip. I didn't want to believe it, but couldn't totally dismiss it either. At one point, I asked Kevin and he told me it was nothing and to just keep it to myself. That's what I did."

"You never told Sandy?"

Marti saw her cheeks flush despite the cool temperature. "No. I never worked up the courage. And I'm still not sure it would be the right thing to do. Would I really be doing her a favor by telling her everyone thought her husband was having an affair? Then he died and the whispers stopped, but Sandy still wouldn't let it go. I feel terrible. Maybe if I had told her, even if it was gossip, she could have confronted him and be more at peace now."

So instead, you leave the dirty work to me, Marti thought. "So, there was never any proof? Kevin never said anything else?"

"No. That's what had me so conflicted. How do you potentially ruin someone's life, or at least their marriage, on a rumor?"

"So why tell me?"

"I was listening to you in there at the table and realized that it could still be relevant and helpful if you knew where to look."

Marti was about to make a disparaging comment about Lisa's lack of backbone when the outdoor lights went on, the front door opened, and Sandy poked her head out. "I thought you'd left already. What's going on?"

Lisa glanced up with a stricken look, like a child caught cheating on a test. Marti moved around her to the Subaru and opened the door. She grabbed the laptop off the seat and held it up. "Just walking Lisa out and bringing Bill's laptop inside."

Lisa took the opportunity to escape. She waved vaguely in Sandy's direction and jumped in her car. Marti followed Sandy back inside to the kitchen. She mulled over what Lisa had said as she stood at the kitchen sink and washed the grime off her hands from the office boxes. There hadn't been a whiff of it, but Marti chastised herself for not considering the other woman theory more strongly. After a health issue, it might have been the most obvious and most logical thing to drive the type of behavior that Sandy described. The kids might not be aware, none of them lived at home, and it was the type of thing that his colleagues and friends might try to keep quiet. As she dried her hands, she thought it might also explain those yet to be identified, but frequent phone calls. If she didn't hear back in a day or so on the message she'd left to the first number, she'd get Neon to poke around for her.

"Can I make you some dinner?" Sandy asked. "Nothing fancy, but I picked up a roasted chicken this morning. And I think I have some vegetables and rice."

Marti had been craving some downtime to sort through the sudden onslaught of new information, but she also didn't want Sandy to think she was padding her expenses and they still needed to discuss the phone numbers. She might as well knock that off her list.

Sandy might have sensed her hesitation and continued, "I also have some wine."

"You should have led with that bit," Marti said and smiled. "What can I do to help?"

Sandy put her to work making a salad, while she prepped the rice and warmed the chicken she'd taken out of the refrigerator. Sandy pulled out a bottle of merlot from a small wine storage rack below the butcher block prep island. She hunted around for a moment in a cabinet before finding two glasses.

She opened the bottle and poured. "Bill is more a beer and bourbon guy. I like the occasional glass when we go out to eat," Marti noticed she had slipped into the present tense, "but rarely open a bottle at home." Marti sensed it was a preemptive apology. "I think someone might have brought this for the holiday party last year. But wine gets better with age, right?"

Marti smiled and braced herself as she took a sip between peeling and chopping a cucumber, but the wine wasn't vinegar nor overtly offensive. It was a cheap, mediocre merlot. Marti recognized it. It was exactly the kind of vintage that Marti could afford and often bought from Luis at Delgado's bodega. "It's good," she said, which was only a small lie. From experience, she knew it would improve with a second glass.

As they set the food on the table and prepared to sit down and eat, a noise from the entryway near the garage startled Marti. She tensed for a moment, but then a male voice called out, "Mom?" and Marti relaxed. Sandy's face lit up with a surprise and joy that Marti had yet to witness. It made her look prettier and less severe. A moment later, a young man dropped a bag of laundry and a backpack in the doorway and entered the kitchen. This must be Brian, Marti thought. As mother and son embraced, Marti took in Sandy's youngest son. She knew from previous conversations that Brian was still in college and in his early twenties. He had his mother's smile and an open, friendly face. Marti remembered the wall of photos from the hallway and could still recognize the smile of the little boy in the soon-to-be adult. His brown hair was slightly shaggy and tousled, and his attire was casual—jeans and a frayed college sweatshirt.

Sandy quickly set an extra place at the table, and they all sat down for the meal. There was more than enough food for three. Marti was happy now that she took Sandy up on her offer to stay. She'd likely still need to talk to Brian again without his mother sitting next to him, but it was still a good opportunity to get a sense of him without driving up to the college.

"So, Brian, your mom tells me you're in college. What are you studying?" Lame, but she was too hungry to think of anything better.

"Yeah, I'm majoring in environmental science. I've always been interested in the environment, so I figured I'd study something I'm passionate about."

"He and Bill used to go off camping when he was younger," Sandy chipped in. "He always had a soft spot for nature."

Marti kept her eyes on Brian, but the mention of Bill and the camping trips didn't seem to faze him one way or another. "That's great," Marti said. "What year are you? Any plans for what you want to do after college?"

"I'm a junior, so I've got a little more time, but I'm thinking about working for an environmental nonprofit or maybe doing some research. Still exploring my options, though."

They spent a few more minutes on college life, hobbies, and Brian's future aspirations. Marti found herself drawn to Brian's natural affability. He had a relaxed and carefree demeanor. He was self-deprecating and easy to talk to. He lacked the hard-bitten outer shell of his older brother and the jittery nervousness of his sister. Of all the siblings, he appeared to be the most well-adjusted and comfortable in his own skin.

After the meal, Brian excused himself to put in a load of laundry and finish some schoolwork upstairs.

"He seems like a good kid," Marti said.

"Yes, he was the easy child. I'm sure he went through a typical teenage spell, but it was mild compared to the other two." Sandy smiled as she looked toward the stairs.

Marti kept her thoughts to herself. It didn't take a genius to realize that commenting on another person's children wasn't a good idea, especially when that person was paying your wages.

They cleared and washed the dishes and put everything away.

"Coffee?"

"I'd better not if I want to sleep tonight."

"I always like a cup of tea after dinner. Settles the stomach, you know?" Sandy put a mug of water in the microwave and pulled a tea bag out of a canister next to the stove.

That had probably been one of the healthier meals Marti had eaten in the last month. Her stomach was probably more in shock than anything else. "I'm okay, really," she said. "It's been a long day, but before I go, I wanted to ask if you'd looked at the phone bills I left."

"Yes, I did," Sandy said. She grabbed a stack of paper from a little nook desk in the corner of the kitchen and then collected her tea before carrying it all over to the kitchen table. They spent the next 15 minutes going through the numbers together. As they reviewed the list, Sandy pointed out the ones she recognized, while Marti took notes. Marti also noted that the recent statements Sandy reviewed did not include the unidentified number that Marti had called earlier or the Sundowner's number.

"So that's it," Sandy said, the unexpected joy of having Brian show up for dinner now gone and replaced by the wan and tired face that Marti recognized.

"Not quite," Marti replied and then almost regretted saying it.

Sandy looked at her across the table and tilted her head. "When you came in earlier, when I was working with Lisa, you seemed frustrated and out of sorts. It was all over your face and body language, but now? What happened? It wasn't the phone numbers."

There was a sudden eagerness in Sandy's face that Marti found heartbreaking if the rumors Lisa heard were true.

"Can you give me another day? I don't want to jump the gun and get your hopes up with false leads."

A shadow passed over Sandy's face and Marti thought she knew what the woman might be thinking, but it passed quickly, even if the smile that took its place seemed brittle. "That makes sense. We'll talk tomorrow?"

"Yes, of course."

Depending on what she found out in Rehoboth Beach, it could be an ugly conversation. Avoiding those no-win conversations was the primary reason she did her best to avoid marital work. In those cases, the messenger always bore the blame.

Maybe she should have quit when she knew nothing.

Chapter Twenty-One

Marti felt a sudden and powerful urge to get out of the house. She needed time and space to think. A lot had suddenly changed in the last couple of hours. Or potentially changed. Or hadn't changed at all. Murky uncertainty was the bread and butter of a private investigator. Marti stood and scooped up the marked-up phone bills.

"I'll call tomorrow," she said and headed down the hall. She left Sandy with her ritual mug of tea, staring at something only she could see.

Marti walked past the collection of school photographs again and looked at Brian's nine-year-old smile, frozen in time on the wall. Then, instead of heading out of the house to her car, she turned left and climbed the stairs, her footsteps muffled by the plush carpeting that lined the hallway.

A small landing greeted her at the top of the stairs. To her right was the open door to a bathroom, followed by two more bedrooms with the master suite at the end of the hall. To her left was a closed door with soft light seeping from beneath it. More family photos—baby pictures, vacations—hung from the walls in the hall.

She turned away from the light and went down the hall. She'd been through the house previously when she was looking for things about Bill. She knew the first door was a guest room and the second door was Olivia's. She glanced in the guest room, but then continued on. It all looked the same.

She nudged open Olivia's door and hit the light switch on the wall. It was a space that seemed frozen in time, like a snapshot of a teenager's life. The room was small, but neat, with posters of various bands and TV or movie stars, none of which Marti knew, adorning the walls. The decor ran to pink with splashes of purple. There was a beanbag chair in the corner and a ruffled canopy over the twin bed. It all appeared unchanged from when Olivia had been 12 years old. Marti knew Sandy's daughter still occasionally stayed here. It felt a little strange. She tried to remember when she'd redecorated her room growing up. She drew a blank, but this room felt like the space of someone very young.

She stepped over to the bedside table and opened the drawer. Hair clips, a paperback book, a book light, lip gloss, and a bookmark. She was about to close it when she caught a glimpse of something at the back. She pulled the drawer out farther. An empty orange pill bottle. A five-year-old prescription in Olivia's name for Topamax. Marti didn't know it offhand. She took out her phone and did a quick search. It was a medication to treat certain types of seizures or to prevent migraines. She put the empty bottle back and shut the drawer.

She went over to the small desk that sat framed under the window. She pulled out the drawers. Paper, pens, charging cords, packages of gum, stray paperclips. She pulled a small book out. A diary. But it was empty. Not even a token entry or two. She closed the drawers and moved to the bookshelf next to it. Three of the four shelves were populated with young adult mystery and fantasy titles that Marti didn't recognize other than *Harry Potter* and *The Hunger Games*. At the end, there was a selection of dog-eared Golden Age mysteries. She pulled one out. *The Death of Roger Ackroyd*. A personal favorite of Marti's. The fourth shelf was full of pictures and photos A few of the family when it was younger and smaller, before Brian and long before Bill.

There were also a number of Olivia and various other girls. The friends changed slightly over the years, other than one in particular. She was in every photo. Marti picked up a framed photo that appeared to be similar to the one Bill had in his office but from a different angle. This one showed the two girls, younger, both in white altar server robes, near the altar. She could see little Brian and Ethan in the background. She put it back and picked up another. The girls were older, maybe 12 or 13, on the cusp or in the midst of changing into women. The other girl was blonde, in contrast to Olivia's darker hair, with a small, upturned nose, wide and expressive eyes, and a slightly pointed chin. She wasn't quite beautiful but she was striking. There was also something familiar in her face. Marti was good with names and faces. She had to be in her job. She studied the picture, the last one, tried to conjure up the connection, she went back and looked at the other photos, but whatever it was, it danced away.

The photos tapered off and, other than a stiff portrait from high school graduation, appeared to have stopped around 14 or 15. Marti did the math. Maybe around the time that cameras became phones, or vice versa, and all photos became trapped in the cloud.

"What are you doing?" Marti flinched at the sound of Brian's voice and almost dropped the frame she was holding.

"Just looking around."

"Must be nice to get paid to snoop."

"The pay's not that good."

"That's Sam. She was Olivia's best friend. She …"

"Died. I know. The desk clerk at the inn told me about it."

They both looked at the photo before she put it back.

"I came up to talk to you. You have a minute?"

"Sure, but let's go back to my room."

Brian's room was small, the youngest always got the smallest room, but neat, with posters of various bands and sports stars, none of whom Marti knew, adorning the walls, all seemingly unchanged from when he was in middle school. There was a twin-size bed with a rumpled duvet, a small desk cluttered with thick textbooks and a laptop, plus a bookshelf stuffed with trophies and mementos from over the years.

Brian went and sat at the desk then swiveled around in his chair to face Marti, who leaned against the wall. His sandy hair fell casually over his forehead.

"What did you want to talk about?"

"I just wanted to ask you a little more about Bill."

"Without Mom around?" He smiled.

"Something like that."

"It wouldn't change the stories. I loved Bill." He said it without hesitation or embarrassment. "I was younger than Ethan and Olivia when Bill and Mom got together and I don't really have any clear memories, at least good ones, of my biological dad. Maybe that helped. He definitely had his own way of doing things. But when it counted, when you really needed someone to listen or lend a hand, he was always there. He took me camping. Taught me how to throw a football. I remember one time when I had this big school project due and I was stressing out about it. I didn't even have to ask for help. He just showed up with a bunch of art supplies and helped me put together this amazing diorama. It was like our little secret project."

"That sounds like a memory worth holding onto."

Brian nodded, a faint smile touching his lips. "Yeah, it was. And there were other times too, you know? Like, when he'd surprise me with tickets to a concert of a band we both liked. Or he at least said he liked. He wasn't the type to say much. I'm not sure he ever told me he loved me, but he showed it in other ways. I miss that. I miss him."

He shifted in the small chair and cleared his throat. He seemed genuinely saddened by Bill's death, reminiscing about the man who had been a steady presence in his life. There was an earnestness in his words that touched her.

"How about in the last few months?" she asked. "Did you see him much or notice any difference in his behavior?"

Brian nodded thoughtfully, his voice carrying a touch of regret. "You mean what Mom's been obsessed with?"

"Not just that. Anything, really. How was he?"

"Well, I'd been mostly away at school," he began, "but the few times I came back, I noticed some changes. It wasn't like he was a different person but more of an amped-up version of himself, you know? He was more short-tempered, withdrawn, and distracted."

"Did he say anything to you about what it might be?"

"Bill never talked about himself or his work. I tried a few times but barely got more than one-word responses. It was often hard to get him to talk about the weather, never mind what might be bothering him."

That didn't surprise Marti. Bill and Brian might have had a better, or different, relationship when Brian was younger, but the taciturn man he described just now matched up with the person Ethan and Olivia described. Whatever bond the pair had in the past had frayed. Marti sensed Brian knew it too and regretted it, even if it wasn't his fault. She realized, like his mother, that this young man was also carrying his own emotional weight.

Marti pushed off the wall. "Thanks. I don't want to take up more of your time."

"I'm not sure if I want you to find anything or not," he said as she left. "Those memories are all we have left."

Marti had no trouble finding a parking spot on the street in front of the inn. That was one thing she'd give to Cedarwood over Jersey City. She had her pick of the whole strip. Parking might be competitive during the day, but that ended by nightfall. She slid into a space directly in front of the inn's walk.

As she gathered up her laptop bag from the passenger seat, Marti realized in the commotion with Lisa that she'd left her purse behind at Sandy's house. In her mind's eye, she could see it sitting next to the boxes beside Bill's desk. She could grab it tomorrow but wanted to get an early start on the drive to Rehoboth Beach. "Shit," she muttered to herself. She didn't feel like driving back to Sandy's now. All she wanted right now was her big tub, a warm bath, and some decent wine, but knew she'd have to settle for a lumpy mattress, some potpourri, and a good book.

She pulled her phone out of her pocket and called Sandy.

"Marti?"

"Sorry to bother you, but I left my purse in Bill's office. I wanted to get an early start tomorrow. I know you don't enjoy going in there, but do you think you could grab it and stick it in your mailbox? That way, I can grab it in the morning without disturbing you."

There was a slight pause as Sandy digested the slightly unusual request. Marti could hear movement. "I'm walking to the office. Okay, I see it by the desk. Small, red thing, right?"

"That's it."

"Jeez, you've at least made a lot of progress cleaning this place out."

At least. Marti heard the unspoken rebuke in that phrase. You have made no progress on my case, but you're a decent cleaning woman. But Marti couldn't disagree, either. Not yet.

"If you're sure about this," Sandy said, "I'll put it in the mailbox now."

"I'm sure. Not much worth stealing in there. Thanks, Sandy," Marti said before disconnecting.

Before she exited her car, Marti paused and looked across the street toward the town green. She felt the nerves flutter in her stomach as she recalled the red, beady eye of the cigarette glowing near the gazebo. She stared into the shadows now for a long time but saw nothing moving other than cars traveling in the opposite direction on the far side of the square.

She watched a Cedarwood police car drive slowly around the green and then slide to a stop next to her Subaru. The passenger side window came down. Officer Ackerman's teeth almost glowed in the dark. She lowered her own window.

"Marti Wells, back in town."

"That's right." She'd been gone for one day. This place was like living in a knitting circle. Everyone knew your business. She would need to remember that. "You in charge of keeping Mayberry safe tonight? That's a very old TV reference that you probably don't understand."

"Let me see. I think my great-great-great grandmother used to watch Andy Griffith." Another smile. "To answer your question, yes, I'm on duty tonight, so you can sleep soundly. Making any progress on your case?"

"I'm talking to a lot of people, so it's a type of progress," Marti said, mostly dodging the question.

"I heard."

"You heard what?"

"That you've been out there beating the bushes, talking to folks."

"That all you heard?"

He looked away. No big smile this time.

"So, people are talking," Marti said.

"It's what people in this town do."

"Gossip."

"Most people pay no attention to it."

"But not everyone."

He shrugged. "Maybe not but you can't pay attention to gossip." The car radio squawked. "I'd better get going." He waved and raised the window before driving off. Marti put her own window up and was left staring at the dark gazebo again.

"Just a dog walker," she muttered to herself and got out of the car. She tried to put a little steel in her voice if only to convince herself, but it didn't really work. She knew it hadn't been a dog walker. She told herself she would not look back. She wasn't spooked. She kept her pace natural and her eyes on the door. It was early enough that it would still be open. She hopped up the steps and pulled the door open. Only after she turned and calmly, but carefully, pushed the door shut with a satisfying snick, did she raise her head and look.

The green was empty and unchanged. Just like she knew it would be.

Chapter Twenty-Two

Going in the front door left her no choice but to go past the small reception area before climbing the stairs. She hoped the young woman, Holly, was again on duty and Marti might skip past with just a polite nod. No doubt Holly's head would be hovering over her phone. But she had no such luck. Or maybe karma was paying her back for her sly side door exit the other morning.

Marti was a trained investigator with decades of experience, and she put all of those years to good use in keeping her face neutral when she saw Lucille standing behind the desk. She wore a blue, flower print housecoat with a white-frilled collar. Her hair was done up in classic pink hair curlers that Marti remembered her own grandmother using in the early 1980s. Most disturbing of all was the gleam in Lucille's eyes. She would not be put off tonight with a polite nod or banal small talk.

"Hello, Marti. I haven't seen you in a few days."

"Good evening, Lucille. Yes, I've been working." Marti immediately realized her mistake. Being busy working would imply some sort of lead or progress.

"Is that right?" Lucille said and leaned forward.

Marti decided she might as well play along and see if she could get anything useful out of the woman. "Listen, did you ever hear any rumors about Bill and other women?"

Lucille boomed out a laugh that made her ample bosoms shake. The big, historic Polk desk might have even jumped a few inches. "Bill? You gotta be kidding me. Sandy kept that man on a tight leash. Not just about sex. It was everything but his work, as far as I could see. His diet. His religion. His vacation plans. I wouldn't be surprised if she scheduled his toilet time."

"So, that's a no."

"A definite no. And, to be fair, at least the sex might not have been all down to Sandy. From what I recall when we were kids, and I saw nothing to change my mind after he moved back, Bill was uptight about sex."

"Or serious about his marriage vows," Marti said, feeling a strange need to defend this man she never met.

"Okay, sure. That's another way of looking at it," Lucille said, her mouth pinched. "Probably a more charitable way. Bill was serious and dedicated in everything he did. That's just the type of guy he was. Dotted his I's. Crossed his T's. Didn't jaywalk. Probably drove the speed limit. I never heard him make any off-color remarks or saw him flirt with another woman. Why do you ask? Did you hear that from someone in town?"

Marti wasn't about to tell this scurrilous woman about the Sundowner. "No, I didn't, and that's exactly why I'm asking. I can't find anything that might point to why Bill was stressed or acting strangely right before he died. It doesn't appear to be health related. I talked to the coroner. I've talked to his colleagues. No one has said anything about work stress beyond the usual caseload. So I …" She let it hang out there.

"Well, I hate to tell you, but you're going to hit another dead end barking up that tree. If you are stepping out or fooling around in Cedarwood, just about everyone would know. Gossip is the currency in this town. It's all fair game. Someone would have ratted him out. The sex would have to be spectacular to be worth the risk."

Marti thought about that. She didn't doubt that Lucille was right, but maybe they started out being careful. Maybe they drove out of town. Maybe they even drove out of state. Maybe to Delaware. But that was a hike. Maybe as time passed, and no one caught on, maybe the temptation to stay closer to home and skip the long drive and cheap hotel rooms became too great. Something to think about.

"Everyone knows about me in town?" she asked, switching gears.

"Oh, sure. Just about everyone knew about you on Monday."

"What's the vibe?"

"Oh, you know, everyone has an opinion."

She thought of the red eye in the dark. "Anyone upset?"

Lucille tilted her head back and forth. "I wouldn't say upset, no. A few complainers. Folks that like to run their mouths on just about any subject, so I wouldn't take it personally. I heard a few of the lonely hearts noticed you don't have a wedding ring."

"Bullshit," Marti said.

"Oh, no. That's the God's honest truth. Viable prospects are few and far between in small towns."

Marti shook her head and thought of Lawson's earlier comments. That was the last thing she needed, especially when the only decent place to eat after dark was the town tavern. "You tell them I might not wear a ring, but I'm in a committed relationship and not looking for local love."

"Bullshit," Lucille said and smiled.

Marti rapped her knuckles on the desk and backed away toward the stairs and her room. "That's the God's honest truth, Lucille. He's six-foot-four and full of muscles."

Lucille laughed. "Now I really know it's bullshit. You're too happy to have been married a day in your life."

Marti started up the stairs but half turned and called over her shoulder, "You'd be surprised."

She dug the big brass key out of her laptop bag, thankful that the antique was too bulky for her small purse, and opened the room's door. By habit, she paused in the doorway and let her eyes sweep the room. Everything looked to be in order. Housekeeping had been in to make up the bed and presumably swap in some fresh towels in the bathroom.

The musty heat and the smell were still cloying. She put her laptop bag down and strode to the window. She glanced again at the shadow of the gazebo. It still appeared empty. She'd halfheartedly tried to get the window open the first time she was in the room but had been tired and distracted. This time she double-checked the latch was open and put some genuine effort into it. The window yielded with a grinding, groaning upward movement that stopped and held firm after two inches. She strained for another 30 seconds and tried different grips and angles, but that was all she was going to get.

She dragged the room's chair over to the window so she could feel the fresh air on her face and grabbed her laptop out of her bag. She next spent a half hour going through her notes and transcribing them into a file on the computer. She learned nothing new, but her habit was to turn over the same ground as she worked on a case. It was also a necessary chore. She liked the redundancy of having her notes in physical and digital form. Satisfied with the notes, she created a report detailing the day's activities for Sandy, even if she had already filled her in over dinner. Again, it was professional and gave her a paper trail if an audit of her activities was ever necessary.

Work done, she showered and did the nightly rituals required of a 50-something-year-old woman. Marti didn't believe in the magic of wrinkle-reducing potions or lotions, but she believed in the power of soap, moisturizer, and dental hygiene, even if she despised flossing.

She pulled her latest cozy mystery out of her bag and read about an antiquarian bookseller in Paris who had an unfortunate habit of stumbling upon murders. She read until her eyelids drooped and then turned off the light.

Marti rarely remembered her dreams, and when she opened her eyes, vague visions of dark shapes pressing her into the bed disoriented her. The smell brought her back. She tapped her phone, sitting next to the discarded book on the old bedside table. Three thirty in the morning. The line of glass visible between the closed curtains was pitch-black. Why had she woken up? She remained still and stared at the canopy above her head. Despite leaving the window cracked open, the room remained hot, and she kicked a leg free of the heavy quilt. She heard nothing outside except the occasional rustle of leaves. No passing cars. No distant sirens. No shouts like she might hear in Jersey City. Cedarwood was sound asleep. Maybe that was it. Maybe it was the preternatural quiet that had woken her up. Maybe her mind and body needed those city stimuli to assure her sleeping body that everything was okay.

And then she heard it. A light scraping of metal on metal. It was close. Not a key, but the sound of someone trying to get in. A tool or a pick going at the lock in the old door. Adrenaline shot through her body. She slid out of bed and moved toward the door. The room wasn't completely dark. There was some ambient light from the window, despite the curtains. Marti was careful not to cross in front of it and throw any shadows at the door. There was no peephole or security chain on the inside. Just the flimsy lock. But it appeared to be giving the intruder trouble. Maybe its age would buy her a few extra seconds, but she didn't think it would hold for long. She moved back to the bed and stuffed the pillows under the quilt. Again, not something that would hold for long, but it might buy her precious time. She grabbed her sneakers from the floor and her phone from the nightstand and ducked into the bathroom.

She eased the door closed and dialed 911. She knew at this time of night there would be a skeleton crew on duty and any response would likely be slow. The call connected and the dispatcher asked what her emergency was. She didn't want to risk talking. The element of surprise was her biggest advantage right now. She left the call connected, wrapped a towel around the phone to muffle any additional sound, and placed the bundle on the floor. She was counting on every emergency call requiring some type of response.

She slipped on her sneakers but didn't waste time tying them. She looked around. The bathroom was darker than the bedroom, and she tried to remember if there was anything that might serve as a good weapon. She cursed herself for leaving her purse behind. She could have used that pepper spray. She felt around with her hands. Shower rod? It was metal, but very light and likely useless. Rug? Hangers? Shower cap? Soap? There was nothing. She thought of the toilet tank lid but then remembered the toilet was tankless. Had she seen an iron in the room? She couldn't recall. Maybe in the closet? She opened the door and took a step out into the bedroom, only to realize she'd run out of time.

She'd picked her share of locks over the years and recognized the click of the tumblers. There was a pause and then she saw the door handle slowly turn. She froze in place as the room's door inched open and gloved fingers gripped the edge like a dark spider. She pulled her gaze away and grabbed the only thing in sight, her own brass room key on the table next to the room's chair. She tried to wedge it between her fingers, but it was too long. She ended up just grasping it in her hand and hoping it added some extra weight to her fist. She backed up into the bathroom again as a body followed the hand through the crack in the door. Marti felt her breath catch at the familiar sight of the black ski mask with the crooked, red-stitched mouth. She watched as the intruder entered the room and crept toward the bed. He raised a hand. It held something. Marti couldn't make it out in the dark. Short and stubby. A pipe? A bat? But the intent was clear. He, in her mind it was a man under that mask, something about the way he moved or maybe the cowardice of attacking a woman while she slept, was going to bust her up, or worse, while she lay in bed. Her fear suddenly burst into anger. She charged across the room.

The squeaky old floor gave her away. She was fast, but he was quicker than she expected. She swung her fist, but he ducked away and the blow glanced off his shoulder and only grazed his neck. He was surprised, but not hurt. Then he was angry. But she had gotten him to drop whatever he'd been holding and preparing to hit her with. She heard it hit the floor and roll away. But he still had his fists. He came up with a snarl and caught the side of her head with a sharp punch. Bright stars burst out of the room's darkness. Before she could get her hands up and recover, she was falling. He had swept her legs out from under her and she hit her head on the floor. She dropped the key with a thunk. Gloved hands groped in the dark, pressing her face hard into the warped pine floor. His weight squeezed down on her. A knee in her back pushed out all her air. She tried to buck him off, but he was too heavy. She squirmed, but a hand on the back of her neck held her still. He was strong. She smelled something sour, like vinegar. Blood? Sweat?

Her own fear? She heard his ragged breathing. She had the sense that he was both angry and confused. He'd expected a sleeping victim. Not someone fighting back. He was pissed, but not sure what to do. She waited for the inevitable bash to the back of her head. Would she feel it?

They both heard the siren at the same time. She felt him shift. She sucked in a small gulp of air. It felt like a miracle. Then her ribs exploded. Once, twice, three times, the intruder slammed his knee into her side. The weight lifted from her back, but was followed by more pain. Kicks to the same ribs. She curled up and tried to make herself small. She sensed him standing over her. There were no last words. The message had been delivered. She heard the door slam shut and then his footsteps descending the stairs.

Marti rolled over and placed her hands across her chest. She could breathe, that was a relief, but it wasn't easy. She had at least one broken rib. Probably more. She hoped she didn't have a punctured lung. Sweat ran down the back of her neck. Her stomach rolled over, and she fought back the urge to vomit, even if it might improve the smell of the potpourri. She struggled up to her feet and almost went back down as a wave of nausea and dizziness swept over her. She stumbled into the wall. The stars came back and her vision narrowed. She began to shake. She couldn't stop. Was she going into shock? She made it to the hallway before she went to her knees. She hissed in pain. She heard footsteps and looked up. A dark shape came around the corner. She squinted. No mask. No ragged red line.

"I need help," she said before she passed out.

Chapter Twenty-Three

Marti slowly opened her eyes, her other senses gradually coming back to her. A nurse in pale-blue scrubs stood nearby, peering intently at a monitor then tapping notes on a handheld tablet. The sterile scent of disinfectant lingered in the air, mixing with the faint pervasive aroma of antiseptic.

She looked around. The room was typical hospital chic—bleached white walls, an assortment of medical equipment, and a low hum of activity. A curtain divided the room in two. She lay in a narrow hospital bed with hard plastic rails, her legs tucked under crisp, starched sheets and a drab mustard-yellow blanket.

The bed's angle was elevated, putting her in a semi-upright position. She wore one of those flimsy hospital gowns, its fabric felt like old, used tissue paper against her skin. As she shifted slightly, a mild discomfort pulsed through her. Her head throbbed, and her ribs ached, but she felt like she was feeling the pain from across the room. As if she were standing 50 feet from a raging bonfire.

Glancing to her right, Marti followed the IV line from the crook of her elbow to a clear bag hanging on a stand. Whatever was in that bag was doing wonders to numb the pain for now, and she welcomed the respite. She knew the agony would return soon enough, but she was content to have it muted for the moment.

The nurse looked up from her tablet. Her expression was one of professional detachment. "What happened?" she inquired, her voice tinged with a hint of weariness.

"Someone broke into my hotel room and tried to kick me to death," Marti replied matter-of-factly. The nurse nodded as if she'd heard variations of this story countless times. Maybe she had.

The nurse continued, "You've got two broken ribs on the left side. No internal bleeding or punctured lungs, fortunately. The doctor wants to keep you overnight, just in case."

Marti gave a nod of agreement. "I'm in no hurry to leave."

"Good," the nurse responded. "How's the pain?"

Marti thought for a moment. "About a three right now."

"That's the morphine, but it'll get worse before it gets better."

"I figured as much."

"We'll have you off the drip later today, but you'll be on pain pills for seven to 10 days before you're left with just Tylenol. There'll be some discomfort with deep breaths and lifting movements for a while, but you should be back to normal in six weeks."

Marti offered a wry smile. "Normal being relative, of course."

The nurse managed a thin smile of her own and reached over to press a button on the monitor. "Everyone becomes a comedian on the drip," she remarked before exiting the room, leaving Marti to the ragged, phlegmy breathing of the patient on the other side of the curtain. As the cocktail of pain relievers coursed through her veins, Marti welcomed the embrace of sleep.

The second time she roused from her medicated slumber, her neighbor's labored breathing had finally quieted down. And Jessica Lawson sat in a nearby chair. Her brown hair was tied back in the same practical ponytail, but this time she wore a light-gray suit.

Marti blinked, her mind still shrouded in a pleasant, foggy haze. She couldn't be certain how long she'd slept, but she didn't think it had been too long. Unless you were in a coma, did anyone sleep long in a hospital bed?

"What time is it?" Marti croaked.

"A little after eight." Lawson took a sip from a cup of to-go coffee. "Want to tell me what happened?" she asked.

Marti took a moment to gather her thoughts. The pain in her head and chest still throbbed in rhythm with her heartbeat. "Sure," she replied, deciding there was no reason to hide the truth. A small, rational part of her mind spoke up from behind the gauzy curtain of opioids. Talking to Lawson in her current state about Bill Thompson was probably a bad idea. But she could tell the woman her own sad story of tonight. So she did.

Lawson kept quiet as Marti talked. She jotted down a few notes on a small pad. The only time her face changed was when Marti mentioned the mask and the red mouth. Lawson's eyes widened ever so slightly.

"Any theories?"

"It wasn't a robbery. Best guess? He wanted to discourage me. Scare the hell out of me. Hurt me."

"Why?"

Marti gave a dry laugh. "You tell me, Detective. I have no idea. I just finished telling Sandy tonight that all I've been doing is digging dry holes."

That wasn't totally true. There was Rehoboth Beach, but she'd told no one about that potential lead. Marti didn't see how the attacker would even know she'd found that information. She didn't yet know herself if it was relevant or useful.

"You think this is connected to Bill?"

"You don't?"

"I'm not convinced, no."

"And I can't prove it, either, but it would be a hell of a coincidence." Lawson didn't agree or disagree. Marti continued, "So where does that leave us?"

"It could have been something else. You're a lone, attractive female. It could have been—"

"It was not an attempt at rape or sexual assault, Lawson. The guy made a beeline for the bed with some sort of weapon. He wasn't looking to incapacitate or subdue. He was looking to harm me."

"Ax handle. Just the handle. The blade had been sawed off."

"Huh." That was all Marti could say. She hurt bad enough and the asshole didn't even get to use the toy he brought along.

"We found it under the bed. That was a first for me. I've seen some odd things in my brief career. Assault with a chicken. Assault with a meat thermometer. Fruit. Samurai sword. But a sawed-off ax is a new one."

"You'll have to tell me the meat thermometer story sometime."

That got a thin smile from Lawson. "Any idea who it might have been?"

"Not a clue. I've talked to half the town, but no one's said much."

"How about a physical description? Height? Weight?"

Marti looked up at the ceiling and tried to put herself back in the room. She saw the man moving through the dark and then stopping by the bed. She lined him up against the bedpost supporting the canopy. "Maybe a little taller than me, but not much. He had no trouble holding me down, so he must outweigh me by 50 pounds. He isn't big or bulky, but he is strong."

"How tall are you?"

"Five ten."

"Scars, marks, tattoos?"

Marti saw the woman's fingers twitch and noticed her left leg doing a little cha-cha. She needed a cigarette. "It was pitch-black, Lawson. He had on a mask and gloves. He was trying to brain me in my sleep."

Before Lawson could respond, a young doctor, perhaps in his early 30s with thin sandy-brown hair and a round chin, walked into the room. He had a buzz of caffeinated energy about him; he checked her monitors and glanced at something on a tablet he carried. He asked Lawson to step out while he examined Marti.

"Hello, Ms. Wells. I'm Dr. Harris," he said with a toothy smile as he moved to the head of the bed. "The hacks in the ER told me you took quite a beating. Let's have a look and make sure everything's okay."

Dr. Harris checked her over, asking about headaches, dizziness, and nausea. She sucked in a hissing breath as he probed a tender spot just above her ear. Marti explained the dull pain that lingered in her head but confirmed she didn't feel disoriented or nauseous. He flashed a light in her eyes and then asked her to track it. She did it without issue.

"If it's a concussion, it's minor," he said.

Next came the examination of her ribs. She slipped the gown off one shoulder and winced as the doctor gently pressed around the area. The bruise was large and dark as a ripe plum. "They took a quick x-ray when you came in. It looks like you've got a couple of cracked ribs on your left side," he said. "But nothing worse, which is good news." He glanced again at the monitors. "And things have remained stable so far, so I think we're okay, but I'd like to get a few more pictures, different angles, just to be sure. If those come back clean, as I expect, then I think we can get you out of here later today with just some pain management."

Marti nodded, her gaze shifting to the IV bag, which still delivered a steady stream of relief. She wasn't in a rush. "That's fine," she said.

"I'll get an orderly to wheel you down to Radiology. We'll try to make it quick."

It must have been a slow night. Or was it morning now? Marti had lost track. An orderly and a nurse arrived within five minutes, moved the IV bag, and helped Marti into a wheelchair. There was a jolt of pain from her ribs as she shifted off the bed, but it remained distant, like hearing a train whistle far, far down the tracks. But it was getting closer, Marti knew.

In the x-ray room, the process was swift but the room was cold and Marti was continuously aware of her bare backside hanging out in the breeze. The technician positioned her carefully and took the series of images. Then it was over, and the orderly pushed her back into her hospital room within minutes.

Once back in her room, she settled into the bed again.

The nurse returned and hooked up the IV line to the port again. "Just saline at this point. Let me know if the pain gets worse."

"Okay," Marti said. It wasn't great, but it was manageable right now. She knew the longer she was on the strong stuff, the longer they'd try to keep her here. She also didn't like how the pain meds filled her head with cotton.

"Once the radiologist and doctor look at the x-rays, you're free to go."

The nurse adjusted the blankets and left. Marti felt tired, so tired that even the stiff hospital mattress felt comfortable. Her eyes started to slip closed when Lawson appeared in the doorway. Marti was a little surprised she'd stuck around. She looked more relaxed now, her face less pinched and intense. The wonders of nicotine. It will tar up your lungs but mellow you out.

"Anything else you can tell me?" Lawson asked. She didn't sit this time, just leaned against the door.

With an effort, Marti pulled herself back up to consciousness. "He smelled sour. At least, I think he did. That could have been me."

"Sour?" From her tone, Lawson hadn't been expecting that, but it was the first thing that Marti's slightly addled brain had coughed up.

"Yeah, like slightly spoiled cheese. It was body odor, but it was not like a regular funk BO or sweaty feet. It was a little different. Almost like vinegar."

"All right." Lawson jotted a note. "Did he say anything?"

"Only the grunts as he was breaking my ribs."

"Got it." Lawson looked ready to wrap it up and maybe get outside for another smoke. Nicotine drove a hard bargain. "That it?"

"It wasn't the first time I'd seen him," Marti said.

That got Lawson's attention and probably made her forget about the cigarette, at least for a few minutes. "Tell me." She looked like she wanted to say more, but held her tongue.

"I can't swear to it. I didn't see the guy's face either time, but it was the same mask. It was Monday. I was walking back to the inn after a late dinner at The Blue Haven. I was coming up one of the side streets heading toward the center of town when a car started stalking me."

"A car?"

"Yeah, you know, it was rolling slowly, keeping pace. Eventually, at the intersection, he pulled up and gave me a look before peeling out in the opposite direction."

"A look?"

"We sort of had a stare down. The guy eventually made a little trigger gesture with his hand, you know," Marti demonstrated making a gun with her hand and Lawson nodded.

"He do anything else?"

"No. That was enough. I think he was trying to intimidate or scare me, like tonight, but without the ax handle. And it worked. I know it doesn't sound like much now, but in the dark, late at night, it was more than enough."

Lawson made a couple more notes. "Anything you can tell me about the vehicle?"

Marti brought her hands up and rubbed at her face. Just that bit of movement made her ribs sing. "Shit, Lawson, I don't know. I was almost peeing my pants. It was a sedan of some sort. Four doors, dark color, decent engine." She closed her eyes, but all she could see was that crooked stitching. "Taillights were square. I didn't notice the plate. I'm guessing it was a Jersey plate, otherwise it might have caught my attention more."

Lawson nodded, but Marti noticed she didn't take down any notes. It sounded thin even to her ears and she felt a rush of frustration and sympathy for all the previous witnesses that she'd interviewed and silently chastised for not paying better attention.

Lawson tucked the notebook into her suit coat pocket. "I think that's it then. I'll pass this information along and make sure it gets into the system and whoever ends up with your case."

"It's not you?"

"Might be. Gotta talk to the chief. I said I'd pitch in this morning and talk to you because we'd met before and the other officers were working the scene."

"Okay. Well, I appreciate it. You guys find Bill's notebook yet?"

Lawson put her hands in her pockets. Her pose reminded Marti of those big catalogs that used to come in the mail a few times a year for department stores. Filene's, Bullocks, Strawbridges, Marshall Field's, Jordan Marsh. All long gone now.

"No, it hasn't turned up. I know it wasn't on his desk or a drawer. I cleaned that out myself."

Marti had been banking on it being with his personal effects at the office. Maybe dumped in a desk drawer or left on the desk at the end of the day but never picked up the next because Bill never saw the next day.

"You don't find that odd?"

Lawson shrugged. "The entire situation was a little unusual." Marti noted she used the past tense. "Things get shuffled, moved around. Unusual, yes. Deliberate, no, I don't see that. Odds are, it was just misplaced. Maybe for good."

Marti couldn't refute anything Lawson said with actual evidence. Bill's case notes were missing. Or misplaced. But what did it mean? A simple mistake in the wake of a tragedy or something else? "Maybe the notebook doesn't matter. Can you tell me the department's procedure for reports? Could his notes have already been written up?"

"It's possible. He'd have kept copies of his reports. The originals, if the case was closed, would have been sent to Records. Those are stored by the county over in Easton. Reports are supposed to be submitted at regular intervals, but there's no set schedule or expectation. A guy with Bill's experience would be given a lot of leeway. He'd write them up when he wrote them up. No one would get on his back about it."

Marti thought about it. "Would there be any way to cross-reference his current caseload and submitted reports? Work backward to figure out what he was currently doing by what he hadn't submitted?"

Lawson pulled a face. "I'm not sure what that would tell you. You wouldn't know where he'd been or who he'd talked to or what he talked to them about."

Marti felt deflated and it wasn't just the injuries and being woken up in the middle of the night by an armed intruder. It was the thought that the answer was out there, but it was buried in paper. "Do you think he could have been working on developing information on a case?"

"I'm sure he was. That's what detectives do. Bill was always working. He was a police officer first, last, and always. I'll tell you one thing; I don't think it was a recent case. We had been meeting regularly and splitting those as I got more up to speed."

Marti thought of the box of cold case files in Bill's office. "Did he mention working an old case?"

Lawson thought about it and then shrugged. "No, but there's always the chance that new information had come in and we hadn't discussed it yet." Marti watched a thought occur to Lawson.

"What?" she said.

"Maybe it was sensitive information or for Internal Affairs."

"You guys have IA?"

"Yes, not specific to our department, but we're subject to oversight from the county and state."

"So maybe sensitive information or something he didn't know how to handle."

"Yes, I could see that, though I still think he might have mentioned it or hinted at it. We talked a lot about the job."

"What if it was about you?"

Lawson gave her an icy stare and looked ready to turn on her heel and leave. "Sorry," Marti said, holding up her hands and then wincing as the pain raced down her ribs. "Don't get touchy. I had to ask. What if it wasn't about you but about a fellow cop and he was protecting you?"

"Better than your first suggestion, but I still don't think it rates all that high."

"But it could explain his mood, right? He was a man who dedicated his life to law and order and now he finds a fellow officer betraying that calling. Maybe someone close to him? That would be a tough thing to handle."

Again, Lawson thought about it. "It would be difficult and it would hurt, but it happens. I don't think it would send Bill into a tailspin. He was a law and order guy and he'd see this the same way. If anything, he'd be angry about it and anxious to root it out. I don't think he'd be conflicted."

Marti thought that made sense. "Okay, one last question. Do you think Bill could have been involved with another woman?"

"No." No need to think about it.

"Why not?"

"He was a deeply moral man."

"Wouldn't that explain his behavior? He was fighting against himself."

"No. Whatever you're thinking, it's not that. I think we're done. You need a ride? I can wait and take you wherever you want to go."

Marti guessed Lawson's preference would be to drop Marti off somewhere over the town line but, as the saying went, beggars couldn't be choosers.

Chapter Twenty-Four

The hospital made up for the quick x-rays with an interminable wait for discharge. The affable Dr. Harris had no pull with the hospital bureaucracy. It rolled on at a glacier's pace. Marti was pretty sure Lawson regretted her offer. Although it gave her ample time to smoke half a pack of cigarettes and work on an increasingly creative palette of curses. It took three people, two hours, and a stack of forms thicker than the King James Bible before she cleared the maze of administration and was allowed to leave. They insisted on providing her with a wheelchair for her exit, citing hospital policy, which Marti translated to mean insurance policy.

The same orderly returned and wheeled her through the hospital's automatic sliding doors. She soaked in the warmth of the rising sun, relieved to escape the sterile, institutional air of the hospital. Just beyond a line of trees to her right, she could hear the rhythmic hum of traffic from the nearby freeway.

She might have initially balked at the wheelchair, but she didn't hesitate to accept the script from the pharmacy. The pain in her ribs was now off the morphine leash and nipping at her heels. She'd be careful, but she knew she'd need help in the coming days. She clutched the orange bottle tightly in her right hand.

As Lawson pushed her down the ramp toward the parking garage, Marti noticed a 1972 blue Ford Bronco parked in a nearby red zone. A police placard sat on the dash. She wheeled Marti over and locked the chair's wheels. Marti admired the car as Lawson dug in her purse for a set of keys that she used to unlock and open the passenger door. Then she leaned in and rearranged things so the seat was clear.

The vintage truck exuded a rugged and timeless charm. Someone lovingly restored and maintained it. Light tan, well-worn leather seats and a touch of chrome that gleamed in the sunlight complemented its deep-blue exterior.

"I didn't peg you as a classic car type, Lawson," Marti said as she admired the distinctive round headlights and fiberglass hardtop on top of the classic boxy body.

"Not many people would consider this a classic," Lawson replied. She finished clearing a spot and stepped back to look at the truck.

"Those people would be just plain wrong. What option is under the hood? The straight six or the V8."

Now it was Lawson's turn to be surprised. "V8, my daddy wouldn't have had it any other way. Didn't peg you as a gearhead, Wells."

"Don't let the Subaru fool you. That's purely utilitarian and goes with the job. And, I'll admit, maybe financial, too. But my third husband was a talented mechanic, and his one conversational skill was talking about cars. Luckily, he had a few other useful skills outside the garage, but that man's biggest passion was American muscle cars. I'll bet I know more about 1960 Chevy Impalas than any other woman alive."

"Lucky you."

"You'd be surprised how often it comes in handy in my line of work."

"Third husband, huh?"

"That's right. Daryl. Maybe I'll trade you that story for the meat thermometer one sometime."

"Deal," Lawson said.

It took Marti almost a full minute, but she managed to climb out of the wheelchair and into the passenger seat. She was sweating slightly, but she hadn't screamed. She took that as a win. As Lawson pulled out of the parking spot, she said, "I talked to the guys at the scene. They're going to need a few more hours to finish up. Might not be until the late afternoon that you can get back in your room."

Marti had no intention of stepping foot in that room again if she could help it. She certainly wasn't going to spend another night there. Her thoughts must have shown on her face.

"I can stop by later and grab your stuff if you're thinking of pulling up stakes."

"I've been thinking about leaving ever since I got here, but I'm not going to do that, not yet, not without talking to my client. But I'm done with the Cedarwood Inn."

"Fair enough. Where to then?"

That was a good question. She didn't have a lot of options. Unless she went back out to a chain place on the highway, there was really only one. "Could you drop me off at Sandy's?"

As Marti and Lawson pulled up to the house, they noticed Sandy standing in the driveway. She wore black leggings and a yellow long-sleeved top. Her hands were on her knees as she caught her breath. Squinting against the morning sun, Sandy watched the truck pull to a stop along the roadside.

Lawson, puzzled by the sight, couldn't help but mutter to Marti, "What the hell? Is she okay?"

Marti recalled her recent conversation with Sandy about taking up running to deal with her grief and stress. "She's fine," Marti reassured Lawson. "She's just taken up running."

"Why?" She sounded genuinely confused.

Marti shrugged. "People process things in different ways. You've got your cigarettes; maybe she's got her running shoes."

Lawson didn't say anything else, but her expression was one Marti recognized well, having seen it on the faces of many dedicated non-runners over the years. With a last shake of her head, Lawson hopped out of the truck and headed toward Sandy. Marti moved more slowly, mindful of her injuries.

Sandy noticed Marti's labored movement. "What happened?"

Marti briefly sketched out the early morning attack at the Inn.

Sandy's hand went to her mouth. "I feel terrible. Absolutely terrible. I did this. This is my fault."

"Sandy, please. This isn't your fault." Marti glanced at Lawson. "If anything, it tells us you might be right about Bill. This wasn't random."

She looked somewhat placated, but not completely. "I didn't think you'd get hurt. You were just supposed to talk to people."

Marti felt a rush of impatience. She felt the pain meds ebbing away more, the deep bass drum pounding in her head and ribs getting louder, and a bone-deep weariness settling in. She needed to lie down again. She'd prefer the house, but if the small talk continued, she'd settle for the front lawn.

"If you're feeling guilty, I need a favor."

"Anything."

"The police are still processing my room at the inn. Could I crash in your guest room?"

"Of course. That's the least I can do."

"Thank you," Marti said.

If the out-of-breath Sandy in running gear was a new persona, the Sandy who turned to head inside was one Marti recognized. This was Sandy with a purpose. The Sandy who filled out seating charts and volunteered at the church.

She turned to Lawson. Marti wasn't sure why the woman had done it. Maybe she was feeling a little guilty herself. "Thanks for hanging around and giving me a lift."

Lawson looked uncomfortable with the gratitude and shifted her feet. "I'll bring your stuff around when I get the all-clear. You'll be here?"

Marti wanted to get down to Rehoboth Beach and chase down her one slim lead, but at that moment she might as well have considered swimming the English Channel, too. "I don't think I'm going anywhere today. I'm toast."

"Okay, then," Lawson said and started back toward her truck.

Marti shuffled along after her. Lawson heard her and turned back. "Forget something in the Bronco?"

"No, I just need to get my purse. It's in the mailbox."

Marti's journey up to the second floor was slow and laborious. Each step felt like a monumental effort. It took her over 10 minutes to retrieve her purse, navigate up the porch steps, enter the house, and ascend the Everest of steps to the second floor. By the time she reached the landing, a sheen of sweat had formed on her brow.

She caught her breath. She could hear Sandy bustling around in a bedroom to the left. The linen closet door, midway down the hall, stood open. She followed the sounds. Sandy was just pulling up the duvet cover on the bed as Marti entered the room.

The guest room exuded a placid tranquility with its earth-toned decor and wooden furnishings. The queen-size bed, adorned with a quilted coverlet and plump pillows, sang her name like a mythical siren. The only thing Marti wanted to do was fall face first onto it.

Sandy turned to her, a warm and welcoming smile on her face. "There are fresh sheets on the bed, and there are towels and washcloths here on the chair if you want to use the shower. It's just across the hall. Do you need anything else?"

Marti shook her head, appreciative of Sandy's hospitality. "No, but thanks again. I think I just need some rest at this point."

Sandy nodded and took the hint. "I have one errand to run in the afternoon after lunch, but otherwise I'll be around. Just holler if you need anything."

Marti managed a tired but grateful smile as she limped over to the bed. She was still holding the orange pharmacy bottle. It had become a talisman of sorts on the ride over. She carefully placed the bottle on the bedside table within easy reach. Sandy dropped the shades on the windows and closed the door gently on her way out.

Marti kicked off her shoes and settled onto the bed. After some careful experimentation, she found the most comfortable position her injuries afforded, then stared at the ceiling for five minutes as her mind skipped like a water bug across disparate thoughts. Then the exhaustion crashed down on her like a tidal wave, and she fell into a deep and dreamless sleep.

Chapter Twenty-Five

When she woke up sometime later, her mind felt rested, but her body remained battered. She figured it would be that way for a while. She'd just have to get used to it. There was enough money squirreled away in her bank account that she could afford a month or so to recuperate. Maybe be choosy about her cases. Take the ones that she could do from behind a desk. But that didn't solve her immediate problem. Her Bill and Sandy problem. She would not solve this one with a laptop. She knew that for certain. She also knew some thug and his ax handle would not run her out of town.

She slowly pushed herself up and looked around, but didn't see a clock. The house was quiet and she guessed Sandy was out on her errand. She half rolled, half slid out of bed and stood up. It wasn't pleasant. She preferred being in bed. She let a brief wave of dizziness pass, then shuffled a few steps and peeked out the window. The long shadows spreading across the lawn told her it was now late afternoon. She hadn't meant to sleep that long, but maybe it was for the best. She didn't know what else she could accomplish today other than recover.

She picked up the bottle of painkillers and dry swallowed one, then turned on the bedside lamp. At some point, Lawson had made good on her promise. Sandy had put her travel bag and laptop bag from the inn just inside the door.

Suddenly, she felt a desperate urge to get out of the dirty pajamas that she had been forced to put on back at the hospital. She went into the bathroom and felt the urge to open the medicine cabinet like a sneeze coming on. She'd given it a cursory look during the initial house search but had concentrated on the master bath, assuming that's where anything related to Bill would be.

She opened the mirrored cabinet above the vanity and found about what she expected—small bottles, compacts, ointments, and over-the-counter allergy and flu and cold medicine. There were three additional prescription bottles on the lower shelf. All for Olivia. One was the same drug she'd found in Olivia's bedside table. Topamax. She wasn't sure of the other two but thought they might be antidepressants. Society might have gotten most kids under 30 off cigarettes but a whole lot of them ended up on anxiety meds. She shut the cabinet and then glanced at the space underneath. In for a penny, in for a pound. She slowly lowered herself to one knee and opened the lower cabinet. Cleaning supplies, a bucket, extra toilet paper, a sleeve of paper cups, a first aid kit, and a stack of hand towels. Plus, two boxes of insulin pump pods. She picked up the purple and white box. There was a layer of dust on the lid. Not something that was used frequently or recently. Maybe for one of the kids when they were younger. She put it back and then pushed herself back to her feet while she suppressed a groan. Then she carefully stripped off her clothes and took a moment to gape at the large, black and purple bruise that was spreading across her ribs and torso. It looked like a dark slick of spilled ink.

The needling spray of the shower made her long for the big tub back in her apartment. It felt like she was being attacked with Lilliputian ice picks. She washed her face but kept her hair out of the water. Before she'd been discharged, Dr. Harris had decided sutures would be better than a bandage and had quickly and efficiently stitched her head wound closed with five stitches while he cheerily told her about practicing his technique on pig's feet he'd bought at his local butcher. He appeared to think of the anecdote as a bit of homespun bedside manner. Marti could only think of his stockpile of pork feet in his refrigerator and if he had a roommate.

She felt halfway human again as she gently dabbed the water off her body and dressed in fresh clothes. She found a brief note on top of her bag from Sandy: Will be out until 5. Left some soup on the stove.

She hadn't been hungry until she read the note, but her stomach suddenly rumbled to life at the thought of warm soup. It was as if her body was slowly moving through its hierarchy of needs. She dressed in jeans, a T-shirt, and her St. Peter's sweatshirt, the most comfortable clothes she had available, and then took her laptop and phone and limped her way downstairs to the kitchen.

There was a pot of chicken soup warming on low on the stove along with a thick slice of white peasant bread on a plate next to a crock of butter. An empty bowl and spoon sat next to the plate. Marti spooned out a bowl and spread some butter on the soft white bread. She ate the bread standing by the stove then immediately cut another piece, carried the bread and the bowl over to the kitchen table, and sat down. She scrolled through her phone as she slurped up some soup. There were several missed calls and two voicemail messages.

Marti savored the warmth of the soup. There was nothing like chicken, noodles, and salt to soothe a battered body. She had to tell herself to slow down. She picked up her phone and looked at the voicemail numbers. The first, from her sister Emily, sent a subtle tremor of worry fluttering in her gut. Emily typically only called for one reason, their father, but Marti reassured herself with the thought that if it were a dire emergency, there would have been more calls.

She moved on to the second number, unfamiliar, but a local number from Jersey. She tapped it and, after a moment, Brenda Martinez's voice flowed through the tiny speaker. "Hi, Miss Wells. This is Brenda Martinez from the Cedarwood Police Department. We spoke this afternoon out by the CC." It took Marti a moment to puzzle out that the initials must be the local moniker for the enigmatic Country Corner Store. She could think of a few colorful monikers of her own for its peculiar and surly proprietor.

Brenda's message continued, "Anyway, the reason I'm calling is that I thought of something. Might be nothing, probably is, but thought I'd pass it on. Call me back when you get a chance."

Marti noted the timestamp, recognizing that the call had come in late the previous night. Her phone automatically activated its Do Not Disturb mode after

10:00 p,m. Brenda had left the message before Marti's violent encounter, but after she'd retreated to bed with her book.

Finishing her soup, Marti contemplated whether to indulge in a second helping, but Brenda's message tugged at her curiosity. She called back while she had the house to herself.

"Brenda Martinez."

Marti realized this must be her personal cell number. "Hi, Brenda, this is Marti Wells. I'm returning your call."

"Hi, Miss Wells."

"Please, call me Marti."

"Okay, Marti. I just heard about what happened to you. I work nights and just came on duty now. Are you all right?"

"Yes. Well, mostly." She gave Brenda a brief recap.

"Sounds like the guy meant business."

"No concussion, according to the hospital. The bruise is spectacular, but I'll be fine in six weeks or so." At the moment, even after the warm bowl of soup, that felt like a lot of false bravado. "You said you remembered something," Marti prompted.

"That's right. I didn't put it together in my mind until after we talked and I was running through that night again in my head. Before I came up on Bill's truck, I was cruising west, out to the town line, then over to 78, and then back. It's my usual loop and how I like to start and end the shift. Anyway, I was heading out toward Fairmont, headed away from the CC, like we drove yesterday, and a woman was walking along the road."

"A woman?"

"Yes, I think so. It could have been a man, I suppose, but my first thought was a woman. She tried to get into the trees when she saw me coming."

"She tried to hide? She was walking toward you?"

"Yes, she was coming toward me, and I don't know if she was trying to hide or not. The shoulder isn't wide there and is not in good shape. She might have just been trying to put a little space between an oncoming car and herself. You know, be a little safer."

"Okay." Marti thought about that stretch of road. It was pretty empty by her recollection. A string of trees, firebreaks, hunting cutouts, and utility poles. "Is it unusual to see someone walking along there like that?"

"Yes, especially at that time of night. There are very few houses out there. I remember thinking maybe she had a flat or ran out of gas and was walking back to the CC for help. Not great cell service out there, either."

"Did you recognize her?"

"No. Too dark. I didn't get a good look. Like I said, she sort of scampered down the embankment and into the trees. I went past in a flash and then came up on Bill's truck and ... his body and forgot all about her." There was a pause. "If it was a her. Talking to you and driving out there must have jogged it loose."

Marti tried to read into that pause. She knew sometimes you saw things late at night on patrol. Her dad had told her stories. Brenda didn't strike her as the type to invent something, even after-hours alone in her car on dark roads. Or, if she did, she wouldn't disclose it to a virtual stranger. No, Marti was pretty sure Brenda had seen someone along that roadside, but like everything else so far, Marti was left unsure if it was relevant to Bill's death or not.

"How far from Bill's truck did you see her?"

"Couldn't have been far. Less than half a mile. I remember seeing the hazard lights pretty quickly after that and thinking it must be hers until I recognized the truck."

"Do you think this woman, or this person, was with Bill?"

"I don't know. If she was going for help, why not flag me down? Why get off the road? If I hadn't come up on Bill, I would have gone back in case she needed help, but ... that didn't happen."

No, it didn't. Instead, Brenda had come across a colleague dead, or dying, in his truck. It wouldn't have been easy for a veteran cop, never mind someone relatively new like Martinez. In the rush of emotions and actions to try to save Bill, she had forgotten about the lone woman. It was curious, but at the moment, Marti couldn't think of any more questions for Brenda. It wasn't yet winter, but it was getting cold at night. She wouldn't want to walk far. She should check out a map. Maybe the person was walking home for whatever reason. "Thanks for calling and letting me know. I'm not sure what to make of it."

"Me either, in retrospect. Do you think I should have told Lawson or the chief? Should I tell them now?"

"Up to you, but I don't think it would have changed the outcome at all."

"Yeah, you're probably right."

Marti would later realize she'd been very wrong about that assumption.

Chapter Twenty-Six

As Marti drove from Cedarwood to Rehoboth Beach the following morning, she mulled over the events of the previous evening. Shortly after her call with Brenda Martinez, Sandy returned home. They engaged in polite small talk about the church and Sandy's volunteer efforts, while Sandy ate a bowl of soup, and Marti toasted and buttered another slice of bread. Marti had abandoned organized religion long ago, but she considered herself spiritual in certain ways.

Once they had tidied up, Marti ventured back to Bill's office and conducted a slow but thorough search for his missing notebook. She knew it wasn't in his office, but she couldn't think of anything else to do and didn't want to join Sandy in the living room watching a nature documentary. She even revisited Bill's truck out in the driveway for good measure. Predictably, both attempts proved fruitless. The notebook was not in Sandy's house. She did, however, find the Subaru in the driveway. Lawson must have arranged for someone to retrieve her car from the inn and deliver it to Sandy's, which was a thoughtful gesture. After the events of the last day, and their brusque start outside the precinct, maybe she should revise her opinion of Detective Lawson.

Despite sleeping most of the day, the search had left Marti drained. She'd said goodnight to Sandy, telling her she'd likely be up and out of the house early the next morning. The other woman hadn't responded, just nodded, and continued to stare at the television as if lost in another world. Eventually, Marti turned, made the slow climb up the stairs, and went to bed.

She made good time in the early morning traffic, but the Subaru's cranky suspension did her injuries no favors. Her head felt full of cotton as if she'd drank two bottles of merlot from Delgado's bodega. She didn't want to space out during the drive, so she'd only taken half a dose of Percocet. It muted her headache to a tolerable level but did little for her ribs, which only hurt when she breathed or hit a pothole. Both occurred frequently as she drove south on 278 until it hooked up with the turnpike through the farmlands of lower New Jersey and then hopped onto Route 1 into Delaware.

She'd started just after six. Carefully making her way downstairs in the dark, trying not to wake Sandy. She'd stopped once for gas, a cheese Danish, and more coffee and was parking along a mostly empty stretch of boardwalk by 10:00 a.m.

It was well past the peak of tourist season, and as she stepped out of her car, the sight of a nearly empty beach and boardwalk greeted her. A few solitary figures strolled along the wooden planks, their heads bowed against the persistent onshore breeze. She stood for a moment. The sky was a canvas of shifting grays and whites, the sun hidden behind a thick blanket of clouds, turning the air cool and crisp. It felt invigorating after the long drive.

She walked gingerly, her steps measured, her body stiff and aching, up the steps to the boardwalk. She walked a quarter mile until she came to the first bench and sat. She felt winded and physically tired. For someone in good physical shape and used to relying on her body to do what she asked, it was a depressing and disconcerting feeling. And she hated it. She felt a wave of anger at her attacker. She promised herself that she would find the crazy SOB with the creepy ski mask and hold him accountable. But she would be smart about it. Anger would not help. Not right this second.

She took in the wide sandy beach stretched out before her and tried to let it calm her. She breathed in the scent of saltwater mixed with the familiar tang of carnival food that clung to the wooden stalls and food stands. Even now, mostly shuttered for the season, Rehoboth Beach held a certain charm. The buildings that lined the boardwalk, with their colorful facades and quaint storefronts, were old and weathered and seemed to lean against each other in solidarity. The beach town seemed to exhale in the offseason as if taking a well-deserved break before the tourists would descend again next summer.

Beyond the boardwalk, the sea itself was a study in shades of blue and gray, the waves crashing with a steady rhythm against the shore. Marti stood and shivered slightly in the breeze. She knew that Rehoboth Beach, for all its charm, held secrets like any other place. It was time to find out what exactly had brought Bill to the Delaware shore.

She let the GPS guide her four blocks west, away from the water, and three blocks south into the Sundowner's parking lot. There were three other cars in the lot. One parked near the office and the other two farther along. She parked near the office and climbed out. She was developing a system to mitigate the worst of the pain. She'd unlatch the door, kick it all the way open, and shimmy sideways in the seat so her feet were on the ground. Then she'd grab the side of the car and sort of pirouette up and out of the car with minimal strain on her damaged ribs. In theory. It still hurt.

She shut the door and studied the old motel. The Sundowner was a midcentury relic that had seen better days. It looked like it was one good storm surge away from being knocked down and carried away. The building was an artifact of a bygone era, and its facade bore the scars of time and neglect. The once-vibrant turquoise paint on the exterior had faded to a pale, tired blue, and the wooden panels showed signs of peeling and warping. An orange neon sign that might have once boasted the motel's name now only lit up partially, the letters flickering intermittently.

The parking lot was sand and gravel, its surface uneven and rutted from years of use. A few wind-worn trees swayed in the ocean breeze around the edges, their leaves yellowed and tattered. The motel might be close enough to smell low tide, but the ocean was nowhere in sight. Marti was certain that on a hot day, the idea of walking would deter all but the most determined or budget-conscious beachgoers.

The surrounding area was quiet, away from the bustling beachfront, but still exuded an air of shaggy dignity. The Sundowner stood as one of the more prominent structures, surrounded by modest beach houses, a dog park, and lower-rent commercial properties. A block to the east, on the corner, she could see a convenience store with a fading sign advertising bait and tackle painted on one side. Next door was the Surfside Diner. Looking in the opposite direction was a laundromat, gas station, and Gary's Liquor World.

As she walked up the narrow strip of cracked sidewalk that led from the parking lot to the motel's office, she recalled the clerk's description of the Sundowner when she'd called. Food, a bed, liquor, and laundry. This stretch of Rehoboth Beach had everything a divorced dad might need. Except for a family.

Marti entered the Sundowner's office, a dimly lit room that seemed frozen in time. The air carried a musty scent of old sunscreen and faded memories. Flickering fluorescent lights buzzed overhead and cast a pallid glow on the worn linoleum floor. The once-vibrant patterns of the linoleum had faded over time, worn down by countless flip-flops. Scattered scuff marks and water stains told the story of a motel whose best days were long gone.

Faded photographs of happy vacationers, their colors muted by time, hung in cheap frames interspersed with surfing and beach scene posters frayed and tattered at the edges. Marti had the surreal feeling she'd stepped into an old family scrapbook.

Behind the front desk sat a bored clerk, his disinterested eyes fixed on a smartphone. His face wore the expression of someone who had seen too many guests come and go without leaving an impression. He was just the guy manning the conveyor belt. He looked up as Marti entered, absently patted down what remained of his disheveled hair, and then put the phone face down by his elbow.

The furniture in the office, much like the rest of the place, showed signs of wear, neglect, or simple disinterest. The front desk, made of dark wood, bore nicks and scratches from years of use. An old rotary phone sat beside an antiquated cash register, each looking incongruous in proximity to the clerk's smartphone.

Pamphlets and faded brochures in little plastic stands promoting local attractions crowded the desk. Marti expected that at least 75 percent of the advertised businesses were now bankrupt. A small oscillating fan in the corner circulated the stale air, doing little to ease the stuffiness of the room.

Marti approached, her footsteps slick on the linoleum. Up close, she could see the clerk's nametag read 'Ron.'

"Good morning. My name is Marti Wells. I'm a private investigator." She pulled a business card from her wallet and slid it across the desk. The guy glanced down but didn't read it. "Do you still use that thing?" She pointed at the old register.

"Nope. That thing is solid steel and I'm not going to throw my back out moving it. It's more a curiosity for folks."

Ron was a middle-aged man with a classic receding hairline. A pair of wire-rimmed glasses perched precariously and crookedly on the bridge of his substantial nose. There was a weariness in his brown eyes, and Marti wondered just how long he'd been sitting behind that desk.

"Bet you could sell it on eBay."

"Thought about it. The boss would probably never miss it. The issue is the weight. It would cost more to ship than it's worth. To be honest," Ron said, slowly coming alive and warming up to the conversation like a rusted engine sputtering to life, "thought about trying to sell the whole kit and kaboodle." He circled a finger in the air. "The boss," now he used his fingers to make air quotes, "lives down in Boca and I haven't seen her since before COVID. It might take her another five years to notice, but my job comes with a rent-free room. Where would I live?"

"Probably the right decision. Eventually, someone like me would come looking and you'd end up living in a jail cell."

Ron nodded and deflated a little. The temporary dream of escape put back on the shelf. "A private eye, huh? Well, what brings you to my door?"

"I'm here to inquire about a guest who stayed here recently. Can you help me with that?"

"I can try."

She pulled out her phone and brought up a picture of Bill Thompson that she'd downloaded from one of the local newspaper stories. It was a department head-and-shoulders shot of him in uniform. She turned the phone around and put it next to the business card in front of Ron. "You recognize him?"

He stared down at the picture and then leaned back in his chair and looked at the ceiling. "Yes."

"Really," Marti said, maybe surprised Ron could recall Monday, never mind a visitor from almost four months ago.

"Bill ..." he paused.

"Th-"

"Wait, don't tell me. He wasn't in uniform. He said he was a detective. Not from around here. That helped me remember. Thompson. Bill Thompson. Came in, I don't know, back in the spring before the summer season."

Marti was astonished. This was more than she'd hoped for, and she was momentarily struck dumb. "That's right," she finally managed. "That's amazing."

Ron's cheeks colored slightly. "I've got a thing for memory. I'm studying for Jeopardy, or some other quiz show. As you might imagine, I spend a lot of time by myself. Gotta fill the time somehow." He flipped his phone over and turned it around. She could see a list of presidents and vice presidents in chronological order. "The trick is to give most everything a little mnemonic. Sort of pin it in your mind with some sort of aid or association. With Detective Thompson it was his last name. Thompson. Like a Thompson submachine gun. The guy was a cop, but he was also old-school. Or gave off that vibe. I could see him in that old Costner movie, *The Untouchables*, where they went after Capone. So, give me the bill for the machine gun became Bill Thompson to me."

"That's good. And very helpful to me."

"Did something happen to him?"

"He died about a month ago. Heart attack."

"Damn, that's too bad." Marti noticed he'd unconsciously put a hand on his chest. His physique wasn't all that dissimilar to Thompson's. "He didn't look that old."

"He wasn't, but he didn't take great care of himself, either. Does that big brain of yours happen to remember why he came in?"

"Yes. We often get the local cops in here for fights, domestics, or bodies or … well, to be frank, prostitution, but we rarely get a detective and never one from far away." He glanced down at the business card and frowned. "I don't think he was from Jersey City, though."

"He wasn't. He was from a small town called Cedarwood. It's in central Jersey. About four hours away."

"Okay, I don't think he told me that. Maybe he did, or maybe he flashed his badge, though everything about the guy said cop, or maybe it was just a sense I had. He was from away. Not the shore. He was in here looking for a guy."

"So he was here on police business of some kind?"

"Oh, definitely."

"What about the other guy? The guy he was looking for. You remember his name?"

"Hold on. What did I use for that?" He screwed up his face, which Marti thought was mostly theatrical, but she didn't mind the dramatics if Ron kept coming up with leads. "Thomas Foster! Thomas Foster, the fishing forecaster. I didn't use imagery this time but alliteration. I linked the first and last names. The repeated F sound in Foster is reinforced by the phrase fishing forecaster, which also starts with F. This creates a mental connection between the first name, Thomas, and the last name, Foster, making it easier to remember both together."

"What made you go with fishing and forecaster?"

"Well, Thomas was always going out surfcasting. He'd stop by most evenings and shoot the shit with me for a bit. It always included a weather forecast for the next day as he was leaving. So, fishing forecaster."

Marti nodded as if it all made perfect sense to her. "So, Bill hooked up with this Thomas Foster?"

"No, unfortunately not. He missed him by a few weeks. Thomas left on May first."

"Any idea why Bill was looking for him?"

"No, he didn't say anything specific. Just said it was for a case."

"Is there a forwarding address for Foster?"

Ron gave her a look that said she should know better. "No, we get payment upfront and take down the license plates of the cars in the lot, but as long as you don't trash the room, once you check out, we lose interest."

"Gotcha."

"Do you want to know about the other detective?"

"Other detective?" Marti said.

"He came in earlier in the month, before Thompson, but still a day after Foster had checked out."

"Coincidence?" Marti said, more to herself, but Ron answered.

"Probably not."

"Yeah, probably not." Marti wasn't sure what to make of this new piece of information. "Okay. What was this other cop's name?"

"Can't help you there. Paul was working, and he doesn't really do names or details like me. It was a cop; he had a warrant and he was looking for Foster. Frankly, I'm surprised Paul retained that much." Ron tapped his temple. "He's a little slow, but he's reliable with the basics. I can't be here 24 hours a day. I think he only told me because he knew Foster and I were sort of friendly."

"Did you tell Thompson this?"

"Yup, same way I'm telling you. I figured maybe they were colleagues or knew each other."

"Since you were friendly, do you have any idea why two different detectives were suddenly so interested in Thomas Foster?"

Ron scratched at his neck. "I asked myself the same question, but the answer is no, I don't. When I say we were friendly, it's relative to the other guests but still superficial. Thomas and I talked about fishing, the weather, the news somewhat, and occasionally baseball. I got the feeling he was a lonely guy. We get those a lot around here. I asked Thompson but sort of got the standard company line. He said he had to ask him some questions."

"Other than fishing, did he hang out anywhere or with anyone? Someone that might know where he went?"

"I know he ate quite a bit at The Surfside up the street. It's convenient even if the food mostly runs toward soft and brown. You could try there. There's also The Dawn Patrol, that's the informal name of the group of morning fishermen that meet up at the 7th Street pier around sunrise. That's another good bet. But you don't really need to do all that. I don't know where he went, but I can tell you where he ended up."

"Oh, thanks, I'd appreciate that."

"Don't thank me yet. He's up at Rose Hill. Thomas Foster is dead."

Chapter Twenty-Seven

Marti sat in her car in the Sundowner's parking lot and tried to figure out how this new information might fit. Bill Thompson had been very stressed out, or very worried, leading up to his death. He'd driven four hours looking for a Thomas Foster at a down-and-out motel in Rehoboth Beach. Another cop, this one with a warrant in hand, had also shown at up the Sundowner at one point looking for Foster. Popular guy. He took off, but he didn't get far.

She pulled out her phone and googled 'Thomas Foster, death, 2022' and found a handful of short wire stories. She tapped the link on the top result from the *Star-Ledger*.

BODY FOUND IN THE PINE BARRENS

STAFFORD - The partially decomposed remains of 65-year-old Thomas Foster were found by a hiker in a remote and dense part of The Pine Barrens on Wednesday morning.

An autopsy was expected to be completed Friday but the cause of death may not be immediately known for some time. Stafford police Capt. Mark Anderson said it was not clear how Foster ended up in that area. Authorities are investigating the circumstances surrounding his death. More details are pending the ongoing investigation. Anyone with information is asked to contact Detective Laura Parker at the Stafford Police Department.

Marti browsed a few more stories, but they were all a variation on the same generic press release and she didn't learn anything new. The *Star-Ledger* story was from late June. There had been no follow-ups in the media since then. She pulled up the website for the Stafford Police Department and tapped connect on the main number. It took five minutes and three transfers, but eventually, she got Detective Parker on the other end.

"Parker." Her tone was flat and professional. Polite cop, but not friendly. It immediately made Marti think that Parker and Lawson might make good friends. Marti could also tell just from those two syllables that she would not get much help from Detective Parker.

"Hi, my name is Marti Wells. I'm a private detective working on a case that might be related to the death of Thomas Foster."

There was a pause. Marti was about to prompt her with the scant details she knew of Foster's death when she responded, "How?"

That was going to be tricky to explain because Marti didn't know. She decided that bullshitting this woman would not work, so she went with honesty. "I'm not sure. Could you tell me if there's been any change or update since June? I saw nothing online." She hastily added, "Nothing confidential, of course."

"What exactly is your client's connection to Foster?"

Marti blew out a breath. "I don't know if there is one. I'm working for the widow of a detective in Cedarwood. Bill Thompson. You recognize that name?"

"No. That doesn't sound familiar."

"The widow firmly believes that he was deeply troubled by something when he died. She would like to know what that was."

"Uh-huh."

Marti worked to keep her tone easy, but it was like talking to a bland, obtuse houseplant. "Thompson drove down to the Sundowner Motel in Rehoboth Beach last May to talk to Thomas Foster. He missed him at the motel. I'm not sure if he caught up to him before he died or not. I'm assuming it was part of an active investigation. Another detective had also visited the Sundowner looking for Foster."

"Okay."

Marti couldn't tell if this was new information to Parker or not. She pushed ahead. "Is there any record of Thompson getting in touch with you guys after the body was found?"

Another pause, but this time Marti could hear keys lightly clicking in the background.

"No. There's no record of that in the file."

"And there would be if he'd gotten in touch?"

"Yes."

Marti worked to keep her frustration in check. She knew before she called that this was going to be mostly a one-way street. Parker might answer direct questions, but wouldn't volunteer any information. "Could you tell me if Thomas Foster had any outstanding warrants at the time of his death?"

"No, not that I'm aware of."

"Huh. The front desk guy at the Sundowner said the other detective, not Thompson, came in with a warrant looking for Foster."

"Not us."

"There are no outstanding warrants for Foster?"

"Not that I can see."

"So, what was the connection? Why would Thompson drive all the way down here?"

"I don't know, ma'am. If this is just a matter of satisfying the widow, why don't you talk to Cedarwood PD? Thompson didn't contact us, but we reached out to Cedarwood. They might be your best bet."

"So, you do have information?"

"Ma'am, look at it from my perspective. I just received a random phone call asking about an ongoing investigation. You could be anyone. A journalist."

"God forbid."

Marti could feel Parker smile through the phone and felt like she'd at least scored a point.

"You want to come in and take it up with my lieutenant? Feel free."

"Has there been a resolution to the case?"

"It's still open."

"You're in Homicide, so Foster's death wasn't natural?"

"That's right."

"Any suspects? Any leads?"

"Not that I'm going to share with you. Why don't you leave me your number and if anything changes, I'll give you a ring."

"I'll wait by the phone," Marti said.

Parker laughed. "Have a good day."

After Marti hung up, she did her shimmy dance to get out of the car and reentered the motel office. Ron glanced up from his list of vice presidents. "Don't tell me you want a room?"

She tried not to grimace at the thought. She didn't want to insult the man. Though he seemed to have a pretty clear-eyed understanding of the Sundowner's place in the greater lodging ecosystem. "No, but I was wondering if the Sundowner has any security cameras?"

She wasn't thinking about Thompson but rather the second detective Ron had mentioned, the one with the warrant, the warrant Parker said didn't exist, not in any jurisdiction she could see. Marti would love to find that guy and pick his brains about what was going on.

Ron's response was a mixture of amusement and disbelief. He shot her a sidelong glance. "Lady, does this place look like somewhere folks want to be recorded coming and going?"

Marti got the message but pressed a little. "Isn't it required for insurance or something?"

Ron let out a gruff chuckle. "If you think the boss is shelling out premiums for insurance on this dump, you're way off the mark. On the day she left," he continued, reaching down and unclipping a chunky keyring from his belt, "she handed me these." He tossed the keyring onto the cluttered desk, where it landed amidst brochures and old coffee cups. "And this." Ron reached beneath the desk and retrieved a gleaming blue steel .45 revolver. The firearm was so large that Marti figured she could stick her thumb in the barrel and there'd still be room for the bullet.

"That's our insurance policy," Ron stated flatly, then slid the massive gun out of sight. Guns were a necessary tool in her line of work, but she had never been comfortable around them.

Marti pressed on. "All right, no cameras. Can you do me a favor, though? Could I get Paul's contact information? I'd like to talk to him and see if he remembers anything about this other detective's visit. I didn't know about him. I want to track him down and see what he knows about Foster and Thompson."

Ron leaned back in his creaky office chair. "Paul won't be on duty until tomorrow night, but I can call him." He picked up her business card from where she'd left it earlier on the desk. "If he's okay with it, I'll pass your contact information along. Will that work for you?"

Marti nodded. "Yes, that works."

Ron glanced at the old clock on the wall. "Paul's a creature of the night. Most days, he doesn't surface until late afternoon. Like I said, I wouldn't expect much, though. Paul's memory is … mmm … unpredictable."

"Can't hurt to ask."

Ron shrugged. "Suit yourself."

Marti drove the short distance back to the boardwalk and parked along Seventh Street. She walked up the steps and found the plain wooden pier jutting 100 yards into the Atlantic. The sun had banished the clouds and cast long shadows across the boardwalk. The wind off the water picked up. Both the pier and the surrounding stretch of beach were empty.

Now what? According to Ron, she had hours to kill before the fishermen might show up for some sunset casting. Her gaze swept the surroundings, finding only one open shop, a pizza place, Mario's, on the corner. The shop must rely on the locals and takeout orders to weather the offseason. Still, pizza was almost always a safe bet.

Inside, the pizza joint was small and humble. The front of the house was an unassuming seating area with a few worn plastic tables and chairs. The place smelled of olive oil and cheese, mingled with the tang of tomato sauce. The far end was a counter spanning the width of the restaurant with a menu board suspended above. There was a clear display case next to the register for the pizzas on offer and a soda fountain setup to the right. Today the case was empty save for a lone plain cheese with nine slices remaining.

She reduced the slice count to seven and added a Diet Coke. The slices were dripping with oil, saturating the paper plate, but they were hot and her hunger made them taste better than they probably were.

She spent a half hour nibbling the slices and reading her book, then, as she disposed of her trash, she asked the curly-haired counter guy if he knew a Thomas Foster. He shook his head and then disappeared behind the long oven without a word. Marti took the hint and exited the shop.

She let the ocean breeze revive her. The boardwalk remained empty other than a pair of seagulls eyeballing her from the far rail. She pulled her coat tighter and headed for the stairs. The excursion had taken its toll, leaving her tired and the painkillers wearing thin. Still, her determination to talk to The Dawn Patrol and chase down this lead on Foster kept her moving. She knew returning to Cedarwood tonight was unlikely.

Marti returned to her car and drove three blocks north to an oceanfront hotel, another relic of an independent era that had avoided the Sundowner's fate by either luck or its prime location. The lot was barely a quarter full, and she haggled an offseason rate from the front desk before she rode a rickety old elevator three floors up. The room was simple, with a queen-size bed, a low bureau with a television on top and a long mirror behind, plus a bathroom with a snug shower stall. It was plain but serviceable and clean, suitable for a night. She closed the curtains tightly, took off her shoes, set her phone alarm for 4:30, and slipped beneath the covers.

Chapter Twenty-Eight

She woke to her alarm and moaned as she sat up and kicked off the covers. Maybe a nap hadn't been such a good idea. Her whole body felt stiff, like an old, forgotten marionette tangled in its strings. She was used to feeling a little sore when she got out of bed. She was in her fifties. It was par for the course. She accepted waking up with rusty hinges no matter how much running, yoga, or stretching she did. It was an age tax everyone had to pay. But she'd been harboring a secret hope that she'd wake up feeling better. That her body would bounce back, maybe not with the snap of a rubber band, but at least with the slow grace of a Slinky. No such luck. If anything, she felt worse than when they'd wheeled her out of the hospital.

She checked her phone after she turned off the alarm. Several missed calls. Her sister again. Three from Sandy. She dropped the phone on the bed. She should call them both back, but just the thought made her head feel even fuzzier.

She limped to the bathroom, swallowed two more painkillers with tap water, and then used as much hot water as she could to loosen her joints. Twenty minutes later, she felt marginally better and took the elevator back downstairs.

The lobby bar was surprisingly full, tempting her to further loosen her joints with a glass of red wine. However, with the sun sinking fast, she didn't want to miss this opportunity and get stuck down here for another whole day. She walked outside, left her car in the lot, and walked down the boardwalk toward the Seventh Street pier. The wind had picked up even more and, without the bright sun, it knifed through her light jacket. Her breath puffed out in little rings as she walked.

She was the little engine that could. I think I can. I think I can. She put her head down, pulled her jacket tighter, and stuffed her hands in her pockets.

Marti reached the end of the Seventh Street pier, where she counted five men, each deeply engrossed in their own bait and tackle. If they were friends, they formed a motley crew, as diverse in age and appearance as the fish they probably pulled out of this part of the Atlantic.

One appeared to be in his late teens or early 20s, his youthful enthusiasm clear in the way he cast his line with an air of carefree optimism. And complete lack of arthritis. He wore a baseball cap pulled low over his eyes, shielding them from the fading sunlight.

Another man, in his 50s, stood out like a sore thumb. He sported business suit pants paired incongruously with a parka and a winter hat as if he'd rushed from a meeting to make it here in time. His line was out, but drifting, his gaze fixed on something distant and introspective. Marti envied his hat as the tips of her ears slowly froze in the wind.

The remaining three were older, their white hair contrasting with the deepening hues of the evening sky. They stood together along one rail and were dressed comfortably in faded blue jeans, sturdy shoes, and hooded windbreakers. Each sported a large, floppy-brimmed hat, each a different color, navy, white, and tan, that was firmly secured by strings tied under their jowly chins. Two large white buckets and several tackle boxes lay scattered nearby.

One of the white-haired men glanced up and smiled as she approached. Marti took that as an invitation. "Are you guys The Dawn Patrol?"

"That's us. I'm Walter," the white-haired man with the tan hat said. He had big, square teeth that filled his mouth like rows of pristine ivory dominoes when he smiled. He motioned to the man next to him. "This is Edgar."

"Pleasure to meet you, miss," Edgar said and doffed his navy fishing hat.

"Next to him is George," Walter continued. "He's mostly deaf, so don't be offended if he ignores you. He's also mostly an ass and only pretends to be hard of hearing." George flipped them the bird and didn't take his eyes off the water. "The guy in the suit is Henry. And the young buck is Jake." Henry was reeling but made a grunt that might have been a greeting. Jake turned and sketched a quick wave. "Who's asking?"

"My name is Marti Wells. I'm a private investigator. Do any of you remember a guy named Thomas Foster?"

"Sure," Walter said. He appeared to be the group's spokesman. Or worst fisherman. He placed his pole against the wooden rail and turned to face her. His ivory smile faded. "And I'm sorry to be the one to tell you, miss, but Tommy is dead. Has been since the spring. If you're looking to collect any debts, we can't help you."

"Yes, I know. Ron at the Sundowner told me earlier. I'm here for another reason."

"All right then," Walter said. The other four had lost interest and gone back to fishing, though Marti had thought Jake, the young guy, had shot her a look when she mentioned Foster's name. "Why don't we sit down on the bench? My sciatica is acting up something fierce. Always does as the weather gets cooler. I could use a break." Marti followed him over to a nearby bench. She perched on a spot that wasn't completely covered in seagull shit. Walter didn't seem to notice and sat down with a heavy sigh and straightened his left leg before pulling out a thick joint and lighting up.

"You mind?"

"Not at all."

"It's the only thing that really helps with the pain. I don't want to get hooked on that Oxy. After my nephew almost died, I ground the rest of mine up in the garbage disposal. You don't mind me saying, but you look like you went through the wringer recently, too." He motioned at her head.

"Yes. Car accident."

"They didn't prescribe you painkillers, did they?"

"Just heavy-duty Tylenol. Not Oxy."

"Good. Nasty stuff. Believe me. Here, give this a try." He held out the joint, and she took a hit and handed it back.

This conversation had taken a strange and unexpected turn and she decided to get back on track before Walter pulled a tab of acid out of his pocket and things got truly bizarre. She took a minute to fill him in on the job that Sandy Thompson had hired her to do.

Walter nodded along. "I remember Bill. He must have gotten the same story from Ron that you did because, now that I think about it, he showed up at about the same time of day that you did. That wasn't long after Tommy had left, a week or so, maybe 10 days, so I told him Tommy was probably around someplace. From what I understand, he was probably already dead when Bill was asking his questions."

"How long was Foster here in Rehoboth Beach before he took off?"

"Let's see." Walter looked out over the water. "He wasn't here last Christmas. I know that. I organize a thing each year with fishes over at the Scully. I would have remembered." That entire sentence didn't make a lick of sense to Marti, but she just smiled and let the man talk. She had the feeling that after fishing, talking was a favorite pastime for Walter. "Then again, maybe that's not true. He might have been around, but he wasn't with The Dawn Patrol yet. That's probably more accurate. You should ask Ron. If he was staying at the Sundowner the whole time, he'd have a record."

"Good idea," Marti said. And it was. She should have asked when she was in the office.

"You think he was planning on staying? Making this a permanent home?"

"Unless you own a business along the beach or you're retired, Rehoboth Beach doesn't encourage long-term plans. You end up here because you're a hustler, a tourist, or you're restless."

"Which one are you?" Marti asked.

"I'll let you draw your own conclusions," Walter replied and flashed those big teeth again.

Hustler, Marti decided. "What about Foster?"

"Good question. I'd say restless. He was a nice guy. Or, appeared to be. He showed up one morning with a reel and then kept coming back. He was a talker.

Like me. That's a bit of an outlier among fishermen. It's more of a solitary thing. Even with our group, you can see," he waved a hand at the four silent men staring down at their lines, "we're not the most garrulous bunch."

"He mention where he came from or how he ended up here?"

"Nope, can't really help you there. First rule of fight club," Walter said with another smile, "we don't ask personal questions. We fish. We speculate about the weather. We bitch about the local sports, and we complain about the government. You know why I come out here twice a day, just about every day of the year?"

"You really like the taste of fresh cod?"

"Honey, I'd have to swim out five miles before I sniffed any cod. We mostly get bluefish, the occasional striped bass, or flounder. The point is not the catch. They all taste mostly the same, like silty shit fried in breadcrumbs. I come out there to kill the time. I don't sleep much anymore. I got 18, sometimes 20, hours to kill each day. Prepping, getting here, fishing, getting back. That takes care of at least six."

"And that's worth it?"

"Hell yes, but my point is that all of us are here for selfish reasons. We aren't here for therapy. We talk to pass the time, not to make new friends or get to know someone."

Marti wasn't sure how much she bought that argument, but men, especially men who spent so much time fishing, were a strange and unknown species to her. "Surely, you must have picked up a few things."

"Surely. I can tell you Foster served overseas, likely in the Army, but he never said specifically. I can tell you he was a spiritual man of sorts. I can tell you he knew baseball but didn't care much about football. I can tell you he was educated. And I can tell you he probably spent some time in jail."

"That's a strange mix. Why jail?"

Walter shrugged. "I might be wrong. He never said it directly. It was more just a feeling I had. He was most comfortable out here on the pier. Sometimes after the morning session, we go up to The Surfside and if we land in the back booth, it's kind of tight. Tommy's eyes always got jittery in that back booth. He didn't like tight spaces."

They turned and watched as Edgar hauled up a fish, neatly unhooked it, and dropped it into the white bucket near his feet. Marti noticed Jake looking in their direction, but he looked away again when he saw her looking.

"You must have talked about it after you learned he was dead. You guys develop any theories?"

"None, other than he wasn't killed for his money. I know he picked up occasional work around the motel from Ron, to offset his room cost, but he was mostly broke. I usually ended up picking up his portion of the check from those breakfasts."

"Any idea what made him bolt?"

"Nope. The cops asked me the same thing. He came down the morning he left. Maybe to say goodbye. Maybe not. He was usually a talker. He was a good fit with the group. But that morning he stayed mostly quiet, fished a little, but quit early. I got the impression he was nervous, but he never said why."

"When Bill came down and found you guys, did he mention why he was looking for Foster?"

"No, he just said he wanted to talk to him concerning a case."

"He thought Foster was a suspect?"

"No, he didn't say that. He said he was a person of interest, but isn't that the same thing? I think maybe he was, but he thought we might be more open or cooperative if we thought Tommy was just a witness. I will say I don't think he was a killer. I never got that vibe."

The ellipsis at the end of that comment was practically visible in the air. "But you got some type of vibe?" Marti asked.

Walter rubbed at his leg and didn't answer for a time. "Yes, I guess I did. Tommy could be a little unsettling."

"Like he was crazy?"

"Crazy, but in a very subtle way. Almost like you'd only see it if you were looking at him from the corner of your eye."

"Huh," was Marti's only response.

Walter must have read her face. "Not that helpful, I know. I guess you had to meet him."

No chance of that happening now, Marti thought. She was running out of questions, but she had one more. "Did Bill mention how he found Foster down here?"

"Oh," Walter said as if he'd never considered it. "Now that you mention it, I don't know. It's not like the Sundowner was his permanent address."

Chapter Twenty-Nine

Marti found a sheltered spot along the boardwalk, escaping the wind while still keeping a watchful eye on the end of the pier. The sun had dipped below the horizon and the lights that lined the boardwalk had flickered to life. As she shuffled her feet, she thought she could smell taffy and buttered popcorn. Maybe it was baked into the boards. Or maybe it was her imagination trying to conjure up a softer summer night.

Fifteen minutes later, the members of The Dawn Patrol made their way down the pier—the three older men, Walter, Edgar, and George, walked together, while Henry and Jake followed separately. Henry stopped by the stairs and said something to Jake, but the wind took it and Marti didn't hear. They separated. Henry headed down the steps and disappeared. Jake walked along the boardwalk away from Marti.

She trailed Jake, who carried his rod and tackle box in one hand, his footsteps a soft echo on the boards. The three old men had already reached the far end of the boardwalk, their forms dusty shadows in the dim light. Jake didn't look back, but Marti thought he was aware of her presence. Maybe he had been expecting it. Finally, he slowed his pace and allowed her to catch up.

He set his fishing gear down and leaned against the rail near a bench. Marti joined him. They were each silent for a minute and gazed out at the darkening sea, listening to the crashing waves carrying secrets to the shore. Or taking them out again.

Finally, Marti broke the silence. "Walter told me he got a vibe from Thomas Foster. That maybe he'd spent time in prison. You get that same vibe?"

"Walt's a good guy, and he's pretty perceptive," Jake said. He turned his head and looked at Marti. Up close, he had rugged features, and despite still being only in his early 20s, deep lines and creases etched his face and spoke of years spent in the sun and wind. Even this deep into September, his skin remained deeply tanned and, under the glow of the streetlights, she could see his eyes were a foamy shade of green.

After a pause, he continued. "My mom was a drunk and all of her boyfriends' conversational skills started and ended with a bottle or their fists. I've been living on my own since I was sixteen. I spent some time on the street before I got myself set up with a job at the arcade and got my apartment. You learn to size up people quickly and trust your gut."

"What did your gut say about Thomas Foster?"

"He tried to hide it, but I'd seen it before. Same look a few of her boyfriends had. They never lasted long. Maybe my mom saw it, too. I wasn't their type." He turned and looked back at the black water. "I wasn't Tommy's type either. But if I had been a few years younger ..."

He picked up his rod and tackle box and walked away without another word.

Chapter Thirty

Marti returned to her hotel room. The encounter had left her feeling emotionally drained. Now, it wasn't her injuries that weighed her down the most. The conversation with Jake had stirred a troubling unease that gnawed at her thoughts.

She retrieved the orange pill bottle from her bag, but, hearing Walter's chiding voice, opted to take only half of her prescribed painkiller dosage. She settled back onto the overly firm hotel bed and attempted to distract herself with a book. However, the trials of the retired schoolteacher, now bookstore owner, as she tried to unravel the mystery of a stolen quill to protect her town's history refused to hold her attention and she set it aside after a few pages.

She felt empty and wrung out, like an old, frayed dishrag twisted to its limits. Restlessness coursed through her without a clear outlet. The words of the men on the pier, Thomas Foster, Bill's missing notebook, and the mystery woman by the side of the road all swirled in a whirlpool of muddled thoughts. She finally knew more than when she started almost a week ago, but somehow it felt like less.

Her phone rang and snapped her out of her reverie. Her sister. This was the third call in the past two days. Marti couldn't keep avoiding her. She tried to ignore the sudden queasiness in her stomach as she put the phone to her ear.

"Hi, Emily."

"Hey, you. Everything okay?" Emily asked. "I tried to call you yesterday."

It was a mild rebuke, for Emily, and Marti let it go. She knew she deserved it. "Yeah, everything's ... well, it's complicated right now."

"Complicated? What's going on?"

She rarely discussed her cases with her sister, and her sister rarely asked. It wasn't how their relationship worked, but Marti knew neither one of them were eager to get into the real reason for the call so she explained the recent events in Cedarwood, leaving out the more dangerous aspects, like the assault, and focused on Bill and what he might have been up to before he died.

"I'm getting closer to something, Em. I'm not exactly sure what it is, but I think Sandy was right. Whatever Bill was working on contributed to it. It pushed him over the edge."

"And you're retracing Bill's steps. I know Dad asked you to do this as a favor," Emily replied. "But please be careful, Marti."

"I will," Marti assured her. "What's going on with Dad? Is everything okay?"

Emily's tone shifted, becoming more somber. "Not exactly. There's been another incident at the assisted living place. He's been having trouble distinguishing between different shoes lately. He wore a mismatched pair of loafers to lunch the other day."

"Did he at least have them on the right feet?"

"This isn't funny."

Marti's heart sank. "I know, Em. I just … don't know what else to say or do. Maybe it was dark in his room. Maybe he couldn't find the matching pair. Maybe he's reached the age where he doesn't give a shit about things like that. Did anyone ask him? Probably not. I sometimes feel like they see what they want to see." Marti knew she was deflecting, but she wasn't in the mood to admit it right now.

"Dr. Evanston mentioned we might need to consider a higher level of care soon," Emily replied.

"Of course he did."

"We don't have to make any decisions yet."

"Good."

Marti still had trouble picturing her father as retired, as a man without a badge, as a man with wrinkles. She was not ready to think of him as a man with dementia.

"You should go see him."

"I will. As soon as I finish this case, I'll go see him and tell him about Bill."

They spoke for a while longer. Marti asked about her nieces and nephews. She tried not to yawn when Emily told her about the suburban real estate market and her upcoming open houses. After she disconnected, she sat in the dark. She could hear the waves crashing against the beach. Each wave slowly eroded the shore, carrying fragments of sand away, and she fell asleep with an ache in her heart.

Chapter Thirty-One

Marti woke up the same way she'd fallen asleep, to the sound of the waves hitting the shore. Time was fragile but relentless. She stared up at the textured white ceiling and wondered if she lived here if she would eventually stop hearing it? Would she go selectively deaf? She didn't plan to stick around to find out. She tried to sit up, let out an audible groan, and dropped back onto the bed. Time was not healing her wounds. Not quickly.

Trying to ignore the pain in her ribs and the stiffness in her body, she made a second attempt and pushed herself out of bed. The prospect of a morning run to clear her head and work out the stiffness seemed wildly optimistic, given the simple act of standing up made her break into a light sweat. Instead, she settled for making it to the bathroom without having to pause for a break.

She made it, and after 10 minutes in a shower that felt like wading through a field of stinging nettles, she didn't feel any better, but she did feel awake. She toweled off, skipped the hopeless hotel hair dryer, allowing her long, wet hair to cascade down her back, and slowly dressed. What normally took two minutes was now a laborious 10-minute process. Mentally giving Walter the middle finger, she swallowed two pain pills.

After taking the elevator down to the hotel lobby, Marti walked outside and located her car in the parking lot. It wasn't difficult. There had not been a flood of overnight guests. The lot remained mostly empty. She carefully climbed in, without groaning, and the Subaru turned over on the first try. Maybe the salt air was doing one of them some good. She pulled out and headed back toward the Sundowner. But the old motel wasn't the destination she had in mind.

Marti found a parking spot along the street and climbed the short flight of steps to The Surfside Diner. As she stepped inside, the low hum of conversation and the clinking of silverware greeted her ears. It was busier than she'd expected, but then she remembered it was Saturday. She'd received the call from her father about Bill Thompson one week ago.

The interior of The Surfside had that distinct feel of a classic Jersey diner. Rows of laminated booths lined one side, while a long, worn counter with spinning stools stretched along the other. The vinyl seats showed the wear of countless patrons over the years, and the countertop gleamed with a shine of constant polish. Behind the bustling counter, she could see a man and a woman managing a big flat-top grill. One worked eggs and pancakes, the other turned over a big pile of diced potatoes. A waitress moved down the line of stools, refilling mugs.

The smell of sizzling bacon and freshly brewed coffee hung in the air, mingling with the faint scent of syrup and butter. A waitress with a notepad tucked into her apron and a pencil behind her ear swung by, a warm smile on her face.

"Morning, hon. You look like you could use a good breakfast. Right this way." She gestured toward a booth in the corner, away from the hustle of the counter.

Marti followed, her stomach grumbling. She'd eaten a small bag of almonds from the minibar for dinner, otherwise she had eaten nothing else since the two slices of pizza the previous afternoon. Maybe they would screw up the food, but they had the smell right.

Marti settled into the booth, and the waitress handed her a large, laminated menu.

"Coffee?"

"Definitely."

The waitress swiftly moved on to serve another table but returned quickly with the steaming coffee in a thick, plain white mug.

"Ready?"

"I'm always ready to eat. I'll have the scrambled eggs, with bacon and home fries, and a short stack of pancakes."

The waitress scribbled it down, offered another quick smile, then hustled off again. Marti couldn't help but feel weary just watching the woman's frenetic movements.

Marti had planned to seek out someone at the diner who might have known Thomas Foster, hoping to gather more information before heading back to Cedarwood. However, the bustling scene she had walked into on this Saturday morning was not what she had envisioned. It was far from the sleepy, sparsely populated place she had expected from Walter's anecdote. She figured that imagined scene was likely reserved for Tuesday afternoons. Scanning the room, she couldn't spot any obvious candidates who might be part of the extended Dawn Patrol or associated with the Sundowner. She contemplated asking the harried waitress but decided against it, sensing the woman might spontaneously combust if made to stand still for too long.

As she pondered her next move, her phone vibrated in her bag. She pulled it out and looked at a vaguely familiar number that didn't register immediately. She answered, inserting a finger into her opposite ear.

"Marti Wells."

"This is Jennifer Anderson, returning your call."

Her voice was flat and even and completely unfamiliar to Marti. She ran the name through her mental Rolodex and came up empty.

"I'm sorry. I don't remember calling you. What case is this regarding?"

"You left a message two days ago about Bill Thompson."

Marti briefly pulled the phone away from her ear and tapped the call history. This was the other number she'd picked up from the pad by Bill's desk phone. The first had been the Sundowner's office and the second had gone directly to a voicemail with just an automated message that repeated the phone number. She put the phone back to her ear.

"Hello?" Anderson said.

"Sorry. I'm here. That's right. I appreciate you calling me back. Well, like I said in the message, I think, the reason I called is that I'm a private investigator from Jersey City—"

"I know who you are. I checked you out before returning your call."

"Okay, good. I can skip that part then. Uh … you know Bill Thompson is dead, right?"

"Yes." That was it. Her tone remained neutral and careful.

"I've been hired by Bill Thompson's widow—"

"Sandy."

"You know her?"

"Never met her, but Bill talked about her."

"Okay, Ms. Anderson—"

"Call me Jennifer."

"Okay, Jennifer, I'm going to be honest with you. I found your number on a notepad in Bill's office and then I checked his phone bills. You guys talked a lot in the months before he died."

Marti liked to use silence to draw out answers. She tried it now with this guarded voice and willed the other woman to speak first. She did, but not with information, just more deflection.

"A lot is a relative number. Might be a lot to you, but not to me."

The waitress dropped off her food. Marti was sore, cranky, and hungry. She wanted to eat, not verbally joust with Jennifer Anderson. "Where are you, Jennifer? Could we do this in person? It's a little complicated to get into on the phone while I'm sitting in a booth in a diner."

There was a pause before Anderson replied, "I'm in Jersey. We could meet."

"Tell me where and when."

Another pause, a little shorter. "Molly Pitcher. There's a Starbucks. Three o'clock today."

Marti did the rough travel math in her head. Roughly a three-hour drive, but also roughly in the same direction she needed to go. "See you then." She disconnected and dove into the pool of maple syrup, meat, and carbs.

Chapter Thirty-Two

After finishing her lumberjack-size breakfast, she drove over and strolled the boardwalk down to the pier but didn't find Jake or the rest of The Dawn Patrol. Instead, she encountered a few persistent seagulls. The gulls quickly lost interest in her when they realized she wasn't carrying any funnel cake or caramel popcorn. She retraced her steps to her car, returned to the hotel to check out, and then headed north, leaving Delaware and crossing back into New Jersey.

She took her time on the drive but still arrived with plenty of time before she met with Anderson. You couldn't do better than the Molly Pitcher rest stop, Marti thought, as she took exit 8 near Cranbury, on the New Jersey Turnpike. Molly Pitcher might or might not have been a Revolutionary War heroine, but the rest stop named in her honor was very real.

The rest stop had many things you'd find at other stops along the New Jersey Turnpike: gas pumps, thin strips of spotty grass around a picnic area, an anonymous convenience store, a Roy Rogers, a Nathan's Famous, a Cinnabon, and a Dippin' Dots vending machine. But it also offered airy windows and arching ceilings. And a Starbucks.

But there was another hidden gem to Molly Pitcher. A cherry on top of what was already an elevated rest stop experience. There was a second convenience store. It existed almost like a strange genetic aberration inside this mostly typical roadside ecosystem. Tucked at the far end, away from the moribund, normie convenience store near the gas pumps, this second store had a minimalist design with blond wood shelves displaying slightly more upscale offerings, dark chocolate, and fresh produce. And, nestled in the back like a fever dream from a Willy Wonka-inspired short story, was an old-timey penny candy section.

To Marti, who had spent a lot of time in her career in her car and subsequently had mapped out the best public bathrooms and fast-food, the Molly Pitcher stop was, in a word, flawless. The perfect place to pee, stretch your legs, and grab a childish sugar rush.

She used some of that extra time to contemplate between jawbreakers, caramel creams, and various flavors of Chuckles. In the end, she didn't decide at all, just scooped portions of all three into her bag and carried her sugary nostalgia to the register, then out to the picnic area.

The weather had shifted overnight and the afternoon was warm, perhaps the last gasp of summer. It felt good after the biting wind of Rehoboth Beach. She ate her candy and read her book at a picnic bench until a shadow fell across the page. Marti looked up and shielded her eyes from the sun.

Jennifer Anderson was in her mid-40s with sandy-blonde hair tucked beneath the wide brim of a park ranger hat. She wore no makeup and subtle lines around her eyes and mouth showed under the shadow of her hat.

The hiker had discovered Thomas Foster's body in The Pine Barrens. Marti knew that at least part of that vast tract was parkland. This must be how Anderson and Thompson came into contact.

Anderson recognized Marti. There was no hesitation or question in the woman's green eyes. She'd likely spotted a photo online when she checked her out. She nodded her head toward the Starbucks. "Coffee?"

"Sure, small, black," Marti replied. She pulled her bag over and took out her wallet, but Jennifer waved her off.

"I'll buy," then she turned and walked off.

Marti watched her go. Anderson's tan and forest-green uniform was clean and pressed, and her boots appeared worn and broken-in but polished to a shine. She carried a sidearm and radio on her belt and walked with an athlete's balance and fluidity.

Marti read three more pages and ate a caramel cream before Anderson returned with two cups.

"Thanks," Marti said. She closed the book and tucked it into her bag. Anderson sat across from her at the table but stayed quiet. "This is my favorite rest stop on the Turnpike," Marti said, to fill the silence. She sipped cautiously at the hot, bitter drink. She would be wired until Monday afternoon with the afternoon coffee and the sugar rush from the candy.

"I like the bit of green space," Anderson finally said. "The little knoll. The trees. Feels natural. Most of the other ones are too ... industrial. You can tell they rolled out the grass."

"You work for the parks?"

"Parks and Forestry Police, it's part of Environmental Protection."

"They have their own cops?"

"Yup. We're responsible for law enforcement in all the state parks."

"Huh, I didn't know that. I mean, I know the parks have rangers, or something, for help and supervision, and staff for maintenance, but I guess I never considered how crimes were handled."

"They happen, believe me. In serious cases, local or state agencies may also get involved to provide support."

"How'd you get into that?"

"Family tradition, of sorts. My grandfather was a state trooper. Dad was a sheriff. I've got two brothers who also have badges, one a statie, one local. I went in that direction, too. Attended the State Police Academy and served as a state trooper before transferring to the Park Police. It was a better fit. More time outdoors. I was born and raised in a little town in northwest Passaic and spent most of my youth outside. Park Police gets me the best of both worlds. Been there about 10 years now." She shrugged. "Suits me."

They each took sips of their coffee and glanced around at the cars and trucks coming and going. "How about you?" Anderson eventually said. "How'd you end up as a PI?"

Marti gave her the postage-size resume recap. "My father was a cop, like you, but it took me a little longer to follow him. Went to college, got a mostly useless English degree. Hated teaching. Wasn't a writer. Married and divorced four times. Eventually became a cop, but it didn't stick." Marti sidestepped the messiness that ended her brief career. She watched Anderson's face. The woman said she'd checked her out. That story was out there, but it was 20 years old at this point. Anderson looked back, her face calm. Marti shrugged. "Too much politics. Too much bureaucracy. Way before the Me Too movement. Working for myself was a better option. Suits me." She echoed.

"Got it," Anderson replied.

"Did I pass?"

"Pass what?"

"I'm guessing this whole tête-à-tête was you sizing me up. Figuring out exactly what or how much to tell me."

"Sure, I guess. Look, Bill came to me and confided in me. Even if he's dead now, I need to think carefully about betraying that trust."

"Maybe you can help him finish what he couldn't."

A dog on a long retractable leash wandered close and Anderson turned to watch it for a moment. "I'm not sure this is about Bill anymore. It sounds like it's about his wife."

"True. She's looking for some peace of mind."

"Aren't we all? I'm not sure any debt or feeling of obligation to Bill extends to his wife, so I'm not sure I care about her peace of mind."

"What about your own?"

"That's got nothing to do with you."

"I could use the help. I feel like I've got a lot of the pieces, but I can't see the entire picture. You could help me sort them out."

She finished her coffee and stood up. "Let me think about it."

"One question before you go?"

She didn't answer, but didn't walk away. Marti stood, as well.

"Who handled the autopsy on Thomas Foster?"

Marti didn't think she was going to answer, but after a pause, she did. "State Police."

Marti knew she wouldn't get anything else. Not right then. What was with all the people involved in this? Extracting useful information was like trying to squeeze water from a stone. She glanced down at the bag of candy. There were only two black Chuckles left. People who enjoyed black licorice were aliens to her. She dropped the bag and the empty coffee cup in the trash and headed to her car.

Marti merged onto the Turnpike, the miles of concrete strung out like a dark ribbon under the afternoon sun. She settled the Subaru in the middle lane, secured the Bluetooth earpiece, and tapped Gary Mitchell's number from her contacts.

"Five minutes," he whispered and immediately hung up.

She smiled. In her 20-plus years in business, Marti had accumulated contacts and cultivated relationships with people at just about every level and location of New Jersey bureaucracy. Gary Mitchell was her contact at the State Police crime lab and had provided the occasional help and support on Marti's cases when law enforcement wasn't in a sharing mood.

Five minutes later, Gary called back. "Hey, Marti! Long time no see," he said with a tone that matched the easygoing grin he'd wear if they were face to face.

"Yeah, it's been a bit hectic on this end," Marti replied. "Listen, I need a favor."

"Of course, assuming you still have those sweet 50-yard line seats, what can I do for you?"

Marti smiled. Gary was a lifelong bachelor, but he had a nephew who was a die-hard Giants fan. "I've still got them. You working?"

"I'm on call. You know the single guy somehow always ends up with weekend duty."

"I'm looking for some information about an old autopsy report. Thomas Foster, found in The Pine Barrens back in June."

Gary made some shuffling noises on his end. "Thomas Foster, you said? Rings a vague bell, but I don't think I worked on him. Let me see what I can do."

"Listen, I'm just down the street. Can we meet up? Might be faster and I can get a look at any photographs."

Gary was never careless with the information he provided her, and neither was she. The trust she gained over time was almost invaluable. He also wasn't as paranoid or insular as most police she came across. He knew that she'd cracked more than a few cases that had hit a standstill with detectives. After a pause, he relented. "Sure, okay. It's pretty empty here. The boss should be outta here in an hour. Pull around back then. I'll let you in."

Gary stood casually against the brick exterior of the lab building. Gary was a slender man in his late forties. He wore jeans and a wrinkled lab coat over a light blue Oxford. He waved a hand in greeting as Marti maneuvered her Subaru into a nearby parking space.

"What the hell happened to your head?" he said as a greeting when she approached.

She touched the bandage above her ear and could feel the stitches through the dressing. "Got jumped in the middle of the night in my hotel room. I've got a bruise that looks like a map of Asia across my ribs."

"Same case?"

"Yup."

"Huh," was all he said. Gary was most comfortable behind a microscope, not out in the field. He shook off whatever feeling her beating had stirred up. "Come on back. I'll show you what I found."

He used a key card attached to his belt and held the door open for her.

"So, how are you involved in this?" he asked as he led her down a dark, tiled hallway. At this hour, on a weekend, the place was largely deserted.

"I came across Foster's name through a detective out in Cedarwood. Bill Thompson. Did you see any reference to him in the file?"

"No, not that I noticed."

"Thompson himself died a little while back. Natural causes. Heart attack. I talked to the ME. I'm working for his widow. She's looking for answers of some kind. Says he was very stressed out and distracted leading up to his death and she wants to know why."

"Cedarwood PD didn't say?"

"No, I haven't made much progress with them. They're all being very tight-lipped. I don't know if it's on purpose or just a reaction to my natural charm."

Gary led her to a small bare box of a room at the end of the hall. There was a round conference table, two chairs, and a speakerphone. "Take a seat. I'll grab the file."

He returned a minute later with a laptop and placed it on the table between them. He took a seat and let her work through it on her own. She'd read her fair share of autopsy reports over the years. Each jurisdiction was slightly different, but largely the same overall. She started with the photographs. It had taken a while for the body to be found. There was evidence of animal and bug activity. The remaining skin was dark, almost black. The surrounding terrain was rough. Thick trees, low shrubs, and rocks. She recalled the newspaper report mentioning the body being found in a remote and dense part of The Pine Barrens. Looking at the photos, Marti thought it was lucky that someone found the body at all.

She paused and stared at one photo. "Are those stakes?"

"Yes. That's why it was vaguely familiar. The guy's hands and feet were bound."

"That wasn't in the papers."

"No, it wasn't. Sort of surprised it didn't get out."

Marti agreed. "He was tortured?"

"No. Not in the traditional sense."

Marti glanced over at him. "What does that mean?"

"It means it's probably why it didn't get out, or if it did, the press didn't know what to do with it. There were no signs of trauma on the body. No wounds. No broken bones. The skin around the wrists and ankles was abraded, but that's it."

"Other than the stakes."

"Right. A stake as a murder weapon is unusual. First guess was a suicide of some kind. But no note and it doesn't really hold up anyway."

"So, what? He was subdued to death?"

Gary shrugged. "The official cause of death was ultimately ruled dehydration."

She suppressed a shiver. It wasn't torture, by a strict definition, but it wasn't a pleasant way to die. "How long would that take?"

"Our bodies are 50 to 70 percent water, which means an average man contains up to 10 gallons. So, probably about a week. When our bodies are deprived of water, they take water from other organs. It starts with the kidneys and ultimately leads to organ failure and brain shrinkage as the blood thickens and blood pressure drops. Everything... dries out. You become like a piece of jerky. If you were cut, you wouldn't even bleed. Dehydration is considered one of the most painful and protracted deaths a human can experience."

"Ah, God, Gary. That's a disturbing image and sounds very much like torture to me."

Gary nodded. "Slow, painful torture. Nothing remarkable about the ropes or the stakes. Garden variety hemp rope that's available at every Home Depot or local hardware store. Stakes were made onsite. Cut from a nearby sapling."

Marti frowned at that bit of information. Whoever had killed Foster was confident in their skills. She flipped through more pages. No personal effects were found with the body. "He started as a John Doe. It's in the initial notes. How did you get an ID? Missing persons reports?"

"Nope. That's another interesting bit. As far as I know, no one ever reported Foster missing. We were able to get a partial print, despite the body's deterioration, and that led us to Tom Nixon."

"Tom Nixon? Who's that?"

"Tom Nixon is Thomas Foster. Army Chaplain Tom Nixon. That's how we were able to make the ID. His prints are in the system. He served in Desert Storm and the aftermath. Was over there from '91 to almost '95."

"And eventually changed his name."

"That's right. Lucky for us, he changed it in New Jersey or we might not have found it. The petition came up in a routine record search once we had the Nixon surname."

"When was the petition filed?"

"Uh, I can't recall. I only glanced at it. It's in there. There was a copy of it along with the summary sheet of his Army discharge papers. It's at the back."

Marti jumped to the end of the file and then scrolled back. She scanned the Army summation. Honorable discharge in '95 due to the end of service term. He was eligible for reenlistment but declined. The rest were dry details and shed little light on Chaplain Nixon. He'd served, apparently adequately, but with little distinction. The section for additional comments or notes from superiors was blank. There was a small photo in the upper right corner. She realized it was the first time she'd seen Thomas Foster, though he would have been Tom Nixon at the time. The photo showed a man in his late 20s with a clean-shaven face, bright eyes, and a serious, yet somewhat somber expression. Her eyes lingered on a faint scar on his left cheek below his eye, and she realized she'd likely never know if it was from a combat wound or just a boyhood accident. She considered snapping a photo of the headshot with her phone but then thought it would be useless. It was a 30-year-old snapshot of a dead man. She scrolled farther back in the file.

The page before the Army record was the name change. It was also a straightforward rote government document that stated Thomas Nixon was changing his legal name to Thomas Foster. It was dated July 18, 2010.

"Why do you think he changed his name?" Marti said as she pushed back from the table and rubbed her eyes. "You don't need to state a reason to change your name as an adult, but there are some basic checks run before the petition is approved. You can't do it to dodge prosecution or hide from debt collection. The court would catch that and deny it."

"True," Gary said, "but you could do it to escape the past."

Chapter Thirty-Three

The day caught up to Marti as she drove back to Cedarwood. Her eyelids grew heavy and she struggled to focus. So much for the power of candy and caffeine. She lowered the car windows. The cold breeze slapped her face and jolted her back to a semblance of alertness. She realized with a sinking feeling that it might be a longer road back to normal than she wanted to admit.

As she pulled into Sandy's driveway, relief washed over her. She only wanted to get inside, crawl into bed, even an unfamiliar bed, and surrender to sleep. But her plans were derailed when she spotted Sandy on the porch. The woman was pacing back and forth, her hands nervously wringing together.

Marti parked the car and climbed out, ignoring the burst of pain from her ribs. For the moment, the sight of Sandy had chased away the last remnants of Marti's fatigue.

"Sandy, what's going on?" she asked, coming up the steps. "Are you all right?"

"Someone's been inside," she said. "I just called Kevin. He's on his way."

"Are they still here?" Marti said as she looked over the woman's shoulder through the open front door and into the hallway. She thought of her gun, still locked up back in Jersey City. Given her current physical limitations, the attack on her at the inn, and now someone potentially breaking into Sandy's house, maybe she should drive back and get it. She didn't like guns, but they were effective tools that served a purpose, and it wasn't going to help her a whole hell of a lot locked up back in her apartment. Something to think about.

"No, I don't think so. I haven't heard anything. I think they're gone."

"What happened?"

"I know this sounds odd, but I'm sure someone was inside while I was gone. It's not trashed. I can't spot anything missing, but I have a hinky feeling. Something's off. I know my own home, especially since Bill died. You get a feel for it, you know? Like putting on an old coat."

Marti had lived most of her life alone and she knew exactly what Sandy meant. "Maybe one of the kids stopped by?"

"No, I called all three."

"Maybe it's just me, having me around as a houseguest?"

"No, I don't think that's it either."

"How'd they get in?" Marti asked. She moved over to the door and bent to examine the lock. Sandy hesitated, and Marti knew what she was going to say. "You left it open?"

"I just had to run over to the church. I was barely gone an hour. Maybe a little more. No one locks their doors around here for something like that."

"Okay," Marti held up her hands. "What about a neighbor? Or someone else? Were you expecting anyone?"

"Please, I know what people have been saying. I know what they think about me, especially since Bill's death. I hear the whispers." She glanced down at her feet. "I don't think anyone stopped by for a visit."

Marti didn't know what to say to that and was saved from responding when a Cedarwood cruiser came down the road, no lights, but driving quickly.

Kevin pulled up close behind the Subaru and stepped out. "What's going on?" he said as he stepped out, one hand on the butt of his service weapon as he looked around.

"I think someone's been in the house," Sandy said. "Maybe searched through Bill's office."

Marti glanced at her. She hadn't said that the first time. They all met up near the steps.

"Searched Bill's office? Why?" Kevin asked.

"I don't know." She ran her hands through her hair. "I'm sure someone was inside, but I can't explain it. Like I told Marti, you just know your own house and you know when things have been ... disturbed."

Marti moved toward the door. She didn't need to hear Sandy's story again. She wanted to look at the office, but Kevin called out. "Hold up. Let me take a run through the house. Unlikely that someone is still here, but better safe than sorry." He gave Marti a look and she knew he was thinking about the hotel room assault. She backed away until her knees hit the edge of one of the Adirondack chairs. She sat and the fatigue crashed back in.

Kevin mounted the steps and disappeared inside. Sandy came over and sat down in the opposite chair. After a moment, she spoke up. "I tried to call. A few times. You disappeared Friday morning without a word. I've been waiting to hear from you."

Marti looked over, but the other woman wouldn't meet her eyes. Her tone was injured, almost aggrieved. Marti felt the heat rise on the back of her neck, but she was too worn out to get worked up about it. "I told you Thursday night that I would be gone early." It sounded defensive.

"Yes, I remember, but you never said where or what you were working on. Was it even Bill's case? Have you given up?"

Marti felt the anger kindle again but not catch fire. "This situation is a little unusual. I don't usually stay in my client's guest room. I work the case and you get reports. You need to give me room to do the job you hired me for."

"I understand." Even though the whining tone in her voice said she didn't.

"I'm here now." She spent the next five minutes briefing Sandy on her trip to Rehoboth Beach, Tom Nixon, The Dawn Patrol, and Jennifer Anderson. She kept a few things a little vague. The conversation with Jake. Bill's frequent calls to Anderson. It was harder to tell just small lies, even if she was trying to protect Sandy. It didn't appear that Bill and Jennifer had anything other than a professional relationship, but why put even the suspicion in her head? "For what it's worth, I think whatever was bothering Bill was about work and had nothing to do with you."

"Then why didn't he just tell me?"

"You told me he liked to keep things separate. Work and home."

"I know. I know, but if this was just about a case, then why won't anyone just tell me that? Why did someone attack you? Or break into my house?"

All good questions that Marti didn't have answers for yet. "Do you remember Bill taking a trip? This would have been back in June. Maybe overnight?"

"Yes, I think so. He was gone two days. Is that when he went to Delaware?"

"Probably."

"Why was this Tom Nixon so important? If the body was found up in The Pine Barrens, how was Bill even involved?"

"I don't know. If it's an active homicide investigation, even a cold case, we might hit a dead end. As a PI, I don't have a lot of leverage in those situations. It doesn't appear Bill or Cedarwood PD were officially involved. Even if you back me up, I'll likely get stonewalled."

"What? Why? They can't stop you from asking questions."

"No, they can't, and that's exactly what I've been doing around here, but they can refuse to answer. I'm effectively a concerned citizen who is allowed to carry a gun."

"And you'll just give up? That doesn't seem like a good use of my money. If you're going to roll over, just tell me now."

Marti sat up straight in the chair and felt a jab in her ribs. This time, the anger caught. This was a side of Sandy she hadn't seen but matched up with some stories she'd heard from others in town. "Why are you angry with me? I'm doing what I can. What do you expect? I've talked to everyone relevant. I've been stalked and assaulted and ended up in the hospital. I think you've gotten your money's worth."

Before Sandy could respond, Kevin stepped out the front door. She hadn't heard him approach and Marti wondered how long he'd been standing there and what he'd heard. "No one inside. Nothing broken. No sign of anything missing. Did you check?" he asked, looking at Sandy.

She gave a half nod. "I didn't see anything either, but I'll look again. I was a little frazzled."

"No signs of forced entry on any of the doors or windows. Nothing out back." It was clear from his tone he thought Sandy was seeing ghosts.

"Okay," Sandy said. "Thank you for coming so quickly, Kevin. I appreciate it."

Kevin went down the steps. "Any time, you know that." He gave them both a wave, got in his cruiser, and backed out.

"Listen," Marti said, and carefully pushed herself to her feet. "I need some sleep. I'm sorry I didn't stay in touch better, but trust me, I'm working the case."

"I know," Sandy said. "I apologize for jumping down your throat. This has me …"

Marti waved her off. "Let's start over in the morning. I've got a few more leads. Let's see where they go before deciding what to do next."

Marti lay in the guest room and couldn't fall asleep. Sandy's words had gotten under her skin, and she now felt restless and frustrated in the face of her accusations. Had she done all she could on the case? What was she not seeing? Who else could she talk to in town? Her legs twitched under the sheet and she stared at the ceiling as her mind wore grooves in the familiar questions. When her phone lit up just after midnight, she was still awake and welcomed the distraction, despite the time.

"Hello?"

"I don't even know why I'm calling."

It sounded like Jennifer Anderson had been drinking.

"Because you liked Bill."

"True."

"And you want to tell someone the rest of it."

"Maybe, but more the first thing."

"I never met him, obviously, but everyone tells me he was a solid guy. Good husband, a dedicated officer. When did you first meet him?"

"He showed up at my office asking about Thomas Foster. I'm not sure how he got my name. Bill was good at digging up information. We hit it off, which is rare for me, I'll admit. We traded war stories, histories, experience, the usual stuff between cops."

"I don't want to ask this, but I have to. There were some department rumors in Cedarwood about another woman and Bill. Was that you?"

"Someone trying to stir up trouble, huh?"

"I think it's just a small town." Marti thought of Lucille's comments. "They like their local gossip more than Netflix."

"No law against flirting, but I can tell you Bill lived up to his reputation. Nothing ever happened. It was always about work first."

"Thomas Foster aka Tom Nixon."

"How'd you hear about that?"

"I wouldn't be very good at my job if I didn't have my own sources. Did Bill ever say why he was interested in Foster?"

"He was cagey about it. He thought it might be related to a case he was working on in Cedarwood."

"Did he say which one?"

"No, he just said he had a body that shared similarities."

"Body? So, it was a homicide?"

"Yes."

"He didn't tell you any more than that?"

"No, he didn't tell me any specifics."

"You didn't find that strange? You were also a cop."

"Not really. Wasn't my case. I didn't need the extra work."

"I have his phone records. You spoke several times."

"True. He called regularly to check in on the investigation." Despite what she'd said earlier, Marti wondered if that was all they talked about. Anderson continued, "I'm sure if he discovered anything relevant to Foster, he would have shared it, but I had the sense that his case up there might have been old or stalled out just like ours." Marti thought about the stacks of cold case files in the office. "I do know he felt responsible for Foster's death."

That made her inch up on the pillow. "What? How?"

"He believed someone had used the information he'd gathered on Foster to track him down and kill him before he could get to Foster himself."

"Really? How did he think that happened? Sandy keeps telling me the man was a vault. He never talked about his work outside of the job."

"That might be true."

The realization hit Marti like a sledgehammer. "He suspected a fellow officer?"

"That's my guess. He never came out and said it, but it makes sense to me. Either someone overheard him, or he discussed it with someone, or someone got a look at his notes. It would also explain his dilemma. Why he might have felt so stressed and conflicted. Bill had blue running through his veins. If someone betrayed the department, the brotherhood, it would have hit at the very core of the man's beliefs. I think that's what could have been tearing him apart."

"Foster was living in a cut-rate motel doing odd jobs for cash. He was mostly off the grid, from what I can tell, and I think that's the way he wanted it. How did Bill even track him down?"

"I told you Bill was good at digging things up. He might have looked like a big, dumb ox, but he was no dummy."

Marti could almost hear her smile through the phone. She really had liked the man. Maybe more than liked him. She thought about it. How would she do it if she'd had to find Foster? She ran through her mental playbook and came up with only one answer. "He followed the money."

"You're no slouch yourself. Foster might have been working for cash down in Delaware, but it wasn't his only source of income. He had an Army pension from his days as a chaplain. He would take a regular monthly draw off of it from ATMs. It wasn't always the same ATM, but they were all clustered in or around Rehoboth Beach. After that, it was just logic and a little legwork. He called all the cheap hotels until he got a hit."

"Pretty good detective work."

"I thought so."

"Do you really think he suspected a coworker in a double homicide?"

Marti thought of the officers she'd met at the small-town department: Kevin, Bill's brother; Lawson; Martinez; Ackerman. Could one of them be responsible for two bodies? The town also used the sheriff's department to fill in. That potentially broadened the pool. Then another thought hit her. The person who she'd fought in the hotel room. He'd been efficient and skilled. Did he have training? Maybe from the police academy?

"It's all speculation on my part. Bill never said anything to me directly so I can't be sure. It's one reason I did nothing. Never called IA or anyone down in Cedarwood. What would I say? I had no proof."

"If it is true, with Bill dropping dead, they must have thought they were off the hook."

"And then you come along."

"Bad luck for both of us. I start asking questions. They are confident that Bill never got his information into an official report, otherwise some additional action would have been taken." She was thinking aloud now. "But his notebook is missing."

"Maybe they've already got it."

"Doesn't make sense. If they had it, why come after me?" She thought about the break-in tonight. "I'm only dangerous if I have the notes."

"Then you better find them fast."

Chapter Thirty-Four

The night clung to Marti like a shadow she couldn't shake. She lay in bed, staring at the ceiling. Her eyelids felt heavy, her body yearning for rest, but her mind raced in a disorienting loop. The conversation with Anderson played out again and again, a relentless reel of unease that kept her eyes open. She knew she couldn't afford to be sleep-deprived, not now.

Her heart hammered inside her bruised chest and a fluttering anxiety battered her resolve. The idea that she might be stalked by someone in uniform, someone she should trust, someone with the power and authority to protect her, left her shaken. Is this what had driven Bill out into the night to die on a deserted road?

Her logical mind recognized that most in law enforcement were like Bill, dedicated individuals committed to the public good. But the seed of doubt had been planted. What if one had crossed that line? The thought gnawed at her. It raised the stakes dramatically. Would she even survive the encounter? Bill hadn't.

Marti knew one thing: she couldn't give in to fear. She pushed herself out of bed with a determination that overrode the fatigue. The house was quiet, just the occasional creak and groan of the house's foundation. A clock ticking somewhere in another room. Bill stared back at her from a photo hanging in the hallway. Her bare feet felt cold on the wood as she descended the stairs.

She stood in the office doorway and tried to feel what Sandy had felt earlier, a presence, a change, but it didn't work. It wasn't her house. She didn't have the familiarity. It remained only a cluttered, half-packed home office. She moved inside, turned on the light, and shut the door. She rummaged through the boxes stacked on the left near the bookshelf until she found the one she wanted and then carried it over and placed it on the desk.

If Anderson was correct and Bill believed Foster's death tied back to something that happened in Cedarwood, the answer might be in the box of cold case files Bill had collected or copied from the police station. She had wondered before why they were in the office. Now, she might have the answer. She'd scanned each file the first time she'd discovered the box but hadn't paid close attention. Nothing had jumped out at her as specifically important or potentially related to anything she knew Bill had been working on at the time of his death. Now, she read more carefully.

First, she went through all the files and made two different piles by date. Bill had left Paterson and moved back to his hometown 23 years prior. She put all the crimes that happened before Bill arrived in one pile and those after in another. Then she started reading.

It was a history of small-town crimes in forms, reports, and photos packaged up in manila folders. Small-town crime, like crime in urban areas, had undergone several notable changes and trends. As she read the files, she saw traditional property crimes, like theft and vandalism, drop away while new challenges, such as methamphetamine production and prescription drug abuse, rise. Cedarwood was not immune to the effects of the opioid epidemic and the proliferation of other drugs. Drug-related crimes, such as trafficking, theft, and domestic disputes, had risen sharply in the last 15 years.

After almost three hours of reading, she made it through the first pile, the unsolved crimes that had occurred since Bill returned to town. She'd pulled three files that she thought deserved a deeper look.

In 1999, Abigail St. Clair, a wealthy heiress, disappeared under baffling circumstances in Cedarwood. She was last seen leaving her house for a charity event but never arrived. Her car was found abandoned on the outskirts of town, but no trace of Abigail. The case gained national attention, but despite extensive investigations, there were no leads. Bill was the lead detective and it was by far his highest-profile case. Marti remembered it, even if she hadn't immediately connected it to Cedarwood. The pressure on Bill at that time must have been intense. There was no body to compare to Foster's, but had this case left a mark? Had it stayed with him over the years? Did he feel guilty? Professionally wounded?

In 2005, a young couple, John and Lisa, ventured into the remote woods of Cedarwood for a romantic getaway in a secluded cabin. Their belongings were found in the cabin, including their packs, but the couple was never seen again. Search efforts yielded no results and the case went cold. Because the disappearances happened in the remote wilderness, similar to Foster's in The Pine Barrens, she set it aside.

Finally, in the summer of 2008, the town was shaken by the discovery of Father Joseph Moran's body in the woods behind St. Mark's Parish. Reading through the interview statements, Father Moran was known and loved by the community, and his death was a profound shock, but the investigation soon hit a dead end. The autopsy revealed no signs of foul play but noted heatstroke and subsequent dehydration as the likely cause of death. The parallels to Foster, the mention of dehydration and religious life, made her add it to the follow-up pile.

Marti's eyes fluttered open at 10:00 a.m., much later than her usual wake-up time. She lay there for a moment, feeling slightly sweaty and disoriented. Her sleep had been restless, plagued by a sense of unease, but she couldn't remember any specific dreams and chalked it up to the accumulation of stress and exhaustion. The fear she'd felt last night over the potential involvement of a cop wasn't gone but had receded. She could feel it lurking at the back of her mind.

From downstairs, the sounds of clinking dishes and the aroma of freshly brewed coffee drifted up to her room. Sandy was up. Marti knew her client had probably been awake for hours. She was probably silently judging her for sleeping so late. With a sigh, Marti swung her legs over the side of the bed. Stiff and sore. Check. It was hard to believe the attack in her room at the inn had only been two days ago. She slipped across the hall to the bathroom and forced herself to strip and look in the mirror.

The bright-white light did her no favors. She removed the dressing over her ear and gingerly touched the stitches. Tender but healing. She could strategically cover them with her hair. She tossed the old dressing in the trash. The left side of her body was a horrifying, mottled bruise that extended from her shoulder to her navel. There were new bruises on her arms and legs, vibrant shades of purple and black that she hadn't known existed, but at least this morning she could move without the searing pain that had previously accompanied every breath.

"Progress," she mumbled to herself. Progress was all she could hope for right now.

She turned on the shower and let the scalding water wash away the previous day's miles. She toweled off, dressed slowly, and then descended the stairs. The scent of coffee grew stronger with each step. She found Sandy in the kitchen, her back to the door, pouring coffee into two mugs. She glanced over her shoulder.

"Morning," Sandy said. "There's cereal and granola bars in the pantry," she pointed at a slim, tall door, "or eggs in the fridge if you want to make something hot." She handed Marti a mug.

"Thanks," Marti said. Making scrambled eggs was actually within Marti's limited kitchen skill set, but not at a stranger's house. She went to the pantry and found a peanut butter granola bar before taking a seat at the kitchen table with her mug.

Sandy still looked tired and subdued. Marti noticed the pot of coffee was half empty, so she'd been awake for some time but was still wearing a pink bathrobe topped with disheveled hair. No morning run today.

"Were you in Bill's office last night?" she asked. "The light was on this morning."

"Yes, sorry. I came back down because I couldn't sleep. Figured I might as well work."

"Find anything?"

"Yes, actually. I think I might have an idea about what Bill was working on. What might have been bothering him."

"Really?" She set her mug down and leaned closer.

"I haven't nailed down the details, but I'm getting close, still mostly guesses and hunches at this point. It can't go any further yet, understand? I need to firm this up before we involve anyone else."

"Okay, but what was it?"

"I'm not sure how to tell you this, Sandy."

"Jesus, just say it. It can't be worse than anything I've already imagined."

"I think Bill suspected someone in the department or someone in law enforcement of a double homicide."

Sandy raised a hand to her mouth and stared across the table at Marti as she absorbed the information. "No, I don't believe it."

"I know. I don't want to believe it either, but that doesn't make it less of a possibility. Think about it. It had to be something harsh and almost unbelievable to affect him so much, right? Wouldn't this do it? If he found, heck, even suspected, a link between murders and it was a fellow officer? It would shake him up. Bad. It would affect his behavior and moods like you observed."

Marti watched her fight against it.

"Where did this second body come from? Last night you told me about a Tom Nixon that they found out in The Pine Barrens. Who's the other body?"

"I don't know. That's the hunch part. That's what I was doing in the office last night and will continue working on today. I want to find out what led Bill to Tom Nixon. We know that wasn't his case, but if I can find the link and work backward, it should lead us to what he was working on. I know he played everything very close to the vest, but did he ever mention any old cases? Cold cases he was looking at?"

She watched Sandy go back through her memories, but she shook her head. "No, not that I recall."

"I found a box of the last 50 years' worth of cold cases from Cedarwood in his office. I believe it is something in there, a case from Cedarwood's past, that put him on the trail of Tom Nixon and potentially looking at suspects in his own department."

"Bill gave his life to this town and that department. I don't want to ruin that legacy. I'm not sure I want to even raise the question based on hunches and guesses."

"They are educated guesses, Sandy, not wild conjecture. We'll never know anything for sure unless someone comes forward and confesses. And that seems unlikely."

Sandy looked down at her mug, then out the window into the backyard. "I hope I didn't make a mistake in hiring you." Her tone was bitter.

Marti felt irritation rise in her throat, and she fought to keep it out of her voice. "What did you expect, Sandy? I made no guarantees. In fact, I tried to talk you out of hiring me, if you recall. I can only follow the information where it leads. Sometimes it leads to unpleasant places. I won't apologize for that. I'm doing the job you wanted. Or thought you wanted."

Sandy waved her hand as if dismissing Marti's objections, but she dropped that line of personal attack. "Who told you this? Who told you Bill thought it was another officer?"

"A source in law enforcement."

"You don't want to tell me?"

"A confidential source."

Marti didn't see any reason or benefit to telling Sandy about Jennifer Anderson or the small torch Anderson might have carried for Bill. It could only lead Sandy to imagine other reasons for Bill's behavior.

"If what you are saying is true, their name will come out eventually. These are serious allegations."

"You don't think I know that? This is serious and scary shit. I don't like the idea any more than you do. I don't want to go up against the cops."

"You'd be out of your league."

Marti was getting whiplash from Sandy's mood changes. She had to get out. She stood and carried her empty mug to the kitchen sink.

"It's not just me. Maybe I've just got the common sense to see it. Anyone would be out of their league. Bill was out of his league. It broke his damn heart."

Chapter Thirty-Five

There was nothing like sitting with your fear and staring it in the face. Marti sat on a bench next to the gazebo in the town square and sipped an Americano from Harmony's Brew. The quaint town center was vibrant and bustling on this sunny Sunday morning. No sign of a masked man. No sign of a crooked red smile. No sign of a solitary cigarette. Families were out. Kids were running around. Dogs were sniffing the grass. Death and murder seemed inconceivable in the face of such wholesomeness. But light needs darkness and Marti knew evil was out there, even if it was hard to see. It only needed a crack to get in.

The Americano was good, but not as good as the one she could have gotten from Sophia at Cafe Grand back in Jersey City. She wanted to be back home with Rita and her quirky neighbors. She wanted to go for a run along the river and eat garlic fries from JJ's. She did not want to dig any deeper into the darkness that killed Bill Thompson. But she wouldn't quit. She was stubborn. You had to be in her business. But she wasn't stupid. You didn't go up against evil emptyhanded.

She took out her phone.

"Blossoms and Buds."

"Have you ever heard of a town called Cedarwood?" Marti asked.

"Actually, I have. Smudge on the map, right? Speck of a place off 78 somewhere, I think? We've done a few weddings up there. I remember a lot of woods," Gwen Torres said. Gwen owned a small flower shop called Blossoms and Buds, nestled in the heart of Greenwich Village. But that simple description didn't tell the whole story.

Gwen's past was a web of contradictions, as intricate as the city she called home. Raised in Corona, in Queens, she found herself sucked into gangs and the criminal underworld. Yet, her grandparents offered a starkly different world, a tranquil Upstate farm where Gwen spent summers. The contrast between city and countryside, darkness and serenity, eventually pulled her out of gang life and drove her to open a flower shop in the Village, an unexpected twist for those who knew her history.

Marti often grappled with the guilt of drawing her friend back into her darker side, but Gwen embraced it. She believed it was a necessary counterbalance. Their paths first crossed in a self-defense class, with Gwen as the instructor and Marti as the student. Their unlikely friendship formed the basis for their continued, occasional, partnership, where Gwen's unique skills and background often proved invaluable in Marti's cases.

"How would you feel about a Sunday scenic drive?"

"I do like to look at the foliage."

Marti spent the next few minutes filling Gwen in on Bill Thompson and what she'd been up to for the past week.

"And you're getting the bad juju?"

"The worst. Not just vibes. You should see my ribs."

"And you want me to bring you your gun? Maybe you should walk. You have nothing to prove, Marti."

"Oh, come on, Gwen. I'm a woman PI. Of course, I have something to prove. I can't let this guy intimidate me and think he can just run me out of town with a good rib kicking."

Gwen gave a soft laugh. "Okay. I had to try, but a girl's gotta do what a girl's gotta do."

"I know I'm being stubborn, but I'm not being naïve. This is bad, Gwen. All of it. I can sense this dread closing in like an oncoming storm. He fractured three ribs when I was clueless. What's he going to do when he realizes I'm closing in?"

Marti placed her phone back in her bag. Her Americano had cooled to the perfect temperature, and she savored the last few sips. Her gaze drifted to a young boy, three or four years old, toddling along in the grass after his older sister. They laughed and played a game that only they could understand. Marti watched them, feeling a mix of emotions. She tried to let the simple joy of their interaction fill her up, to hold onto a fragment of that unspoiled world. She knew she might need it. She hadn't been joking with Gwen. The creeping dread was almost a physical presence on the path she was headed down.

Marti was a private investigator to her bones, a woman who thrived on untangling mysteries, large or small. Fear and apprehension were not unfamiliar companions. It was time to get to work.

She stood and tossed her cup in the trash and then turned her back on the idyllic town square. Her thoughts returned to Bill Thompson and the cold case that had led him to Thomas Foster/Tom Nixon. That was the thread she needed to pull on. She could feel it. She'd been at this long enough to know. It was the subtle vibrations—like tiny tremors—that told her she'd finally caught the scent. The case had been lifeless for the past week, but had sparked to life in the last 24 hours. If she could unravel the connection between those two cases, she might finally understand the puzzle that had consumed Bill's last days. Who killed Thomas Foster and who might have feared the truth Bill was closing in on?

Gwen wouldn't arrive for a few more hours and she knew just the person who could help her pass the time. She strolled across the town green and through the vibrant Cedarwood Inn gardens until she reached the little house nestled at the back. Lucille was already waiting by the door, a wry smile playing on her lips.

"I wondered when you would show up again," she said.

Inside, the small living room was cozy, if Marti was feeling polite, filled with the lingering cooking scents of fry oil and onions with the briefest hint of hot plastic. It was like stepping into a time capsule, a room filled with chipped furniture, yellowed doilies, and peeling floral wallpaper. A large, boxy television took up most of one wall. Two trays leaned against the wall and Marti understood why the room smelled like microwave dinners.

Lucille led Marti past a leather recliner that didn't match the other furniture in the room. A man sat in it, his eyes glazed and distant. "This is George, my husband," she paused, maybe to see if he'd respond, "he's mostly not here anymore."

Dressed in a faded plaid shirt and worn, comfortable jeans, George continued to stare at the television and didn't appear to recognize their presence. There was a crisp side part of his full head of silver hair, and his cheeks were smooth of stubble. Marti could see the man he used to be in his broad shoulders and large hands that now trembled slightly as they gripped the arms of the recliner.

Lucille gestured for Marti to take a seat, and they settled into a pair of well-worn armchairs that faced a picture window that overlooked the rear of the inn and the gardens. "I'm glad they didn't run you off," Lucille said, her voice tinged with gratitude and maybe a touch of sadness.

Marti tilted her head slightly. "Who's 'they'?" she asked.

Lucille waved away the question with the same smile. "Just an expression," she replied, her gaze distant. Then, returning her focus to Marti, she asked with genuine concern, "How are you feeling? How are the ribs?"

Marti guessed this reaction was less about her well-being and more about the potential for her to sue the inn over being attacked in her room. Marti had no intention of doing that, but she thought the vague threat might be useful during this interview. "Lucille, someone ambushed me in the middle of the night and I spent a day in the hospital while they checked my lungs for bone chips. How do you think I feel?" She delivered these words with a smile, but also a hint of menace. "I feel like a wounded animal trying to stay ahead of the hunter," Marti admitted, her smile fading as she spoke.

"I'm just so relieved you are already up and about and weren't more seriously hurt. People are talking. They looked you up on the internet. You've killed people. More than one."

"All of those were in self-defense, Lucille. I'm not going around executing people for my clients."

"Oh dear, I didn't mean that. I just meant that you are no pushover. Nobody's going to scare you off. You might have disappeared for a day, but now you are back on the case." She said this with a smile that showed too many teeth and put cracks in the foundation on her cheeks. Marti thought it was curious that her trip to Delaware and absence around town had been noted. She was being closely watched. She'd have to remember that. Maybe she could even use that.

"I stopped by to ask you about some local history," Marti said. She wasn't about to justify her own history to Lucille.

"Of course, dear. I'll try to help however I can."

She pulled her notebook out and glanced at the notes she'd taken while reading the cold case files. "I want to know everything you heard about the couple who disappeared from the cabin near Wacha Lake in 2005. What did the folks around here say that might not be in the official file?"

Lucille sighed and her gaze shifted to the dusty curtains as she remembered. "That case has been the subject of endless whispers around here, especially this time of year. It happened right around now."

Marti raised an eyebrow, encouraging Lucille to continue. Not that the woman needed much encouragement. She was in her element. Her voice dropped to a hushed tone. "People say that lake is cursed. That even the animals avoid it like they know something we don't."

Marti tried to hide her disappointment. She didn't believe in ghosts and she didn't think Bill did, either. "Cursed? How so?"

"They say strange things happen around that cabin. Whispers in the night, ghostly figures at the edge of the woods, and voices carried by the wind. Some even claim to hear laughter echoing through the trees."

"And what about the cabin itself? Anything unusual there?"

"The cabin, they say, was like a time capsule, locked in the moment they left. Food on the table, clothes folded neatly, and the old FM radio still turned on. It's like they vanished into thin air."

"So, the locals think it's more than just a missing persons case?"

Lucille nodded solemnly. "In this town, dear, we've learned to trust our instincts. Sometimes, there are monsters in the dark."

Marti knew that while most of Lucille's story was nonsense, just fiction filling the gap when lacking facts, she thought the last part was true. She'd seen a lot of darkness in her career, and it was often stranger and more twisted than she'd imagined, but it was never supernatural. It was always human.

"I want to ask about two more cases if you have the time. Tell me about Abigail St. Clair. The official story is weird enough, but I have a feeling you have a theory."

Lucille's eyes again took on a far-off look. "Oh, Abby's disappearance. Another story that's been whispered about for years. A wealthy heiress gone missing from her own life."

"What's the local take?"

"People say she was tired of that life, all the opulence and pressure, even though anyone in town would have likely traded places with her in a hot minute," Lucille said. "Most believe she vanished deliberately, to escape from her responsibilities, like some sort of runaway princess. She siphoned off some money, went south, someplace warm and cheap, and lives like a local."

No whiff of the supernatural. "And the car they found? Abandoned on the outskirts of town?"

Lucille chuckled softly. "Money can buy you a lot of things."

"What do they mean by that? She had help?"

Lucille nodded. "Maybe. Her purse, her shoes, everything was inside that car. If she didn't pay someone, then people around here think that it was a message, a riddle she left behind."

"A riddle? Why?"

"Abby could be a little eccentric. I could see her doing that. Setting up some kind of game." Marti saw the gleam in her eye and realized this wasn't something people around here said, it was what Lucille said. This was her pet theory. "She lived alone up there on the hill. She was rich, but also lonely. Maybe she was looking for a spark in her life and liked the idea of leading everyone on a wild goose chase, with the answers right in front of them. The estate hasn't been sold. Maybe there's a reward."

And there it is, thought Marti. A reward. A long-shot lottery ticket. Impossible not to speculate about on long winter nights.

"But that didn't happen. She was never found."

Lucille sat back in her chair. "That's right. If she left a trail, she's been waiting over 20 years for someone to find it."

Marti wasn't ready to write this one off. Bill had been the lead detective and it generated a lot of publicity. Coming up on retirement, maybe he wanted to go back to the beginning and tie up loose ends. This would be a big loose end, but Marti knew from her father that it was a fool's errand. By dumb luck or pure chance, sometimes the bad guys are going to get away or sometimes the mystery is going to remain unsolved. You could drive yourself crazy trying to close every case at all costs.

That thought stopped Marti. Maybe that's exactly what happened to Bill. Maybe it wasn't one case, but the weight of all the unsolved cases that eventually dragged him down. A sobering thought, but not helpful. If that was the case, she'd never get an answer for Sandy. And what about chasing down Thomas Foster? No, she had to think it was more specific. It wasn't a slow slide into depression; Sandy had said it was more distinct than that. It was in the last six months that his behavior noticeably changed. There was a trigger.

"There's one more case—the priest found in the woods," she looked down at her notes, "Father Moran. What can you tell me about that?"

Lucille's expression grew solemn. "Ah, Father Moran. That one sent shockwaves through Cedarwood, let me tell you. Father Moran was a kind soul, deeply loved by the community. His death was like a dark cloud over the parish."

"Did you attend his church?"

"Yes, before ... George got sick. We went to St. Mark's. Father Moran was a good man. A good priest."

"What happened?"

Lucille's lips pinched into a frown. "A lot of nasty rumors. Any time you mix the church with a tragedy, you get the usual gossip. Satanism, the occult, old religious secrets, cryptic texts."

"You didn't buy into that?" Marti asked, a little surprised given how much she seemed to enjoy sharing the ghost stories about the missing couple.

"Of course, I didn't believe any of that poppycock."

"What do you think happened?"

"I certainly don't think it was murder. I think it was a terrible tragedy. I think he was walking in those woods and had a medical episode and God called him home." Marti did not believe in organized religion, not anymore, she'd had her fill as a child, and maybe that showed on her face. Lucille continued, "You don't have to take my word for it. Ask Sandy."

"What do you mean?"

"Sandy has been involved with St. Mark's for as long as I can remember. If anyone would know the inside story, other than the police, it would be her."

Chapter Thirty-Six

Marti left Lucille's and stepped back into the late-morning light. She felt the innkeeper's eyes on her as she followed the crushed stone path through the inn's gardens back onto the sidewalk. She took out her phone. Lucille was right, and Marti should have realized it sooner with the church connection. She needed to talk to Sandy, but her call rolled directly into voicemail. Annoyed, more at herself than Sandy, for missing the opportunity, Marti sighed and watched an elegantly dressed older couple walk past in the direction of one of the steeples. She realized Sandy was likely at mass. It was easy to lose track of the days out here. For a moment, she considered driving to St. Mark's and waiting, but she had to meet with Gwen in half an hour at the scenic overlook off Route 78. There wasn't enough time for both. Sandy would have to wait.

Then she had another thought. She briskly walked across the green to Harmony's Brew. She had taken her Americano to go earlier and hadn't noticed if Olivia was working, but if she was, maybe she could tell Marti something about Father Moran. Marti remembered the photo in Bill's office. The one that showed the siblings posing near the altar. The kids had been involved in the church. Marti was sure Sandy would have insisted on it.

The café was bustling with late-morning weekend diners. Three waitresses darted between crowded tables and additional counter staff handled takeout orders, but Olivia was nowhere in sight. Perhaps she was attending church with her mother. As Marti went back out, she thought, if there was a higher power, this is what her heaven might smell like. Dark roasted coffee, butter, syrup, and chocolate croissants.

Twenty minutes later, Marti arrived at the scenic overlook just off Route 78. It was a quiet spot with a breathtaking view of the rolling hills and dense forests that populated western New Jersey. Now close to noon, the sun was high and cast the landscape in flat shadows and stark shades of orange and red from the fall foliage.

Gwen was already there, waiting patiently on a wooden bench that looked out over the valley. There was a black backpack at her feet. Gwen had a unique presence, not someone you'd easily forget. She was almost a foot shorter than Marti, petite and small-boned, with a stylish black bob haircut; her hair's aquamarine tips gave her a touch of eccentricity. Most wouldn't guess at the depths of her knowledge and experience just by looking at her. People made assumptions. That was Gwen's biggest advantage.

Gwen was a high-level expert at Brazilian Capoeira, a mix of dance and martial arts. She was equally proficient in the precise strikes of Muay Thai. Along with owning the flower shop, she was a sought-after bodyguard and security expert among certain clientele. Her less-than-savory past also gave her knowledge and contacts in the criminal underworld, and she had information on some of New York's most dangerous individuals tucked away. People she had grown up with, just street rats then, like her, now ruled over some of the most dangerous gangs in the city.

Marti couldn't help but smile as she approached Gwen, happy to see her friend. Gwen's sharp eyes softened as she stood and greeted Marti with a warm embrace. Which immediately made Marti yelp.

"If a hug makes you chirp like that, I'm not sure I should give you this bag." Gwen nudged the backpack at her feet.

"Believe it or not, I'm feeling better, but I'm going to be sore for weeks."

"Ribs are the worst," Gwen agreed.

They sat on the bench and looked out at the colorful canopy of leaves. It was a companionable silence. Traffic whisked by behind them. The occasional crow circled overhead.

"I could take a few days off, come down, and watch your back," Gwen eventually said. "Or you could call Bear. I'm sure he would help."

Bear was their mutual friend, a hulking giant of a bail bondsman, who resembled a grizzly bear in size and stature, but had a gentle demeanor that made Rita Mae resemble a furious lion in comparison. Still, his six-foot-six, 300-pound frame was often enough to stop any threat of violence.

"I know, but both of you would stick out like a sore thumb in this town."

"Maybe that's not so bad. Word would get around that you've got a badass posse on your side and the next attempt will not go unpunished." She said it with a smile, but Marti knew she wasn't joking.

"I need to get some less conspicuous friends," Marti replied with a smile. "But I appreciate it. If things escalate any more, I might take you up on the offer."

"What are you going to do next?"

Marti filled her in on what Lucille had told her about the three cold cases and her decision to look into Father Moran first.

"And if that doesn't pan out?"

"Then I'm stuck. Unless I can find his notebook."

She left Gwen and headed back toward Cedarwood. The black bag sat in the passenger footwell of the Subaru. Marti's emotions swung between reassurance and unease regarding her decision. It was a familiar conflict for her, one that arose any time she contemplated carrying a gun on a job. She didn't need a shrink to tell her it was a dangerous feeling. Carrying it while being conflicted could be more perilous than not having it at all. In her line of work, being ready to use it was crucial.

Lost in this internal struggle and considering her next steps, Marti didn't immediately notice the car tailing her in the rearview mirror. She was unsure how long it had been following her. It was an unremarkable dark sedan with boxy headlights and a bouncy suspension. The slanting afternoon sunlight hindered her visibility to see much more. She tried various tactics—slowing down, speeding up—but the car shadowed her every move. Finally, she took a random turn, away from Cedarwood, and the car continued the pursuit. Marti weighed her options. The Subaru could barely outpace a bicycle and reaching a police station seemed unlikely. She didn't even know where a police station might be. She reached for her phone to use the maps app, only to discover she had no signal on the rural road.

The car lingered about 50 yards behind for two miles before abruptly speeding up. Marti debated slamming on the brakes and letting the car go past, but maybe it would end up rear-ending her. Even if it flew past, it would only be a brief respite. There was nowhere to go on this road. No escape. Just as her foot hovered over the brake, the car pulled alongside, and she glimpsed the silver aviator frames of Jessica Lawson staring back. Marti exhaled, a wave of relief washing over her. Lawson signaled for her to pull over. Marti nodded, and Lawson allowed her car to drop back.

Marti spotted a driveway coming up on her right, marked by a faded, lopsided For Sale sign. The property appeared abandoned, with an overgrown lawn and shrubbery. She spotted a few shingles missing from the roof as she turned in and parked next to a crumbling retaining wall. Lawson parked behind her and stepped out, revealing a holstered gun on her hip as she adjusted her jacket and surveyed the surroundings. Marti's gaze darted to the bag. For an ambush, this place seemed almost ideal. Would Lawson do that? No, she thought that was pretty unlikely. Someone in the Cedarwood PD might be involved, but she didn't think it was Lawson. She hadn't been on the force when Moran had been killed. Hell, she'd probably still been in high school. She saw Lawson watching her, likely wondering why she hadn't exited the car yet. Deciding to leave the bag behind, Marti finally opened her door and got out. She leaned back inside to grab her phone and activated the voice recording app. Her gut feelings had been wrong before.

"Hello, Detective Lawson."

"Marti, at this point, I think we've been through enough together to use first names."

Marti wasn't sure Lawson had exactly been through it with her so much as come along in the aftermath. She certainly didn't have her ribs kicked inside out, but Marti wasn't going to turn up her nose at any thawing in the relationship.

"How are the ribs?" Lawson asked.

"I won't be square dancing this weekend, but they're improving." Marti did a little spin to prove her point and then tried not to wince in pain. "Were you following me?" she said to cover up her discomfort.

"No, not really. Saw your car driving back."

"And then you followed me?"

Lawson took off her sunglasses and slid them into her jacket pocket. Marti was surprised to see unease in her eyes, not the coldness or combativeness she expected. Lawson didn't answer, instead, she said, "I have something for you." She turned back, opened the rear door, and pulled out a copy paper box. Marti assumed it was not full of paper. "It's the rest of the things from Bill's desk. Lisa Wilkins told me you'd asked her about them. Or, maybe Sandy was asking."

She took the box and placed it on the hood of the Subaru.

"That's right, Sandy was asking about a few things. Mementos she might pass on to the kids or something."

Marti knew there was no chance that Bill's missing case notes were inside. She was sure that Lawson had gone through each item carefully before deciding to release it to Marti.

"I called Jersey City and asked around about you," Lawson said.

That caught Marti off guard. "Really? Who did you talk to?"

"Couple detectives. Someone at the ME's office. They told me to call an NYC dick named Klein. That guy gave me an earful."

Marti felt her heart bang against her injured ribs. She and Klein had a long and bumpy history. "Doing your due diligence on the town gossip that's going around about me?"

"That's right." She paused. "As far as I'm concerned, and I'll tell the chief this too, you're okay in my book, but, Marti, you need to be careful. Not everyone might see it the same way. I haven't been here that long. My word doesn't pull the same weight as a long-time townie."

"I'm not sure what else I can do. Trying to argue or fight against rumors is only going to make me look guilty."

Lawson put her hands in her pockets and looked toward the woods and weeds slowly encroaching on the lot. "Listen, I know about your suspicions. Why don't you tell me what you've got and I'll see if I can help."

Marti stared at her for a moment and then the penny dropped. Sandy. She'd told Sandy and Sandy must have told Kevin and from there it spread like a match to an oil slick. If she didn't have a bullseye on her chest before, she did now.

"Here's one. A detective showed up at a beach bum motel in Rehoboth Beach—"

"Or someone posing as a detective."

"He was confident enough or crazy enough to bluff an arrest warrant for one Thomas Foster. I don't have access to check if it's bogus or not. I could find out back home, but not out here."

"Okay, I can do that. What else?"

Marti chose her words carefully. "I think this guy was bogus. Maybe he really was a cop serving a warrant, but something feels off. He was blowing smoke in some way."

"Did you get a name?"

"No, it was a different clerk on duty when he showed, and the guy I talked to said the other guy didn't get a name. The Sundowner is not the type of place to be all that concerned with recordkeeping."

"But you still think it was a cop? Someone from our department."

"Maybe."

Marti could see that her equivocating was useless. Lawson saw right through it.

"Based on what?"

"The timing and Bill's reaction."

"How?"

"Bill wanted to talk to Foster in connection with something that happened in Cedarwood."

"Foster is the guy named on the warrant."

"That's right."

"What did Bill want with him?"

"I'm not sure." Marti didn't know how much Lawson knew about Bill's cold cases. She guessed not much but she would keep that to herself for now. She didn't mind the help, but she wanted to stay a few steps ahead if she could. "Bill wanted to talk to this guy. That's all I know. Bill eventually drove down to Rehoboth and located him, or at least where he had been staying, but this other guy had shown up first and spooked Foster. He splits and a few weeks later his body is found in The Pine Barrens. From there, Bill starts to spiral. He's acting tense and nervous."

"According to his wife."

"The person closest to him. Isn't it possible that this is what Bill was worried about? I haven't found anything else that would come close to explaining his behavior."

"And looked at another way, the lack of evidence you've found, or didn't find, could prove my point. Bill was a great cop for almost 40 years. Of course, some cases affected him more than others, but were there any that kept him up nights at the end? No, I don't think so. Did any cause his heart attack? No."

"You don't think work could have been a contributing factor?"

"Yes, I do, but not in the way you mean. I don't think it was one thing. I think it was his entire career. Years of low-level stress. Years of eating poorly. Years of maybe a little too much drinking. You get the point. Why would this Foster guy's death cause him any more stress? Investigating death was his job."

"I think he felt responsible in a way for Foster's death."

"How?"

"He found Foster. The guy was living pretty well below the radar. I think Bill believed someone in the department used that knowledge to get to Foster first and kill him."

"How do you know what Bill believed?"

"Because that's what he told another officer."

"Who?"

"Jennifer Anderson. She was working the Foster case for the Park Police because the body was found in the Barrens."

"And Bill just told her this?"

"No, not exactly. It's what she thought from talking with him, but who else would have access to his notes?"

"Just about everyone. Bill didn't exactly lock up his notes. He left them in his truck. On his desk. Probably at home on his dresser. Plenty of people had access. It doesn't have to be someone in law enforcement."

She had a point. "You're right."

"Why don't you let me handle this?"

"Are you saying you're going to follow up on this?"

"I'm saying maybe it would be better for you to go home and recover and let the police take it from here."

"What about Sandy?"

"She was married to a cop for almost 20 years. She understands how these things work, even if she might be slow to accept it."

"No law against asking questions."

"Probably depends on who you ask." She glanced at her watch and pulled her sunglasses back out and slipped them on. "Did anyone ever fill you in on Cedarwood's history?"

"I got some of Lucille's childhood."

That produced a slight smile. Marti was sure Lawson had had her own dealings with Lucille over the years.

"Cedarwood started as a logging town." She waved a hand around. "Not hard to imagine in this area. It thrived on the timber industry, with sawmills and logging operations providing a livelihood for the residents. Over the next 150 years, Cedarwood became a close-knit community of loggers and mill workers.

"But it didn't last forever. As the logging industry waned, the town pretty much went belly up, and most residents had to leave in search of work elsewhere.

Cedarwood's isolation and economic decline led to a ... mmm ... insular and secretive culture. Some even believed that the town was cursed because of how much timber it had cleared. How greedy it had become."

Marti thought of Lucille's reaction to the cold cases, but she hadn't pegged Lawson as the type to buy into curses and hexes. "You think if I stay and keep poking around that one day I might disappear like that couple up by the lake?"

Lawson stared back at her. "This town's picture-perfect surface?" Lawson's hand swept across the overgrown lot, the crumbling retaining wall, the empty house with its missing shingles. "It's like wallpaper over rotting wood. The people here learned generations ago that survival means protecting their own. At any cost."

Marti laughed a little uneasily. It wasn't anything she hadn't thought of on her own. Or a close variation of it, but to hear it come from someone carrying a badge, like Lawson, was a different matter.

"Am I being warned off by the sheriff? Is this a John Ford western? The stranger has until sundown to get out of town?"

"Not a warning. Just a suggestion," she replied and walked back to her car.

Chapter Thirty-Seven

The dread that had settled in Marti's chest only deepened after meeting Gwen and hearing Lawson's warning. Even the familiar sight of Sandy's house seemed different now - the windows darker, the shadows deeper, the whole place holding secrets behind its peaceful suburban facade.

When she pulled into Sandy's driveway, there were two unfamiliar cars parked behind Bill's truck. Sandy hadn't mentioned any visitors. Marti hesitated, reluctant to intrude. Sandy would have to deal with the interruption. She needed to talk to her client. She could also use the excuse of returning the box. She climbed out, grabbed the box, and approached the front door. She left Gwen's black bag in the car. She knocked and was surprised when Ethan answered. For his part, he didn't appear surprised to see Marti. He gave her a nod and held open the door as he invited her inside.

The smell of a hearty, home-cooked meal greeted her as she stepped into the entry hallway. The scents of roasting meat, butter, and potatoes enveloped her, momentarily easing the tension in her shoulders. She followed the smells into the kitchen and found Olivia and her mother prepping a meal.

Ethan went past, picked up a beer from the counter, and drifted toward the living room, where the low murmur of a football game played on the television. Sandy, stirring something on the stove, glanced over and offered a smile. There was no trace of the animosity from their porch conversation the prior night.

"On Sundays, we like to have an early family dinner after church," she explained, the domestic scene appearing so ordinary, so utterly normal. "Nothing fancy. Pot roast, mashed potatoes, and green beans. Would you like to join us?"

Five minutes earlier, her stomach churning with nerves, she didn't think she could have eaten, but now, inside the Thompsons' warm kitchen, her stomach rumbled. It was a common response to butter. "I'd love to, if I'm not imposing."

"For I was hungry and you gave me something to eat, I was thirsty and you gave me something to drink, I was a stranger and you invited me in," Sandy said.

Marti gave a small smile and held her tongue. She wouldn't let any Bible verse ruin her appetite, but she wouldn't be rude either.

"Is Brian coming, too?" Marti asked.

"No, unfortunately. He has an exam tomorrow," Sandy replied.

"Anything I can help with?"

"No, no. Take a seat. It should be ready in a minute. We can talk while Olivia and I finish up." She used a slotted spoon to scoop string beans from a pot of boiling water while Marti watched Olivia pull a quarter-sheet pan of puffy rolls from the oven. It was clear, as Marti watched them move around each other, that this was not the first meal they'd cooked together.

"What's in the box? You were up and out of the house early this morning. Done for the day?"

Marti wasn't sure if the last comment was another dig at her progress, or lack thereof, on the case. Never mind that it was Sunday. Marti knew people expected you to work 24/7 when they were footing the bill. She gently bit her tongue. She didn't want to jeopardize her room and board. She tapped the lid of the box. "Jessica Lawson gave me this box from Bill's desk to return to you."

"Is that right?" She wiped her hands on a dish towel and came around the counter to the table. She pulled off the lid and started removing items from the box and placing them on the table. Marti had done the same thing in her car after Lawson drove off. There was no notebook. She had been correct. There was nothing remotely useful in the box. She watched Sandy now repeat the process. Two small, framed photos. One of her and Bill and one of the three kids when they were at least 10 years younger. Marti watched a tear roll down Sandy's cheek. She palmed it away and regrouped. She removed more things. Pens, a Lucite block celebrating 10 years of service. A couple of certificates and commendations.

A folded newspaper. A paperback dictionary. A small pocket-size book of the psalms. A stress ball with a logo that Marti didn't recognize. A novelty desk decoration, a plastic plant, and various office supplies that had been swept into the box or dumped in from a drawer. Marti stood and excused herself to use the bathroom. When she returned, the items had been placed back in the box and the box had been moved to a corner. Sandy had returned to the stove.

"The box wasn't the only thing I wanted to talk about. I actually have some questions for you."

Something in Marti's tone made Sandy look up. She wiped her hands on a dish towel and put the bowl of beans on the table. "Yes?"

"What do you know about Father Moran's death?"

Marti watched a look of surprise flash across the woman's face. Whatever she might have been expecting, it was not a question about the priest's death. She noticed Olivia pause while cutting the meat and look over at them.

"Father Moran?"

"Yes, he was the pastor at St. Mark's? That's your church, right?"

"Yes. That's our parish. Of course, I knew him. I worked on several committees with him. That was sad. A terrible situation. He was a good man. A good priest."

Marti recognized those were the same words she often heard used to describe her husband, and yet both men were now dead.

"Did Bill ever talk about that case? He must have known it interested you, given your involvement with the church."

"No, if anything, it made him even more tight-lipped. He wanted to avoid any hint of impropriety. Everyone knew we were involved with St. Mark's. It wasn't a secret. He wanted it clear that this case was being treated like any other. There was no special treatment."

Marti heard Ethan come in from the living room. "What's this about Father Moran?"

Marti shifted in her seat so she could see all three of them.

"I was asking your mom what she remembers about the case. What about you? What do you remember?"

"Not much. That's gotta be, what, 15 years ago? I was just a kid. I remember he died, of course, and I remember there was a commotion, but that's about it. It was happening in the adult world," he put air quotes around this phrase, "it made an impression, but I didn't pay attention. Didn't they determine it was a heart attack or something?"

"It was likely complications from heatstroke, but the autopsy was a little fuzzy. It was ruled a suspicious death. The case is still officially open."

"Is that right?" Sandy said. "I don't think I knew that. Why are you asking about Father Moran? Is this connected to the other body you told me about last night? The one Bill went down to Delaware for? How are they connected?"

"Yes, it might be. I think Bill might have been looking into a potential connection between the two men."

"What other body? I feel like I missed something," Ethan said.

"There was another man, Thomas Foster, also known as Tom Nixon, who Bill traced to Rehoboth Beach. He went down there to talk to him, but he was too late. Foster was gone and later turned up dead in The Pine Barrens."

"Tom Nixon is Thomas Foster?" Sandy asked.

Now it was Marti who was confused. "What?"

"You said Thomas Foster and Tom Nixon were the same person?"

"That's right."

"I don't think you told me that last night. I think you only said Bill was tracking Foster. I'm sure of it or I would have said something."

"You knew Tom Nixon?"

"I knew Father Tom Nixon. He was also a priest at St. Mark's."

Chapter Thirty-Eight

Marti felt a sense of vertigo, but also, finally, a solid sense of connection. Two men had died, both under similar circumstances, both priests at one of the local parishes. This must have been what Bill was investigating. But why? Lawson's words came back to her. Investigating murder was Bill's job. What was it about these cases that would have caused him so much stress?

"Thomas Foster was also a priest at St. Mark's?" Marti had heard Sandy, but she didn't know what else to say.

"Tom Nixon was. You're telling me he's the same man? That he's also dead?" Sandy looked just as shocked as Marti.

"Yes, a hiker found his body in a remote part of The Pine Barrens. It appears it was lucky they found it at all."

"And Bill knew about this?"

"Yes, he found out about it. I know that for a fact. He contacted the Park Police about it. He was looking for Foster but never got in touch with him before he was killed. The death never made the news here?"

"No, not that I recall." She glanced at her two children. Olivia was studying her fingernails and didn't reply.

"No, definitely not," Ethan said. "Not in the city. I would have recalled hearing about that. Maybe there was a story, but they didn't mention Father Tom or his connection to Cedarwood."

"How far are The Pine Barrens from here? Two hours? The distance plus the name change might have kept it out of the local news in Cedarwood. Maybe the police held the Nixon part back. When was Foster at St. Mark's?" Marti asked.

Ethan shrugged. "I was still just a kid. I remember him, but not when he was around."

"I think about the same time as Father Moran," Sandy said. "They might have overlapped for a time. The parish was bigger back then. At one time, we had three priests and a permanent deacon, plus occasional visiting priests to say the different masses," Sandy said.

"Could you find out the exact dates for me?"

"Sure. That shouldn't be a problem. The parish will have records."

"Do you know why he left? He was not a practicing Catholic priest at the time of his death when he was living down in Delaware. I didn't get the impression from a few of his acquaintances that I met that they even knew he had been a priest."

"Is that right? That's a shame. He was a good priest. Warm and kind. I remember his sermons being interesting and relatable." Marti glanced around the room. Ethan nodded along with his mother's words. Olivia made brief eye contact but didn't add anything. "I don't recall why he left St. Mark's. I assume it was just one of those things. The diocese is always changing and moving priests. He was fairly young. Maybe it was a promotion to pastor."

"Is that something you could also find out, along with the dates?"

"That might be a little more difficult, but I can ask around."

"Thanks, I'd appreciate it."

They sat for dinner, moved on to other topics, and finished the meal. Marti helped clear the table. Ethan took up a station at the sink. Marti grabbed a towel and dried. Olivia drifted out of the room while Sandy made a pot of tea.

As she dried, Marti remembered what Walter had said about Foster/Nixon and it matched up with Sandy's recollection of the Sunday homilies. Foster/Nixon was a talker. She certainly didn't forget the veiled conversation with Jake along the boardwalk and darker thoughts swirled in her mind about why he might have moved on from St. Mark's, but she kept those to herself. For now.

It had grown dark but it was still early when the dishes were cleaned and put away. Ethan, Olivia, and Sandy retired to the living room to watch television. Marti begged off and then slipped back out the front door.

Chapter Thirty-Nine

Like most everything else she had encountered in Cedarwood, St. Mark's was charming and traditional. Its exterior adorned with timeless Romanesque architecture, a solemn stone facade, and a tall steeple that reached up toward the heavens. If that's what you believed.

Marti eased the Subaru into the empty parking lot. She glanced at the signboard listing a verse of scripture and the mass times. Daily mass at 8 a.m. plus a Saturday evening mass at 5:00 p.m. and two masses on Sunday morning.

The sun dipped below the horizon, casting long shadows across the brief strip of grass and landscaping in front of the church and extending into the parking lot. Something made Marti step around the dark shape of the steeple as she climbed the steps toward the church. She looked again at the signboard and its weekly scripture verse.

'God will not permit a greater trial than we can bear.' She didn't recall where that passage came from, but she always wondered how God felt about the sin that spoiled His perfect creation. Was He annoyed? Indifferent? Angry? Did man's capacity for evil take Him by surprise? She'd asked these questions of the nuns during school and was told year after year, grade after grade, not to question God's plans but to work with Him for the greater good. Marti never liked that answer, and she didn't particularly care for such an aloof deity, either.

She pushed through the sturdy oak doors and into the hushed sanctuary. Despite her long-lapsed faith, the scent of incense and old hymnals triggered a rush of childhood memories that almost buckled her knees. The last time she'd been in a church, the last straw for her with that distant deity, had been her mother's funeral. She sat in the last pew, the polished wooden bench cool against her palms as she gathered her composure.

In the dim light, she gradually became aware of someone else in the church. The figure of an older man in a sweater and clerical collar was moving around near the altar, perhaps preparing for Monday morning's mass. She took a deep breath, stood, and walked up the aisle.

The priest heard her approach and turned to face her. He was older than she'd thought from her view in the last pew, maybe late 60s, medium height with a slightly stooped posture and graying hair neatly combed to the side that matched a well-trimmed beard framing his face. He possessed a stillness as he watched her that spoke of an internal contentment in his calling or an utter lack of personality.

"Excuse me, Father," Marti said. "I'm looking for information about Father Joseph Moran and Father Tom Nixon. I understand they both served this parish in the past. I was wondering if you might have known them or have any insights into their time here."

"I am a deacon, not an ordained priest." He held out a hand in greeting. "Deacon Michaelson."

Marti wanted to respond, Private Investigator Wells, but she held her tongue. "Marti Wells."

"Nice to meet you. What has you interested in our past priests?"

"I'm a PI working for Sandy Thompson. I believe she's a parishioner."

"I know Sandy well. She does a lot of positive things for St. Mark's."

"Then you also know about the recent loss of her husband."

"Of course, I helped at his funeral. It was held here. But how does that involve Father Moran or Father Tom? It's been a long time since either man served here."

"That's what I'm trying to find out. Did you know either of them?"

Deacon Michaelson stepped away from the altar and indicated the first pew. They both sat and then he continued. "Yes, I remember them," he replied, a mix of curiosity and caution in his gaze. "I've been part of St. Mark's for close to 40 years. What do you want to know?"

"What can you tell me about Father Moran? What was he like as a person?"

Michaelson's eyes softened with recollection. "Father Moran was here for almost 20 years himself. My hair was glossy and black when he first arrived." They both smiled at his thin joke. "That's actually a more difficult question to answer than you might realize. The collar that priests wear often keeps them separate, by design or necessity, from the congregation and it becomes hard to see the man outside of the priest. I saw Father Moran mostly here, in the church and in the context of the mass. I know little outside of that."

"I understand. I'd still like to hear your thoughts."

"Father Moran was a good pastor, Ms. Wells. It's not always the case that a good priest turns out to be a good pastor, too. There is some overlap, but also some unique skill sets. I've seen both good and bad. We were fortunate to have Father Moran for as long as we did. He cared deeply for the parishioners and the Cedarwood community, always willing to lend an ear or offer guidance."

Marti nodded. "And his death. Do you remember anything about that?"

A shadow crossed the deacon's face. "It was a tragedy. He was getting older and had some health problems, but it was still a shock. He wasn't frail or infirm. Father Moran loved his walks, especially along the wooded paths behind the church. That day, it was unbearably hot. They said it was heatstroke. He became disoriented and maybe confused. He never made it back from his walk."

"Heatstroke," she repeated, more to herself than the deacon. "Did anyone ever question the circumstances of his death?"

"Question? No, I don't think so. The police did an investigation, of course, but while it was tragic, it was still natural causes."

The weight of the past settled between them and Marti's mind buzzed, fitting these small pieces into the larger story growing in her mind. Marti, sensing an opportunity to gather more pieces of the puzzle, continued her questioning. "And Father Nixon, Father Tom, was he also a good pastor?"

The deacon took a moment, reflecting. "He wasn't the pastor here, but he was a good priest. Different from Father Moran, though. Father Tom was more guarded, you could say. He delivered powerful sermons on the Gospel, but there was always a sense of something haunting him, perhaps from his time in the service. He served as chaplain in one of the Gulf wars. It left a mark on him, I think, that kept him slightly apart from the congregation."

"Do you know why Father Tom left the priesthood?"

Deacon Michaelson's expression turned from solemn to confused. "He's no longer a priest? I didn't know that."

Marti realized he also wasn't aware that Nixon was dead. "He's also now deceased."

Michaelson crossed himself in what Marti took as an almost unconscious gesture. "I didn't know."

"Does it surprise you that Father Tom eventually left the priesthood?"

"It caught me a bit off guard. I'd say it's unexpected but perhaps not surprising. There always seemed to be something holding Father Tom back. People, even ordained priests, lose the call sometimes. It happens. God will be waiting if they ever hear it again."

"Is there anyone else who might have known Father Moran and Father Tom well, someone else I could talk to and learn more about them?" Marti asked.

Michaelson took a moment to think. "Yes, Edna Harper might be helpful. She's been the secretary in our church office for decades."

"Do you have contact information for her?"

"I'd have to look up a phone number, but you could probably walk over and see if she's around. She lives just a few blocks away on Evergreen. It's the purple house." He smiled. "You can't miss it."

After leaving St. Mark's, Marti consulted her phone for Evergreen Street and found out that the deacon had been correct. Edna Harper lived quite close. After walking north for a block, she turned east and walked through a neighborhood of small post-war homes lining quiet streets. A few showed signs of neglect, but many were meticulously maintained. And most followed a particular conservative pattern. White or gray or brick with black shutters. Edna's did not. It blazed like a beacon amidst the sea of subdued colors. The bold choice made Marti smile as she opened the low gate, walked up the path, and knocked on the front door.

Edna Harper's love of purple extended from her colorful shingles right into her living room. Marti wasn't sure she'd ever seen a purple sofa outside of Graceland or an animated cartoon. Surrounding the sofa was an eclectic mix of vintage furniture, not exclusively purple, thankfully, and knickknacks, all bathed in the soft glow of gold-burnished lamps that might have come with the original house. The sound of a football game echoed from another part of the house.

"My husband," Edna said.

Edna herself was a stout woman in her 70s, dressed in comfortable slacks with a bosom that pushed the structural limits of her floral blouse.

"Something to drink, hon?"

"No, thank you."

"Right to business. I've heard that about you."

"You have?" Marti couldn't wait to escape back to the relative anonymity of Jersey City.

"Don't be offended, dear. Most people in town know about you at this point. Plus, Sandy is active in the church. I see her almost every day. I knew about you before you even arrived. And I like it. The attitude, I mean. A woman's got to ask for what she wants and never apologize. Small talk has its place, but this isn't a dinner party. So I know why you're in town, but I don't know why you are in my living room."

"What do you remember about Father Moran and Father Tom?"

"Oh dear," she murmured, though she didn't seem quite as surprised as Sandy by the question, "we better sit down."

Marti sat on the purple couch, she couldn't pass up the opportunity, while Edna took an armchair across from her.

"You worked there while both priests served at St. Mark's?" Marti asked. It prompted Edna to let out a chuckle.

"It sometimes feels like I've been at St. Mark's since Jesus and Peter got together and started the whole church thing. Don't get me wrong, it hasn't been a bad job.

Quite the opposite; it's just questions like that remind me of how long I've been at it. When you become the unofficial historian, you know you are part of the history yourself."

"I know how you feel," Marti replied with a sympathetic smile.

"Pish," Edna dismissed the comment with a wave of her hand, "you're still a young thing. Call me back in 20 years."

Marti sensed Edna's hesitation with the direction of the conversation and decided to push a little. "What do you recall from the day Father Moran died?"

A canned cheer erupted from the other room, momentarily distracting the woman. Or providing a distraction. She broke eye contact and glanced toward the noise before answering. "I mostly remember the heat," Edna said. "This was before the new air conditioner had been installed, and even working down in the basement offices, it was hot." She looked back at Marti now. "Father Moran liked his routines. And he took his walk after his lunch. It didn't matter if it was raining, snowing, or sweltering. He said it was good for digestion. Maybe it did. But the heat outdid any benefit that day. The devil himself would have taken a pass. He shouldn't have been out there."

"I spoke to Deacon Michaelson at the church. He mentioned Father Moran had some other health problems?"

"Nothing serious. Typical getting older stuff. High blood pressure. Some arthritis. I don't know all the details. It was the usual greatest hits when you get to be my age. You'll find out eventually. None of the big ones. Not cancer or anything like that."

"How long was Father Moran at St. Mark's?"

"Oh, I don't know the exact timeframe. I could get you the dates if that's important. I remember the 20-year anniversary barbecue party we had, so longer than 20 but not by much. Maybe 22 years? There was never a 25th anniversary party."

"Did he get along with the congregation?"

"Sure, for the most part. There were difficulties occasionally. He was here for a long time. Bound to be some friction over something. I remember some people were upset about the growing acceptance of gay marriage, and abortion is always a hot-button topic in the church, but he handled those pretty well. Talked it out one-on-one with the person, typically. I do sometimes wonder how he might have handled certain situations today. Things are changing so quickly now and the church does nothing fast. So it can sometimes create some tension and put parish priests in a tough spot."

Marti noted the one big thing Edna didn't mention. She could see in the woman's eyes that she knew it, too. "Were there ever any accusations of abuse against Father Moran or Father Tom?"

If Edna had pearls, she would have clutched at them. Instead, she stood and left the room. Marti frowned. But a moment later, the sound of the football game became muted as if the door had been closed and Edna returned. Marti noticed the woman's fingers twisting her wedding ring. What Marti first took as shock or offense at her question appeared to be more nerves. She kept quiet and waited her out.

"I'm sorry. My husband doesn't like any discussion about all that."

"So there were allegations against one or both of the priests?" Marti pressed.

"No, there weren't." The way Edna paused and how her eyes flitted around the room, Marti knew there was more, and she eventually coughed it up. "Not during their time at St. Mark's."

Chapter Forty

At Edna's urging, Marti pulled out her phone and searched for a recently released diocesan report on clergy abuse. She downloaded the publicly available report. The list was long, and just thinking of the innocent lives twisted and betrayed by these men turned her stomach. She searched within the document. Tom Nixon was not on the list, but Joseph Moran appeared. There was a credible allegation listed from St. Cecilia's in 1987. He must have been a young priest then, barely out of the seminary. Church leaders assigned Moran to two additional parishes before naming him the pastor at St. Mark's. Was there anyone better at circling the wagons than the bureaucracy of the church? She heard the Catholic school nuns' voices of justification in her head as they quoted the Bible: 'On this rock I will build my church, and the gates of Hades will not prevail against it.' The evil of man might not prevail over the promise of heaven, she thought, but it sure could do a lot of damage along the way.

"What about Father Tom?" Marti asked when she finished skimming the report. "What do you remember about him?"

Edna shifted in her chair. "He mostly kept to himself. I didn't know him as well as Father Moran."

"Were they both at St. Mark's at the same time?"

Edna's eyes went distant for a moment. "Yes, they were. For about three years before Father Tom moved on to another parish."

Marti stood and Edna walked her to the door.

"Were you surprised Father Moran's name appeared in the report?"

"I never heard about any incidents at St. Mark's."

They both knew that didn't answer the question and sounded very much like: I was only following orders.

"Do you have any children, Edna?"

"No. George and I were never blessed by God in that way."

"If you had, would you have left them alone with Father Moran or Father Tom?"

There was a long pause before she replied. "No."

She returned to Sandy's house and tried to figure out what to do next. Ethan and Olivia were still in the living room watching television. Sandy's car was outside, but she wasn't around. Maybe she was upstairs.

"There's a pot of tea on the stove if you'd like some," Olivia said.

"Thanks," Marti replied. She occasionally had a cup of tea before bed, but that felt like hours away. She grabbed Bill's personal effects box from the corner of the kitchen and carried it back to Bill's old office.

Despite all her efforts, the room still looked like a confetti bomb had gone off inside. She ignored the mess and carried the box to the desk. She took the lid off and went through it all again. The desktop filled up and she placed the remaining items on the floor and then dropped the empty box next to them.

The only thing of mild interest was the old newspaper. Why did he keep it? She scanned the headlines and turned the pages. She found the likely answer on page four. And thought of her father. One of his favorite sayings when he was on the job was 'If you look for coincidences, you'll find them.' It was a small one-column story about the release of the diocesan abuse report. The same report she'd just downloaded in Edna purple living room. She glanced at the date in the upper corner. March 5th. Sandy might not have been able to pinpoint when Bill's behavior changed, but now Marti could. She felt the threads converging. She thought she heard footsteps in the hallway, but no one appeared in the doorway.

She picked up the copier paper box, scooped the items on the desktop back inside, and put it on the floor. Next, she went over and found the binder of

Cedarwood cold case files by the bookshelves and flipped the pages until she came to the section regarding the suspicious death of Father Moran. She started reading. She made it as far as the autopsy report.

When pushed to explain her job, she'd often tell people it involved talking to a lot of people until two different pieces of information clanged against each other unexpectedly. That, or going through lots of spreadsheets. The talking thing sounded more interesting.

Father Moran had a small, partially digested meal in his stomach when he died. That made sense, given that Edna Harper had told her he liked to go for his walks after lunch and believed they aided digestion. Nothing was surprising there, but it sparked a thought about Bill's autopsy. She grabbed her bag, pulled out her notes, and found Dr. Turner's number.

"Office of the medical examiner."

"Dr. Turner?"

Marti wasn't surprised when the medical examiner herself answered the main office number late on a Sunday. It was the type of work ethic that got you promoted to boss.

"Speaking."

"This is Marti Wells, we spoke a few days ago about Bill Thompson."

"Yes, I remember."

"I have a quick question if you have a moment."

"Sure, how can I help?"

"What were the contents of his stomach?"

Chapter Forty-One

Marti drove back to the state road where Bill had been discovered. She spotted the cracked utility pole that Martinez had pointed out and slowed to a stop. There was no other traffic on the road. She reset the trip odometer to zero and drove two miles in each direction. She checked out each turnoff. There weren't many. It only took 30 minutes. Two farms, three homesteads, two that appeared to be seasonal homes near a lake, and a single-wide ranch house that appeared to be abandoned, plus a firebreak and a utility access road. That was it. The only other place nearby was The Country Corner Store.

She parked in the same spot as the last time, when she met up with Martinez. As she walked toward the porch, she noticed the metal silo on the farm in the background canted slightly to the left. It reached out like a crooked finger toward the store. Marti couldn't decide if it was accusing her of something or pointing the way.

She climbed the porch steps and nudged one of the rocking chairs. It was too still and quiet. She went inside. There wasn't an old-fashioned bell over the door, but there must have been a tell somewhere because a moment later the same sour woman Marti had met previously emerged from a door behind the register. Her face was pale and pinched and she squinted under the store's lights. Marti wondered if perhaps she slept in a coffin behind that door.

Marti strode to the cooler and grabbed a grape Moxie and then circled the penny candy display and grabbed an assortment of saltwater taffy, placed it in a paper bag, and carried it to the register.

"Hi," Marti said.

"How many pieces?"

"Oh, I'm not sure." Marti opened the bag and dumped the candy out on the counter. "Looks like an even dozen."

The woman might have grunted or shrugged and then hit some keys on the register. "$6.57."

Marti handed her a ten. "Quiet tonight."

"Quiet every night, mostly."

"Why stay open?"

"Gotta eat."

Marti unwrapped a green and blue taffy and popped it in her mouth, chewed, and tried to figure out the flavor. Pineapple? Pear? She wasn't sure. "That your farm out back?"

"Yeah."

"You work there, too?"

She shrugged. "When I gotta. Milk the cows in the morning. Mostly hire out a couple of guys for the rest of it."

"Turn a profit?"

"You got a lot of questions, lady."

Marti took a sip of Moxie. "Sort of my job. My name's Marti Wells." Marti paused and watched the woman's face but saw no flicker of recognition or even curiosity. This strange creature might be the only person in Cedarwood who didn't yet know who she was. "I'm a private investigator." Still nothing. Or, she was a master poker player.

She didn't offer her own name. Marti put out her hand, and after a pause, the woman reluctantly took it.

"Heather," she finally said. Her grip was cool, almost clammy.

"Did you know Bill Thompson?"

"He was a cop."

Was. So she knew he was dead. "That's right. He died a couple of months ago, just a few miles up the road here. You get a lot of cops in here?"

"Sure, I guess. They do patrols along 47." She nudged her chin toward the road that passed the store. "They stop in. Get a drink or snack. Maybe use the bathroom."

"You comp them?"

She hesitated, but then said, "No. I need every sale I can get."

"Did Bill Thompson stop in?"

"Not usually, no. He didn't do patrols. I think he was a detective or something. He didn't wear a uniform or drive a regular cop car."

"That's right. He was a detective. But he stopped in here at least one time, didn't he?"

She crossed her arms. "You want to cut the bullshit and tell me what you want? I got things to do."

Marti resisted the urge to look around the empty store and ask what exactly those things were. Maybe it had to do with the farm. "You're right. I'll get to the point. The night he died, Bill Thompson met up with someone. I believe that person was you."

"Why would he do that?"

"I don't know. That's why I'm asking."

She made a show of frowning and shaking her head. "I don't know. I think you might be mistaken."

She was not a good liar.

"I'll tell you what, Heather. I just spent the past hour driving up and down that road and unless there's an underground bunker that I missed, this store and your farm are the only places he might have met up with someone at that hour." Marti could see she was going to lie again, so she played her last two cards. "Plus, Bill's autopsy showed a partially digested colored mass of sugar, corn syrup, butter, and cornstarch."

Heather's face screwed up in confusion or disgust. "What?"

"Those are the primary ingredients of taffy. I bet with a little more testing, they could narrow down the type, or flavor, or hell, even the manufacturer." Marti glanced over at the penny candy bins and then down at her purchase on the counter between them. That last part was a bluff. There would be no further testing and those ingredients made up most candy, but she didn't think Heather knew all that. Every cop show on television made it appear like science could solve everything. Why should Heather believe any different? Plus, Marti had one more thing she hoped would knock down the woman's last resistance. "Oh, and someone also saw you walking along the side of the road."

"Who?"

"Officer Martinez. She was in the cruiser that passed you. She was the person who found Bill in his truck after you left."

"Then why hasn't anyone been out to question me?"

"What for? The autopsy came back with no signs of foul play. No one thinks you killed him. He had a heart attack. Tragic, but plain and simple."

"Then why are you here?"

Marti smiled. "It took me all week to figure that one out and I still don't have all the answers, but I'm getting closer. No one thinks you killed him, me included, but something was going on. Bill was working on a case. I'd like to know what you talked about."

She looked like she wanted to argue some more, Marti was getting a sense that it was in her nature, but then she sighed and said, "It wasn't much, to be honest. Some chit-chat. We mostly talked about Sam and Olivia and, you know, the glory days before everything went to hell and I ended up behind this counter six days a week."

Marti was confused. Sam? Olivia? Why was Bill asking this clerk about his stepdaughter and her best friend? And then she saw it. Maybe. Working the farm and keeping the store afloat had taken a toll, but if she looked carefully enough. Maybe in a better light. Marti thought of the photo in Olivia's room. "Sam was your sister?" It came out sounding like half a statement and half a question.

"That's right. Younger sister. Olivia's best friend, but we all hung out occasionally. I think Mr. Thompson felt bad about how it all worked out." She looked around. "Or, didn't work out. After Sam … died. My parents fell apart. My dad into the bottle and my mom just drifted away. I know you can't wish yourself dead, but that sure seemed to be what happened. They both joined Sam within two years."

"And Bill was asking about that?"

"Maybe. Not about my parents, but about Sam and Olivia. He was working up to something, but I wasn't sure what. Then he started sweating and got really pale. I started freaking out a little. It scared me. I said I would go back to the store and call for help. There's spotty reception for cell phones out there. I jumped out of the truck. He told me not to tell anyone about talking to him and locked the doors. Then I took off. But by the time I had walked back, I saw an ambulance pass." She paused. "Turned out neither of us made it in time."

"He didn't say why he wanted you to keep the meeting quiet?"

"No. Maybe to protect me?"

"From whom?"

"I don't know. He didn't mention anyone by name."

"Is that it?"

"Yes." Though Heather wouldn't meet Marti's eyes.

"I'm looking for a small notebook. It was Bill's. He carried it on him all the time so he could keep notes on his cases."

"So?"

"It's disappeared. He didn't have it on him, and it wasn't in the truck when he was found. It also isn't at his home or the police station. Everyone assumes he was alone in the truck when he died. But that turned out to be wrong. You were in the truck, too. Any ideas where the notebook might be or who might have taken it?"

"You don't have any proof." Which told Marti all she needed to know.

"Nope. Not a shred, but all logic points to you having the notebook. I think Bill knew he was in trouble, but maybe not how much. I don't believe he thought he was going to die right there in the truck. Maybe he thought he'd end up in the hospital, but he didn't want someone, probably a colleague, going through his stuff. He wanted to protect his leads, he'd been burned once on this case and a man died, so he gave you the notebook until he could come back and get it."

"But he died instead."

"He's never coming back, but I can still help."

There was a long pause as they studied each other across the counter, and then Heather said, "Okay," and she reached forward and hit a button on the register. The cash drawer popped out, and she lifted it and took out the notebook.

As she held it out, a set of headlights swept across the front of the store. So other customers did frequent the old store. Marti was beginning to have her doubts, but she was glad the person wasn't a minute earlier or it might have broken the tenuous connection she'd made with Heather. She took the notebook and slipped it into her pocket.

A moment later, Officer Ackerman walked in with his big, blinding smile.

Chapter Forty-Two

Marti hadn't noticed before quite how big Ackerman was. He was at least an inch over six feet, maybe two, with wide shoulders and a flat stomach. She was tall and she had to look up to meet hi eyes. She felt a worm of paranoia in her gut. Was there something else hiding in that smile? Was he following her?

"Two of my favorite ladies," Ackerman said as he strode across the old wooden floor to the drinks cooler and pulled out a Coke.

"What brings you out here?" Marti asked. Her throat suddenly felt dry. Each word was like pulling cotton out of her mouth.

"On patrol, doing the rounds." He cracked the can of soda open with a pop. "Wanted to check in and make sure my big sister was okay. It's dark and lonely out here most nights, but she won't give it up and move to town."

Marti's head spun in another direction. "Heather is your sister?"

"That's right," Ackerman replied. "All my life. She's mostly a pain in the ass, but she has her moments." He smiled at her. Heather was looking down at the floor.

"I didn't know that," Marti said.

Ackerman took a long swallow and then suppressed a carbonated burp. "No reason for you to know."

But should she have known? Did it factor into Bill's case? She wasn't sure. The notebook felt like a lump of hot charcoal in her pocket. She needed time and space to go through it and piece this thing together.

"I guess not."

She scooped up the remaining taffy pieces and stuffed them in the bag, then dropped the empty Moxie in the garbage can by the counter. "I better get going." She turned to leave.

"I'll walk you out." He waved toward the door. "Unless you need something, Heather."

"Just some peace and quiet."

"How about more customers?" Ackerman responded.

"I've had my fill for tonight."

"Fair enough."

Marti felt his presence at her back as she walked out. Ackerman had access to the notes. He had known Bill since he'd been a kid. He was Samantha's brother. Could he also be Foster's killer? Her attacker? She had to fight back the urge to run to her car, jump in, and lock the door. She turned and faced him on the porch.

"Why don't you help with the store?" Her tone was sharper than she intended.

His ever-present smile faltered. "I do help, at the farm and the store, when I can. I took the job with the police so I could stay close and we'd have a steady income. As you can see, this place isn't exactly setting us up for retirement. Most months it barely breaks even."

"Why not sell the land?" Marti held up her hands. "Sorry, you don't have to answer that. It's none of my business."

"Occupational hazard, right?"

"More like a character flaw."

"Nah, nosy people are more interesting." The smile was back. If he was a killer, he was the most cheerful one she'd ever met. Of course, a sociopath just might be.

"That's a generous interpretation."

"To answer your question, I've tried. The farm and property, including the store, are in both our names. We'd both have to agree to sell. Heather ... isn't ready." Both turned to look toward the farm, but only the dark silhouette of the crooked silo was visible against the stars.

"Making any progress on your case?" Ackerman asked. "Is that what brought you all the way out here?"

"I wanted to see the spot where they found Bill," Marti said, only lying a little. Ackerman nodded and didn't make any comments about why she'd want to see it in the dark. She followed up before he became more curious. "You patrol out here a lot? Any idea why Bill might have been driving out here?"

"I take this section when I can, so I can swing by and check on Heather. It's typically pretty quiet. The store mostly scrapes by on the tourists in the summer who come to hike the trails and the weekenders in the fall who come for the foliage. But during the week, it's mostly farmers, locals, and deliveries. The only reason I can think of that he'd be out here, especially at night, was just to pass on through. It's what most people do on this road. It's a waystation to somewhere else. And not a very popular one. I can count on one hand the traffic I've passed in the last week out here at night. And that's including the deer and the racoons."

Ackerman's radio crackled, but it must not have been a call for him. He made no move. Just stood on the porch. The yellow lights were dim and his face was in shadow. "Then again, maybe I'm wrong. Bill always struck me as a guy who had a reason for just about everything he did. You hear any different?"

"No, I think you're right. I think thoroughness went along with his dedication. That's why I'm out here. Went up and down the road looking for the reason but came up empty."

"Huh. Heather tell you anything?"

"Heather? No. I just stopped in for a soda and a snack," she waved the paper sack of candy, "before I headed back to Sandy's. What would she tell me?" She tried to keep her voice even.

He looked over his shoulder. "Probably nothing. As you might have noticed, she's not big on customer service."

"I noticed."

"It has a kind of gruff charm."

"If you say so."

"She's family, so I guess I have to." Now, he did move toward the steps. "You take care, Marti. Lots of strange things happen out here in the dark."

She sat for five minutes in her car after Ackerman pulled out of the lot and kept an eye on her mirrors on her way back to Sandy's house. She told herself she wasn't being paranoid, just careful. Bill might have suspected a fellow officer, but nothing she'd found so far pointed toward Ackerman. Still, she watched the mirrors. At one point, a set of headlights appeared behind her, but they never came close enough to be threatening or for her to identify if they were Ackerman's patrol car.

The road behind her was empty when she pulled into Sandy's driveway a little after nine. Ethan and Olivia's cars were still parked next to Bill's truck. Maybe they planned to stay the night. If that was the case, she didn't look forward to sharing a bathroom. She missed her tub. She needed to wrap things up and get home. The notebook pulsed in her hip pocket. A few days ago, the possibility of answers felt murky, but now she felt like she had a chance.

She took her things out of the car. She wouldn't say the house was isolated, she could make out a light on at the neighbor's through the trees to the left, but no one was tripping over each other out here. It was at least a quarter mile, maybe more, through the woods or walking along the narrow, twisting road, to get to the next driveway. She took one last look but neither saw nor heard any other cars approaching. She hustled inside.

Olivia was alone on the couch in the living room watching a reality show where women were pointing long, painted fingernails at each other and threatening to throw their drinks. Marti didn't recognize it.

"Ethan still here?" She asked.

Olivia looked up, her eyes slightly glassy. Probably a side effect of the reality TV. "I think so. He didn't say goodbye, at least. Mom's upstairs. I think she's done for the night."

"Okay."

"Where'd you run off to?"

Marti debated asking Olivia more about Samantha but decided she wanted to read through Bill's notes first and get a better understanding of what he suspected before she talked more with Olivia.

"Just needed to talk to someone in town."

Olivia glanced over at her, but then someone on the screen finally threw her drink. "I made more tea," Olivia said as she focused back on the show.

Marti walked into the kitchen, poured a cup of tea, and carried it to Bill's office.

She sat at the cluttered desk, surrounded by stacks of papers and files. The tea steamed at her elbow giving off a flowery and medicinal scent. She took a sip. It was bitter. She liked chamomile or lemon verbena. This was something more assertive. She pictured Sandy harvesting roots and bark from her garden.

She took another sip and looked around. The dim light from the desk lamp cast eerie shadows across the room, adding to the sense of mystery. Or her own melodrama. Everyone thinks they're the star of the show. She'd managed to tame most of the paper and make a dent in the clutter, but it was still a lot. She did her best to ignore it. The needle in the haystack now sat on the desk blotter in front of her. She picked up the notebook. It was frayed and worn around the edges from being carried around in pockets or tossed on the passenger seat of Bill's truck. There were only a few empty pages at the back. He'd carried this notebook for almost six months. He would have filed this one away soon in the basement and cracked a new one.

Bill's handwriting was small and cramped, but legible. All of the notes were in blue ink. She leafed through the pages, her eyes scanning the shorthand notes and cryptic abbreviations. She puzzled out most of his system. It wasn't complex. It wasn't meant to hide anything, just to get something down quickly and jog his memory later for reports or follow-ups. Occasionally, she needed to cross-reference something with her own notes. With each page turned, she felt a growing sense of confidence as she pieced together the steps that Bill had taken in his investigation. Many of them mirrored her own, just not always in the same order.

Bill's investigation had been dogged and straight ahead, much like the picture she'd built up of the man over the past week. It had stalled out a few times, or been overtaken in priority by more pressing recent case work, but he always returned to it at some point and picked up the threads again. Something about it had gotten under his skin. He needed to find the answers. Marti recognized that feeling, too.

As she reached the last few pages, she couldn't shake the feeling of stiffness and fatigue creeping over her body. She stood and stretched. Or tried to. The pain in her torso had eased enough that she could breathe without the reminder that her ribs had been kicked in, but her body was still very sore and wasn't shy about reminding her it needed to rest and recover. The house had grown silent and still. She was almost getting used to the way it creaked and settled. She took her empty mug and walked back to the kitchen. A single light was on in the kitchen. She was surprised to see it was past eleven. The living room was dark. Olivia had left or gone to bed. Ignoring the growing weariness and her body's need for sleep, she poured another cup of tea from the kettle on the stove and heated it up in the microwave. She wanted to read through the notes one last time tonight. She felt like she was close. It would be nice to have answers for Sandy in the morning. The microwave beeped and she took the tea back to the office.

She didn't need to decipher the notes this time and read more carefully. She paid attention to the steps Bill had taken and the likely conclusions he'd drawn. She paid particular attention to the last few pages. This is where things became muddled. She still couldn't figure out what had led Bill to drive out to The Country Corner Store to talk with Heather. She said it felt as if he'd been leading up to something. What? Something with Father Moran or Nixon? Heather had appeared as confused as Marti. Maybe Bill didn't quite know, either. Maybe he'd been uncertain and fishing for a way forward. Still, something had led him to seek out Heather. She sipped her tea and tried to see the connection but came up empty. Whatever it was, Bill hadn't put it in his notes. At least not directly. There was nothing triple underlined with an exclamation point. Still, she felt the final thread had to be in there.

She went to the final page. There was a phone number scribbled beside a doodle of a machine gun and a chain-link fence. The phone number's area code was for New Jersey and it triggered a memory from her own notes. She pulled out her own notebook and quickly found the three numbers she matched up from Bill's cell phone records. It was the Air National Guard number. She had dismissed it before, thinking it was unrelated and maybe having to do with Bill's prior service. That might have been a mistake. It now seemed more significant. Beneath the number was an email address, jsperching@njang.af.mil, with a looping line connecting it to the doodle of the fence.

A sudden wave of dizziness washed over Marti as she jumped up to retrieve Bill's laptop from the bookshelf. Black curtains swam at the edge of her vision. She struggled to maintain her balance for a moment, grabbing the edge of the desk for support. She waited for it to pass and promised herself she'd go upstairs and rest once she'd checked out the email address. She grabbed the laptop and returned to the desk. She powered it up and bypassed the password prompt, thanks to Neon's prior work.

Opening Bill's email, she did a search on the address and found two messages—one sent to jsperching and one received. The first was a request for information and included Bill's name and police details, like his badge number. It did not contain details of what he was requesting. He'd likely told jsperching that over the phone. This was more of a CYA email. The National Guard covering their ass in case Bill's request somehow went sideways. She imagined jsperching had checked Bill out after receiving his details, making sure he was legit, before complying with his request. Two days later, a week before he died, jsperching had responded to Bill's request. His email included an attachment. She opened the attachment, a comma-delimited data file. It wasn't large, but it still contained a dizzying amount of information. Many of the columns appeared as random strings of numbers and letters.

She emailed the file to herself and took her own laptop from her bag. She used Excel to import and organize the data. There were no column headers to make the information easier to understand. Some columns were obvious. Dates and timestamps and coordinates. Others remained obscure. She spent an hour plugging in sample strings to Google. Sometimes it returned an answer. Sometimes it only added to the confusion. She was so tired. The information on the screen started to blur before her eyes. Then she noticed her fingers shaking as she typed. She stared at her hands until the shaking stopped. She kept going. Again, she could sense she was close. She felt like she was chasing someone through a maze and they remained just out of sight, always turning the next corner just ahead of her.

It took another half hour, but eventually, she made a breakthrough.

She knew what Bill had found. And what had ultimately killed him.

Chapter Forty-Three

The Excel sheet had 15 columns and 7,742 rows of data. She'd ultimately identified two as latitude and longitude coordinates. One was a timestamp that included the date. The dates covered two weeks in July. Another column was a device ID or name of some sort. The rest of the columns remained opaque. Combinations of numbers or letters. Or just single numbers. Ones and zeroes with the occasional two. Or just Boolean values of True or False. She spent some time trying to parse those opaque columns but ultimately came up empty. She'd need more context to make any sense of them. She had decided to concentrate on the columns she could reasonably identify. This was likely the approach Bill took. Unless there were further calls or emails to jsperching that she didn't yet know about. But she didn't think so. She thought Bill had a reason for keeping this investigation quiet.

She plugged in a random sample of the latitude and longitude coordinates to Google Earth and was not surprised to find them all tightly clustered within the Warren Grove New Jersey Air National Guard Base. Warren Grove sat within the greater confines of The Pine Barrens. She didn't have any coordinates for where Foster/Nixon's body was found, but she was willing to bet it was within spitting distance of the base. She glanced at her phone to check the time. The numbers swam around before settling. She shook her head to shake the cobwebs. Way too late to call Anderson and ask about the location of the body. The best she had to go on were the newspaper reports. She quickly googled that again, but found nothing specific. No reference to Warren Grove. Just vague descriptions of 'dense and remote' which, in her experience, described the vast majority of The Pine

Barrens. She searched 'Warren Grove' and then clicked through a series of pages, paying attention to the images. A few images showed the base and the grounds, including a security fence, but Marti couldn't see anything special about it. Maybe Bill had just been doodling and passing the time while he waited on hold. She remembered his other doodles of cats and dogs. Was she chasing her own tail here?

She went back to the data and the column with the device ID or name. Marti recognized a few of them because they were fitness watches, lifestyle trackers, or step counters. Apple. Or Garmins. Or Fitbits. She did her runs with a Garmin to track her mileage and time. Those were the big names in the industry and most of the entries. Why was the National Guard collecting coordinates on soldiers through their fitness watches? She had no idea.

She stared at the screen. God, she was tired. Each time she moved, it felt like she was dragging boulders through quicksand. She needed sleep, but she knew she'd just lie upstairs in the strange guest bed, eyes wide open, until she had an answer. She forced her hand to move. She might not know what the Air National Guard wanted, but she bet someone out there had the same question.

Marti remembered something her sister Emily had told her once. For a parent, the internet was terrifying. You could search on symptoms, and it would tell you your child likely had ebola or something worse. But it could also be a balm. No matter how strange the string of words you put into the search box, it was likely some parent before you also wondered how to get a blue crayon out of an ear canal.

She typed 'armed services fitness watches' into the box and hit enter. The results returned a slew of stories about how the military, after initial security concerns, was using the watches to track soldiers' sleep, habits, and overall health. Marti amended her search to include 'security concerns' and hit enter again. This time, the list of results pointed to an extensive report in 2018 about how the watches inadvertently could leak troop locations and mission intelligence. She scanned several articles. The third article from *The Washington Post* made her sit up straight. The article talked about the many benefits the watches could provide, both for soldiers and military leadership; it then explained the growing use of geofencing on foreign bases to capture, log, and most importantly, shield GPS and other data from being intercepted.

Marti knew about geofences from a previous insurance claim case that had her tracking missing inventory from a warehouse. A geofence was simply a virtual boundary around a geographic area or an object so that every time a user or employee entered ore left the imaginary perimeter, actions or notifications could be triggered. If Warren Grove was set up with a geofence, it would log anyone broadcasting a GPS signal when it passed a tower or boundary defining the fence.

Bill had noted the proximity to the base and either spotted something in the crime scene photos or knew about the military's policy. This explained the fence and gun doodles, but not exactly what Bill found. She looked at the columns of data. What had he seen? The only unique item was the device ID. She scrolled through the first 200, then another hundred. That was useless. She didn't even know what she was looking for. Maybe she could call or email jsperching in the morning and try to figure out what Bill had asked. Maybe that would give her a clue. If they'd even talk to her. She idly kept scrolling. Garmin. Garmin. Garmin. Apple. Fitbit. If it was the device ID field that held the answer, she didn't think it would be one of those. Too common. That gave her an idea. She sat up straighter. She used the sort function to group all of those together and then she hid them from view, leaving only the more unique IDs. Still more than a hundred, but much better. She scrolled down but reached the end of the list with nothing stopping her. She forced herself to read each one, saying it aloud under her breath. She stopped at number forty-seven. Dexcom. A faint bell. Where had she seen that name?

She wracked her brain. Dexcom. Dexcom. Dexcom. It was in there somewhere. She closed her eyes and tilted her head back. She felt the room spin, but the answer spun away, too. She couldn't force it. She opened her eyes. But maybe she could give it a nudge. She typed 'Dexcom' into the search box. The results loaded and she clicked the top link. As she watched the purple and white page load, the answer clicked into place.

"Oh, shit."

Chapter Forty-Four

She stood and the black curtains at the edge of her vision returned. Her view narrowed and her legs buckled. She put both hands out on the desk to keep herself upright. Something wasn't right. This wasn't just a need for sleep. She moved one hand in front of her face and watched four hands trail after it. She looked at the empty mug. Her stomach did a slow backflip. The door to the office appeared very far away, down a long, narrow hallway. She looked back down at the desk and tried to find her phone. She needed to call someone. She needed help. She reached for it, but it kept moving and slipping out of her hand like a fish jumping on the end of the line. Eventually, it fell off the desk and out of sight.

"That's not good," she said and then laughed. She heard a noise. Someone was there. They could help. She looked up. The man in the ski mask stood in the doorway. His red stitched mouth mocked her with a crooked smile.

"Oh, shit."

This time, when her knees buckled, she went to the floor and landed in a boneless pile next to the desk. She'd become one more piece of clutter. Just one more thing someone would eventually have to sort through and clean up. The curtains closed. She sank into the quicksand and it all went black.

She didn't think she was out long. She could hear the man moving around the office. She kept her eyes closed and her breathing soft. When unarmed and faced with mortal danger, if she couldn't run away, she favored the possum's approach. Pretend you were dead, or at least unconscious, until your circumstances changed.

Last time, kicking her or bludgeoning her with an ax handle hadn't been enough for the asshole, so this time he'd gone Agatha Christie and somehow drugged her. With a sinking realization, she understood how Foster and Father Moran likely met their untimely ends. Something slipped into his food at lunch. Or into a drink at a bar. It would make a person easier to control and less likely to fight back.

He'd moved around to the left, near the bookshelves. He was looking for something. She thought of the recent break-in Sandy reported and doubted if it was the first time he'd searched this office. She opened one eye in a narrow slit and saw his back. She seized on the moment of distraction. Her hand darted to the nearby personal effects box and her fingers found the Lucite block. She tucked it near her side and went limp again.

He moved back behind the desk. Even if she hadn't sensed him, she could now smell him. She remembered the strange, almost vinegar tang to his sweat when they grappled in the dark hotel room. She could hear him putting papers and other items into a bag. She couldn't let him leave.

With a sudden surge of adrenaline that overrode whatever crap he'd given her, her hand lashed out and she cracked the hard piece of acrylic against his ankle. He yelled in surprise and pain and hopped backward, away from her. He got tangled in the desk chair and fell. Now they were both lying on the ground. Down and dirty. Most of his strength and leverage was gone. She never did like to fight fair. She clambered closer to press her advantage and swung the block again. It caught him on the side of the head. He grunted and tried to cover up. She reached out and wrenched the mask up and around. It didn't come off, but the eye holes shifted. He was effectively blind. She went back on the offensive. She swung again, but he tried to roll away and this time it only glanced off his shoulder. He reached out an arm and tried to push her away, but it was feeble. She felt nothing. She felt strong and invincible. She felt afraid. His movement only provided an opening, a better target. She swung and hit him behind the ear. She swung again. And again. He went limp. Someone was screaming. She put a hand over her mouth. The screaming stopped. She didn't turn her back on him, but reached for her bag and pulled out the flex cuffs she kept in the side pocket. She slipped them quickly over his wrists and pulled them tight. Very tight. She did the same to his ankles. Blood soaked into the mask and pooled on the floor. She pulled the mask off. She put a finger to his neck. He was alive.

She staggered to her feet and fought off the urge to rain down some retaliatory kicks. She wasn't entirely successful. She gave him two good, bruising strikes to his ribs. Paused and then added a third. For good luck.

As she stepped back, her legs shaky, triumph tinged with exhaustion and whatever else coursed through her veins, she caught sight of Sandy in the doorway, pointing a gun at her. Marti's own gun.

"Get away from him. I've lost my husband. I will not lose my son, too."

Marti stood with a hand on Bill's desk to steady herself, breathing hard, but not feeling much more than that. She was wrung out. No panic. No fear. No anger. She felt detached. This was another problem to deal with. One down, one to go. She took in the details. Sandy's eyes were red and her hair mussed. She wore a pink robe and matching slippers. Marti ignored her and moved behind the desk and found her phone. This time she managed to pick it up.

"Stop moving. Put that down. I'm warning you," Sandy said.

Whatever she'd been dosed with, the side effects had passed. Or the adrenaline overrode them. She felt tired, but she recognized this kind of tiredness. The heaviness, the bone-deep weariness, the strange stereoscopic vision were gone. There was no quicksand. No boulders were pressing her down into the muck. Still, she felt a complete lack of concern or curiosity at the black-eyed emptiness of the gun barrel. That didn't feel right.

"I tried to tell you to stop. Everyone did. That the answers might not lead anywhere good. But you wouldn't listen. How much do you know?" Marti asked.

"What are you talking about?" Sandy almost screamed back. Sandy held the gun with both hands. It wavered in her grip. Marti put the odds of Sandy hitting her at 20 percent.

"A mother always knows," Marti replied and egged her on a little more. Like kicking Ethan, she couldn't seem to resist. "Edna knew and she never got the chance to be a mother. Jake knew, too."

"Who's Jake?"

But Marti kept talking. "Maybe you didn't witness it. Maybe Ethan never said anything. Maybe you never asked. But on some level you knew something had happened. Something bad. And yet, you kept right on going, bringing the kids into the lion's den."

"Stop it."

"Did you know all along? Was hiring me ever about Bill or was it about making someone hold you accountable because you were too were too weak to do it yourself."

"Stop it!"

"I'll stop. I'm done. You lost Bill. And now you've lost Ethan. If you pull that trigger, you might even lose yourself."

"I have not lost my son." Ethan moaned and rolled over on his side. Sandy took a step toward him and raised the gun higher. "Put the phone down or I'll shoot. I really will."

"Fine. Do it."

Marti then watched in detached amazement as Sandy closed her eyes, turned her head away, and pulled the trigger. There was a bright flash and a loud roar. The gun recoiled and the slide bit into Sandy's hand. She screamed and dropped the gun clutching her hand to her chest. Marti dropped her phone. Two feet to the right, Bill's old desk chair took the round right in the stuffing. Sandy dropped to her knees beside Ethan and started crying.

Chapter Forty-Five

"Don't say it."

"What?"

"I know you can't resist. Just get it out of the way."

"We have to stop meeting like this."

"Feel better?"

Marti looked out the window. This time, she had a private room. It even came with an armchair for Lawson to sit in. Today's suit was gray with a light striping over a white blouse. She appeared calm. The wrinkles around her eyes were less pronounced. Marti guessed she'd had a cigarette before coming inside.

"Not really. I think it might be a while before I feel better."

It had been three days since Ethan had attacked her in his stepfather's office and Sandy had tried to shoot her. Ackerman had been the first officer on the scene to respond to Marti's 9-1-1 call. The thing she remembered most when he'd stepped into the doorway was that he hadn't been smiling. She remembered little after that. An ambulance ride. The unpleasant experience of having her stomach pumped in the ER before landing in this room and spending a day or two drifting in the warm waters of saline and morphine. Walter would have been disappointed, but she didn't give a damn. Still, she requested they take her off the strong stuff on the second day and step her down to something else. The doctor had agreed and told her there was nothing wrong with her physically. Nothing new, at least. She just needed rest and if she could manage the pain on aspirin, all the better.

The only thing she regretted was her lack of a book. Hospitals could be very boring. She'd had a lot of visitors, but there was still a lot of downtime. Without a book, her tub, or some red wine, the small hours of the night seemed to last forever.

"Any update on Sandy?" Marti asked.

Lawson had come by yesterday to take an official statement. She'd brought the Cedarwood police file on Father Moran, along with a copy of the Foster/Nixon file that Anderson had sent down. They'd gone through the files. Marti had talked Lawson through both her investigation and Bill's notes. Lawson talked to jsperching at Warren Grove. His name was Jordan Persching. He was an Administration Airman. Bill had talked him into providing the the geofence data to help catch a killer. And it did. Eventually.

The Dexcom insulin pump that Ethan wore for his diabetes broadcast a GPS signal in case of emergency. Caregivers or first responders could locate a user if they went into diabetic shock. Ethan hadn't known about the feature. Or hadn't thought about it. He'd used the same pump to treat his diabetes since he'd been five. Marti had seen the old boxes in Sandy's guest bathroom. He'd been smart enough to leave his phone and car in the city. But he couldn't leave his insulin pump behind, even for a short time. The thing that kept him alive also would likely keep him in jail.

Did Bill know he was chasing down one of his step-kids? Marti didn't know, probably not at first, but she suspected he might have come to that conclusion. And it was tearing him apart. He faced an almost impossible choice. Arrest Ethan and destroy his marriage or bury the evidence and destroy everything else he believed in.

"Sandy has lawyered up and she's put up the house as collateral for Ethan. They've both pleaded not guilty and are out on bail."

"And yet, I'm the one still locked up in here. Ain't that typical. Our justice system is screwed up."

"You don't have to tell me, but you're not locked up. You've been cleared of any charges and are free to go whenever they release you."

"Yeah, yeah." She pretended to pout.

"Do you think Sandy knew?"

"I've been thinking about that. I don't think she knew, not at first. She was in shock and grieving and wanted answers. That's why she hired me. Was she aware it would all lead back to her own son? Was she aware of what he'd done? Did she know I don't know. She certainly chose to protect her family when she found us in Bill's office."

They were both quiet for a moment and Marti thought about how far we'd go to deceive ourselves and what we might do to protect our families. "Did they find out what he drugged me with?" She finally asked.

"Yes, the tox results came back. It was something called ..." Lawson pulled out her phone and tapped at the screen. Mobile phones were the new case notebooks. She wondered how many cops would embrace them. Notes in the cloud. Cops could be a paranoid lot. "Here it is. Topiramate. Probably crushed it up. They found trace amounts in the bottom of your teacup."

A faint bell pinged in Marti's brain. She'd learned to pay attention to these pings. Topiramate. Topiramate. It was in there somewhere but she was tired and her brain felt muddy. "What is it?"

"The doc told me it was typically used to prevent epileptic seizures."

"Huh. Where would he have gotten that?"

"Not sure. We're looking into it."

"Did you check the house?" Marti told Lawson about the old prescription bottles she'd seen in the guest bathroom and Olivia's room.

"I didn't do the search, but I don't recall seeing that on the inventory." Lawson frowned and flipped through her phone notes again. "No, nothing like that is listed."

Sandy had woken up and confronted Marti that night, but Olivia never had. She claimed to have slept through the whole thing.

Olivia had also made the tea.

They talked for a few more minutes before Lawson left. A nurse came in a futzed with some machines. She felt something warm flow into her arm.

She thought about Ethan and Olivia. Brother and sister. She thought about the wall of photos and how the two older siblings' smiling faces had changed into something else after a certain point. After a certain age.

Brian's smile had never faltered in any of the photos. Had the youngest sibling been spared? Was Ethan's motive more than just revenge? Was it premeditated, but also preemptive?

She thought about Samantha and Heather. One sister had committed suicide. One sister was just barely hanging on.

All of them friends.

She thought about the stack of cold case files Bill had brought home. David Manning, the science teacher who had disappeared, had taught at the kid's high school. Was that a connection? Was he a perpetrator, too? Had it been a triple murder?

She felt herself drifting off. Not her case, but she'd tell Lawson when she woke up.

How deep did the rot go?

Would the truth ever fully come out?

Does it ever?

About the Author

Mike Donohue is the author of the Max Strong and Marti Wells thriller series. He lives with his wife, two daughters, and Dashiell Hammett outside Boston. Dash is the family dog.

Mike doesn't think reading during meals is particularly rude. Quite the opposite.

You can find him online at mikedonohebooks.com

Milton Keynes UK
Ingram Content Group UK Ltd.
UKHW041329301124
451950UK00014B/155/J